THE
YEAR
THEY
FELL

THE YEAR THEY FELL

DAVID KREIZMAN

{Imprint}
MAKE YOUR MARK

New York

SQUARE
FISH

An imprint of Macmillan Publishing Group, LLC
120 Broadway, New York, NY 10271
fiercereads.com

Our books may be purchased in bulk for promotional, educational, or business use. Please
contact your local bookseller or the Macmillan Corporate and Premium Sales Department
at (800) 221-7945 ext. 5442 or by email at MacmillanSpecialMarkets@macmillan.com.

Library of Congress Cataloging-in-Publication Data is available.

ISBN 978-1-250-25098-8 (paperback) / ISBN 978-1-250-17986-9 (ebook)

{Imprint}
MAKE YOUR MARK

@ImprintReads
Originally published in the United States by Imprint
First Square Fish edition, 2020
Book designed by Elynn Cohen
Imprint Logo designed by Amanda Spielman
Square Fish logo designed by Filomena Tuosto

1   3   5   7   9   10   8   6   4   2

The Curse of the Sunnies:
Steal this book and be permanently unfriended.
Each party you host will be minimally attended.

For Tash

THE
YEAR
THEY
FELL

1

DAYANA

ON THE NIGHT THEIR PARENTS' PLANE DID A header into the Caribbean Sea, Josie and Jack Clay threw the biggest blowout River Bank High School had ever seen. Wait. That came out really shitty. It's not like the twins knew about the crash during the party. Nobody in attendance did, especially not Archie Gallagher and Harrison Rebkin, whose parents were on the same doomed flight. I got *my* party on the way I always did: alone in my tiny, sweltering room, in front of the computer, stalking them all on social media.

I prepared my usual dinner: one blueberry Greek yogurt, two cans of Rock 'n' Roar energy drink, unicorn puke in my vape pen, and as many pills as I could swipe from Papi's stash. With my parents away on vacation, I had my pick of the in-home pharmacy. I lined up the bottles at the edge of my laptop like a tiny audience. Alprazolam, clonazepam, sertraline . . . the names of at least four different doctors on the labels. My father didn't move his ass for much those days, but he never missed an opportunity to score from his enabler of the week.

I rattled out a few yellows with a name I recognized from the commercials. You know, the one starring White-Lady-Riding-Bike-with-Cat-in-Basket and Whiter-Dad-Climbing-Tree-with-Adorable-Kids. I swallowed the pills and washed them down with the energy bevs. Now *there's* a commercial I could get behind. Brown-Teen-with-Purple-Hair-and-Face-Full-of-Piercings swallows a magic pill and suddenly the world comes to life in vibrant colors. Birds sing and a butterfly lands on her shoulder. Her clothes explode in flowery pinks and ruffles. The rings and studs drop from her ears, nostril, septum, eyebrow, and upper lip. Mami would empty the rest of the bank account for that little miracle. What wouldn't she give to have her precious little princesa back?

While I waited for Papi's little helpers to do their thing, I joined Josie Clay's #epicClayparty #LastPartyBeforeSenior Year, already in progress. I clicked on a photo of blonde, beautiful Josie and her ginormous shaved-headed brother, Jack, on the porch pre-party. I hit print and watched as it rolled out.

Cyber lurking wasn't something I was super proud of. It's just what I did. It had been a hundred years since Josie, Jack, Archie, Harrison, and I were in the same class at Sunny Horizons Preschool. Josie dropped me as her bestie a long time ago. Or maybe I dropped her. Whatever. Things happen. People change. I wasn't bitter or anything.

If I'm being honest—and why the shit not at this point—

I kept watch on a lot of people. Their Snapchats, Instas *and* finstas. I was pretty much up-to-date on Jack, his whole football team, and the rest of the student council; pretty much all of Josie's followers. And she had A LOT of followers. All those characters I saw in the hallways. Spray-tanned white girls in miniskirts, making out with their hoodie-wearing boyfriends. I'm not saying I wanted to be part of their group. They were mostly asswaffles anyway. Their music was poser urban electronic techno-crap. They were fake to everyone outside their group and even faker to each other.

But they had drama. Stories. Lately my story was just a lot of me sitting home by myself getting high.

As #epicClayparty #LastPartyBeforeSeniorYear cranked up, Josie and her crew of look-alikes seemed to be spending more time posting pics, showing the world they were having fun rather than actually *having* fun. All of her *new* besties must have wanted a selfie with Josie. Josie in her clean white dress, holding a red cup and smiling like she'd just won Miss Teen New Jersey. Cody Salamone wearing a scarf and winter beanie with his board shorts, hugged her from behind. Was he her newest boyfriend? How long would *he* last? Josie was everywhere, that grin at the center of every post from the party. The smile wasn't real though. I knew that smile, the one that said "I'm not really here right now." It never quite reached her eyes.

While their house was under siege, Josie's 'rents were on their way to the islands with Mami and Papi, Archie's parents, and Harrison's mom. They'd become friends when we

3

were all in preschool together. And they were still friends, even if we weren't. I wondered what would happen in a few days when the Clays got home. Maybe they already knew about Josie and Jack's party and didn't care. By the time they returned, the cleaning lady would've fixed it all up anyway.

'Course my parents wouldn't have given two mouse balls if I'd thrown a party, invited the entire high school, and provided free meth at the door. Papi wouldn't even notice, and Mami would be thrilled that I'd at least done something "normal." Not that anyone would come to my shindig anyway. And who could blame them for avoiding me? I'd heard the rumors: that I'm a vampire or a Santeria witch or a Santeria vampire-witch. That I eat babies for breakfast. Didn't matter that I was a vegetarian. Most of the time. Not like anybody would talk to me to find out. Mami would say, "Daya, maybe if you try to look a little less . . . *rough*, people might not be so afraid to get close to you." I was okay with the distance. Really, I was.

I scrolled back through the latest posts in my feed, all filtered to perfection. But to me, the action in the background was the real show. There you got to see people in their natural states, when they didn't know the camera and I were looking. Frosh chick nervously fixing her lacy bra straps. Hot-shit wrestler gazing longingly at his teammate. I was about to scroll past a picture of a bored-looking Jack Clay when I spotted something really fucking weird over his left shoulder.

I clicked and zoomed in on two sad and lonely figures hovering near the snack table. Archie Gallagher clutched the bulky sketchbook jammed under his arm, his thick-framed glasses so smudged with Doritos dust I could barely see his eyes. I'd say he was the last person I'd ever expect to see at Josie's party, but he was at best tied with the pale, awkward creature looming above him. As far as I knew, Harrison Rebkin hadn't been to a party since his eighth birthday was shut down when he had a panic attack at Chuck E. Cheese's. What in Satan's name were these two doing there? We were all buds back at Sunny Horizons Preschool, but those days were way gone. Our little group had scattered to the winds years ago. No chance Josie invited those two and not me. Right?

With my brain starting to fuzz around the edges, I closed my eyes and saw myself gliding into the party. Atop the perfectly manicured lawn, the crowd would part for me. I'd feel the beat from the sound system going right through my body. Some of the less douchey guys might even check me out. Josie, in the middle of a conversation with a horde of her followers, would sense me at the door. She'd turn and smile, like no time had passed. Like we were four years old and she was my lifeline in the scary world of the Sunny Horizons Preschool playground.

I. Am. Your. Friend.

Just like she did then, she'd take my hand and lead me inside, where Jack, Archie, and Harrison were waiting. The five of us, the way it used to be back at Sunny H.

I pulled open the fridge. On shelf after shelf were perfectly lined-up containers, each labeled in Mami's neat lettering. Food from our native Costa Rica right next to our adopted American "cuisine." Casado cozying up to pasta with meat sauce and broccoli casserole. I had no desire to touch any of it. I wanted Mami to come home in a few days and see it all still sitting there. Rotting.

I cracked one of Papi's beers and took a few gulps, leaving the refrigerator door open. Was it possible I could hear the music from the party this far away? I let my head bounce forward and back to the beat I may have only been imagining. What if I *did* take a stroll over to Chez Clay. You know, for research. I could roll in all coolio, grab myself one of those red cups, and chill in the yard. It's not like I'd be bothering anyone. I mean, could I possibly be any more toxic than my old amigos Archie and Harrison?

My legs were getting a little rubbery, but I figured I could make the ten-minute walk to Josie's house if I started now. She would be happy to see me. I was really starting to feel that. Stopping by this party would change things between us. Maybe the pharms were doing a job on me, but I was starting to feel . . . hopeful? Like senior year could actually be different. Less lonely. Less . . . tragic. Jack and Josie had thrown a rager and somehow Archie and Harrison showed up. And now I was going, too. It had to mean something.

I stuffed a bottle of Xans into my shoulder bag; you know, for the road. Losing my buzz halfway there would be disastrous. I reached for the door, but before I could open it, two beams of light flooded the kitchen.

Headlights were coming up the driveway. A car door slammed. Then another. Papi's car? It didn't make any sense. I looked out to see him trudging up the front steps, Mami tearing after him, screaming in Spanish. I wasn't completely sure this was really happening. Why would they be here? It felt like they'd left just a few hours ago.

Mami usually tried to keep her English and Spanish separate. But when she was pissed, she was pissed en español and inglés.

Papi kissed me on the head and walked straight for the bathroom. Mami blasted through the front door after him. I wasn't sure this was actually happening.

"Wait. I don't . . . Aren't you supposed to be in Antigua?" I blurted.

"Anguilla," Mami snapped. "And no! We are not there because your papi's passport expired last month. Ask me when he checked. In the airport!"

"You didn't go?" I tried to shake out my brain. I thought I still heard the beat from Josie's party.

"¿Estás sorda? Six hours and a half trying to find a way to get on a plane. After what it took us to get *into* this country, and now we can't leave? So now Jennifer and the Gallaghers and the Clays are drinking margaritas on the beach while I'm here in this house on this street with this—" She stopped as she noticed the bag slung over my arm. "Are you going somewhere?"

"Oh, this?" I slurred. "There's this, um, senior year party thing at Josie and Jack's and weirdly Archie and Harrison are there so it's kinda like this reunion thing maybe—"

Papi walked out of the bathroom holding several pill vials in his hand. Shit. "Daya, did you take some of Papi's medicine tonight?"

Mami walked over, pried open my eyes like oysters, and shook my bag. "¿Drogas? You know what they do to you, how they pull the life from you?" She glared at Papi.

"So, can I get rolling to the shindig or what?" I asked.

"No," snapped Mami. "No party! You will sit here with me and wait until the drugs are gone from your body."

"What? You have no right to—"

"You could overdose. I will not find you tomorrow morning floating in Richard Clay's pool."

Mami's rant was interrupted by a blast of music from her phone. She put it up to her ear. "¿Hola? Hello? . . . Yes, this is Vanesa Calderón. No, we did not get on the flight from Newark. We were not permitted to board." She glared at my father. "Yes, connection to Island Hopper Airlines from St. Martin to Anguilla. With our friends. I booked it through—"

Her voice sounded far away. I leaned against the wall. I was starting to fade, and feeling like I could be sick. I let out a big yawn only a moment before the phone fell out of my mother's hand and smacked on the cracked, yellowing tile. The rest, I have to admit, is kind of a clusterfuck in my brain.

Mami crying, choking out what the guy said to her on

the phone . . . Completely giving up on English. Papi coming to hug us . . . I was slipping away and scrambling out of the house . . . Almost plowing into a neighbor walking her yappy little dog . . . Running through the dark . . . Every block looking the same . . . Cars parked everywhere in the Clays' neighborhood . . . Loud hip-hop music . . . Nobody on the giant front lawn at Josie's like in my fantasy . . . Shoving the gate . . . Opening the door . . . Everyone looking at me . . . Thousands of eyes . . . The followers whispering at me, pointing . . . Some dick in his varsity jacket grabbing my arm, trying to drag me out . . .

Josie's new best friend, all in my face with fake lashes and her nasally voice that goes up at the end of everything she says. "Um, hi? Not trying to be rude? This is Josie and Jack's private party? You're not invited? You should probably find somewhere else to be?"

Josie, walking toward the door to investigate the disturbance at her party . . . Jack right behind her . . . Harrison and Archie hugging the wall near the stairs . . . We're all here, I thought. We're finally all here . . . The Sunny Horizons Preschool Class of 2007 . . .

I was so out of breath and wrecked out of my mind I could barely form a sentence. I braced myself against the wall, hoping just to stay on my feet. A different person might have planned a speech while she was staggering over to Josie's house. She would've had soothing words and a comforting tone. She could've eased into it and told them to sit down first. 'Course, a different person wouldn't have gotten so messed up in the first place. Josie stared blankly as I reached out and touched her face. It was like it took her a few seconds to even recognize me.

"Dayana? What are you doing here?"

The only way to describe what happened next is to say it vomited out of me. "D-dead. I had to come say . . . the plane . . . It went down . . . Nobody made it . . . They're all dead . . . Fuck me, I'm so wasted . . ."

I don't know if there's a right way to tell the four people who used to mean more to you than anyone in the world that their parents died in a plane crash, but I can confirm with absolute fuck-all certainty that there is a wrong way.

2

ARCHIE

I CAN SEE THE FUTURE. THAT'S WHAT I USED to tell people. Also in my wheelhouse: mind control, super-speed, and X-ray vision. Oh, and I was born on another planet to genius scientists killed in an intergalactic civil war. Who wouldn't want to hang with someone like that? That last part could've even been true. It's not like I ever met my birth parents. And I know one thing: wherever I came from was much different from where I ended up.

In the comics, being different meant you were special, gifted. In real life, different is just *different*. Being black with white parents doesn't really get you much, other than a million stares and insulting questions. Still, most of the time, dudes don't just start out as superheroes. Their powers only come out later, like after some experiment goes wrong or there's a terrible accident. A terrible accident, yeah.

All I'm saying is maybe there was a reason Jack Clay invited me to his party that night I ran into him at the

7-Eleven. I mean, in the last three years of high school and the previous three years of middle school before that, Jack and Josie had never even added me to one of their massive group chats, much less a guest list. So what inspired Jack to invite me that day if it wasn't, you know, fate or whatever?

Okay, so I did bust him loading up on red cups, Doritos bags, and other assorted party swag, which means guilt could be in the mix. Plus, he must've noticed how the rat-faced clerk was following me up and down the aisle making sure I didn't steal anything. I wanted to be like, yo, this giant angry bald white dude is a way bigger threat to store security than the black art nerd in the thick glasses. But that's the way it goes, even in a "progressive" town like River Bank. Different is different.

I lied again when I said I ran into Jack. More like he ran into me. Through me. I was just sucking down a Slurpee and looking at my sketchbook one second and the next I was counting the lights and covered in orange goo. I scrambled through the book, making sure none of my drawings were wet or smeared.

"Archie," grunted Jack. "Didn't see you there."

When I get nervous I have this habit of talking nonstop. Dad called it Jabber-Jaw. "My bad. I was looking down and I didn't see you and . . . It's hard not to see you. You take up the whole aisle. Practically the whole store. I don't usually do the orange Slurpee thing, but the Coke one was all watery and I like a thicker consistency. Anyway, I was on my way to see this girl and she asked me to get her one. Okay, that's a lie. There's no girl. The orange was for me. But that guy was following me and—"

Jack reached down his paw and yanked me off the ground so hard I was momentarily airborne. "My parents are out of town for a few days," he said once I'd landed. "Yours too, I guess."

"Oh yeah. I'm solo, too. Well, not solo. I've got Lucas. Little brothers, right? What are you going to do? I didn't even see my mom and dad when they left for the airport this morning. They let me sleep in. We're cool like that. Plus, I had nothing to do, so . . ."

"Uh-huh. Anyway, we're throwing a party. Jo is. End of summer, beginning of senior year thing. You should come."

"I should?" My voice cracked with surprise.

He shrugged. "Sunny Horizons forever."

Did Jack really feel that? Is that why he invited me? Did he really still think about the days when he and Josie and Harrison and Dayana and I were friends? Why would he? He had football and hot girlfriends and scaring ninth graders so much that they memorized his schedule and took elaborately planned detours to class. Of course, I still thought about our little group enough for all of us.

My house was like two and a half blocks from Sunny Horizons Preschool. I rode my scooter past the playground just about every day. Like a boss. Sunny H had changed since we were there. The faded blue awning with the yellow sun still hung above the entrance to the school. But years back, the people in charge decided that it was more important for kids to be safe than to have fun. So now the play area was all soft and round. The huge oak we used to run around and climb up was now just a stump. Dad said the tree got some kind of virus and they had to put it out of its misery. I didn't even know that was a thing.

I know it's pretty sad that thirteen years later I still missed preschool. I get it's not normal. But it was never *normal*. I mean, who else makes the only real friends they've ever had when they're four? Guess I'm not really made for groups. I'm not sporty enough for the athletes, or smart enough for the brains. I'm not artsy enough for the other artists, or weird enough for the weirdos. I went through a phase where I tried to be black enough for the black kids, but I felt like a fraud and they knew it. But of course having white parents wasn't enough to make me blend in with the white kids either. So I was lost somewhere in the middle. But back at Sunny Horizons, Josie and Jack and Harrison and Dayana and I were all already different. We weren't one thing. We were everything. And somehow that made it work.

I always knew I was different. It wasn't like Mom and Dad could hide it from me. No one could look at us and think, *He came from them*. But they always told me skin color meant nothing. I was their son. Mom explained how hard they tried to have a baby the regular way. They did a bunch of shots and operations, and spent almost all of their money— that's how much they wanted a kid. But nothing worked, so they brought me home when I was two in what they call a closed adoption. Mom and Dad never got to see my original birth certificate, or even learn the name of my birth mother. I wondered about her sometimes, but the law said I couldn't find out who she was until I turned eighteen. Laura and Phillip Gallagher were German-Dutch and Irish and they were the only parents I ever knew.

Mom said even though we were a family, it was important for me to hold on to my "culture." She would try out "soul food" recipes she'd found online and Dad would play jazz and hip-hop in the car. We'd have "African American Pride Night" where they'd rent movies about people like Jackie Robinson, Rosa Parks, and Madea. I never told them how uncomfortable those nights made me feel. Mom used to complain that there were no other black kids my age in the neighborhood. She set me up on playdates with Dayana Calderón, whose father had met Dad at work or something. Dayana didn't look anything like me, but she was born in Costa Rica and her skin was darker than their other friends' kids. The problem was, Dayana didn't speak English and I didn't speak Spanish. I don't remember much about those awkward playdates except feeling like Mom and Vanesa were watching us like pandas in the zoo.

So I discovered drawing. And comics. A place where people who are different can be heroes, where a group of freaks and oddballs can become a superteam and save the world. Every good comic starts with an origin story. But not every origin story ends with an ordinary loser becoming a costumed crusader fighting for truth and justice. Sometimes, an origin story is just about how a lost boy finds people who change his life, and how a bunch of very different kids get put in a room by their parents and become something bigger.

Dayana only really knew one English sentence at first. Jack was always sick, and when he was in school, he spent most of his days in time-out. Harrison was full of worries and fears. It was Josie who brought us together. And it was Josie who kept us that way.

I've been told that most people don't remember much from preschool. But I have my drawings to remind me. They're sort of like a record of our time there. Mom kept them all. At least all the ones I didn't give to Josie.

In my first week at school, we were all playing hide-and-seek on the playground. Josie put a finger to her lips and silently showed me how to get up to the lowest branch on the big tree. She bounded up there in three seconds and when I struggled, she reached down and pulled me up with her. We sat there together and watched everyone run around below us. It felt so good to be up there with her. When we got back to the classroom that day, I drew a picture of Josie and me in the tree. I wanted to show it to her, but I was too scared. So at snack time, I walked over to her cubby and slipped it into her Yankees backpack. After that, I drew another picture every day. Sometimes it was of her or Jack or a squirrel on the playground or all five of us. I'd drop it into her backpack when she wasn't looking. She never mentioned the drawings to me, but I saw how she'd run to her cubby at the end of school. Like she couldn't wait to open it.

Dad took to calling us the World's Cutest Gang: "The

Sunnies." We may have been cute, but we operated like the Hells Angels or any other badass gang. The Sunnies stuck together. We didn't let anyone else in. And we were not afraid to fight for each other. Like when Jack got really sick the week of preschool graduation. Everyone thought he wouldn't be able to leave home to be there. As the legend goes, Josie, Harrison, Dayana, and I decided that if Jack couldn't be at the ceremony, then we wouldn't go either. We did it together or not at all. Nothing our parents said would change our minds. Finally, Mr. and Mrs. Clay offered to host the graduation in their backyard so Jack could come outside and we could all graduate together. I've gone over my drawings from that day a lot of times. In a lot of ways, it was the beginning of the end of "The Sunnies."

The Clays and the Rebkins and the Calderóns—these were Mom and Dad's friends. As my parents told it, when they started trying to have a baby, they had moved out to the suburbs. Dad scored a civilian accounting job at the local army base, Fort Benson, and Mom found work as an ER nurse. They were pretty isolated until I came along, so my school gave Mom and Dad their social network. The four families came from different places, but they were all young parents and they formed a group, just like we did. They'd stick us kids out in the yard to play while they'd hang out and drink wine and laugh. At some point, they all decided they needed a couple of days in the sun without us around. So they called in babysitters or grandparents and they flew someplace warm for a long weekend. Which instantly became a tradition; after that first trip, they went away together every year. And it all started at Sunny Horizons.

There's one part of preschool graduation I don't need drawings to help me remember clearly. We were sitting near the pool in Josie's backyard. Mom tried to take a picture of Dad and me, but he insisted she be in it. Mom hated having her picture taken. She always avoided it, but Dad said she'd be sorry one day when there were no photos of her at all. He handed his camera to Harrison's father, Bobby.

Bobby squeezed us together. "Hey, Arch, you psyched you're gonna be a big bro soon?"

I felt Mom and Dad stiffen behind me. Before Bobby could take the picture, Jennifer grabbed her husband by the sleeve and dragged him off so they could fight. Mom and Dad shared a weird look and she reached into her bag and handed me an oatmeal raisin cookie and a juice box. And that's how I learned I was going to be a big brother. In the six months since they'd discovered the news, Mom and Dad hadn't been able to find the right time to tell me they were having a baby.

"Is this baby going to be adopted, too?" I asked.

"No, kiddo. Your mom is pregnant. You know what that means, right?"

"I thought you couldn't have a baby like that. You said your tummy had a boo-boo."

"We thought so, too, sweetheart. It just . . . happened. I don't know why. Even the doctors say it's amazing. Maybe it's because you got me ready to be a mother."

"I was just here to get you *ready*?"

"No! No, of course not. I didn't mean it like that. I just mean that being your mom . . . I don't know . . . Phillip?"

"This is going to be a great thing, pal," said Dad. They each took one of my hands.

I kept looking at Mom's belly, picturing the baby inside it. "What color will his skin be?"

Mom and Dad looked at each other again. "He'll be white," said Dad. "Like us."

They did their best to say the right things. They'd only love me more. I'd always be their first. Nothing was going to change.

Everything changed.

The baby in Mom's belly turned out to be my little brother, Lucas, who was a miracle before he was even born. Once out in the world he was the best infant and the cutest toddler. He slept like a dream and talked early and he ate all his veggies. Dad's prayers had been answered. Lucas had this thing called coordination that somehow escaped me entirely. He could kick a soccer ball with both feet and throw a baseball harder than I could by the time he was four. He didn't need glasses to see things that were far away. His palms didn't sweat when a grown-up talked to him. He had Dad's red hair and blue eyes and Mom's smile. Everyone said so.

It's a total bummer when you realize your baby brother is cooler than you are. He had more friends. Girls texted him. Coaches begged him to be on their teams. And the worst part of all—Lucas was a great kid. He wasn't all cocky like some of the athletes. He pretended to look up to me, even though I knew that wasn't possible. Why would he? He'd ask me to have catches with him or play *Call of Duty*, and never rubbed it in my face after crushing me in both. He didn't make fun of my drawings or ask why I never had a girlfriend.

Life would've been so much easier if Lucas were a dick. At least then I could've hated him. At least then being jealous would've been acceptable.

After Sunny Horizons, Josie, Jack, Dayana, Harrison, and I headed to River Bank Elementary for kindergarten. And we stayed friends for a while. We'd always been such different people, but it didn't really matter. Until it started mattering. I was the first to see the little cracks. Jack picked everyone else to be on his team for kickball; Harrison's mom cancelled playdates while she was going through her divorce; Josie hung her backpack in her classroom lockers. My drawings stayed in my sketchbook. As the years went on, the cracks grew. Somehow when we walked out of Sunny Horizons, it's like the spell holding us together was broken.

It's a freaky thing, watching your friends change from a distance. Like that time-lapse photography where the buildings stay the same, but the clouds and the people race by. Jack, who'd always been small and sickly, hit a growth spurt and hulked out. Dayana spent middle school wearing pink, sparkly skirts, but showed up in high school in oversize black T-shirts and combat boots. Harrison started busing to math classes at the local college. Josie . . . well, Josie is a whole different thing.

I'm sure I changed, too. But not that much. I still wore glasses and read comics and rode my scooter. I still only felt right when I was drawing. I thought about girls and sex, and sex with girls. But I never got anywhere close. And besides, there was only really ever one girl who mattered.

I tried to keep the gang together, but it was already too late for the Sunnies. I don't think the others even noticed. And if they did, they didn't seem to care. When the five of us were first drifting apart, I'd see one of them in the hallway and we'd talk or walk home together. But after a while we started running out of things to say to each other. So then it turned into a quick "hi." Before long it was just a nod. And then, finally, nothing at all. By the time we finished our junior year of high school, I guess you could say we were pretty much strangers to each other.

Until the day our parents fell out of the sky.

3

JACK

THE LIFE DRAINED FROM JOSIE'S FACE. HER mouth drooped open. Her arms turned to rubber. She fell back against the wall and her knees collapsed.

"Jo?" I tried to yell over the music, but my voice came out like a whimper. "Jo . . . ?"

A minute ago, Jo had commanded the living room. Pouring drinks, dancing on the bar, flirting with her boyfriend, directing the DJ. This was her party. Her world. Now my twin sister was a puddle on the floor.

I finally found my voice. "Get away from her!"

Dayana kept cursing and crying and saying how sorry she was and how beautiful my parents were.

"Shut up! Stop. Stop talking so I can think."

Get Josie out of here. The one clear thought in my head. Get her somewhere safe. Her dress was riding up her thighs, so I leaned over to tug at the bottom, and that's when I got a close look at her eyes. Fixed. Empty. The black parts swallowing up the green. I didn't know if Dayana was telling the truth about Mom and Dad, but Josie was gone. And I was alone.

I scooped her up into my arms. I hadn't carried her like this since that time on the softball field four years ago. Back then I could barely lift her. Now I hardly felt her weight at all. All around us, the party went raging on.

Her best friends didn't even notice she'd gone down. All those worshippers, trading loyalty for selfies and perfect parties. Feeling important because she let them be around her. Now they were too busy getting wasted and hooking up to even move aside for us. But if I was good at anything it was making people move out of the way.

Archie put his hand on my shoulder and I almost took a swing at him. "What happened to her?" he asked.

Earlier that night, Josie had found me alone by the keg in the backyard. When I stayed inside the party too long, bad things started to go on in my head. The music, everybody yelling at once, flooding my brain with noises and information. My girlfriend, Siobhan, kept trying to have "a talk." I couldn't concentrate on a word she was saying so I gave up and came outside for air.

Josie had slid open the glass patio door, sneezing as she walked outside. "I always get sick when I'm stressed out," she said.

I handed her a napkin and she pushed it away. "I thought we understood our roles on planning the party," she snapped. "I do the heavy lifting and you lift heavy things."

"What's wrong?" I went back over the assignments she'd

given me. Keg, snacks, cups. I'd written it on my right hand so I wouldn't forget anything this time.

"Did you invite Archie Gallagher?"

Oh. I could see inside where Archie was nursing a beer by the snack table. Harrison stood next to him. I know I didn't invite *him*. "I didn't think he'd actually show up. Did he bother you or something?"

"No. No, it's not like that. It's just . . . tonight's supposed to be perfect. I need it to be."

"You want me to throw him out?"

Cody appeared at the door and smiled at her through the glass.

"It's fine," Josie said, making herself smile back at Cody. "I'll be fine."

She'd been planning this party all junior year. Maybe even longer. She'd decided who would be there, what they would eat and drink, what the DJ would play, even how they would hashtag the event. Both our names were at the top of the invites, but Jo ran the show. I moved the furniture and rolled up Mom's expensive rugs, carried the kegs to the yard, chatted up neighbors, and traded football stories with the cops to make sure we wouldn't get shut down. She'd never risk giving me more responsibility than that. And that was fine. I knew my role.

When I was about eight, I found one of those sonogram pictures the doctor took of Mom's stomach when she was pregnant. Fetus A—Josie—was facing forward, looking straight at the camera. Fetus B, on Josie's left, was curled up and turned toward her. They found out later that the way we were stuffed in there kept me from getting all the nutrients I needed. But Dad said it just looked like I was waiting for her to tell me what to do.

I looked down at motionless Josie in my arms. Archie was still blocking our path. And now Harrison was there, too. They were the only two people in the party who'd noticed.

"Did she pass out?" asked Archie.

"It's very hot in here," said Harrison. "She looks flushed."

"Can I get her water? I think I should get her water. Where is the water? All I see is beer and—"

A thought sliced through my head. *Their parents were on the plane, too.* I pushed that aside and used Josie's legs to shove Archie and Harrison out of the way. Then I carried her upstairs and punted open the door to her bedroom.

Josie's room was one massive collage of wall-to-wall pictures of Josie with her friends. Thousands of smiles and duck lips and peace signs. So forced and phony. I eased her down onto the bed and propped fluffy white pillows under her head. Jo's eyes were open, but she didn't look at me or at anything else.

"We're going to figure this out, Jo. I promise."

I slammed open her laptop, typed in her password, and googled *plane crash*. 56,500,000 results. A jumble of words and images. Like all fifty-six million results were on the screen at the same time. Plane crashes in Germany, in South Korea, in Salt Lake Fucking City. What island were they on?

What island were they flying to? Aruba? St. Something? Shit, I wrote it down somewhere.

I dug through my pockets for the paper where Mom wrote her instructions, but all I could find were two dimes and an empty gum wrapper. Why hadn't she just texted them to me? What was the name of the island? Something with an A . . . Antigua? *Plane crash Antigua*. Nothing within the last year. Anguilla! Mom said they were flying to one island and then transferring to one of those little puddle jumpers. She hated flying, especially small planes . . . *Plane crash Anguilla*. First result.

I squeezed my eyes. Locked them in. Focused. One word at a time. *If it's hard to concentrate, try harder*, Dad used to say. *I know you're smart. You're my son. But you'll never get anywhere if you don't apply yourself. Don't listen to those labels from your teachers. Labels are excuses for being lazy.*

"Six Americans Dead in Offshore Plane Crash." I gripped the laptop until my knuckles turned white. The bass was thumping downstairs. The ceiling fan whirred over Josie. My heart beat in my ears. I tried to read the full article, but my eyes jumped all around. Words popped off the screen . . .

KILLED   SMALL PLANE CRASHED
NEW JERSEY   INSPECTOR   WALLAS LAKE POLICE
TWIN-ENGINE   RESCUE AND RECOVERY
SHALLOW WATERS
NEXT TO IMPOSSIBLE   DECEASED PERSONS   NTSB
NO SURVIVORS   VICTIMS' IDENTITIES

No survivors. Victims. Deceased. I hurled Josie's laptop across the room. It shattered against the wall and she still didn't budge.

"They're gone, Jo," I whispered. "They're gone."

I grabbed a blanket and threw it over her legs. "Wake up. Please."

A loud *WOOO* exploded through the open door from downstairs. Up here, the world had just broken forever, but downstairs everything was the same.

I wandered down to the living room barely feeling my legs. It's like I was watching it all in a movie. The lacrosse guys were standing on the couch doing shots. A pack of drunken girls were attempting to rap along to the music near the DJ. Some wasted idiot was leaning his head against a photo of our family trip to the Cape.

I felt rage and pressure building up inside me. Like on the football field. Or when Dad got in my face. I hated this fucker touching our picture. I wanted to hurt him and everyone else in the room. I shoved two people aside and headed straight for him. But before I could reach the guy Siobhan came up and stuck her hand in my back pocket.

"Sorry about before, babe. You know I hate it when you don't listen to me? Where've you been? Someone said Josie's really messed up?" The music was pounding my head.

"Jacko!" Cody was holding Dayana by the arm. "What did 'Walking Dead' say to Josie? What's going on, dude?"

I grabbed Cody by the throat and slammed the back of

his head against the door. Then I dragged him out to the porch and launched him down the steps. When I walked back inside, the party had suddenly gone quiet.

I shoved the DJ and snatched his mic. "Get out!" I shouted. "Get the fuck out! All of you."

When they didn't move, I moved them. When they resisted, I got rough. When they tried to reason with me, I got rougher. Soon they were running out on their own.

Siobhan tried to talk to me, but I shut her down, too. "Go. Just go with your friends."

I don't know if it took five minutes or two hours to clear the room of all but three. When I finally slammed the door I was breathing heavy and bleeding from a scratch on my arm. Only Archie, Harrison, and Dayana were left. The three who were never supposed to be here in the first place.

Archie looked panicked. "We were just about to—"

"Go upstairs," I growled. "She's already in there." Dayana covered her mouth and stumbled past me.

Archie used the back of his hand to wipe his glasses. "You want us to go up to Josie's room?"

Upstairs, Josie hadn't moved. I couldn't be sure she'd even blinked. Her feet were poking out of the blanket, her shoes resting on the clean, white comforter. I carefully unstrapped them and tossed them on the floor.

From the open bathroom came a horrible, guttural sound. *"Bluuuuuch!"* Dayana was kneeling in front of the toilet, puking her guts out.

"Hey," said Archie. "You realize this is like the first time we've all been in the same room together in like thirteen years."

"*Bluuuuch!*"

"Well, pretty much the same room. I mean, I'm not sure you count the bathroom, but we did walk in at the same time so that probably counts. Not that it matters, but I'm just saying."

Harrison reached down to pick up the pieces of Josie's laptop. "What happened to this computer? You're going to need it for the start of school. I think I could fix it if you'd like me to . . ."

"Jack," said Archie, "what's wrong with Josie? 'Cause it seems like she's—"

"Don't go near her!" I shouted.

Archie pushed up his glasses and backed away. "Sorry. Has she said anything? Anything at all?"

On the wall behind Josie's bed hung a photo of Mom and Dad holding us at our Sunny Horizons backyard graduation. Dad was smiling and gripping a bunch of balloons, Mom was wearing her tennis whites. It was the last time the five of us had all been in this house together with our parents. "Something happened." *Small plane crash. No survivors.* Archie and Harrison looked at me with these dumb expressions on their faces. "There was . . . an accident. That's what Dayana came here to say. There was an accident." *Victims' identities. Deceased persons.* "Our parents. The plane. It was like one of those little shitty ones that go island to island. They didn't make it."

They weren't getting it. Or didn't want to get it. Archie clutched the sketchbook under his arm. "What do you mean, they didn't make it?"

"Didn't make it. The plane went down."

Harrison looked curious. "You're saying there was a crash?"

"Yes, that's what I'm saying. The fucking plane carrying my mom and dad and your parents—"

"My parents?" asked Archie.

"Yes, yours, too." I wanted to bash their heads together.

Harrison already had his phone out, tapping it frantically. "Mom, it's me. Call me as soon as you get this. It's urgent."

What was wrong with them? "She's not calling you back. Are you listening? They fucking crashed. There were no . . . There were no survivors . . ."

"Oh, God," moaned Archie as it finally hit. He leaned over and the glasses slipped off his face as he put his hands on his knees. "Oh, God. Oh, God."

Harrison stared at his phone. "She didn't call. My mother had an international plan on her phone. If the plane were going down it would've taken minutes before it crashed. If she was aware of what was happening, she would've—"

"Oh, God. Oh, God."

My hand clenched into a fist. "Stop saying that!"

Archie bolted straight up. "Lucas. My little brother. I have to tell my brother. Oh G—" He caught himself and took a step away from me.

Dayana stumbled out of the bathroom, wiping her mouth on her sleeve. "Do you have Lysol? Shit. It's a mess."

"How did you know?" I asked.

"Huh?"

"About your parents. Did the airline call you?"

"No, my parents weren't . . . They're not . . . Papi—his passport. They couldn't go. They weren't on the plane . . . I'll grab some paper towels to clean up and then I'll leave. I should go."

Wait. Her parents were alive?

Archie was crying and sucking in big gulps of breath. "Josie?"

"She'll be fine," I snapped. "Don't worry about her."

"But is she . . . ?"

"I said she'll be fine!"

He swiped an arm across his nose. "Jack, I think . . . I think I saw her like this once before. Well, not this bad, but quiet and—"

I ordered them to leave. All three of them. I wanted them out. I needed to be alone with my sister. I would take care of her this time. I would protect her.

I heard the front door close. Josie's chest moving up and down was the only sign she was still alive.

"Don't do this to me, Jo. Please, talk to me." She didn't move an inch. Not even her eyes.

I took off my shoes and climbed up onto the big, soft bed. My weight made it creak and sag in the middle. The house was silent now except for Josie's breathing. It sounded ragged, like she'd taken water into her lungs. Just like in that old sonogram, Josie was facing forward. I curled up on her left, turned toward her.

Waiting for her to tell me what to do.

When we were kids, lying beside Jo was the only thing that quieted my thoughts and calmed me down. Most of the day, there was this *pressure* racing around in me. Pushing me to move around, to do something, anything. Sitting still in class was torture. I'd yell out or throw a book or kick someone else's chair just to let some of that energy out. And then when Dad came home he'd yell at me for getting in trouble at school again and the pressure would build some more.

But when it got really bad, Jo always knew when to pull me away to her room. I'd lie back, stare at the ceiling, and concentrate on her voice while she talked about softball or her friends or whatever. There was finally peace. And relief. But as I lay next to her the night of the party, she was silent and the thoughts in my head were never louder.

Dad's parents, Grandma Nelly and Grandpa Ralph, arrived after 5 a.m. and found me there, still waiting for Josie to talk. They'd both been crying, but they were dressed nicely like they always were.

"Josie, can you hear me? It's Grandpa. Can you say something, sweetie?"

I told them she'd be fine, that she just needed a little time to deal, but Grandpa called his friend Dr. Mike to ask his advice. Grandma seemed very worried about the mess downstairs. "People are going to be coming here, Jack. We can't leave it like this. Your parents wouldn't have wanted that." So she called Marybeth with the news that her longtime clients were dead, and their house wasn't going to clean itself. Marybeth showed up, shaky and sniffling, and Grandma followed her around the house pointing out spots she was missing.

As soon as the stores opened, Grandpa started making trips to delis, supermarkets, and coffee shops. "Your mom and dad meant something to a lot of people. To this community. You will never be alone. Wait until you and Josie see how they come out to support you."

He was right about the people. But wrong about Josie seeing it.

While Jo remained under, our house filled up and stayed that way. News of the crash spread and by the next morning cousins, aunts, uncles, neighbors, Dad's coworkers, Mom's book club, even strangers started showing up. All I wanted to do was stay with Jo, but Grandma forced me to shower, shave, put on nice clothes, and come downstairs. "At least *one* of you needs to be there. And Dr. Mike is going to stop by later. I'd like him to take a look at Josie."

Everyone asked about Jo. When you're 6'4", 260 pounds, and your parents just died, you can't hide. Without Josie, I had to be the host of the party. Put on a jacket, greet people at the door, thank them for coming, listen to their boring stories, their bullshit clichés. When I tried to disappear to the basement to hit the heavy bag, Grandpa stopped me to deliver a speech about being "the man of the house." His son would be proud.

When we were six, Mom made Jo and me take piano lessons with some lady down the block. For a year, all we practiced was how to play "Heart and Soul," that duet everyone knows. Jo got it right away. As usual, it took me eight times as long. I had a hard time sitting still on that bench. But eventually I got it.

Once we had it down, the lessons stopped. And at every single party in our house Mom would lead us to the piano like a couple of show ponies. We'd sit at the piano, Josie playing the high notes and me playing the low ones. Mom would announce to everyone that this song was perfect for us because her twins really were two parts of a whole. I was the heart and Josie was the soul. I wondered if the people in our house the day after the crash were waiting for an encore.

Grandpa's buddy Dr. Mike showed up looking like he'd just come from playing eighteen at the golf course.

"Thanks for coming, Mike. My granddaughter is upstairs."

Dr. Mike shook my hand and didn't let go. "I'm sorry, pal. Your dad . . . I ever tell you about the time we won the member-guest tournament? So Rich lines up the putt and I'm thinking there's no way. Not even Rich Clay can make this. I mean, you know your dad. The guy was like a god, but—"

"Who the fuck cares?" It shot out of my mouth before I

could stop it. But it felt good. I'd been keeping it inside so long.

"Excuse me?"

"Who. The. Fuck. Cares? He's not a god. He's dead. Mom's dead, too. And Josie might as well be dead. Who the fuck cares about golf and cold cuts and stains on the fucking carpet?"

Grandpa rushed over and dug his fingers into my bicep. "What are you doing, Jackie? Everyone's looking at you."

I ripped my arm away and he stumbled back into the bar, knocking a bottle of vodka to the ground, where it shattered. As Grandma hurried over to clean it up, I bolted out the door, ripped off my sports jacket, and just kept going. I ran down our block and kept going. Past Dayana's house. Then Archie's. Past Sunny Horizons.

My legs were shot and my lungs were burning, but I ran as hard as I could. I only stopped when I got to the beach and I couldn't go any farther. I stood there, sucking in the salty air, staring at the waves. I know the ocean is supposed to calm some people down. I didn't get that. It never stopped moving. Encroaching onto the land. Wave after wave after wave. Relentless. Pulling everything in, smashing it back down.

When I finally staggered back up the driveway at home it was dark out and my dress shirt was soaked through with sweat. My calf started to cramp and I bent over to stretch when I noticed the smell of a cigarette. I limped into the backyard, where a woman in a black dress was smoking behind a bush. She spun around when she heard me approaching.

Dayana's mom. "Vanesa?" I said uncertainly.

"Lo siento. Jack, sorry . . ." Her voice sounded dry and hollow.

The back door slid open. We hung back as Grandpa Ralph walked outside to show off the pool to an older couple I didn't recognize. When they went back inside, Vanesa coughed violently. Her face looked puffy and swollen, like a boxer's.

"Daya . . . She is in the car."

"You can come inside. Both of you."

I heard jingling as Dayana hurried around the corner. Her eyes were red and glassy. "We should go, Mami. I told you this was a mistake."

Why? Vanesa was their friend. She worked with Dad at the law firm. She probably knew him better than most of the people inside. "*They're* the ones who should go home," I said. "I can't deal with everyone saying the same shit, the same pointless shit. 'They were wonderful people.' 'They loved you.' 'They were lucky to have you.' I just stare and nod."

"It's like Mom and Dad are throwing a party, but they're not here. And Jo's gone," I said.

Dayana let go of her mother's arm. "Still?"

"I don't understand," said Vanesa. "Where did Josie go?"

"She's awake and her eyes are open, but she's not there. I don't know where she is. My grandparents want her to see a doctor. I just . . . I just need her to wake up."

36

"If you need help, don't be afraid to ask." Vanesa removed another cigarette from her purse and lit it with a shaky hand. She looked over at Dayana. "Fourteen years and not one smoke," she said, "since we arrived here." The cigarette slipped from her fingers and dropped to the ground. She cursed in Spanish, then said, "Your dad. He was a busy man. I know he was hard on you, but—"

"Mami! He just said he doesn't want to hear bullshit. Come on." Dayana started to drag her mother back to the car.

"What's it like?" I asked, stopping them in their tracks.

"What?"

"What's it like to be almost dead?"

Vanesa stared at me. I wished I hadn't asked that.

She just turned and ran off.

Dayana didn't know what to do. "I'm sorry, Jack. I'm sorry it's all so fucked-up."

I stood there in the driveway. Alone again. Vanesa's cigarette smoldered in the flower bed. I stubbed it out with my heel and watched the smoke float up and slowly drift off into the sky. I dropped to my chest at the side of the pool and dunked my head into the cool water. I thought about how when she was little Jo used to sit at the bottom of the pool and how it always freaked me out. With my face in the water, I couldn't hear anything coming from inside the house. I kept my head under until my lungs burned and I started to feel light-headed. Until I couldn't last any longer. *Almost dead.*

I pulled my face out and gasped for air as the water

dripped off my shaved head. As I stood up, I got a weird feeling someone was watching me. I looked over at the blue house peeking out of the trees behind ours. In a small window on the top floor, a ghostly face pressed against the glass. As soon as I spotted him, Harrison pulled the blinds closed and disappeared.

I turned and walked back toward the house, toward Josie. The house had never been more full of people and it had never been emptier.

4

JOSIE

OF COURSE I HEARD ALL THE RANDOMS coming and going. Grandma kept bringing visitors into my bedroom to talk to me. They had lots of kind and loving words to say about Mom and Daddy. And I could feel the vibration of my phone blowing up next to me. I heard Jack promise everything would be okay. I also heard him go into the bathroom by himself, turn on the water, and scream until his voice was hoarse.

But most of the time it was coming from far away.

When I was little, I liked to see how long I could hold my breath underwater. Daddy would set his stopwatch and I'd fill my lungs and sink to the bottom of the pool. I liked hanging out down there. The sun made these shimmering reflections that looked like the sky on a different planet. You could hear voices at the surface, but it's like they were coming from someplace else.

So when Dayana's words sunk in at the party, it's like this

hole opened behind her, one only I could see. I just wanted to go away, to pretend that none of this was real. So I pinched my nose and I dove in. As a kid, I never got to see how long I could stay down there because Jack would get all anxious, dive in, and try to drag me to the top. He was small and not very strong, but he kept tugging at me until I had to come up. Daddy said it was just like Jack to give up before I did.

He was a lot bigger and stronger now, and he worked hard to drag me to the surface, but I kept going under again. Underwater was peaceful and safe. Time didn't matter. Nothing was real. I didn't have to think about Daddy and Mom.

What was the last thing I said to them? I couldn't even remember. I was in the middle of some text-chain drama over the party guest list when they hopped a car to the airport. Did I even say goodbye?

Jack brought me food and changes of clothes, and I could hear how he was struggling. I know that when things go wrong for Jack, he sometimes does dangerous things. Destructive things. Like when he stole Daddy's car and crashed it. I couldn't let him do that. So I tried to resurface. For Jack.

I'd been down here before. And I'd made it back up. But this time as I pulled and kicked, as much I reached for the light, there were weights on my ankles, dragging me down.

Jack was out for another run when Grandma led Siobhan and Cody into my room. Siobhan had been my best friend since I chose to sit next to her in ninth-grade science. She was tall and popular and you did not want to get on her bad side. But she was loyal to me and she was willing to be mean so I didn't have to. Cody was everything you could ask for in a boyfriend. Hot, sensitive. He was a surfer, so he had a great body and this amazing messy hair. And he never asked for more than I gave him. I watched from underwater as they arrived at my bedside. Siobhan was crying. She'd brought me flowers, and when I didn't reach out for them, she set them across my legs.

You should see your feed. It's so full of love right now.

Cody squeezed onto the bed next to me. *I mean when the party ended like that, we didn't really know what was happening, babe. And then Jack went apeshit and started throwing everyone out. If you guys had told us right away . . .*

Siobhan patted my hand like she was petting a scared dog. *We wouldn't have gotten so pissed. When you didn't text back last night, I was freaking? Like, when do you not text back? And then I was like, what, am I not good enough to be with you when your parents die? Like, aren't I supposed to be there for you and Jack? But then someone said you were, like, in a coma or whatever so we rallied? Wait. Can she even hear us?* She moved to the other side of me. *I think we should selfie this, just so everyone knows you're okay.*

Is *she okay?* Cody whispered.

Jack returned to find them squeezed into my bed as Siobhan tried to find the right camera angle. His voice was tight as he asked them to leave the room. I could hear him unloading on them once they got to the hallway. *Don't come back here without asking me first. I don't care what my grand-parents say. Just go!*

When Jack came back into my room, Grandpa Ralph and Grandma Nelly followed him. *Why did you let them in here?!*

Grandma Nelly picked up my wrist to check my pulse. *They love her, Jack. She can't just stay in here by herself. What if I call over your friends? Archie and Harrison and the Calderón girl.*

They aren't our friends.

Of course they are. You share something. Josie needs that. She needs people..

She needs me.

Grandma Nelly cleared her throat twice and nodded at Grandpa. He blew his nose into a handkerchief. *Jackie, your grandmother and I want to take Josie to see someone. A specialist.*

I let you march Dr. Mike in here to see her. He said she's fine.

He didn't say she's fine. He said give her another day and then bring her in. And Dr. Mike is an orthopedist, not a therapist. Your sister requires professional help.

I'm helping her, Jack insisted. *She'll come out of it. She's eating, right?*

Barely, said Grandpa Ralph. *She's barely breathing. I did a search on this. What she's doing is called dissociating. It's a symptom of post-traumatic stress. It's serious. People come in here and look at her like she's some kind of oddity—*

I don't give a shit about those people. I don't even know half of them. Let them come here and stare and eat the fifty-seven pounds of chicken salad you bought, but you're not taking Jo anywhere.

Today's the day, Jo. They're calling it a memorial service instead of a funeral since the bodies . . . Unless you want Grandpa dropping you off at the hospital, I'm going to need you to stay with me. And if you don't shower and get dressed, Grandma will do that for you. Your black dress, with the stuff on the shoulders, is hanging on the door. Be downstairs in twenty. What do you say before every party? "Game face on."

I turned my head to look at him.

Jack stopped at the door. *Jo*—His voice caught in his throat. *We're gonna be okay, Jo. I mean, not okay-okay. Not for a long time. Maybe never again. If I said different, you'd know I was lying. But okay. I'm here when you're ready. I'm heart. You're soul.*

So I hauled myself off the bottom of the pool and got dressed for my parents' memorial service. But I sank back down when Jack started to cry in the limo.

Archie was right. This wasn't the first time I'd almost let myself sink to the bottom when life on the surface got too ugly. I'd been down here before, when all that stuff happened with Coach Murph. When it got really bad.

'Course it wasn't always like that. At the beginning it was great. He was the best softball coach I'd ever had.

When I was ten, Coach taught me how to throw a windmill pitch. "You put a little action at the end and the ball will rise up right at the batter's chin. She'll be too afraid you're gonna take her head off to even think about swinging. And, JC, you just give her that sweet smile and let her know you own her."

Coach Murph called me "his little machine," and together we won three league championships, two AAU golds, and four all-star tournaments. I'd never had a coach who cared as much as he did. I'd never had an anyone who cared as much as he did. Daddy was always traveling and Mom was on fifteen charity boards, but Coach never missed a game. He even offered to drive me to practice and tournaments in the blue Mustang he called "Shirley." On the road, he introduced me to his "old-guy music," like Bruce Springsteen and Guns N' Roses. For some reason, he really liked singers who screamed. He talked to me like a real person, not just a kid. He told me about life, how he'd wanted to be a pro baseball player but had to give it up when his elbow got shredded. How I should never lose sight of what I want because one day you could wake up and find you're working at a car dealership and coaching girls AAU softball just to stay close to the game you love. Not that he didn't find it rewarding.

Daddy was in D.C. on business when we won states. I'd never seen Coach Murph so happy. After the game, he gave me the trophy and told me to keep it in my room because I deserved it. On the way home, Coach asked if I was hungry. I waited in the car while he picked up some sandwiches. He drove Shirley down near the beach and parked, but he left the key in the ignition so we could listen to the radio.

He handed me my chicken sandwich, and then he pulled out a bottle of wine and a plastic cup. "Do you have any idea how proud I am of you?"

"Thanks." I'd seen him have a couple of beers at a softball picnic, but he'd never had a drink in the car before.

He poured himself a cup, drank it, and refilled. "It's so wrong that your parents weren't there to see what you did today. It's the same thing with Christine. She doesn't understand why I do this, why it means so much to me. To us."

Coach hardly ever talked about his wife in front of me. She'd never been to one of our games. "Christine doesn't want you to coach softball?"

"We were really young when we got married," he said. "It's different now. We're different." He reached down and lowered the radio.

"Are you gonna get divorced?" I asked, in between bites of my sandwich. Coach held out his cup and offered me a sip of the wine. My heart sped up and I got a weird feeling in my stomach. I liked that he saw me as mature enough to drink with him. I liked how he talked to me; even how he looked at me.

That's how it was when it all started. We'd get together and just talk a lot. He really cared about what I had to say. Like he wanted my opinion on things. I told him about how Jack was always fighting with Dad over his grades and how he didn't want Harrison to tutor him anymore because he was embarrassed that he needed help. I told him how it hurt that Dayana never invited me over to her new house. I even gave him one of my favorite drawings from Archie, the one of me in my softball uniform.

Whenever I wanted to see Coach, he was there. If I needed a ride, he'd leave work to pick me up. I could text him in the middle of the night about the dumbest things and he'd write back in like seconds.

You awake?

IM now

Yankees won ☺

Yanks suk. Go Mets

He didn't need me to take care of him like Jack did. And he didn't treat me like I needed to be taken care of either. Jack blamed Dad for always working and not being around. When he told me he hated that I relied on Coach to take me to games and practice, I accused Jack of being jealous. I said he liked it better when he was the only guy I could talk to. And all of that was before anything was even going on.

I did feel bad that I wasn't around for Jack. He was getting into even more trouble at school, ignoring his homework and not even studying for tests. He talked back to teachers and sometimes just walked out of class. Dad was on him all the time. There was so much yelling in the house. But that just made me love the days I spent with Coach even more. I loved the sound of Shirley's engine pulling up the driveway, the shiny blue exterior and the smell of the leather seats. When Coach was driving, I'd rest my hand on top of his. We'd go out to the diner and our knees would secretly touch under the table. It was confusing, but it was exciting, too. I knew we were more than friends, but I told myself there was nothing wrong with it. We were just close. And that could happen at any age. He cared about me. I think I could've stayed like that forever.

During the winter of my eighth-grade year, stuff started changing. Coach said things were getting worse at home, that Christine was being really mean to him. Always criticizing everything he did or said. He'd pick me up and he'd already smell like beer or wine. He didn't want to talk as much, but he was cutting practices short so that we could have more alone time before he dropped me off at home.

In the car one day he watched me put on lip balm and he asked if he could try it. I started to hand it over, but instead he leaned over into me and pressed his lips against mine. I was scared. I knew it didn't feel right, but he was my coach. He went in a second time, pressing his weight against me and this time using his tongue to open my mouth.

After that, kissing became a part of the car rides. Then touching. By the spring he was whispering he loved me. He talked about what it would be like when I was older and we could be together for real. All I ever wanted was to make Coach Murph proud of me. So I kept getting in that blue Mustang, even after the sound of the engine made me want to cry and the smell of the leather seats made me sick to my stomach. I never told him to stop. Not when he reached under my shirt or undid my belt. Not when he took my hand and showed me what to do with it. Not at the overnight tournament in Maryland when he asked me to wait for the other girls to fall asleep so I could sneak into his hotel room. Not even when he took my hand and told me he couldn't wait any longer to be with me.

Everything in my body was screaming to get out of that hotel room. But the screams stayed inside as he led me over to the king-size bed and pulled back the dingy covers. And as Coach lay down on top of me I figured out how to sink to the bottom of the pool.

I worked hard every day to never again be that girl who had to go underwater because she felt helpless and afraid. And I did it all on my own. I didn't ask for help. Not even from Daddy. I knew I could fight my way up again. Because I had to. So I forced myself to surface in the funeral home and I treaded water as hard as I could.

I didn't sink when Jack guided me out of the limo and into a sea of black. Even with all those people surrounding me, hugging me, touching me. When Cody came up from behind me and wrapped his arms around my shoulders, I resisted the urge to scream and to push him away until Jack finally pried him off. When the service was over, I followed Jack into the small lobby, where too many people were crammed in. A man in a wrinkled suit with a bunch of little Band-Aids on his neck touched my arm. This set off Jack, who spun around to face him. It was Nelson, Dayana's father. Dayana stood behind him, her purple hair covering most of her face.

"Jack, Josie, I'm so very sorry for your loss," Nelson said.

"They were wonderful people, your parents. If I could have traded places with them—"

"Papi!" Dayana looked like she was going to say something more, but I turned away. I turned away and that's when I saw *him*.

In the back corner of the lobby, reading a program, was Coach Murph. He'd grown a beard and his hair was shorter. I recognized the brown corduroy blazer he'd worn for every end-of-season softball awards night.

". . . And the MVP trophy goes to . . . Josie Clay. Shocker, huh? Come on up and grab another, JC."

Maybe Coach Murph felt me notice him, or maybe he was only pretending to read the program in the first place. He looked at me. Looked. At. Me. He put his hand on his heart, smiled sadly and mouthed, "Hi, JC."

Suddenly, I was sinking faster than I ever had, rocketing to the bottom, the breath flying from my lungs. I reached for Jack, for anything that might slow me down. I was drowning, watching the world disappear maybe forever this time. And just as I was about to crash, I felt a hand grab mine. It was smooth and clammy, so unlike Jack's rough, beefy paws. I blinked and saw that the hand belonged to Archie.

He leaned in, his breath smelling of mint. "You need to get outside?"

"Yeah."

Behind his thick lenses, his eyes grew wide. "You said something."

"Yeah."

"Cool."

Archie wasn't as good at opening holes in a crowd as Jack, but he made up for it with a complete willingness to knock into any man, woman, or child between us and the door. He used his sketchbook like a shield, battering people out of our way. He led me through group after group, with each step pulling me farther and farther away from Coach Murph.

Finally, we arrived at the twin poster boards near the entrance. The way the photos were placed, Mom and Daddy appeared to be looking at you as you walked in between them.

Daddy flashed his half smile like he'd just told a joke. He told the best jokes. They always cheered me up when I was sad or upset, and when I laughed, he'd hug me and tell me I was his girl.

Mom had this way of making a photo look as if she were caught in the middle of having the best time of her life. Her friends said she could always make the best of any situation. Her giant funeral headshot was no different. *Can you believe our plane crashed? I mean, how crazy is that?!*

Archie must've sensed me falling into the vortex between the photos. He tugged hard on my hand, yanking me through the door and into the blinding sunlight. "You okay?" he asked. "Sorry, stupid question. Of course you're not. But you're talking again?"

"I guess so." I was as surprised as he was.

He handed me a mint from his pocket. "How come?"

"You talked to me and I wanted to answer."

"Is that the first thing you've said? Since the party?"

I nodded. "I was sitting underwater. Even if I'd said something, even if I tried to yell, I don't think it would've come out. Nobody would've heard it."

"Like *Alien*," said Archie. "'In space, no one can hear you scream.'" He took off his glasses and used his jacket to wipe away a bead of sweat as it rolled down his nose. His brown eyes had glints of yellow that bounced around in the light. Like the reflections of the sun at the bottom of the pool. "Josie? Just so you know . . . I would've heard it."

5

HARRISON

TO DO:

-~~Finalize funeral arrangements with Schaeffer Funeral Home. Coffin? (No body)~~ X

-~~Write obituary.~~ X

-~~Submit obituary to the press.~~ X

-~~Choose reading for service.~~ X

-~~Practice reading in mirror so that it seems natural in cemetery. (Look up from cards, speak slowly and clearly.)~~ X

-Prepare Mom's clothes for consignment. (Pickup scheduled for 10 A.M.)

-~~File papers to have Bobby Rebkin (Pop) declared my legal guardian.~~

-Follow up with Jack. Will tutoring continue now that it's no longer required by Mr. Clay?

-Prepare notebooks and supplies for first day of school. X

-Contact authorities about the crash. Why?

"There's nothing more satisfying than crossing off items on a to-do list," my mother used to say, before she—before. Mom preached the gospel of the list. "Wake up each morning and decide what you're doing today to achieve your goals, to work toward The Plan. Write it down in specific steps. Don't go to bed until you're satisfied that you've completed what you set out to do." She'd be proud of all that I've accomplished in the days since her death. Without any assistance, I planned a respectful memorial service, burying an empty coffin in the plot Mom had pre-purchased years ago. I prepared the house for life without her, completed two college application essays, and filed a request to have my absentee father declared my legal guardian. I would've completed the third essay ("Please write page 164 of your autobiography") if not for the arrival of a particularly difficult glitch.

Since the party at Jack and Josie's house, I'd suffered only three glitches, two of which were relatively minor. The last one, however, felt like it was never going to end. They're unpredictable, these glitches. I never know when one will occur or how severe it will be. I only know it's coming when the symptoms start, and by that time it's too late. The room begins to feel warm, my palms perspire, my heart rate increases, and my hands tremble. From there, a glitch can take me down any number of different rabbit holes: numbness in the extremities, abdominal distress, chest pain, choking, absolute certainty that I am dying. I can't remember when I had my first glitch experience. They have always just been a part of my life.

Through the years, they've varied in frequency and intensity. I've learned to power through the minor episodes with a strategy I've dubbed "Pi in the Sky." I find the nearest dark, quiet spot and imagine myself floating above the earth as I recite pi to as many decimal places as I can remember. I continue to soar and recite digits until my pulse returns to normal and I'm able to resume my life. My record is eighty-six, although I average about forty-three. I learned it by grouping the digits into bunches of four and memorizing it in chunks like a song. It sounds harder than it is.

3.(1415)(9265)(3889)(7932)(3846)(2643)(3832)(7950)(2884)(1971) . . .

Major glitches are not powered through. They do not subside with the recitation of numbers, not even if I made it to a googleplex. Major glitches feel as though they will continue until my heart explodes or my brain spontaneously combusts in my skull cavity. They terrify and haunt me. I never talked to Mom about the glitches. She had enough of her own worries to deal with. And they weren't part of The Plan. *Every day at the clinic I see people who have thrown their lives away. That won't be you. My son will be stronger than that.*

I believe I managed to keep my glitches hidden from everyone, in fact, except Mr. Unsinger, the school custodian. Once during third period, he opened the door to his cramped supply closet to retrieve his mop and found me among the cleaning supplies, reciting numbers and struggling to siphon oxygen into my lungs. He wanted to call the nurse, but I begged him not to. I grabbed his wrist and didn't let go until the anxiety passed. Mr. U never tried to pull away. He didn't even ask any questions.

"My sister used to get these episodes," he said. "After her first baby was born. Said she thought she was having a heart attack. Not for me to say, but you should talk to someone. Till then, use the space any time you need it."

On the day after Mom's service, the glitch started while I was filling out an insurance form online. I got to question number four: Cause of Death. I started to type "Plane crash," but I realized that didn't truly answer the question. What was the cause? What was the *reason*?

I went straight for Mom's tiny bedroom closet, which was mostly empty after I'd spent the morning packing her clothes for donation. I'd left only one item hanging there—the red sweater with the cracked button she'd worn on the morning she told me that Pop left. I was seven.

"Where did he go?" I'd asked.

"I'm not sure, sweetheart."

"When's he coming back?"

"I don't know that either."

"Last night when he kissed me goodnight, he said what

he always says. 'I'll see ya when I see ya.' It doesn't make sense."

"No. It doesn't make sense."

I sat on the floor of the closet, clutching Mom's sweater, reciting digits, until the doorbell rang. And rang. I checked my pulse, took a deep breath, and diagnosed myself as ready to step out into the light. I hurtled down the stairs, but my legs tangled and I tripped, landing hard on my tailbone before bouncing the rest of the way to the floor. I limped to the front door and opened it to see Dayana repeatedly jabbing at the bell.

"Took you long enough," she said, a bag slung over her shoulder. Then she saw my face and added, "I mean I'm sure you were busy what with your mom crashing and all. Oh shit, sorry."

"Dayana . . ." Dayana's father, Nelson, walked up behind her. I hadn't seen him in ten years. He looked twenty years older.

He put out his hand. "Hello, Harrison."

When I was a kid I loved hearing him talk. My mother's Jersey City accent sounded like a tin can banging around a washing machine compared to his. Nelson had this formal way of speaking and his accent bounced and flowed like it was carried along by an ocean breeze. I especially liked the way he said my name. Ha-dee-soon.

"We have come by to see if you might be in need of something from us," he said. "Have you heard from your father? I have made attempts to contact him, but the phone number

I had was disconnected. I left a message for his brother. I am not for sure they are speaking these days."

"I sent him an email," I said. "Since I'm only seventeen, I needed him to be declared my legal guardian. He doesn't have to actually guard me. But without his signature they won't allow me to stay in my house. I want to stay in my house."

Dayana looked down and rubbed her hand back and forth against her forehead. Lately she'd been covering her skin in a pale and cakey substance that made her look sickly and hid any trace of her freckles. When we were little, the older kids around the neighborhood sometimes made jokes about those freckles.

Maybe if you connected the dots they'd teach you how to speak English.

She couldn't understand what they were saying, of course. But Josie did. And she didn't like it. She'd take Dayana's hand and march her right up to the bullies and insist that those freckles were marks left by fairy dust. They meant that she was special and magic. That explanation always seemed plausible to me. I knew she was special.

Even as a child, I wasn't one to believe in magic and fairies. But Josie believed and so did Archie and that was enough for me. At home, Mom and Pop were always screaming at each other. Calling each other names. Slamming doors. At school, my friends and I were in this bubble. Archie would draw us as superheroes or kid astronauts. And it felt real. Realer than what was happening in my house.

"You have no other family who is able stay with you? I do not think you should be alone, Ha-dee-soon."

There was no one. Mom's parents died when she was young, and I'd never even met Pop's family. "You're lucky," he'd told me once when I asked about it.

I assured Nelson I would be fine on my own. I preferred it, actually. Nelson invited me to go along for lunch with him and Dayana. His treat. I thanked him for his offer but declined. *Be polite, but don't take handouts. You don't want to owe anyone but yourself.* Mom had broken her own rule once when Pop left, and we nearly lost the house. She never let me forget it.

"If you need anything at all, please do ask," Nelson said. "Your mother—she was very proud of you. You were her everything."

Dayana leaned in and said something softly in her father's ear. He paused, then nodded, and walked back to the car, leaving Dayana behind. She waited until he drove off, then pulled the saddlebag off her shoulder and unzipped it. "I brought you something," she said. As she headed toward the glass coffee table, an irrational thought careened through my brain. *Fairy dust . . . She's brought me a bag of fairy dust. We'll pour it over my head and everything will be back to normal. Fairy dust keeps planes in the air.*

She turned over the bag and onto the coffee table poured pill vials of all variety. "For you."

"Wow, that's . . . Thank you? What a kind thought. No one's ever . . . Are those prescription?" And then I found myself blurting, "Are your parents really alive because he was too lazy to get his passport renewed?"

Dayana blinked. "Have you been talking to my mom? I'm sorry. I mean of all the people to be chosen . . ."

"No, it's excellent. Wonderful luck. I mean, my mother, she— Thank you for the drugs, but I have work waiting and Jack still hasn't gotten back to me on the subject of tutoring, so—"

"Harrison?"

"Yes."

"What're you gonna do?"

"Do?"

"I don't know. I mean, your mom's dead. You're alone in this house."

"Senior year starts tomorrow," I said. "I have to keep up my GPA in order to retain my position as number one in the class over Mackenzie Markowitz. I'll be sending in my application early to Harvard. I'll move to Cambridge, stay in Boston for med school, followed by an internship at Mass General—either cardiology or pulmonology. After that . . . I'm not sure yet."

Dayana clearly didn't know how to respond to The Plan that Mom and I had been formulating for over a decade. Maybe she was expecting me to collapse in hysterics or drain a whole bottle of her pills. But I hadn't cried a single time since I heard about the crash. According to the websites, I was probably in shock. Not like Josie, but in shock nonetheless. Or maybe I didn't break down because Mom prepared me. Over and over again. *I won't live forever, Harrison, and you can't count on your father. But even if I'm gone I won't leave you. Just like my parents never left me when they died.* She told me this the day after Pop left. And at least once a week every week after that.

Dayana picked up a pill bottle from the table, shook several green tablets into her hand, and swallowed them dry.

"I need to go back upstairs and finish my essay," I told her. "I don't want to lose momentum."

She looked disappointed. "Can I hang out? I promise I won't bother you. These are good for anxiety, but after I take them I need to lie down for a few minutes. Plus, I don't really feel like going home. There's a lot of crying."

"Okay, I guess."

She followed me up the stairs and back into my room. I sat down at my desk as she wandered around, checking out the books on my shelves.

"It was Nelson's idea to come over here," she said. "He showered and shaved and everything. He and Vanesa are still barely talking, but since the crash, it's like they've switched places. I know they could've died and all, but it's totally fucking bizarre."

"She wasn't even supposed to go on the trip, you know."

"Your mom?"

"She hated being the fifth wheel or seventh wheel with the other couples. But Jack's and Archie's moms convinced her. I heard them talking when I was tutoring him. 'You deserve fun, too, Jen.' 'We miss you, Jen. The kids are seniors.

We made it!' Jack's mom even offered to pay. They wouldn't take no for an answer."

"Oh." She stopped at my porthole window and peered down onto the Clays' patio. "Why did you go to the party?"

"I don't know. Mom and I had agreed that I'd spend the night outlining my essays. I spoke to her right before they boarded the plane. The music was loud and the connection was spotty. I could barely hear her. I hung up before we even said goodbye. I never did that. I thought she would call back. I waited hours. I was closing the blinds when I saw Archie down there on the patio. He was struggling with the keg and getting beer all over his shirt. I felt . . . affronted."

"Affronted?"

"Insulted. Offended. I'm Jack's tutor. Or I was. Mom baby-sat all three of us for years when we were repaying the loan from the Clays. I thought, *What am I doing in this room? If Archie Gallagher is at this party, then why not me?*"

She put a hand on the streaked glass. "Why not you?"

"But I was sorry as soon as I got there. Archie was the only person I really knew and I don't really know him anymore either."

Dayana turned away and sank down on my bed. She picked up a photo of me and Pop on the beach from when I was four. He was in the water up to his waist while I stood on his shoulders, holding on to his hands.

Dayana lay back, one of her oversize black stomping boots now dangling off the end of her foot. "I remember him," she said. "Your dad. He always called me Dana. And rolled his r's like he was trying to sound Spanish. 'Hola, Dana. Yo soy Rrrrroberrrrto.' Oh, and he wore sandals and he was missing a toenail. Freaky."

I nodded. "His right big toe. He used to say it gave his foot character. He lost it in a surfing accident when he was a teenager. Although every time I asked him about it, he'd invent a different story about the incident. Sometimes it would be a rival surfer who cut him off, or a once-in-a-decade rogue wave that appeared in a flat sea and slammed him into the jetty. Once he told me he'd been attacked by a hungry great white."

Dayana had dozed off on my bed. She murmured and turned her head, leaving a smudged streak of pale makeup on my gray pillowcase. On her cheek, I could see an exposed swath of freckled skin. A girl in my bed. I'd imagined many such scenarios with many different girls. Celebrities, classmates, teachers. Suddenly, the room felt ten degrees warmer. My hands were slick. My heart raced. "Excuse me, please," I said to unconscious Dayana, before rushing back toward Mom's closet and sweater.

When I stepped back out this time, Dayana was gone.

The alarm on my phone trilled at 6:14 A.M., but I had already been awake for hours. I can't say for sure whether I slept at all the night before my first day of senior year. I ran through the day's schedule for the hundredth time. First period—AP calculus. Math had always come easily to me. Math made sense. Equations made sense. $A + B = C$. Everything had a purpose and a reason. I tried to write an equation for Mom's accident. Anguilla + Bad Luck = Crash? But equations have variables and constants. There was no constant here, unless you counted Mom being gone.

I silenced the alarm and walked to the bathroom. To save time, I'd slept in the blue button-down and chinos my mother had bought me for my first day of senior year. She liked to brag that at seventeen I already dressed like the man I would become.

I walked to the mirror and shut my eyes, visualizing my day just as Mom had taught me on the morning I started preschool at Sunny Horizons. It was the same technique she taught her patients at the rehab clinic where she worked as a counselor. *Imagine how you want your day to go. Set goals and picture how you will achieve them, just as I've been visualizing your life since before you were born.* I envisioned myself driving Mom's red Saturn to school, sitting in class, memorizing the course syllabi—attacking senior year with renewed purpose. I saw myself feeling solid and safe and in control, and making it through day one without the use of Mr. Unsinger's supply closet.

I lifted Mom's keys from the hook by the door and was heading for the driveway when I realized I'd forgotten something very important: the traditional first day photo. Mom had snapped the same picture of me on the front porch from preschool to junior year, pasting them in a brown-and-gold album. I'd watched her doing it last year and it struck me how all those photos fit across two pages. Nearly my entire life contained in one collage. How many pages did Mom's life fill? Four? Five? Less than the menu at a diner.

This year, I'd have to serve as my own photographer. I pulled out my phone, extended my arm the way I'd seen classmates do, and took my very first selfie. When I surveyed my work, I almost didn't recognize the face in the photo. Under scraggly beard growth, my cheeks looked concave and my eyes were bracketed by dark circles. I inhaled deeply and started reciting: *3.1415926535 . . .*

En route to the kitchen, I took a wide arc around the coffee table, which was littered with Dayana's pill bottles. I reached into the refrigerator for one of Mom's kombucha drinks.

I didn't have a license, of course. There were too many other things to do. It's not like we could afford a second vehicle. And I'd be moving to Boston next year, where I'd rely on mass transportation anyway. But how difficult could driving be? Everyone did it. I spent ten minutes watching a YouTube video entitled "Learn to Drive," and I climbed into the driver's side of the Saturn.

In the drink holder sat an old tube of Mom's lipstick. Lying there never to be used again. Like an artifact in a museum. Cold and lifeless.

Often when I was struggling with a difficult math problem, I'd walk away from it and allow my brain to keep working while I did something else. It would come back to the problem when it was ready. As I turned the ignition key my brain returned to the unsolvable equation. Mom was here and now she's not. I took the lipstick and wrote on the mirror.

MOM + X =

In the mirror I saw a black Jeep round the corner. Jack and Josie were already on their way to school. I wondered if they were asking these same questions about their parents. When I tutored Jack he struggled with complex equations. Was he struggling with this one, too? Was Josie staring at her mother's lipstick? Was Archie trying to draw answers in his sketchbook? I put the lipstick in my pocket, took a gulp of kombucha, and tried to ward off a glitch as I drove to my last first day of high school.

6

ARCHIE

I WAS ALMOST A NO-SHOW FOR THE FIRST DAY of senior year, but I couldn't stand another minute in the house. Josie and Jack's party had kicked off a week of non-stop events. After the Clays' memorial service there was the one Aunt Sarah organized for Mom and Dad. One for Harrison's mom. A vigil at the hospital. A dedication at the town hall.

Lucas and I went to everything. So did Harrison, Jack, and Josie. Dayana was always there, too. None of us talked much, but night after night, we all showed up. Just sitting near Josie made those minutes go by.

And then suddenly it was over. No more events. No more group. No more Josie. Just Lucas and me and a quiet house.

"Mr. Calderón dropped off some more food. I can heat it up for us," I'd say.

"I'm not hungry," Lucas would reply.

"Okay, let me know if you want something. I mean, not that you don't know how to use the microwave."

Lucas spent most of his time in his room. I barely looked up from my sketchpad.

I should've known something had changed when I woke up one morning to find hundreds of friend requests waiting for me. My previous record was one. But it didn't really hit me what had happened until I showed up to school that first day. I pulled my scooter into the lot at RBHS just as Josie and Jack were parking the Jeep. Josie was wearing an outfit I'd never seen and her hair was perfect, but her eyes looked like she hadn't slept in a week. Suddenly, a swarm of kids moved in, surrounding them. I tried to get close, but a trio of underclass girls rushed up to me. I'd never talked to any of them before and I didn't even know their names. Without saying a word, each of these sniffling strangers took turns hugging me.

A red sedan came screeching into the lot, forcing everyone to jump out of the way. Jack used the distraction to grab Josie's hand and shuttle her toward the school. Harrison stumbled out of the red car and soon he had a crowd gathering around him, too.

I thanked the three girls for their hugs and hustled to catch up to Josie and Jack. It wasn't hard to gain ground since they were slowed down by all the people who wanted to embrace them. I could see how much each of these encounters took out of Josie. Her shoulders slumped more with every step as she dragged her designer shoes across the blacktop.

I hadn't seen Josie since my parents' service. I went by her house a couple of times, but it was always full of people who looked like they'd just left the country club. So I never got past the sidewalk. As I walked behind them, Josie seemed to sense someone was following her. She turned around. I held my breath and raised my hand in a tentative wave. But she didn't wave back. She let Jack hold the door for her as they walked inside. And as the heavy door clanged shut, I wanted to turn around and go home. I didn't belong here with all these regular kids, showing off new haircuts, laughing, singing, and asking about each other's summers.

"You should've asked before you started blabbing to reporters, Arch." Dayana leaned against the wall of the school, covertly exhaling a puff of vapor. "Just sayin'."

It took me a moment to figure out what she was talking about. Then I realized: Aunt Sarah. Her stupid blog. Of course. That's why Josie looked at me like that.

"I needed to talk to *someone*," I said.

Dayana shrugged. "Guess you talked to the wrong fucking someone." She took another inhale. "You don't look so good."

Before I could answer I suddenly found myself wrapped in the long arms of Jack's girlfriend, Siobhan. "I am so so so sorry, Archie!" She knew my name? In heels, she was at least two inches taller than me, so my face sank into her neck. She smelled like cinnamon gum and body spray. I had no idea how to react. Should I hug her back? Or would Jack beat me senseless?

Siobhan didn't seem to notice how uncomfortable I was. "What you guys are going through . . . I can't even? I mean my mom? Doesn't get me at all? And my dad, his drinking's getting OOC. Totally shameful? But I love them so much? Like if they ever were in a crash . . . total devastation, you know?"

"Um. Yeah."

"You're all so brave to be here, you know that? Why don't you sit with us at lunch today? We'll save you a seat. Nothing stinky or gross, though? I have a sensitive gag reflex. Okay?"

She was waiting for me to answer. My jaw started jabbering. "I mean, I usually sit with this other group by the front. The art kids. Do you know them? Probably not. They're not like my good friends or anything. We just sit there and draw and critique each other's work and stuff. They're pretty cool. I guess. I'm sure they're expecting me, but it's not a serious commitment or anything, so . . ."

"Okay?" Siobhan repeated.

"Okay . . ."

Siobhan squeezed me again. "You're the best. What you said on that blog—"

"I shouldn't have—"

"Totally touched me. Tears. Like seriously emoche. Josie and Jack are lucky to have you in their lives."

Believe me, if I'd known it would become a big deal, I wouldn't have said anything to Aunt Sarah. I wasn't trying to get all famous. I mean, it would take a serious evil genius to come up with a plan like that, using his parents' death to become popular. I was just talking. I told her stuff because she asked. I kept talking because she listened.

When I'd stumbled home from Josie's the night of the party, Lucas was already asleep. I went to his door and I could hear him breathing. I stood out there, heaving, choking back sobs, trying not to wake him. I couldn't go in. Instead I wandered into Mom and Dad's room. They'd left without cleaning it, so the bed was unmade and there were clothes on the floor. Without even taking off my shoes, I climbed into the bed and burrowed under the blankets like I used to do when I was little, before Lucas was born. But the bed felt too big. So I grabbed all the pillows and put them around me. Then I reached for all the clothes from the floor and put those on top. But the sight of those empty clothes only made things worse. It was like reaching out for Mom and Dad and only feeling their shadows. When the crying really started, it felt like it would never stop.

I was still huddled in their bed the next morning when I heard Lucas pouring himself a bowl of cereal. He didn't even look up when I came into the kitchen.

"You're up early. I have a game in an hour. Jaden's dad is picking me up. Then I'm going to Sam's, so feel free to go wild."

"I don't think you should go."

"To Sam's? Why?"

I paused, wondering whether I could actually say this out loud. "I was at the party last night and—"

"How was it? Still can't believe you actually went. Did you talk to Josie?"

"No, I—"

"Why not?"

"She wasn't talking," I said.

"What do you mean she wasn't talking? You just have to do it, Arch. Less Clark Kent, more you know who. You like her, right?"

I couldn't figure out how to say it, so I just said it. "There was a plane crash, Luke. A terrible plane crash. Nobody knows how or why, but there were no survivors and Dayana showed up last night to tell us."

Lucas took a spoonful of cereal and shoveled it into his mouth. "Okay."

"Mom and Dad. It was their plane. They died," I added, and immediately started crying again.

"That's not funny."

I was crying too hard to argue.

"Why are you saying this? What's wrong with you?"

I grabbed a kitchen towel and wiped my face while I brought Lucas to the computer to show him the article about the crash. Lucas didn't cry. He didn't say anything. He just turned his back on me, went up to his room, and shut his door. I walked upstairs and placed my hand on his doorknob. I wanted to sit with him and talk about how we'd get through this, but I knew if I walked in there I'd just start bawling and jabbering and that would make things worse.

Besides, I knew Lucas was not alone in his room. He had a massive following of friends online, a whole army of support. At fourteen, Lucas was kind of a rock star in his corner of the social media universe. He was this good-looking, all-state soccer player. He was open and honest and comfortable with himself. And he liked guys. When he wasn't on the soccer field, he tweeted, blogged, posted all kinds of pictures and positive messages. I guess over time he'd become sort of a symbol to gay kids all over who were having a rough time, who maybe had closed-minded parents or lived in places that weren't as accepting. Mom said Lucas helped a lot of young people and teenagers just by being himself. So I was sure that when he needed it, Lucas would have lots of love coming back in return. My little brother would be fine. He always was. All those friends would be better at helping him than I could ever be.

I was sitting by myself in the kitchen, shoveling down spoonfuls of Lucas's soggy, leftover cereal, when Mom's sister, Aunt Sarah, showed up. She was dressed in black yoga pants and a black tank top and she was a hysterical mess.

She took my face in her hands and pressed hard against my cheeks. "We will face this as a family. Your mother was a loving, caring woman and she will always be in our hearts. And I will embrace you and your heritage just as she would have wanted." Heritage, seriously. And those are the only nice words I'd ever heard Sarah say about Mom. The last time I'd seen her was Thanksgiving when she and my mother got into a huge fight. Sarah had called her an uptight bitch, who was *just as bad as Mom.*

Sarah brought Lucas out to join us. He looked annoyed that we'd pulled him away from his phone.

"You two will come stay with us," she said. "You'll sleep in Gregor's room and I'll treat you like my own children."

"Um, okay, that's a really nice offer," I said. "For now I think I need to stay here so I can ride my scooter to school." I didn't want to live with Sarah. "But Lucas, this could be great for you. She can drive you to practice and you can come back whenever you want—"

Lucas got up from the table and walked to his room.

Aunt Sarah took my hand. "I'll talk to him. But I hope you know your mom was a hero. The way she saved people at the hospital. Not to mention adopting you . . . I want people to know about it and to know about you. I'm sure you've read my blog. People say it's a game changer. I don't know. I just like to share. And to listen."

I didn't know Aunt Sarah had a blog and if I did I would've never read it. She was one of the fakest people I knew and I hated how she spoke to Mom. But that morning she was the first person to really ask me questions. The first person to listen. So yeah, I talked. I talked about how Mom and Dad adopted me and gave me a great life. How they worked so hard to make me feel okay about being a black kid in a white family. How they were both so understanding when Lucas came out to them on his twelfth birthday.

I told her how Mom and Dad loved those vacations with their friends and how it had been thirteen years since we were all together at Sunny Horizons.

Aunt Sarah asked me about Harrison, Josie, and Jack, and even about Dayana. I brought out our class picture, along with some of the drawings I made when we were kids. I told her a hundred stories about our group, the Sunnies, and what amazing friends they were to me. Like when we were in first grade, and Mom and Aunt Sarah's mother, Granny Lois, died. While Granny was alive, she wasn't very nice to Mom and especially not to me. She wore her hair pulled back really tight, and I remember she used to yell at me if I spilled a drink or if I even went near her bag. She made Mom cry all the time. One time after Granny left, Mom told me it wasn't my fault that Granny treated me like that. She was *set in her ways* and had *old ideas* about what a family should look like.

Dad said, "Your mother is trying to say Granny is racist."

You'd think Mom wouldn't have been that upset when mean, racist Granny Lois died, but Dad said it was hard because they were fighting and they never made up. *Sometimes grown-up feelings are complicated*, he said. So I was sad for her, too. When I got to school that day, Harrison came over and handed me a piece of paper. It was the answers to the math homework I'd missed the prep for. At lunch, Jack slid his chips and his favorite cookies over to me. And when I saw Dayana at recess, she just ran up and hugged me.

None of them said anything about Granny. They didn't

have to. At the end of the day I opened my backpack and found a drawing in it. From Josie. She wasn't a great artist, but I could tell what she was going for. The picture was of me and Josie sitting together on the branch of the tree. Our tree. I realized when I talked to Aunt Sarah, I left out the part where none of us were friends anymore. It just never came up, I guess.

I didn't even notice when Sarah's blog post, *The Orphans of Sunny Horizons,* dropped a couple of days later. But now, as I made my way inside RBHS, I quickly learned that the story had gone viral and was shared like thousands and thousands of times. It seemed like everybody in the school had read it.

I was ten minutes late getting into the cafetorium for lunch. I'd taken a detour to ditch my stinky tuna sandwich in the dumpster behind the gym. I thought it would look creepy to show up at the lunch table empty-handed, so I stopped at the vending machines. I couldn't decide if granola bars and Smartfood were stinky and/or gross, so I settled on some plain crackers and a bottle of water. By the time I made it to Siobhan's table near the window, Harrison was already planted in the middle seat. I should've guessed that he'd be invited, too, but still . . . His hair was sticking up in the back and his beard was growing in uneven patches. He seemed completely unaware that he'd broken the space-time continuum by sitting at this table. Like he'd always spent lunchtime with the most popular kids in school.

Siobhan had saved me a seat right between her and

Harrison. She checked out my crackers and water and nodded approvingly. Harrison had either not gotten the same warning, or not understood. In front of him were a full-size box of Honey Nut Cheerios and a whole packet of turkey lunch meat. He scooped handfuls of dry cereal into folded cold cuts, before stuffing it all into his mouth. He seemed not to notice that all the guys at the table were staring at him. Or that Siobhan was stifling a gag.

I opened my sketchbook and stared at the blank page. Drawing always made me feel better. Sometimes that sketchbook was kinda my best friend. It had a leather cover and rings that opened so I could take out and add pages. After Mom and Dad's memorial, when the events were over and I was just . . . alone, I started filling the book with my old drawings. Drawings going all the way back to Sunny Horizons. I found sketches I'd made of us as kids: Jack and Harrison playing on the swings; Dayana twirling around in her princess dress. And Josie. All those sketches of Josie. I may have stopped slipping them into her bag, but I never stopped creating them. Josie lived on nearly every page of that book, first as a fearless little girl in a tree and then from afar as I watched her grow up. Somehow carrying those sketches with me made me feel a little less alone.

I closed the book and looked up to see Jack and Josie heading toward the table, *our* table. I tried to act natural and take a sip of water, but I swallowed too fast and started to choke. When I finally stopped coughing and sputtering, the others were staring at me like I was a carrier for the zombie virus. Josie and Jack had stopped about halfway across the room. Josie was arguing with Siobhan. I could hear them from where I sat, although I pretended not to.

"So what are they, your little pets? A charity project?"

"It's not like that, JoJo."

"I get it. You wanted nothing to do with them when their parents were alive. But the Orphans of Sunny Horizons are internet *stars*, right? We're this big famous group, so you want them all to be our friends."

I wiped up my spewed water, swept my cracker crumbs into my hand, and stood up from the table. "Hang in there, Harrison."

"Have you been wondering how it happened?" he suddenly asked.

"Huh?"

"The crash that took our parents' lives. Have you come up with anything? Because as I write out the contributing factors and possible explanations, I'm stuck on what might qualify as a reason."

He blinked at me. I didn't know what to say, and Josie was still standing there. I didn't blame her for hating me. She was trying to mourn her parents. I'd turned us into a *meme*. I gave up and walked out.

After seventh period when I passed Josie in the hall near the teachers' lounge, there was no nod. No smile. Whatever we'd shared at her parents' memorial service was gone. Once I'd gotten her through the crowd and outside to the parking lot, we sat down on the curb and talked for the first time in over three years. I didn't even jabber much.

"They wouldn't have even been home by now," I said. "How can I miss them so much already?"

"I don't know," said Josie. "Maybe it's that we miss the stuff that hasn't happened yet? First day of school. Senior Prom. Graduation. Getting married. Having kids."

I looked back inside. "It must feel good to know that this many people loved your parents."

Josie didn't turn. "It doesn't feel like anything." She squeezed my hand. "Are you scared?"

I didn't want to give her the real answer. "You're going to be fine. I know that sounds weird right now. I just mean that of all of us—Jack, Harrison, me—you're the one I'm not worried about. That sounds terrible, too. Of course I'm worried about you. I always—What I'm saying is you're the strongest, toughest, most amazing person I know. What I've seen you overcome . . . You'll do it again. I know you will."

Josie smiled at me as she wiped tears from the corners of her eyes. "How is it on the worst day of all the worst days, you still manage to find something good to say?"

We sat there holding on to each other's hands until Jack and Cody came outside looking for her. I watched her walk back inside and she turned around one last time to look at me. But that moment on the curb wasn't life changing. It wasn't a course correction or the start of a new chapter. It was a blip. Another momentary anomaly in our awkward and confusing history. It wasn't the first time we'd shared something like that.

Before ninth grade when everything happened with that asshole coach, when Josie and I were together on the playground, I thought . . . Well, it doesn't matter what I thought. Point is, first day of freshman year, she acted like she didn't know me. And first day of senior year, she acted like she wished she didn't. I should've been used to it by now. She needed me and then she didn't.

But this time was even worse. Because *I* screwed it up. And because this time I needed her, too.

7

DAYANA

"THIS MUST BE SO HARD FOR YOU?" SIOBHAN said. Or asked? So freaking hard to tell the difference when her voice goes up at the end of every sentence. It's hard enough speaking two languages. Now I have to learn bitch-speak.

"*What* must be so hard?" I asked.

"Like . . . the crash?" She extended her hand, but she hesitated like she was unsure of whether or not to pet me.

"You know my parents weren't on the plane, right?" Even with a couple of percs dulling my senses, I could feel the eyes on us in the hallway near my locker. Why was *this* person talking to *that* person?

She tilted her head like a dog hearing a strange noise. "That's what I mean? Like how everybody's rallying around Josie and Jack and Arch and whatshisname?"

"Harrison." Siobhan was dangerous. She ruined lives for sport. Last year I watched her unleash hell—and even worse,

Insta Stories—on some girl who supposedly flirted with Jack. The poor girl never came back to school.

I guess I understood why Jack would date someone like her. She was tall and had good skin and he got to be naked with her. It's that simple for some guys, right? But how could Josie let this vicious monster be her best friend? The Josie I knew was . . . Well, the Josie I knew was gone. Replaced by the kind of person who could pal around with Siobhan fucking Hughes. I knew I should be walking away from this conversation while I still could. But I couldn't.

"I heard they were trending again last night? The Sunnies? And Maya Turner? Her dad is like an entertainment lawyer, I think? She said there might be a reality show? And I mean, you're like part of the group, but not really, you know? I don't know if you'd even be on it. It's like you're . . . I don't know, famous adjace?"

Adjace. Without knowing it, my new buddy Siobhan fucking Hughes had stumbled on the perfect definition of me. Adjace. As in adjacent. Next to.

She finally stopped talking and I realized I should respond to the bullshit she was spouting. "Are you asking me if I'm jealous because their parents died in a fucking plane crash and mine didn't?"

"I didn't ask anything? I was just trying to be a person to you? And I thought maybe you knew what's going on with Josie?"

"Why would I know about Josie? You're her best friend."

I was . . . adjace. What kind of person did she think I was, that I would be bummed because my parents *weren't* on that plane? Only a sick fuck would be jealous of kids whose parents died like that. Why, because everybody in the school suddenly started caring about them? Because they were pseudo celebrities who were going to get a reality show and had thousands of people wanting to be their friends? Because the four of them were now sitting at the same lunch table and would forever share a deep connection I could never understand? I was always on the outside anyway. It's where I was most comfortable.

We aren't from here, Mami would say. *So we have to work harder to fit in. Be respectful. Dress nice. Make friends.*

The worst part is, when Siobhan gave up on our conversation and walked away, this heavy wave of loneliness rolled over me. I can't exactly explain it. She was a miserable turd of a person who didn't care about me at all. She was also the *only* person to talk to me in the hallway in the three weeks since school started. Not one actual conversation since Connor and Michaela graduated last year.

Connor and Michaela were my two best friends. My only two friends. We liked the same bands and wore the same clothes. Connor was an awesome bass player with the dopest green hair. Michaela and I got piercings together at the mall and bitched about our parents. They were a couple, but they never made me feel like some third wheel. And Michaela helped me with my makeup even though she was naturally pale and didn't have to work as hard. They brought me vegan lunch and I shared the pills I swiped from Papi's stash. We'd meet out in the woods behind school and wash them down with energy drinks and rip on the sheep roaming the hallways at RBHS.

Connor and Michaela didn't judge me or make me feel like some kind of freak the way everybody else did. They didn't even make it weird that I was in love with Connor. Not that we ever talked about it. I tried to hide my feelings as best I could, but one time I heard them talking.

You don't think it's, like, awkward or whatever? he'd asked.

I think it's cute. Who wouldn't *have a crush on you?*

Not that I ever wanted to get between them. They were the first real friends I'd had since Josie and the crew, and I wasn't looking to screw that up. But still, what if Connor truly loved me instead of her and was just trying not to hurt her feelings? Even Michaela wouldn't want that, right?

Near the end of junior year, Michaela was in Florida for her grandmother's eightieth birthday party. I texted Connor to see what he was up to and he invited me to come hang out. I figured we'd get high in his yard like normal and I'd stumble on home. When I showed up at his house, he was waiting in his basement. His parents were out for the night, so we snagged a bottle of vodka from their bar and watched *Paranormal Activity 3*. I actually hate scary movies and had my eyes closed through half of it, but I didn't want to say anything—not with Connor sitting so close to me. And when he leaned over, nuzzled my neck, and touched my breast, I was pretty sure I forgot how to breathe. I knew I was breaking a million rules by hooking up with my best friend's guy. But he was kissing me and it was moving really fast and I realized this was it. Connor was going to be the guy to take my virginity, and it felt so right. And even though it didn't last long and afterward he said he was tired and had to get up early in the morning, I felt like I'd been waiting for this moment forever. I knew it would be painful once Michaela came back, but we'd figure it out somehow. We were connected. She'd see how my being with Connor would make everything better in my life. The constant shitshow of the last few years. Papi's depression, the hell of school, Mami's secrets . . . It was all going to be better now.

When Michaela came home, things were even less weird than I thought. Connor never a said a word to her about what happened between us. Never said a word to me either. It was like it hadn't happened at all. After a few weeks, I started to wonder if I'd been so drunk that I'd imagined the whole thing. I kept trying to bring it up to him, but we were never alone again. Not ever. At the end of the summer, Connor and Michaela showed up at my house to say goodbye before they left for college. When I opened the door, I almost didn't recognize them. Michaela had taken the piercings out of her nose and Connor's hair was almost fully grown-out brown. He was wearing a red University of Maryland T-shirt and a pair of khaki cargo shorts. He wished me well and told me to have a great senior year and what a great friend I was. They hugged me goodbye and promised to text, and then the love of my life and my only two friends in the whole world were gone.

I stood at the mirror in the bathroom checking my makeup. At the next sink, a ninth-grade girl splashed water on her face. It looked so refreshing. My makeup would never survive a washing like that. Sometimes I wished I could just wipe it all off and start clean. Be the girl with the naturally brown skin and the freckles and the wavy hair. But that felt scary, to be that exposed. I needed my layers.

A toilet flushed and Josie walked out of the stall. She walked to the sink next to mine. Her clothes, her skin, and her hair were flawless. But as our eyes met in the mirror, I could see hers held a spiderweb of red lines.

"Hi," Josie said, like it was the most natural thing in the world. She took the open sink beside me.

"Hi." As we stood next to each other, I let Josie know that I was here if she needed me, that it didn't matter what had happened over the last three or four years. What we had was bigger than that. Older. Meeting Josie was one of my first memories. We'd just moved from Patterson, where everyone we knew spoke Spanish. Cousins and neighbors. Even our landlord. We might as well have still been in Costa Rica. But Papi wanted us to be capital A *American*. Go to an American school, make American friends. So as soon as he had the money, he moved us to River Bank, which felt like a different country. I stood on the playground and watched all the kids playing and yelling and singing. When they talked they looked to me like chickens. Making all kinds of clucking sounds without hardly moving their mouths. I tried talking to a couple of girls playing dress-up, but they stared at me like I was from another planet.

And then Josie walked up to me.

You're Dayana.

I nodded.

Josie, she said. *Josie. I. Am. Your. Friend.*

And just like that, she was. She helped me learn English. She was there when things were good in my family, when the American dream was alive and well in mi casa. And she was with me ten years later when Papi's dream crashed and burned. But when we had to move to a smaller house in a worse neighborhood, I didn't want her to see it. I pulled away. And then she pulled away, too. But now if Josie wanted to talk or just hang out, I'd be there for her. I owed it to her because of our history. And because my parents survived.

Okay, so I didn't actually say any of that out loud. I said it in a look and a nod before she left the bathroom. I hoped Josie got it. I thought about Siobhan's accusation. What kind of person would I be if I had thoughts like that? Wishing my parents died just so I could be close to Josie again? Part of the group? Disgusting.

I was not jealous. Not even a little bit.

When you roam the halls at school and no one talks to you, you notice things. I knew when people got haircuts or gained weight. I knew which married teachers flirted with each other. I saw breakups happening before the couples themselves did. So I wasn't shocked when I saw Harrison slipping into Mr. Unsinger's supply closet before lunch. I'd seen him come out of there before. He'd swivel around to make sure no one had spotted him and then disappear down the hall. I didn't know what he did in there and I have to admit I was kinda curious.

This was the first time I'd actually seen Harrison going *into* the janitor's closet. If it was possible, he looked even worse going in than he did coming out. He was panting and sweating and desperately loping toward the door. I waited outside and tried to listen in. I didn't want to get all up in his business, but I did want to make sure he wasn't having a heart attack or some shit. When he finally came out almost ten minutes later, he walked right past me toward the lunchroom. His hair was matted down, but he was breathing better, and at the very least he wasn't dead.

I followed a few steps behind him as he lurched into the cafetorium and sat down in the middle of Josie's table. I couldn't believe that he and Archie were still there. I thought for sure it would last a day or two, but somehow Siobhan and the others hadn't gotten tired of them yet. As long as social media was still hot on the Sunny Horizon orphans, then by God, so were the popular chicks of River Bank High.

Every day I sat at my table in the back corner watching them, wondering when the natural order of things would be restored, waiting for it all to implode. And then finally, one day it did. When I heard loud voices coming from Josie's table, I slid into the lunch line near the table to see what was going on.

Cody was arguing with Siobhan and not even trying to keep his voice down. "Look, I'm sorry, Shibs. I'm all for charity, but this isn't working. One says weird things and eats like an animal. And the other one is always looking at Josie. And what the fuck is he drawing?"

Archie stammered, "No, I—I don't."

Siobhan tried to pull Cody away from Archie and Harrison. "Don't be a dick, okay? I mean, I know they're a mess, but these two lost their parents? Don't you read my posts? They're just like Jack and Josie, if Jack and Josie weren't rich and hot and cool? I mean, it's fucking tragic?"

"Like you care about them, Siobhan," Josie snapped, standing up at the end of the table. "What's going to happen when some other tragedy hits and the Sunnies aren't trending anymore? Do we just tell them to go back where they came from?"

Archie picked his head up from his sketchbook. "It's okay, Josie. Really. Everybody's cool to us. Right, Harrison? It's a good place to eat. Close to the kitchen and not too close to the garbage."

"See," said Cody. "This is what I'm talking about, Josie."

Harrison kept on eating, even as Jack stepped his massive frame into the mix and glared down at Archie. "Was this the game plan when you had your aunt write that blog? Is sitting at the popular table everything you hoped it would be?"

Archie looked over at Josie. "It's not like that. Josie, you know I'd never—"

Cody grabbed Archie by the collar of his plaid shirt. "I'm over this. Sorry for your loss. Time to go."

Josie begged him to leave Archie alone while Harrison kept his head down, slurping his chicken noodle soup. Cody yanked Archie up and out of his chair. Archie didn't struggle at all. But before Cody could launch him to the other side of the room, Jack grabbed Cody's arm and effortlessly ripped it from Archie's shirt.

"What the fuck, dude?" Cody shoved Jack, and Jack shoved him back, twice as hard. Once he caught his balance, Cody grabbed Archie again. Jack went for him, but another giant football player put himself in Jack's way. Josie rushed up and gave that guy a push, and then two cheerleaders got in Josie's face, and without thinking, I ran and threw my body into one of them.

It all happened in a blur. Bodies pushing against each other. Food spilling off the table. Everyone yelling and cursing. Someone blowing a whistle. I got knocked into the table, stomach first. I looked back as Cody was lifting Archie off the ground. Suddenly a wild fist came flying in from the side and connected with Cody's jaw with a loud crack. Stunned, he let out a whimper as he fell right on his ass and peered up to see Harrison standing over him, fist still clenched, a blank expression on his face.

The principal, Mrs. Walters, seemed more sad than angry when she called us into her office. She spent a lot of time playing with her helmet of hair while telling Jack, Josie, Harrison, and Archie how terribly sorry she was about their parents. She wanted them to know that the administration would help in any way they could and she'd of course work with them to smooth out this regrettable situation.

Her expression hardened as she turned to me. "Ms. Calderón, we both know this is hardly the first time *you've* been in this office. We've talked about your attitude and your unwillingness to adhere to our school guidelines. Unlike your classmates, you have no excuse for your behavior or for getting involved in this incident in the first place. Therefore, I'm giving you two weeks detention."

Whatever.

She let Jack, Josie, and Archie off with a warning that was more like a condolence card. Then Mrs. Walters turned her attention on Harrison. "It pains me to say this," she said sincerely. "You are the most dedicated student in our senior class. Your mother was a driving force behind our enrichment program, and our entire community feels her loss. You have a perfect attendance record and a clear path to being valedictorian. However, Harrison, when it comes to violence, we have a zero tolerance policy. Several witnesses confirm that you struck another student in the face."

Harrison finally spoke up. "It wasn't as hard as I thought it would be."

I grabbed his hand. "No more talking," I whispered.

Mrs. Walters explained that she had no choice but to suspend Harrison for one week. Harrison barely reacted to the news that his perfect attendance record was about to be shit-canned. Instead he flexed his hand and stared at the bruises on his knuckles.

Principal Walters dismissed us from her office, and we all stood around outside the door, waiting for someone to say something. Harrison started to wander off and I snatched his arm. "You okay with this?"

He shrugged. "It's not like she's going to call home and get me in trouble."

"But what if she finds out you're not living with anyone?"

"I gave one of my neighbors some money. He'll pretend to be my father if I need him to. Nobody at the school's ever met my pop anyway."

"You've got it all figured out."

"Mom always wanted me to be prepared if I . . . If I was alone."

"Hey, anytime you want, you can come over for dinner. Papi will pick up some Chinese or something."

"You eat Chinese?"

"Yes, we Latinx people eat Chinese food, too."

"I meant because you're a vegan. Mostly."

"How did you know that?" I asked.

Harrison shrugged. "Hey, did you see the punch?"

"I think the whole fucking world saw it."

"Did it look . . . It was pretty solid, right? Never mind.

Hey, um, Jack, do you need me to come tutor you next week? I have a lot of time on my hands now."

Jack looked down at the ground. "No, I'm good. We can end that now."

"Oh, all right," said Harrison. "I was hoping we could talk though."

"About what?" asked Jack.

"I was wondering. Did your dad do any business with Fort Benson, the army base where Archie's father worked and Dayana's dad used to— What I'm asking is, did he have dealings with the government at all? I know he had some big clients. Maybe he did some casework for the military or—"

Jack cut him off. "Why are you asking this?"

"Yeah," said Archie. "What are you talking about?"

"So you don't know if your father had any government connections?" Harrison continued. "Did he ever talk about it or meet with guys in uniforms or—"

"What are you doing, Harrison?" snapped Josie. "These questions are creepy and we have to get back to class. This day is already such a mess." Jack and Josie walked off down the hall. Archie looked crushed as he headed in the opposite direction, leaving me alone with Harrison.

"You want a ride home?" he asked. "I've got my mother's car. Although I think you should drive."

"Why?"

"The medication I took warned against driving or operating heavy machinery."

"Medication? Are you talking about the pills I left for you? What did you take?"

He scratched his head in an exaggerated display of thinking. "The green ones. WebMD said they help ease anxiety. I took several before lunch. They really work! I may have just screwed up my whole life and I don't feel anxious about it at all!"

It was then that I noticed his giant dilated pupils. "Oh my God," I said. "You're fucked-up."

"You have no idea."

8

JOSIE

HAVE YOU EVER SEEN A SNAIL OUT OF ITS shell? It's just this soft, gooey mess of a creature with no way to protect itself. The simplest thing can hurt it. Rain, salt . . .

Archie sitting at my lunch table. I knew I was treating him horribly. Like what did he ever do wrong except be there for me at the two worst times in my life? But when he looked at me with those deep brown eyes, my shell was gone. No matter how hard I worked to be perfect, to get my outfits right, my hair right, my life right—Archie knew. He saw underneath.

Archie and Harrison and Dayana, they were part of a different life—one I had to leave behind. It had taken me three years to build all of this. My table. My squad. *Josie Clay.* What was I supposed to tell Siobhan? *Sorry, but being near this sweet, creative guy makes me feel dirty and disgusting because he knows what I did when I was fourteen.* What would I tell Cody? He'd never look at me the same again.

After I spent that night in Coach's hotel room in Maryland, we were together after almost every practice. He'd take me to some private spot on the beach or a motel where I'd wait in the car while he paid. Sometimes we'd just do it in Shirley's cramped back seat. I hated it more each time. I hated that car. I hated Coach for making me feel I had to do this to make him happy. Mostly I hated myself for letting it happen.

On the day of the Regional Finals I walked by the mirror in my uniform. I loved wearing the green-and-gold jersey, the high socks, the band I used to pull back my hair. I felt proud and strong. Now I felt like a liar. A phony. I went into Mom and Daddy's bathroom and locked the door. I picked up Mom's pink razor and I pressed it hard against the index finger of my pitching hand. I didn't know exactly what I needed to do, but I was determined not to stop until there was no way I could play in that game. I'd go to the bone if I had to. I dug the blade into my finger and squeezed until it started to bleed. Just a drop at first, then a thin line. I pushed harder and harder until the razor snapped in half. Scrambling, I reached down to pick up the blade and that's when I heard Shirley's engine roar up the driveway. The double beep of the horn. My hand was shaking as I held the broken razor handle.

Mom started knocking on the door. "Josie, Coach Murphy is here! You don't want to be late. Your father is going to the game straight from work."

I stopped. I was willing to cut off a finger on the

bathroom floor, but I couldn't disappoint Daddy. So I wrapped my hand in toilet paper and walked past Jack and out to Coach, waiting for me in the car.

I spent the whole game feeling dizzy and angry with myself for not slicing deep enough. In the bottom of the seventh, I came up to bat with runners on second and third and two outs. We were down by one. A base hit would win the game. As I started toward the plate, Coach Murph stopped me for some last-second advice. He rested his hand on my lower back and he leaned down to whisper in my ear. I didn't even hear what he said. I was too focused on his thick fingers and his dry lips so close to my ear. I suddenly felt so many eyes on me. Like they'd turned on a spotlight and *everyone* saw. Everyone knew what I'd been doing with Coach Murph in the hotel and on those car rides. Jack and all the parents in the bleachers, my teammates on the bench, even the other team in the field were looking at me like I was this gross person, like there was something wrong with me. But worst of all was seeing Daddy there, knowing I *had* let him down.

Coach nudged me toward the batter's box, and I wanted to run or cry or just be swallowed up by the ground. I couldn't do it anymore. I needed it to stop. The car rides and his body against mine and the promises that he'd love me forever. I needed it to end. So when the pitcher windmilled a fastball high and inside I leaned over the plate and let the ball smash me right in the face. I went down in a heap of blood and dirt. I lay there, curled up on the plate until Jack and Daddy ran over and carried me off the field.

That night, after we got back from the hospital, Daddy put me to bed. "Good night, sweetheart. You are one tough son of a gun. You have no idea how proud I am of you."

If he'd known why I leaned over the plate, he wouldn't have been proud. He would've been ashamed and disgusted.

The ball broke two of my front teeth and left me with a black eye and a lot of bruising. But it wasn't enough. When Daddy went back to his office, I snuck down the stairs and out the back door. I didn't know where I was going or why. I was sinking underwater and I couldn't be in the house. I couldn't lie anymore.

So I walked. And walked. And when I finally looked up, I was on the Sunny Horizons playground, where Archie was sitting on the giant stump of the old tree we used to climb. If he was surprised to see me he didn't show it. But he didn't ask me a bunch of questions or try to call my parents. He just made room for me on the stump and quietly drew in his sketchbook. And when I went underwater, it was his hand squeezing mine that pulled me to the surface. When I came up, I told him everything about Coach Murph and about the hotel and the blue Mustang and how it was exciting at first and then turned into something so disgusting. I told him everything I'd done, even the parts that made me sick to say out loud. After I was done he just took off his glasses and looked at me.

"You can't tell anyone," I said.

"I won't. I would never. But *you* should. What he did was wrong."

"I just want it to go away."

"He should be in jail, Josie. I hate him for what he did to you."

"But I was . . . Please, you have to promise me."

Archie stared off toward the school. "Only if you promise me you'll never go near him again."

"I'm a terrible person. I know that."

"Are you kidding? You're like the best person I know. Since the day you pulled me up into this tree."

I ran my hand along the stump. "I can't believe it's gone. I can't believe this is all that's left."

"Yeah. I was here when they took it down. They used chainsaws to cut off all the branches and they went right through the trunk. That tree must've been here a hundred years. It was gone in less than an hour."

I started to cry, and Archie ripped a blank page from his sketchbook. "Sorry," he said, handing it to me to wipe my nose. "It's the best I can do."

I smiled. "I miss the pictures you used to draw me."

"I still draw them."

I touched his sketchbook. "I know a lot of people," I said. "I don't know anyone in the world like you."

I leaned my head against his shoulder. My eye was practically swollen shut and my mouth felt like it was full of glass, but Archie felt warm and comfortable. I turned my head and my lips touched his cheek. We lingered there, barely moving, barely breathing. He tilted his head slowly and brought his soft lips to mine. Our kiss was gentle and slow. It felt so different from everything that happened with Coach. I knew this was someone who really cared for me, who would never hurt me.

When we broke apart, I turned around and ran home. And then I cut Archie out of my life again. I ignored his texts and calls. When he came to the house, I told Jack to send him away. From my window, I watched him head home on his scooter and I hated myself even more. But it's what I had to do to survive.

I never stepped on a softball field again. Just like that, the most important thing in my life was over. Putting on that uniform, standing on the pitcher's mound knowing what I'd done . . . I couldn't anymore. So I walked away. I told Daddy I was afraid of getting hurt again. It was the truth. I'd never seen him so disappointed in me. But I knew it was better this way. I was protecting him from something much worse.

And slowly I started making myself into someone who *wouldn't* be that snail without a shell, someone who would take control so she'd never be hurt like that again. Mom never asked why I gave up softball. I don't think she cared. She actually seemed happy when I started to change. She finally had a girly daughter to take shopping and treat to mani-pedis. That's the thing about parents. If you don't cause any trouble and you *act* happy, that's usually good enough for them.

Even Jack didn't really ask questions. He was too busy going through his own changes. Overnight, he started growing in all directions. He didn't come to my room for help quieting his brain anymore. Instead he went to the gym. He joined the football team and shaved off his hair. My runty twin brother became someone people were afraid of. And I became someone they wanted to be.

When you're Josie Clay, people are always watching, always looking for the cracks. Did she already wear that skirt this week? Do her eyes look puffy? And after the crash, it only got worse. More eyes, more whispers. I couldn't afford to let those cracks show, because once they did, I wasn't sure I'd be able to hold them closed anymore. Only a few weeks ago, my parents died and I dropped underneath the water. If I let go again, I knew I'd slide back under and sink to the bottom, the way Mom and Daddy's plane had. And like them, I might not come back this time.

Cody pulled me aside before school one day. "I think we should take a time-out, Jos," he said.

"You're breaking up with me?"

"We're just both going through a lot of stuff."

"My parents died. What are *you* going through?"

"Your psycho buddy punched me in the face, for one thing. Even Siobhan says it. You're changed since, you know . . ."

"The plane crash?"

"No. Since you got famous."

Famous. People were crazy about the Orphans of Sunny Horizons Preschool: "The Sunnies." I got more friend requests than I could keep up with. A photo of me in a little black dress at my parents' memorial service became a thing. I got offers to publish my diaries and post style videos on my own YouTube channel.

Famous. Except my boyfriend broke up with me, and my best friend thought I'd changed. Maybe I had. I couldn't sit at my lunch table anymore. Because every time I was near Archie or Harrison or even Dayana, I felt people watching us, covertly taking photos on their phones. So I stayed away from them, too. I told Jack I was going to start going out for lunch. Instead, I'd go into the bathroom, sit in a stall, and wait for the bell to ring.

At 1 A.M. the night before homecoming, I was picking out my clothes for the next day, when I heard piercing squeals and thumping bass coming from the yard. By the time I got to the porch, Jack was already there and the cheerleading squad was zooming away in their cute little cars. Our entire yard was covered in toilet paper. Jack held out his hand and looked up at the sky. "It's about to pour," he said. "If it gets wet, this crap'll be stuck here forever."

"I'll help you clean it up." I wasn't going to sleep anyway. Jack turned on the Jeep's headlights and we assessed the damage. Every branch on the big oak tree had toilet paper dangling from it. "Was this Siobhan's idea?"

"I don't know. We broke up."

"You did?" I asked. "But you guys were such a good couple."

"No we weren't."

"I can't believe neither of you talked to me about this. If you were having problems—"

"Problems?"

Jack carried the metal ladder out to the tree and slammed it open.

"We can fix this. Let me text her." Jack never made these decisions without talking to me first.

"I don't want to fix it. I want to get the toilet paper out of the trees. Go. I'll hold it."

I climbed up the ladder. Except for the porch light and the Jeep's high beams, the neighborhood was dark and quiet. We were the only two people in the world. I wondered if Jack was having the same trouble sleeping, the same nightmares about sinking into the ocean. That happens with twins sometimes. Did he miss Mom and Daddy as much as I did?

"You skipped a branch," he said.

I reached out for the paper. "Maybe it's good for you to be single during the season," I said. "You can concentrate on impressing college coaches."

"Who cares?"

"What does that mean?" I asked, stepping down a few rungs.

Jack shrugged. "It doesn't matter now, does it? Football. College. We're going to have plenty of money once the life insurance comes through. What's the point?"

"The point is you're great at it. Daddy said you were a natural."

"Daddy said."

"I thought you loved football."

"I love hitting people."

"Isn't that the same thing?"

"No," said Jack.

"It made Daddy so proud to see you out there."

"And that's all that mattered in this house, right? Making him proud. Making sure he wasn't disappointed in us? Who gives a shit now if I play or quit?"

"You're going to quit? You can't do that!" My voice came out louder and screechier than I expected.

"*You* did."

In that moment, something jarred loose. I forgot that we were standing on our front lawn at 1:30 A.M. I jumped off the ladder and pounded on Jack's chest.

Yes, I'd quit softball, but only because I had to. I gave up the thing I loved most because it was spoiled forever and it was killing me. I quit softball out of survival. This was different. This was—

"A slap in Daddy's face. That's what this is. You think he'd want you to quit?"

"I don't know," said Jack. "Why don't we ask him?"

"What is wrong with you?! You can't talk like that!"

Jack's face was dark red in the headlight beams. He grabbed the ladder and flung it across the yard. It landed with a loud clang. I'd only seen him this angry after one of Dad's rants. "You telling me how to talk is what's wrong, Jo.

We're walking around pretending like it's normal around here. It's not normal." He yelled it again so the whole neighborhood could hear. "It's not fucking normal!"

"Stop saying that," I begged him. I had to get this back under control.

"See? That's what we do. We keep quiet. We stuff shit inside. Grandma's happy, as long as people give her compliments about Dad. And Grandpa spends all day in that shed pretending to be busy. And you? As long as your hair and makeup look good and you're wearing a new outfit, it's fine. It's not fine, Jo. It's fucked. It's fucked forever and there's nothing we can do about it!"

Across the street and next door lights were going on in bedrooms. We weren't the only people in the world anymore. Jack started toward the Jeep, but I threw myself in front of him.

"You know what the real problem is?" I said. "You're lost. You need me to tell you what to do. You always have. And when I'm dealing with my own stuff you don't know how to handle it. You throw away your perfect girlfriend and now you're gonna do the same with football. Since the minute we were born, you followed me. I don't care how big you are. You can't do it on your own. You don't know how. You need me to make you a whole person."

"And you don't?" Jack hopped in the Jeep and drove off, leaving me alone with the darkness.

I waited up all night for Jack, but he never came home. I was surprised to see him at school the next morning, but he didn't bother telling me where he'd been. He barely spoke at all. He'd never done that to me before. When he walked away I stood there, frozen, in the middle of the hallway, watching him disappear around the corner.

I drove myself to the football game that Friday night. I arrived just as our players were running out of the locker room onto the field. When everybody was out, I scanned the numbers. No number 74. Jack wasn't with the team.

I started heading for the field when I spotted him slowly walking out to join his teammates. When he reached the sideline, he shielded his eyes over his facemask and looked up into the stands. As I spun around to see what he was looking at the stadium lights blinded me, covering everything in bright, blurry halos. In the middle of the glowing blur, I swore I saw my parents sitting in their usual seats.

Daddy sported a red RBHS baseball cap and Mom wore a replica of Jack's jersey, number 74 over her turtleneck. Daddy gave me a wide smile and waved as Mom blew me a kiss. I blinked away tears, big, wet tears, and they were gone. They were gone.

Eyes still cloudy, I raced down the stairs, twisting sideways to knife my way through the entering crowd. I kept my head down, hoping no one would notice how hard I was crying.

When I finally made it under the bleachers I squeezed my eyes shut and concentrated on staying at the surface.

I don't know how long I stood in that spot. The game was in full swing and the bleachers above me were pounding with the sound of a mob stomping its feet. The PA announcer's voice echoed from the speakers. "Tackle by number 74, Jack Clay!" When I heard shuffling feet, I opened my eyes and realized I wasn't alone down there. Dayana and Harrison were staring at me.

Dayana took a hit of her vape pen. "Thought we'd lost you again, Jo." I could barely see her in the dim light. Harrison peered down and studied me like a science experiment.

"What are you doing down here?" I asked.

Harrison's eyes looked wild. "I'm not technically allowed to attend school functions during my suspension, so I have to keep a low profile, but Dayana said I shouldn't be alone, so she invited me to come along with her while she sold some of her father's pills to—"

She punched his arm. "I was just . . . meeting some people. Why aren't you up with the screaming douchenozzles? Sorry, I mean, your friends?"

"That's not a nice thing to say," said Harrison.

"You want to know what those douchenozzles say about me? Or how about what they say about you?"

"They like me. I'm one of the Sunnies. Well, they did before I punched Josie's boyfriend in the face. Is he still mad about that?"

"I don't know," I said. "He broke up with me."

"Sorry," said Dayana. "He seemed . . . whatever."

A voice cut in from the entrance. "Hey, it's—it's me. Sorry." Archie walked out of the shadows holding his sketchbook. "I saw you run down here. I wasn't following you or anything, but I saw you were . . . you looked like you were . . . Not that it's any of my business. I just . . . I'm glad you're all right. Are you all right?"

A loud roar above us startled him and he dropped his book.

Harrison picked up the book. "I've always wanted to know what you have in here," he said. "I never see you without it." He opened to the page with a ribbon bookmark in it. His eyes went wide. "It's you, Josie. It's . . . beautiful."

Before I could see the drawing, Archie snatched the book from Harrison and slammed it closed. He looked at me for a second and then quickly turned his gaze toward the ground. "Good thing nobody knows we're down here, huh? This would be a prime photo op. 'The Sunnies reunite to watch Jack play ball. News at 11.'"

"That's not funny," I said.

"Of course not. I just . . . What's everybody doing under here?"

Harrison cleared his throat. "Well, I didn't plan for this, but since four-fifths of us are here, I'd like to raise a question. Or a theory. I tried to bring it up with you at the lunch table last week, Archie, but you were preoccupied. So I've been thinking a lot about . . . probabilities and looking over the statistics of aviation disasters in relation to, well, do you see where I'm going with this?"

We all just stood and looked at him for a few moments before Dayana spoke. "I'm sorry, but I have no idea what the fuck you just said."

Harrison took a deep breath. "The plane crash," he said.

Suddenly I became aware that everything above us was silent, like someone had turned off the volume in the stadium. At first I thought it was in my head, that my brain was shutting out the world again. I wasn't underwater, though. I was still here and something *had* changed in the crowd over our heads. What had been a loud and raucous pounding was now totally still. The whole place had gone dead.

My confusion quickly turned to something else: dread. It started like a tingling in my feet, ran up my legs, and formed sort of a ball in my gut and into my throat, where I felt like I was choking on it.

Jack . . .

I ran from under the bleachers. When I got out to the lights the first thing I saw was Siobhan crying in the arms of another cheerleader. I ran past them onto the track to get a view of the field, begging for someone to tell me what was going on. Players on both teams were kneeling down with their helmets off, while on the other side of the field EMTs worked on a player lying on the ground. When they started to move him, I finally saw my twin brother strapped to a gurney. They'd secured his head with a large neck brace and his eyes were closed, like he was sleeping. He wasn't moving at all. I screamed his name and tried to run out onto the field, but hands held me back, arms surrounded me. Voices told me it was going to be okay, that Jack was tough and that he'd be fine. I struggled to get away from them.

"Jack! Let me see him! Jack!"

A hand reached out and grabbed mine. Archie again. Pulling me through another crowd. "There's nothing you can do here," he said. "Josie, look at me. We'll meet them at the hospital."

Archie helped me into the back of a red sedan and closed the door before climbing into the other side. Soon we were screeching out of the parking lot. Only when we ran a red light and almost plowed into another car did I notice that Harrison was driving, with Dayana in the seat next to him.

"Jesus fucking Christ," she yelled. "Do you even have a license?"

"No," said Harrison. "I learned from YouTube."

Archie sat next to me in the back seat. He never let go of my hand as we flew around corners and scraped against curbs.

"I told him to play," I whispered. "He wanted to quit and I used Daddy to make him feel guilty. I made him play and now . . ."

"Jack's nine feet tall and four hundred pounds," said Archie. "He's the Hulk. No one makes the Hulk do anything he doesn't want to do."

We took another sharp turn and my body got thrown against Archie. He braced me and helped me buckle my seat belt. "I've got you," he said. In that moment, I felt all the guilt and all the shame for how I'd treated him.

"I need to explain why I didn't talk to you after that night on the playground," I said.

"It was a long time ago."

"I'm still doing it."

"I don't care, Josie."

"Please." I took a deep breath. "I'm sorry, Archie. I'm so sorry. What you did for me . . . You saved my life and I treated you like crap."

"It doesn't matter now. We're almost there."

I sat up and looked into his eyes. "Can I see the drawing?"

9

JACK

GODDAMN, MY BRAIN HURT.

Lying in the darkness I felt someone inside my skull trying to hammer his way out. When I opened my eyes, the fluorescent light shot through my head like an ice pick. Blurry people were standing over me. I lifted my head, but the room started to spin, and then everything went dark again.

When I opened my eyes the second time, Josie was by my side. I was in the hospital; that much I figured out on my own. I hated hospitals. All that time spent there as a kid. I was born too small. Caused a lot of complications. Been playing catch-up ever since. I tried to turn to see her, but I couldn't move my head. Panic shot through my body. I yanked the sheet off my legs and wiggled my toes. Arms moving. Legs, too. But the effort made me want to puke.

Josie put a hand on my forehead. "Don't try to move. You're in a neck brace. Just to be safe. Do you remember how you got here?"

My thoughts were a mess. Even more than usual. Like my brain was trying to do ten things at once. Straightening them out just made my head hurt more. I was scared, but I was more tired than I'd ever been in my life. So I let myself drift again. This time when I came back, Grandpa Ralph and Grandma Nelly were with Josie near my feet, while a young doctor in a lab coat poked at my toes with something sharp. I winced.

"That's a good sign," he said.

I tried to read his nametag. So many letters all scrambled together. Keeping my eyes open was a struggle, but I wasn't ready to sleep again. How the hell did I end up here? Focus on something. The scar near Josie's lip from when the softball hit her. Stare at it. Stay awake. "Soul . . . ?"

Josie brushed past the doctor to hug me. "Yes. Yes, I'm here. Oh my God! Heart, I'm so happy you're okay. You don't even know!"

Grandma and Grandpa chattered back and forth. Was everyone talking at once?

"Jack, I'm Dr. Wicentowski. I'm a neurologist. I'm going to ask you some simple questions now. I want you to answer to the best of your ability. Okay?"

"Questions?"

"Do you know where you are?"

"Hospital?"

"Yes. What day is today?"

"It's Saturday, no . . . Thursday, I think. We had school, so. Wait, why are you asking *me*? I've been asleep."

"Do you know why you're in the hospital?"

"Does it . . . have to do with the mashing in my head?"

"Can you describe that 'mashing'?"

"Hurts."

"But you don't remember how you got here?"

"Try to answer his questions, Jackie," said Grandpa.

"I am trying. You talking doesn't help."

The doctor shined a small, bright light into my eyes. Intense pain. I reached up and grabbed his wrist to get the light out of my face.

"Squeeze my wrist. As hard as you can. Don't worry. You won't hurt me." I squeezed hard and he barely reacted. "And what day did you say it is?"

"I don't know!"

"Are you dizzy? Nauseated?"

"What happened? Jo . . . ?"

Josie's details about the game ran out of my head as fast as they went in. Three times I made her repeat it, until I finally got that I went helmet to helmet with Ocean Catholic's running back. I was out cold when they carried me off the field. I imagined what that was like for Jo. Standing next to the stretcher, watching them load my carcass into an ambulance.

The doctor had me follow his finger as he moved it around. No matter how hard I tried I couldn't focus on it. How could moving my eyeballs be so exhausting?

"Mr. Clay, while you were asleep we performed a CAT scan on your brain and your spinal column. There was a minor contusion on the C5 vertebra, which is why you're experiencing some weakness in your extremities. I expect that to repair itself once the swelling goes down. However, you also suffered a serious concussion. The symptoms you're feeling—headaches, sensitivity to light, vertigo, confusion—there is no way to know how long they'll last. My understanding from your GP is that this is your fourth traumatic brain injury in less than two years. Your brain simply hasn't had a chance to fully recover. My recommendation would be that you sit out the rest of the football season and . . ." I shut my eyes and his squeaky voice floated away.

So this was how it ended. I wasn't really going to quit the night Josie and I got in that fight. I don't know why I said it. Maybe just as an FU to Dad.

When I took off from the house that night, I drove to school and lay down on the football field. I felt calm there. I did love football. I could run and hit people without anyone telling me to sit still, pay attention, stop moving. But with my history of head injuries and a less than stellar academic record, no major college coach would want me to play for his team. I was done. No more football. Ever. All that time on the practice field and in the weight room. All of those clinics and private coaches Dad paid for. All the college visits and recruiting trips. It all ended with one collision I had no memory of.

It's weird, though. I felt nothing. Two months ago, losing my football career would've been the end of the world in our family. I guess the end of the world had already happened.

When I finally woke up again, I felt even foggier. *Where are Mom and Dad?* I wondered. *Shouldn't they be here?* And then it all came flooding back at once. Mom and Dad weren't going to be here or anywhere else.

Josie came in with water from the nurses' station, but her hands were shaky and she slipped and spilled it all over me. I was instantly enraged. "What the hell is wrong with you?!" As she tried to help me dry off, I pushed her away. I didn't mean to get upset. If I could just get my thoughts clear!

Josie started to cry. She told me how sorry she was for pushing me to play in the game. "If something happened to you and it was my fault—"

"Stop," I told her. "You weren't . . . I was . . . None of this is . . . Shit, why can't I think?"

I tried to explain I wasn't mad at her, but nothing I said was making any sense. I'd start to say one thing, but then some memory would creep in and I'd be off down another road. Or an image would pop into my brain. Mom taking me to all those doctors' visits when I was little. All the goddamn needles and tests. "Your sister hogged all the nutrients in the womb," Mom told me. "That's why you came out so small. And your body, it just needs a little more help to stay healthy." Nothing good ever happened in a hospital.

Josie in the bed, her face all messed up from getting smacked by that softball. And she'd done it to herself. I knew she leaned her head over the plate. She *wanted* to get hit. And I knew why. Coach Murphy. God, I wanted to make that guy suffer. When I tried to talk to Josie about him, she just accused me of being jealous. She shut me out. What was I supposed to do? Call the police on him?

Fucking protect her, that's what. Three years later, lying in a hospital bed with a messed-up brain, I still felt . . . I don't know what you'd call it. Shame? It didn't matter that I was small and weak back then. I should've thrown myself in front of that bullet before she threw herself in front of a softball. I should've gone to Mom and Dad or the cops, or burned down Murph's house. But I didn't. I let it happen. I watched her get in that fucking blue car three nights a week and I swallowed it. I lived with that every day. Because I couldn't protect her, Josie stuck out her face and ate a softball. That's how it ended for her. She quit sports. She changed. I was the only one who knew why. I kept waiting for her to come talk to me about it, but she never did.

Dad wasn't going to just let her quit. As far as he knew, Murphy was a dedicated coach who was gonna help Josie develop as an elite player. When Josie told Dad she was quitting, he lost his shit. *You have the opportunity to be not just good, but great. You're going to let a black eye and a chipped tooth ruin your life?!* I saw how this was going. He'd continue to threaten or bribe her and never let up until he forced her to play. She lived to make him happy. She was Daddy's girl. But to tell him what she'd been doing . . . I knew she thought she'd break his heart.

One night while Dad was in the city for a dinner meeting, I took his keys, drank half a beer, and drove his Beemer right into a fence outside the school. I didn't do a shit-ton of damage, just enough to make it look ugly. The cops picked me up and brought me down to the station. I gave them

Dad's cell number. When he came down to get me, I made a big stink and blamed him for never being around.

Mom and Dad brought down the ax on me. They took away my allowance, grounded me for months, made me double down on those endless, frustrating tutoring sessions with Harrison. By the time I was finally allowed out of my room, they'd forgotten all about Josie quitting softball.

Jo found a way to move on. But I never did. I made a promise that I would never let her down again. I was done being weak. So I ate. And I worked out. I took every vitamin and supplement and protein shake I could get my hands on. I talked to guys in the weight room and I went to Dad and asked him if he knew a doctor who'd prescribe me growth hormone. He had a golf buddy who was more than happy to help. Anything to make me bigger and stronger. I wanted to be the kind of person no one wants to screw with. The kind of person who can protect his sister.

"Jack? Jack, can you hear me?" Josie gave my hand a gentle shake. My mind had drifted again. That felt like a long one. It was a real struggle to stay anchored in the room. Everything was a distraction. Everything bothered me. People walking in the hallway, car alarms in the parking lot, memories flashing by. *Boom! Boom! Boom!* Loud knocks went off like bombs in my head.

"I want to go home. I don't want to be here anymore."

"You can't leave," said Josie. "The doctor hasn't cleared you. Can they come in to say hi?"

I looked over to see Archie, Harrison, and Dayana

standing in the doorway. "They were with me when you got hurt," said Josie. "They've been waiting out there the whole time."

Dayana produced a bag from behind her back. "We thought you might be hungry, so we got you some food. Can you believe there's freaking fast food in the hospital? They might as well sell cigarettes in the gift shop. *Do* they sell cigarettes in the gift shop? E-cigs maybe?"

Harrison placed a supersized cup on the table next to my bed. "We had no idea how much . . . a person of your size consumes, so I did some quick calculations of body weight and calories . . . I hope it's enough." Dayana opened the bag to reveal that they'd bought me five twenty-piece boxes of nuggets. One hundred nuggets. The smell made my stomach roll.

"Not really hungry," I said through gritted teeth. "You can have them." Harrison came over to sniff around, but Archie hung by the door. He was afraid of me, I could see it. Josie went over to him and put a hand on his arm. I noticed how Archie reacted when she touched him. He adjusted his glasses and coughed.

"Jack, I'm glad you're okay. Really glad. I, um, drew you something while we were waiting. Not that you probably want it now, but I thought maybe, well . . . there were a lot of people sitting out there worrying about you. I thought you'd like to see it. All of us together, you know."

"It's really amazing," said Josie. "You can look at it later."

"Excuse me," Harrison cut in. "I don't know if this is an

ideal time, but we might not all be together in the same room again so I'd like to take this opportunity to—"

Dayana gripped his arm. "Maybe later, huh, H?"

"I'm sorry, but this needs to be said—shared—and frankly I need your help."

"With what?" asked Archie.

Harrison rubbed his hands together and took a breath. "You probably don't remember, but when I was eight, my mother took me on a flight to visit her cousins in North Carolina. I've never liked flying much. It makes me feel out of control. Mom told the flight attendant about my . . . issues. She smiled and took me to see the captain in the cockpit. He was this big blond man with a mustache. He gave me a pair of little metal wings. 'No worries, young man,' he said. 'Planes want to stay in the air.' You see?"

"No," said Archie. "I don't."

"The weather was clear. Perfect flight conditions according to my research. And we're still waiting to hear about cause, so I was wondering if . . ."

Wondering if what? The harder I concentrated, the less clear I got. It was how I felt in English class sometimes—like I was trying to hold on to water by squeezing it tighter. Dad would say I wasn't applying myself. Mom said my brain had to work differently because I didn't get those nutrients as a baby. I put my hands to my face and rubbed my eyes with the heels of my hands.

"Okay, that's enough," said Josie. "Jack needs his rest."

Dayana ushered Harrison out. Archie waited as Josie

kissed my forehead. As they walked out together and slowly closed the door behind them, I caught a glimpse of Archie putting his arm around Josie.

I was in and out the next few days. Coach Hastings brought the whole football team to visit and they all squeezed into my little hospital room and gave me a signed ball. Once they said hi and asked how I was feeling, nobody had much else to say. And when I looked around, I realized I was having a hard time remembering a lot of their names. They started talking about next week's game and I closed my eyes. Already they didn't feel like my teammates anymore.

Siobhan came after school and brought me chicken salad sandwiches from my favorite deli. She acted like our breakup never happened. She wanted to snuggle in the bed with me. She even offered to "relax" me under the sheets, but I . . . I just couldn't. On her second visit I pretended I was asleep.

One morning I woke up with the feeling that someone was watching me. My room was empty, although I noticed a huge bag of Swedish Fish—my favorite candy—on my table. I looked toward the hall and saw Dayana's mom, Vanesa, standing at the window. For a second I wasn't sure if she was really there. It was like seeing a ghost or something. I lifted my hand to wave, but she'd already floated away down the hall.

Harrison came to visit me on his own. "I went to your

house and got your math books from your grandma. She's very worried that you'll start falling behind in school. She said it was very important to your father, and I know that when you start to feel overwhelmed with the amount of work, you tend to have trouble staying focused on—"

"No."

"I could come back another time or—"

"We're done with the tutoring."

"Oh, because your grandma said—"

"We're done with the tutoring."

"Understood. But if you wanted to talk—"

"We never 'talk.'"

"Well, we were always busy with math during our tutoring sessions, and I took pride in helping you succeed and stay eligible for the team. Remember when you showed me that B plus you brought home? That was a good moment, wasn't it? I felt like we were . . . like before, when my mother babysat for you and Josie and me—"

"What do you want from me, Harrison?"

"What do I want?"

"Why are you here?"

"I want . . . I want to understand why my mother isn't here anymore. Because planes want to stay in the sky. People want to stay with their kids, right? They don't just disappear, not without a reason. Don't you want to know that?"

"I want to go home. Can you take me home?"

121

The nurses called Grandpa and Grandma and warned them I'd escaped from the hospital. They were out in front of the house waiting to bust me when Harrison screeched to a stop.

Grandma went right to Harrison's side of the car. "How could you think this was a good idea? You're supposed to be the smart one!"

"He asked me," said Harrison with a shrug.

"He's not well!"

Josie saw me struggling to get out of the car on wobbly legs. "You should go, Harrison," she said.

"He asked me."

"I know. Go home now."

Harrison nodded. "So . . . I'll be in touch."

As he got back in the car and sped off, I looked up at the house. So many thoughts banging around in my brain. Home from the hospital. No Mom in the kitchen. No Dad in his study. Grandma and Grandpa were arguing about whether they should take me back to the hospital. I needed them to shut up. Josie took my arm and walked me up to the front porch.

"Hey, Jackie," said Grandpa Ralph, "wait'll I show you what I did to the shed."

"It's time for you to go, too," I said.

"Go? Go where?"

"Home. You need to go home."

Grandma looked at me like I'd spit on her. "You want us to leave? For how long?"

Grandpa caught on pretty fast. I think part of him was

waiting for this day. He wanted to help. He loved us. But he didn't sign up to be a parent to two teenagers. He'd retired from that a long time ago. "Come on, Nell. Let's pack up."

"What's wrong with you? We're not leaving them. Jackie shouldn't even be out of the hospital. What would Richard and Michelle think about us abandoning their children?"

"We're eighteen," I said. "We're not children."

"You're not? We all saw what happened to this house when you two were left alone. You're not capable of taking care of yourselves."

"Get out. Now!" I didn't mean to hurt her, but I couldn't help myself. I needed them out of my house.

Josie hugged Grandma's tiny bones and whispered in her ear. Whatever she said made Grandma go limp for a moment. Josie held on and kept her on her feet until she recovered her balance. Then she kissed Josie on the cheek, wiped her tears, and said, "What are we waiting for? Let's go pack, Ralph." Ten minutes later they were gone. For the first time since the night of the party, Josie and I were alone in our house.

"So I guess we should celebrate your release."

"You mean my escape?"

"Can't believe you recruited Harrison to drive the getaway vehicle."

"He drives like a maniac. I'm lucky to be alive."

Josie opened a bottle of Dad's fancy wine from the cellar. I didn't even like the taste, but it did the job. Usually I could drink a six-pack of beer and feel nothing, but after one glass, I was buzzing. My bruised brain was half drunk already. When it got dark, we sat out on the patio and had our first drink together as emancipated adults. Lying there on a lounge chair next to Josie, my head finally felt calmer. We were alone.

I'd be lying if I said I wasn't scared. I missed Mom and Dad so much it burned. But I'd also be lying if I said it didn't feel kinda good. We could do anything we wanted. No more events at the club. No more curfew or bedtime or allowance. No more Dad harassing me about my grades and my "work ethic." Josie and I answered to no one but each other.

"I'm sorry," I said.

"It wasn't our first fight. Won't be our last."

"I mean for the game. You probably thought I was paralyzed or—"

"I love you, Heart."

"You too, Soul."

Josie fell asleep in her chair. I grabbed two fleece blankets and tucked one around her. As I lay back on my chair, I heard music coming from Harrison's house. In a downstairs window, I saw a bald guy in a loud shirt strumming a guitar. *Who the hell is that*, I thought as I drifted off to sleep.

When the doorbell rang, I thought I was dreaming. But the throbbing in my head confirmed that I was awake. Josie didn't stir. My vision was blurry, but I somehow staggered into the house. I squinted hard to read the clock. 11:32 P.M.? What the hell would someone be doing here? I opened the door to find Archie standing on the porch, scooter leaned against the wall, sketchbook in his hand. He scrunched his glasses up with his nose. "Jack, hey . . . I heard you were home. That's so good. Really, really good. So, I was wondering if . . . Is Josie around? I just wanted to talk about something."

"About what?"

"Yeah, I mean we've been talking about things and we had plans to hang out . . ."

Seeing him standing there set off an alarm in my brain. Four days of headaches and dizziness. Four days of feeling like crap, with no end in sight. Four days of knowing how badly I'd scared Josie and remembering how I'd let her down before. Finally, she'd found some peace, and now this little shit was here to bother her? Had he been showing up here in the middle of the night while I was in the hospital?!

"What do you want?" I asked.

"Can you tell Josie I'm here?"

"She's asleep."

"She texted me a little while ago. We've been working with Harrison on something." He tried to look past me into the house.

In that moment, I felt like it was his fault that my head hurt so much. Everything was his fault. "Is this about the crash? Are you filling her head with some kind of shit?!"

"No. I'm not trying to . . . I just . . . We've all had a lot of questions and we've been trying to answer them."

"You really think you're going to find answers? Who the fuck are you, TMZ?"

"Look, I'm sorry. I didn't mean to cause trouble."

"But you have."

"You don't understand."

"And you do?" I knocked his scooter off the porch. Some of the pressure blew off and it made my head feel a little bit better.

"If I could just show this one idea to Josie—"

More pressure. When I got like this, it felt like one section of my brain would just stop working. That's not an excuse for what I did, just an explanation. I grabbed Archie by his shirt. Everything started to spin as he tried to pull away. If I'd let go, I would've fallen right off the porch, so I hung on. He tried to push himself away from me and I almost lost my balance. Now I was furious. How could someone like him almost knock me down? I shoved him back, right off the porch and into the hydrangea bushes next to the steps. He tumbled over backward, his glasses dropping into the bushes, and his sketchbook fell out of his hands and landed at my feet.

"Jack, I'm sorry. I'll go."

I leaned over to pick up the book and the vertigo was intense. But I wanted to see. I wanted to see what was so important that he had to carry that thing with him everywhere. So I started riffling through the pages from back to front. Even with blurry vision, I could see that the pictures were of us. Harrison and Dayana and me. And Josie. Mostly pictures of Josie. They bounced around in time and documented years of her life. Josie at a football game last year. Josie looking sad in the cafetorium. Josie sitting on a tree stump on the playground. I stopped on that picture. Josie must've been fourteen in that picture. I concentrated on small pieces of the drawing at a time. Her face bruised, a tooth chipped. Darkness swelling up under her eye. She's damaged. And yet she's beautiful.

As Archie clawed his way out of the bushes, everything became clear for just a second. I knew exactly when he'd drawn this picture. He was with her that night after the softball game. Around 11 P.M., I'd gone in to check on Jo and she wasn't in her bed. I freaked out. What if she was walking the streets? What if she was going to hurt herself again? What if she'd gone to Murph's house? Without telling Mom and Dad I grabbed my bike and went racing around town looking for her. If I found her, I was going to tell her that I knew. I was going to explain how sorry I was for not looking out for her, how I'd never let her down again. I never found her that night.

But Archie did. He sat right next to her on that stump and he drew this picture. Without a word, I tore it from the sketchbook. A long, ragged tear. Archie screamed, but I kept going. Each rip gave me another tiny bit of relief. I tore them out, page by page, one after another as Archie begged me to stop. I ripped each one out until I reached the first page in the book, a drawing of Archie and Josie, sitting on a branch of a big tree.

"Please," he cried. "Please don't."

It was too late to stop now. Like I'd done with all the others, I ripped it from the book, balled it up like trash, and threw it into a shallow puddle at the bottom of the stairs. And for just a moment, my head finally stopped pounding.

10

HARRISON

-Island Hopper Airlines—Safety record? Mechanical issues?

-Captain George Solomon—Flight hours? Incidents? Personal life?

-Phillip Gallagher—Job/responsibility at Fort Benson

-Richard Clay—Clients? Litigation history? Government connections?

-Meet with Archie to compare notes.

Some people are susceptible to the flu or stomach viruses. For me it's always been ideas. A thought enters my central nervous system, makes a home in my brain, and takes hold of me. Once infected, I can think of little else. The thoughts just keep repeating and growing until I feed them. Mom used to tell me it was a strength. I'd envision a concept for a science project or an essay, and I'd have no choice but to commit every waking hour to its completion. *You may not be the most naturally gifted in your class—you have your father's genes to thank for that. Your focus and dedication, that's what makes you special.* Mom didn't understand what it was like to be in the grips of an idea. Sure it could be helpful when the idea was creative and it served The Plan, but sometimes the thoughts that infected me were dark and negative. They were impossible to ignore.

Hard to pinpoint when the idea about Mom's plane crash infected me. At first it was just a question. If planes *want* to stay in the sky, then what caused hers to fall? People don't just disappear without a reason. So I put in a call to the National Transportation Safety Board, which investigates plane crashes. The NTSB told me they were working with authorities in Anguilla and St. Martin and that the crash was still under investigation. That's when I began my own investigation. I read everything I could about aviation accidents and their causes. I read about the model of plane Mom had flown on and about Island Hopper Airlines, which operated the flight. The plane had an excellent record and the company had never had a crash. So why now?

Why them?

The investigation really took hold while I was serving my suspension for punching Cody Salamone in the face. *I love to see you in the throes of a project,* Mom used to say. *It's like watching an artist at work.* I covered my walls with my research and printed copies of every article written about the crash in newspapers and online. But nothing seemed to point to a reason. Until the day I read the blog Archie's aunt posted on her sister's wedding anniversary. Unlike her others, this post focused less on the surviving kids and more on our parents and their legacies. Along with her grandiose descriptions of the five people who had lost their lives (*Jennifer Rebkin, beloved counselor and mother*) was a photo taken at a gala event hosted by the army base where Archie's father worked. In the photo Phillip Gallagher was shaking hands with Jack and Josie's dad while surrounded by a pack of grim-looking officers in uniform. I was surprised to see them in a setting like that and even more surprised when a search revealed that Mr. Clay's law firm often dealt with military and government contracts.

I reached out to Archie and invited him to meet me at the diner. I didn't know if Archie had the same questions I did, but I knew he had a wide-open mind. When we were kids playing together, we made a good team. Archie had a big imagination for crazy stories, but I was good at working out the details so they'd make sense.

Archie would say, "This swing set is a spaceship that's going to take us up to Saturn."

I'd say, "Saturn is just a big ball of gas. We should go to Mars, where the air is poison, but we could live in a giant bubble." And then Archie would pull out his crayons and draw us on the flying swing set in a giant bubble on Mars.

I spent the morning collecting my notes and sorting through documents I'd printed out. I was excited to share what I had found. When I showed up with my research in

Mom's old briefcase, Archie was waiting in a small back booth. He was not, however, alone. Archie and Josie sat next to each other and picked at a plate of well-done french fries. Archie's sketchbook sat closed on the table in front of them. At first, I was pleased to see her there. I had questions for her, too. But as I approached the table, I became distracted by the way their elbows brushed against each other. I imagined their knees were doing the same underneath the table. They were talking so intently that they didn't even notice me until I sat down across from them.

Their closeness threw off my equilibrium. Maybe it's because I'd never experienced that kind of closeness myself. I'd never been to the prom or held a girl's hand at the movies. I certainly wasn't against it. The truth is, I thought about girls all the time. It was impossible not to. The halls of RBHS coursed with sexuality. You literally had to move out of the way or be bumped by some couple with their arms around each other.

It wasn't only the beautiful, popular students hooking up either. The fever spread all over, even reaching my Math Olympics team when calc wizard Greg Chung fell for logic specialist Amber Jenson before States. *This is why you and Mackenzie Markowitz are numbers one and two,* Mom had said when she saw them holding hands at a competition. *You have your priorities straight.* Greg and Amber spent the remainder of our road trips kissing in the back of the bus. Mackenzie Markowitz and I sat in the front, trying not to turn around. She and I had been fighting for the number one ranking in our grade for many years. Our rivalry was intense and often ugly. Mere decimal points separated our GPAs. Every quiz, test, and paper was a battle in the overall war for valedictorian. And while Mackenzie Markowitz was not unattractive if you were someone who appreciated her shiny brown curls and the dimple that formed in her right cheek when she smiled, her personality was as toxic as the air on Mars.

"I should sit in the captain's seat for today's competition," Mackenzie Markowitz said.

"Why, so we can lose?"

"You really have no social skills at all, do you, Rebkin?"

"Luckily I make up for it with my superior skills in mathematics."

"You know I scored higher than you on the last AP calc test."

"A statistical anomaly."

"Can we not talk for the rest of the ride?"

"I can. I have doubts about your capacity for silence."

"Well then let me quiet those doubts," she said, folding her arms and turning her back to me.

I liked nothing more than defeating her, whether in class or in a Math Olympics team bus debate. I thought all the time about ways to get under her skin and prove my dominance. But sitting so close to Mackenzie Markowitz while Greg and Amber were all over each other a few rows back made it hard to concentrate on the competition.

Mackenzie Markowitz and I spent those bus rides in

dense silence as I practiced math equations in my head and tried not to think about Greg and Amber and all the other couples in school who maybe probably definitely were having sex.

I wasn't even safe in my own bedroom. How to explain the torture of overlooking the Clays' backyard from my window? Every warm day since ninth grade, Josie and her friends would sunbathe by the pool in their tiny bikinis, drinking iced coffees and posing for selfies. On days when I tutored Jack, he'd insist that I go around through the front so they wouldn't know I was there. I wasn't certain whether he was embarrassed by the fact that he needed a tutor, or by me. Still I'd pass the patio doors on the way to the study and catch a glimpse. They were less than twenty feet away, and yet they existed in a different stratosphere. They were beautiful and carefree. I had never even kissed a girl and suffered debilitating glitches. But I had goals. And Mom assured me that once I was successful, the women would come looking for me.

In the meantime, I took long showers. Many long showers.

I was not expecting Josie at the diner. I suddenly felt I had interrupted a private moment between her and Archie. When they finally noticed me, Josie scooted over an inch or two in her seat, creating distance between them. "Hey Harrison," she said. "Sorry I can't stay long. I'm going to see Jack at the hospital."

"Maybe I should go visit him. I could help him catch up on his schoolwork."

"That could be good . . . but he's still having headaches and dizziness. Mood swings, too. Like he gets all angry for no reason."

"Symptoms of concussions can sometimes last years and even cause permanent changes to cognitive function and personality," I noted.

Josie stared at me, her eyes welling with tears. "Was that supposed to be helpful?"

"I'm sorry," I said. "It's just something I read."

Archie handed me a menu. "You texted that you had something you wanted to share with me? With us?"

"Yes, so, well, as we discussed, I've been focusing on the . . . particulars of the crash and its causes. Planes want to stay in the air, as I said."

"I don't understand," said Josie. "What is this about?"

"An investigation," I said. "Not the official one. My own. See, there have been no easy explanations. No storm or bird strike or troubling safety record. So I started to wonder."

"Wonder what?" asked Archie.

"Your father worked for the military. But do you know what he did?"

"Civilian stuff. Requisitions . . . accounting . . . administrative . . . uh . . ."

"So no."

"What does that have to do with—"

"And Josie, it turns out your father's firm had contracts with the military and government."

"Daddy?"

"And Dayana's mom, of course. Plus her dad did some work there when they first moved. That pilot told me planes want to stay in the air. But sometimes people have secrets and other people want these secrets to stay buried."

Archie took a gulp of water. "I don't . . . I mean . . . Are you saying the plane, our parents' plane . . . was like . . . sabotaged?"

"It's just a theory. One of several. We haven't heard from the authorities about a cause. They won't even respond to my emails most of the time. I leave messages on voicemails that are never returned— Here, look at all of this." I produced a stack of papers from my backpack. Safety records, newspaper articles, photos of the plane and the crash site. Names and biographies of all involved parties including the Clays and the Gallaghers.

When I looked up from the pages, Josie was holding a photo of her parents and shuddering. Archie put his hand on her back, and it was as if I wasn't there again. He walked her out of the restaurant, and they never came back.

I sat in the booth with my research and ate the rest of their french fries.

When I returned home after dropping off Jack at his house from the hospital there were lights on all over the house. I opened the front door slowly and grabbed an extendable umbrella from the stand. "Hello?! Is someone in there?"

I pressed the button and the umbrella shot to its full length.

From out of the kitchen charged a large, bald man with a gray goatee and a Hawaiian shirt. My first instinct was to run for my life. Before I could flee, however, he grabbed me in a bear hug. "Holy hell, is that you, Bud? Looks like they put you on the rack and stretched you."

Pop? The umbrella tumbled out of my hand.

His scratchy gray chest hair grazed my chin as he swung me around. "Sorry it took so long for me to get my ass in gear. Been chilling down on the Yucatan in Mexico. I'm kinda half off the grid these days. Only way to live."

I backed away to take a better look at him. The last time I saw him he'd had sandy surfer's hair that was always falling in his face. "What are you doing here?" I asked.

He snorted and patted me hard on the back. "Doing here? Your mom's dead, Bud. I'm all you've got."

"I didn't hear from you. I had to forge your name on the forms. I didn't even know where you were."

"Nelson Calderón finally tracked me down. Had to go through a bunch of different channels. Like I said, half off the grid. Probably helped that El Nel spoke the language. Point is, I had to be here. I'm sorry about your mom, Buddy Boy. We had some great times."

He walked to the fireplace mantel, picked up a photo of my mother with her friends from the trip to California

137

wine country years ago. "Those damn vacations," he said. "Always got me depressed. Three nights a year in some tourist trap, trying to make up for the other three hundred sixty-two days of drudgery. Can't believe that's what got them, though. I always thought Rich Clay would drop dead on the golf course."

"He didn't," I said. It was so unsettling to have Pop here in this house that wasn't his anymore. Walking on Mom's rug, drinking from one of her glasses with the cherry on the side. I recognized his voice from his phone calls, but he looked like a completely different person.

"Point is," said this goateed stranger with Pop's voice, "the dude was intense, and intense dudes . . . Well, shit catches up to them. You remember that. No offense, Bud."

"Bud" was what he called me when I was little. Mom hated the nickname and did everything in her power to discourage it. *His name is Harrison, Bobby. Not Bud. Buds drive pickup trucks and drink beer out of cans.* But my father didn't listen. Bobby showed Bud how to karate chop a stick in half and how to drive a car using only your knees. Bobby threw Bud up in the air so high his head would graze the leaves and he never dropped Bud once. It was my favorite game when I was kid. I hadn't been "Bud" since I was seven, since Pop left.

Pop put a hand on my back. "Listen to me," he said. "I've stayed out of this for most of your life because your mother was in charge. But now we've got a chance to reverse some of the damage."

"Damage?" After all this time, he walked into my house . . . Mom's house . . . and called me *damaged?!*

Was I damaged? Was it that obvious?

"Look at you. You're wound as tight as a baseball. You've had nothing but structure and pressure since you were five."

Suddenly I felt like I had to defend myself and prove to him that I was not what he thought. "I drive a car without a license. I busted a guy out of the hospital. And I got suspended for punching a kid in the face." This man meant nothing to me. Why was I trying so hard to impress him?

"I'm sure he deserved it," he said. "Come on, show me your room."

I should've said no. I should've told him that he didn't belong in our house. But for the first time since Mom died, someone told me what to do. So I did it. Pop and his sandals clopped up the stairs and into my room. He circled my space, picking up each of my math trophies, reading my certificates and medals.

"Bet these get the ladies all hot and bothered," he snorted, glancing out the window with a smile.

I imagined cracking him with the hefty Math Olympics MVP award, knocking him through the glass and into the Clays' yard.

"Rich and Michelle still live there? I mean, *did* they still live there." He corrected himself so easily. Jack and Josie's parents existed one moment. Then they didn't. "Pool's new. A little showy for my taste. Rich always had something to prove. Never enough to just have the beautiful wife and the great head of hair. Nope. You still friends with the twins? Wonder how much he left them?"

I couldn't listen to this anymore. "You can't say things like that. You don't know them. You don't even know me! You ran away from us for my whole life and now Mom is gone and you think you can just come back in and take her place? You don't know me. You don't know anything!"

I stood there, panting, waiting for him to defend himself or to punch me or to apologize. Instead he nodded. *He nodded*.

"You're right. Let's go somewhere," he said.

"I have research to do." The crash. I had to get back to Mom's crash.

"It'll do us both some good. Get some air into the lungs and some life into the bones. You look half dead. When was the last time you went outside and did something?"

"Something?"

"You need to get out of this house. Spend too much time chasing a ghost and you become one yourself."

I'd forgotten what it was like when he was in the room. He took up all the air. And it was almost impossible to say no to him. I found myself nodding.

"There you go. Hey, Bud, I didn't get a chance to hit the ATM at the airport. Your mom still keep that stash of cash with her delicates?"

Pop pulled Mom's car into a parking spot and turned off the ignition. "You come here a lot?" he asked.

I raised my seat and looked out the window. A large, plastic palm tree loomed over us. Island Mini Golf on the boardwalk.

"I used to bring you here all the time. You loved to sit on top of the mermaid and look at the ocean. 'Course they always made me take you down. The mini-golf fun police."

I had not been here since he left ten and a half years ago. "I really don't have time to play miniature golf right now."

"There's always time for mini golf. Come on. We'll play a quick eighteen. I remember you were pretty good. Scary concentration for a little kid. Bet you still can't beat your old man, though. I'll spot you a couple of strokes. Loser buys ice cream."

I desperately wanted to beat him into the ground. "I don't need your strokes."

We chose our putters and Pop handed me an orange ball. "Still your favorite color, I bet." I snatched the ball away without giving him the satisfaction of being right. He stepped aside to let me putt first, but from the very first hole he never stopped talking. "I used to cruise down here when I was supposed to be driving you to Sunny Horizons. We'd hang on the beach and eat peanuts and if it wasn't too cold I'd ride waves with you on my back. No matter how much I wiped you clean your mother would always find a spec or two of sand and she'd start in with one of her lectures. She didn't really mean it. You wouldn't know it, but that woman had a wild streak in her. Until you came along, anyway. Not that I'm blaming you."

I shut him out so I could stay focused on my putting. *Your focus and dedication, that's what makes you special.* One hole at a time. I marked our scores on the card with the tiny pencil and we traded the lead back and forth for sixteen holes. We reached the final regular hole in a dead tie.

This was it. Winner take all. Sudden death. As I approached the final tee, my heart thumped harder than it ever did during spelling bees or Math Olympics. I had to beat this man.

As I lined up the putt, Pop put a meaty hand on the back of my neck. "Thanks for coming here with me, Bud. I wasn't sure you'd give me another crack at this, but it means a lot. And I just—" He choked on his last words. Was he crying? Pop swiped at his eyes with the back of his hand. "Sorry. Brings back a lot of memories, that's all. Your putt." Was this real? Mom always told me that Bobby was . . . That he . . . I don't know. It felt real.

Suddenly, my hands were damp. As I stared down at the blurry orange ball I felt the familiar rush of panic coming over me. I couldn't let Pop see this. I tried to fight off the glitch, gripping the club tighter and tighter. Soon I was overwhelmed. I darted my head around to find somewhere I could hide, somewhere to escape. The closest I could find was the mermaid's grotto on hole thirteen. I dropped my club, wedged myself into the fake rock, and attempted to catch my breath.

3.14159265388979 . . .

"Bud?" I opened my eyes to see Pop standing by the

entrance. "This happen to you a lot?" I nodded between gasps for air.

He put out his hand. "Take it." I stared at the thick fingers. "Come on, pal. Take my hand."

Pop's arrival had not been part of The Plan. He insisted I skip school, and come out of my room for meals. He led me on tours around the old neighborhood and to places he called "his old stomping ground." He snuck us through a gate to swim at a private beach and took me for a hot shave from a real barber. He pulled me into the backyard to lie on the grass and look at the stars. Whether I enjoyed any of these spontaneous excursions was not the point. They were very disruptive to my research into the crash.

In my first week back at school after the suspension, I didn't make a single visit to Mr. U's supply closet. In fact I went five full days without a single glitch. But I wasn't much interested in my classes either. I elected for "independent study" in the library, where I'd mostly take naps on the table. One afternoon, I woke to someone pulling me up by my hair. I blinked at Dayana, who was prying open my eyes. "You taking those meds again?" she asked.

"I'm just tired. I went to a midnight movie with my pop last night."

"No shit," she said. "I heard he was here. You good with it?"

I thought about the question. "I have no idea."

"Listen, I'm the last person to lecture anyone about going to school or doing homework or any of that. But it's different for you. You've got something. Like . . . you're going somewhere. Harvard or whatever. And I just don't want to see you fuck it away."

"Fuck it away?"

"You know what I mean."

Dayana studied me some more, her hand still touching my head. I felt her black nails on my scalp. A little shiver ran up my back.

"Nelson wants you and your dad to come over for dinner," she said. "Don't blow it off this time. I can't promise it's not gonna be a fucking disaster, but hey, at least you'll have me and I'm the GOAT at dinner parties. Okay. I'll text you the deets."

When I passed on the invitation to Pop, he thought about it for a while before responding. "Nelson and Vanesa, the sole survivors . . . So is Dayana your girlfriend?"

My face got hot and I snapped at him. "No. No, of course not. Before the crash she didn't even talk to me." I didn't like him asking those questions about Dayana. She wasn't his business. She was with me after Mom died. He wasn't.

"I'll bet she's really pretty. Like her mother. She was a cute kid."

"She's . . . different than you remember."

Pop asked if I'd ever had a girlfriend and when I explained about The Plan and how busy I was trying to beat Mackenzie Markowitz, he grabbed the car keys and told me we were taking a ride. This time mini golf was not on the menu. Instead he swung Mom's sedan into a grubby-looking establishment off the side of route 135 with a large pink sign reading "Delilah's." I reminded Pop that I was seventeen and would not be allowed into a bar.

"Don't worry," he said, "they only serve juice here. That's why they let them go all-out." I had no idea to what he was referring until we walked into Delilah's and I saw the girls.

The room was dim and it smelled like a swimming pool and stale flowers. The music was loud and distorted. But the girls were everywhere. Women. Half to fully naked. They were dancing on the black stage or the bar while several others rubbed against men sitting around small, round tables. As we walked in, a few of the women looked in our direction. They smiled with only the corners of their mouths. One of them, wearing a green bikini she was in the process of removing, winked at me. I averted my eyes to the floor, where popcorn was ground into the dark rug. Even without looking at the dancers, I could feel them around me. Skin and sparkles and perfume. Moving to the pulse of the music. The room was hot, warmed by the energy coming off their bodies.

Pop slapped me on the back. "*They're* the naked ones. You got nothing to be nervous about. It's all good, Bud. Whatever you've got going on in there is natural." It did not feel natural. It felt intense and awkward and terrifying. I stared straight ahead while Pop led me to a table and guided me down into a fake leather seat. I folded my hands on the table, but the top was sticky, so I moved them to my lap, where a lot was happening. Pop pulled out some cash he'd taken from Mom's drawer and nodded to one of the girls on the stage.

She was very small, wearing pink leather bottoms, clear heels, and nothing else. Nothing else. Glitter all over her bare body. I tried to keep my eyes on her face. Looking down at her nakedness was too . . .

Pop leaned toward her and raised his voice over the music. "My son's having a tough time." He slipped her a couple of bills and she turned and smiled at me. Her smile sent a jolt through my body. My right leg started to vibrate uncontrollably.

"You two have fun, okay? Relax, Bud. Enjoy yourself."

Pop went to the bar and left us alone at the table. She leaned in, her lips grazing my ear. "I'm Platinum," she said. "I'm an expert at cheering people up." She slid her back against my chest. I didn't know what to do with my hands or my eyes. What would Mackenzie Markowitz think about me doing this? She was probably at home in those emoji pajamas she wore to school on pj day. What would Mom think about me using her money this way?

"What's your name?" Platinum blew a little cool air in my ear and I shivered.

"Harrison."

"You're cute. I like you. Let's see if we can get you to loosen up."

She rubbed her bare back up and down against my chest, her bikini bottom grazing my lap each time.

"You've got a good dad," she said. "You two must be really close."

I wiped sweat off my forehead, struggling to process the music and her body and the little butterfly tattoo on her back and the pressure of her touching me. "I haven't seen him in many years. He left me and my mother when I was seven years old. He kissed me goodnight and said 'I'll see ya when I see ya.' And when I woke up the next morning he was gone and it was just me and my mother. She died in a crash and I think maybe someone sabotaged the plane."

Platinum bolted up and turned around to see if I was telling some kind of weird joke. When she saw I wasn't kidding, she covered herself with her hands and teetered back on her heels. Up close her face wasn't what I expected. She had big, innocent eyes like a puppy and a little crooked part to her nose. Beneath the long eyelashes and shimmering makeup she looked like she could be my age.

"Oh my God! You're one of those kids. The Sunnies. I read about you every day. It breaks my heart." She grabbed me in a hug. "I'm so sorry, Harry. You must really miss your mom."

Somehow, being hugged by this stranger, her bare breasts pressed against my shirt, made me finally feel the weight of the loss. Mom was the most important person in my world. No one else loved me and protected me like she did, and no one else ever would. She was there when I woke up every single morning of my life. I never went to sleep without her kissing me goodnight. I didn't have real friends anymore. Just memories. I didn't have girlfriends. I had Mom. And she had me. I didn't know a world without her in it and now I was forced to live it every day. I lingered in the warm embrace of a naked stripper and only wished for one more hug from my mother, one more goodnight kiss on the forehead.

I could barely see through the tears flooding down my eyes, but I became aware that Pop was arguing with a huge, bearded man just to my left. The bearded man ripped Platinum away from me and insisted that we leave now. Pop tried to bribe his way out of our ejection, but I was already halfway out the door. He finally caught up to me in the car, where I couldn't stop crying. Crying for the first time since the crash.

"We had a plan."

Pop came out of Mom's bedroom dressed for dinner. "What were you doing in there?" I asked.

"Just looking for toothpaste."

"You shouldn't be in her room."

"It's like the land that time forgot, Bud. It hasn't changed since the day I left this house."

I walked past him to shut the door, but Pop reached out and pulled at my collar. "Hang on. You're a little crooked." He stepped in close to re-button my shirt. As his thick fingers worked the buttons, I caught a strong whiff of his deodorant, the same musky brand he'd used my whole life. I closed my eyes and let it take me back to the days when he was carrying me on his shoulders and tossing me up in the air until my head brushed the leaves.

"Listen, Bud," he said, "I'll be the first to admit I've made a lot of mistakes. I know I haven't been around. Your mother, for all her faults . . . she loved the crap out of you. I'm never gonna be her, but I'm here, so . . . So you don't have to go out with crooked buttons anymore, okay?"

When we arrived at Dayana's house, Nelson opened the door. He pulled Pop into a tight hug and kissed him on the cheek.

Vanesa hovered behind him. "It's been too long." Pop grabbed her, too, but I noticed she didn't hug back with as much force.

I asked myself what it must be like for the three of them. Once, they had been part of a group like us. Eight friends. Now they were the only three left.

I found Dayana in her room, scrolling through Instagram. She closed her laptop as soon as she noticed me. "Shit," she said. "You look kinda strung out. Have you been sleeping?"

"I've had to squeeze it in between school and my plane crash research. Pop has a ton of ideas for us, so I'm out of the house a lot more than I used to be. But I'm corresponding with Michael Boddicker from the NTSB. Archie and Josie are supposed to be collecting research on their parents."

Nelson knocked on Dayana's door to tell us it was dinner-time. As we walked toward the small dining room, he patted me on the back. "It must be wonderful to have your papi home. He is very proud of who you have become. I have not seen him in many years, and he spent ten minutes bragging about all your awards and your score on the standardized testing."

How could that be true? Pop made fun of my awards. And how did he even know about my SATs? I never told him. Why didn't Mom tell me that Pop was following what I did? Did she purposely keep him away from me?

Pop's eyes widened when Dayana walked into the room, playing with her purple hair and jangling her piercings. "Whoa," he said. "Isn't time something?"

I barely ate any of the chicken or rice Vanesa served. They were good, but my mind was infected not only with ideas of who may have killed my mother, and confusion about Pop being here, but by the residual feelings brought on by having been embraced by a sexy, naked woman for the first time in my life. There was little space left for casual small talk at a dinner party. Luckily, Pop controlled the conversation with memories of the old Sunny Horizons days. Nelson kept up as best he could, but he was distracted by Vanesa, who seemed to be adrift in her own world.

After dinner, Dayana's parents went into the kitchen. When Vanesa carried plates to the sink, her hands shook and she almost dropped them on the floor. Nelson steadied her with a hand on the small of her back as he leaned in to whisper to her in Spanish. They lingered there for a moment. Something about that hand placed just above her waist reminded me of

Archie and Josie touching elbows at the diner and of Platinum, pressing her glittery head against my shoulder.

Nelson carried the tres leches cake to the table while Vanesa brought over cappuccino crunch ice cream.

Pop stood up to help her scoop. "It's good to see you guys like this," he said. "I was always jealous of what you two had. Maybe it was because you didn't come from here. Trial by fire and all that. Me and Jen . . . Well, the little things got the best of us. But after all these years the two of you are . . ." Vanesa quickly excused herself and floated away to the bedroom.

Pop was confused about what had happened. "Did I say something wrong? I've been known to do that."

Nelson shook his head. "It is not your fault. We struggle like anyone else. But we are trying, right Daya?"

Dayana pulled me up from the table and led me out to the backyard. It was a chilly night, but she didn't seem to notice. She took out her vape pen, sucked in, and then offered it to me. I looked at the mouthpiece, which glistened from where it had touched her lips. I guided it into my mouth and sucked in. The vapor felt warm in my lungs and tasted like fruit punch.

"Your dad doesn't seem so bad," she said, in between puffs. "I mean the stories are a bit much, but I was expecting him to be a real dickhole."

"He took me to a strip club last night. A girl with naked boobs hugged me and I started crying about my mother. I don't think you're supposed to do that, because we got thrown out."

151

Dayana burst out in a laugh. At first I thought she was making fun of me. The more I thought about it, though, the funnier it became. I started to laugh, too, and soon we were practically hysterical, leaning into each other to steady ourselves on the bench. She was next to me and I felt her energy rushing right into my body. All this energy traveling from her to me. So I pushed my face toward hers and kissed her.

I hadn't planned the kiss and I certainly didn't know what to expect once our lips connected. Dayana froze there for what felt like minutes, but was likely only a second. Then she yanked her face away from mine.

"Oh. Shit, I didn't . . . I mean, was I sending . . . ? I like you, Harrison. I mean, I think you're like the weirdest person I ever met, and that's saying a lot. But there's this guy. Or there was this guy. And I just think you're kinda messed up now and you don't really know what you want. This would be a shitshow between you and me. Especially for you. I'm not . . . I wouldn't be good for you. Sorry."

As Dayana stumbled through explaining why she never wanted to kiss me again, I desperately wanted to take back the last ninety seconds and erase it from my memory banks. Since I couldn't do that, I took off. I didn't say goodbye or thank the Calderóns for a lovely evening or explain to Pop why I had to go. I was just gone.

Running down the street, brain circling in all directions, I clicked back into my research about the plane crash. Probabilities, evidence, equations. I cut through a yard and

found myself rushing toward Archie's house. I rang the doorbell, but no one answered. Lights were on inside and I could
hear footsteps, so I tried the door and found it unlocked. I
walked into the kitchen, where Archie sat at the table, a ball
of wadded-up papers in a pile in front of him. Other sheets,
full of wrinkles and smeared with ink, were stretched out
across the table. He frantically ran his hands back and forth
over the papers, trying to smooth them out.

"The door was open," I said.

A small, wiry kid with spiked hair walked into the kitchen
and waved. "Hey. I'm Sam." Sam grabbed a Gatorade from
the refrigerator and headed back down the hallway.

"Who's Sam?" I asked.

Archie finally looked up at me. "That's my brother's boyfriend. They're tight."

"Oh. Good for him."

"He's here whenever Lucas is. Seems to be helping him
a lot." I thought about what it would be like to have that . . .
intimacy.

"I kissed Dayana." It's not like Archie and I had ever
talked about girls before. Or anything else.

"You did? How'd that go?" he asked.

"Bad," I said. "Really bad. She told me I'm the weirdest
person she's ever met."

"*Dayana* said that?"

"I'm aware I'm different, but my mother used to say
that . . . Never mind."

"You think a lot about what your mother said, don't you?"

I didn't know how to respond. How could I explain? "She's always in my head."

"Still?"

Still.

I picked up a crumpled paper from the pile and attempted to smooth it out. Most of the drawing was destroyed, but I could make out remnants of what it was: Josie sitting in class, a pencil tucked behind her ear. "What is all this?"

"My life." Archie couldn't even look at the remains of his sketchbook.

"How did it happen?"

"Jack."

"Why?"

Archie looked at the smeared Josie drawing. "I don't know. He loves her."

"So do you, right?"

Archie finally stopped smoothing out the papers and looked up at me.

"Do you really believe that someone killed them?" he asked. "I mean, you actually think there was a conspiracy to take out Josie's father and my dad by bringing down their plane?"

"I haven't yet reached a conclusion."

"Yeah. I don't know. Does it really even matter? They're gone no matter what."

I don't think he was ready for me to answer the way I did. "Nothing matters. Not grades or SATs or math awards. Look at this mess in front of you. You spent years drawing these incredible pictures and now they're a useless mess of wadded-up paper. My mother dedicated her entire life to making me a success. But she only saw me become *this*."

"Then why are you working so hard on this investigation?"

"Because it's a problem that needs to be solved and that makes sense to me. I need to know the answer. I need to know why."

Archie thought about that for a long time. In the silence I could hear Lucas and Sam laughing in the other room.

"I do, too," he said. "I'll help you. But only if it's all of us. Because this happened to all of us."

"It did. I guess after all this time we finally need each other for something again."

"If you ask me, we never stopped." He stood up from the table and gathered all of the papers into one large pile. Then he swept them up in his arms, walked over to the trash, and dumped them in. He took a long deep breath and turned to me. "Now what?"

11

ARCHIE

IT'S NOT LIKE I DECIDED TO STOP DRAWING; there just wasn't anything to draw anymore. When I first went dry, I thought I was suffering from some kind of artist PTSD. Watching all those hours of work torn up was like seeing a loved one die right in front of me.

A day went by without any drawings, and then a few more days. And then a whole week. Nothing but blank pages.

I helped Harrison dig into the crash as best I could. Josie didn't come around anymore. While Jack was in the hospital, we saw each other every day. But once Jack came back, she stayed close to home.

I heard people saying that Jack was acting funky in class. Like he'd space out and the teacher would call his name five times before he'd notice. Or he'd suddenly have these really bad headaches and they'd have to turn off all the lights in the room. He was having even more trouble controlling his temper. That part I already knew. I'd escaped our last encounter without any bodily harm and I wanted to keep it that way. So I didn't push it.

How do you miss what you never really had? Before the crash, I understood what Josie and I were. What we weren't. She had her life and I . . . had my drawings. I could live with that. I *did* live with that. Now she had her life and I . . . I just put my head down and kept going. I woke up in the morning and got dressed. Harrison had found the name of the NTSB investigator, Michael Boddicker, and every day we sent him an email with our latest research and theories. But my heart wasn't in it. And I couldn't draw a thing. I even stopped carrying my empty sketchbook. It felt wrong moving through the world without it. Like I'd lost a limb or something. But buying a new sketchbook and then wandering around holding a blank pad . . . It reminded me of this time I saw a guy walking through the park holding an empty dog collar and leash. Tragic.

When someone dies, you start to mark your life by the big occasions that they miss. Mom and Dad's anniversary. Mom's forty-eighth birthday. And now I'd made it to Thanksgiving.

Believe me, I tried everything I could think of to get out of going to Aunt Sarah's suckfest. I summoned up all of my skills as an experienced liar. I tried medical excuses (stomach virus), school excuses (overdue paper), even legal excuses (meeting with a lawyer about Mom and Dad's estate). Sarah refused to let me stay home. Just one year ago, she and Mom had the blowout to end all blowouts, and I wasn't sorry when Mom said we were never coming to Sarah's house again. Now Lucas and I would be there on our own. Sarah would pretend that she and Mom were best friends and that those fights never happened.

And after dinner would be the Performance. At each family gathering, Sarah wrote, directed, and starred in a "musical production" for the holiday. She cast her kids and recruited Uncle Tommy and Dad as stage crew. There is no way to explain how brutal it is to sit five feet from your aunt while she sings love songs to her six-year-old son. I prayed she'd have the decency to cancel the show this year.

Aunt Sarah and Uncle Tommy lived about twenty-five minutes away from us in a new development full of houses that all looked alike. On the drive, Lucas sat in the passenger seat and took control of the radio. He played the music so loud that I had to yell to be heard above it. Not that we had much to say. We hadn't talked much since Mom and Dad died. I *wanted* to talk to him. Some days, I needed to talk to him. Like about Josie and the crash. Or about all the weird people sending me messages on social media. But Lucas didn't need to talk to me. When he was home, he was with Sam.

I was happy for Lucas. At least I tried to be.

In the months after the crash, Sam was this vibrant energy in the house. He had a loud laugh and a nice singing voice and hair that stood up like it was reaching for the sky. Sam made Lucas lighter, happier. But I couldn't stand to be around it. I know that's a horrible thing to say. It was torture, especially once Josie stopped spending time with me. Lucas had what I needed more than anything: a boyfriend. I mean, I didn't want a boyfriend. I wanted *someone*. Someone to talk to, someone to understand, someone to be close to. I wanted Josie. It's like if you were a dog at the pound and they kept you in a crate all day long. All the other dogs had owners who came and walked them and gave them treats and tossed chew toys, but you stayed locked up while you watched them living their lives. Being that close would make you that much lonelier.

The drive to Aunt Sarah's filled me with nothing but dread. And without having my drawing to calm me down, I was a big ball of nerves. I asked Lucas to be my navigator, but he was texting so much that he missed telling me about the first four turns. I tried to be patient. He'd keep his head in the game for a few minutes, but then his phone would start blowing up again and he'd be tap tap tapping away, probably sending little love notes back and forth with Sam. When we drove past the exit off the parkway, I finally snapped at him. "Could you stop sexting your little boyfriend for like ten minutes so we can actually get there?!"

Lucas put down his phone and stared at me with—what, pity?—in his eyes. "Sorry, bro," he said calmly. "Take the next exit." He didn't get angry or defensive. Not a flicker. I couldn't even have the ugly satisfaction of knowing I'd hurt his feelings. He wouldn't call me jealous or homophobic or any of the other things I deserved. Why bother? I wasn't worth it. He felt *sorry* for me. That's the worst.

Aunt Sarah greeted us at the car to tell us she'd invited several of her friends to join us. She wanted Thanksgiving to be "a fully supportive and inclusive experience" for us. As soon as she said the word "inclusive," I knew who I'd find filling Mom's and Dad's seats at the dinner table. Aunt Sarah brought me and Lucas inside and introduced us to Harold and Kimberly Hunt, the young black couple who'd recently moved in across the street along with Jim and James, her friends from art class.

Kimberly awkwardly hugged me. "It's great to meet you, Archie. We've heard so much about you." I didn't have to ask what they'd heard. Luckily, the addition of the two couples meant that Lucas and I could hide at the kids' table with our little cousins, Gregor and Emma. At least there, I wouldn't have to make uncomfortable small talk about my "culture" while Aunt Sarah patted herself on the back.

The kids' table was covered in a brown paper tablecloth. Aunt Sarah brought over a large cup full of crayons to draw on the paper. "Your cousin Archie is one of the best artists in the world. He's going to be famous one day! I bet he can show you guys how to draw some awesome turkeys!"

As Aunt Sarah headed back to the kitchen, Emma handed me the crayon cup while Gregor barked orders. "I want a pilgrim and a Native American and a turkey, and they're all in a car together and the car is really a boat, and it's flying. Do that!" Gregor showed me where he wanted his masterpiece.

Lucas was back to texting away on his phone.

I stared down into the deep hole of the crayon cup. How do you explain artist's block to a five-year-old? *See, the thing is, Gregor, my guts were crumpled up and tossed in a puddle by a giant football player and since then I've lost my drawing mojo.*

"See, the thing is I don't really do animals Gregor and crayons they're not like my favorite drawing utensils 'cause it's hard to get shading right and if you press too hard you end up breaking the crayon and the point gets all worn down and I don't see a sharpener here and it's just not like ideal and I think you two are expecting something great after your mother's big buildup and well I haven't been sleeping all that great and the person I was usually drawing she's not even . . ."

Blank expressions on their faces.

I picked up a black crayon and pressed it to the paper. Nothing. Not even a freaking hand outline turkey. "Sorry," I muttered. "This never usually happens to me."

I spent the next hour shoveling as much food into my mouth as I possibly could. The meal was as bland as ever, but I didn't care. I just wanted to stuff myself, to bury everything under a mound of carbs, to be too full to think. I wanted more plates to cover the blank tablecloth. I wanted to watch my fork scrape the leftovers instead of watching Lucas sending witty texts back and forth to his boyfriend.

I would've kept on eating all night, but Aunt Sarah and Kimberly Hunt and James stopped by to clear the table.

"Show starts in five," said Sarah. Oh God no. "This year's theme is 'Thanks for the Memories.'" Oh dear God no, no.

The Thanksgiving show was a tribute in song and performance to Mom and Dad. Uncle Tommy ushered us into the living room, where we took our seats and waited. Tommy hit the lights and the room went black. Then *fwwwip!* A floor lamp turned on, aimed toward Aunt Sarah like a spotlight. There were already tears rolling down her cheeks.

"Memories," she said. "We thank you for the memories." Uncle Tommy touched his phone and the music started. This was worse than I even imagined. But before Aunt Sarah could start singing or reciting poetry or God knows what else, a phone buzzed. I turned and glared at Lucas. If I was going to suffer through this horror show, then so was he. But he wasn't looking at his phone. When it happened again, I realized the buzzing was coming from my own pocket. Someone was texting *me*. I discreetly fished out my phone and gave it a quick look.

Where are you Rn?

Need to C U

I jumped out of my chair, bumping into Jim and knocking over his glass of wine. Everyone in the room looked at me, including Aunt Sarah, who signaled Uncle Tommy to pause the music. "Arch? You want to say something?"

I felt all the eyes on me as Uncle Tommy swung the light around and shined it on my face. Now I couldn't see anyone else's face, except for Lucas's, lit up by his phone. He was so hard to read. Once in the spotlight I could've said something nice. I could've found a story to tell about Mom and Dad. Maybe I could've talked about how hard they worked to bring me home. Or all the nights they let me sleep in their bed even though I tossed and turned and Dad had to get up early for work. Or the way Mom walked me to school and kept touching my arm, but did it in a cool, secret way so that it wouldn't look like she was holding my hand.

I could've said all of those things, but I didn't. "I had four plates of food and my stomach is . . . You do not want me to . . . I have to go. I'm sorry."

Uncle Tommy said he'd drop Lucas home in the morning. I was already heading for the door.

I barely remember the drive home. My brain was spinning and my stomach was doing flips. As I pulled the car into our driveway, Josie was sitting on the steps, her arms wrapped around her knees. She was shivering and I instantly hated myself for leaving my jacket back at Aunt Sarah's. It always seemed like such a cool move when the guy takes off his jacket and puts it around the girl's shoulders. "Come inside," I said. "You're freezing."

"Ease up, Granny. I'm fine."

I ran inside and grabbed the quilt off the couch. My stomach gurgled. Coming home to Josie Clay on my porch didn't exactly do wonders to settle things down, intestinally speaking. I came back outside and draped the blanket over Josie's shoulders. I wasn't sure what to do next. Sit down with her? Slide under the blanket? I chose option three: stand and hover. All of it was very confusing. My house was a place where I only *thought* about Josie. She was never actually here.

"Why have you been avoiding me?" she asked. Her breath shot out under the light.

"What?" She thought *I* was avoiding *her*?

"Do you blame my dad for the plane crash or something? You think he got involved with bad people and your dad got in the way and—"

"What? No, that's crazy. I didn't . . . No."

"Then why'd you go radio silent? You haven't texted. You look away when I see you at school. You're totally blowing me off." She wiped her eyes with the blanket.

"Josie, I . . . I thought you didn't want me around. After Jack . . ."

"After Jack what?"

Josie dropped her head into her hands.

I started to reach out to touch her shoulder, but I still wasn't sure how that would go over.

"Jack's not . . . Jack's still dealing with a lot of problems. I did a search on WebMD. I know you're not supposed to do that because everything you look up says cancer, but . . . They said concussions make ADHD like a million times worse. I know he never really admits he has it, but he's, like, all over the place. He gets furious for no reason. It's scary and if he said something to you . . . He doesn't mean it. And I . . . I missed you."

"Oh." For once I didn't feel like jabbering around her.

"Where's your sketchbook?"

"I . . . left it inside. Why did you text me?"

Josie wrapped the blanket tighter around her. "We were

at my grandma and grandpa's for Thanksgiving, you know. I didn't want to be there. I'm just sitting there freaking out and I see this little picture hanging on the wall. A picture from Mom and Daddy's wedding day. They're cutting the cake and Mom's laughing with her mouth open like she always did in pictures. I couldn't believe how young they looked. Even though they were getting married, they didn't look like two adults. They looked . . . like us. And we're going around the room saying what we're grateful for. But I can't say it. How am I going to say thanks for what happened to us? Everyone's just looking at me. Waiting."

"What did you say?"

"I left. I ran out and I texted you."

"I don't blame you."

"I want to know, Archie. Did someone do this to them? To us? Why are people always hurting each other?"

"I don't know yet. I mean, Harrison and I talk every day, but half the time I don't understand what he's saying. I've gone through Dad's stuff and called his friends at the base to ask about the kind of work he did. They pretty much say nothing, which is exactly what they'd say if they were trying to cover something up. There's no way we're going to get anyone from the government to talk to us about it. I think—I think this investigation is gonna have to get more personal."

Josie tossed off the blanket as she stood up. "So let's do it. Let's make this personal. I mean, it is personal. Someone killed our parents, right? Or they might have," she said.

"Daddy's firm keeps calling and asking if Jack and I would stop by to help clean out his office. I've totally been avoiding it for months."

"His office is still there? Everything?"

"Dayana's mom is a paralegal at the firm and I don't think she's been back to work since the crash. The other partners are really worried about seeming cold, so they just . . . waited for me and Jack to come around. We can go over there right now. Will you do it? Will you come with me? Please."

"Of course I will."

We stopped off at her house for the office keys. "Come inside," she said. "Jack's still out and I don't like being in the house alone."

We walked in the door and Josie went off to grab the key. I looked around the massive white living room. A towering stack of mail sat on the bar. And if quiet can be loud, then the house was deafening. I remembered what I felt in here the night of the party. The first day of senior year was coming and everybody was high on possibility. Even me. I showed up that night with this feeling that something was going to change in my life.

I guess for once I was right.

The offices of Tovaris, Kesselman & Clay occupied an entire building in a large industrial complex off the highway. In my mind, Rich Clay's office would be in the penthouse of a huge skyscraper like Tony Stark's in *Iron Man*. This building was big and modern, but mostly it felt like an office. Where were the retinal scans and the laser alarm system? Not even an old security guard on patrol. Josie opened the glass door and flipped on the lights in the outer office, which was filled with dozens of cubicles, each personalized with family photos and novelty calendars.

We walked by Dayana's mom's cubicle. On the desk was a framed photo of Dayana as a tiny girl in a white dress on a sandy beach I assumed was in Costa Rica. Josie entered the office and I almost ran right into her back when she stopped short. I saw inside the office and understood why she froze. His desk was untouched. Nothing seemed to have been moved since the day Josie's dad died. They didn't even take away the newspapers he'd been reading. It was like they were afraid to disturb anything.

Josie was practically shaking. I touched her hand and she jumped. "Maybe this was a mistake," I offered, pulling my hand back. "We can call Jack . . ."

"It smells like Daddy," she said. "Mom never let him have his stinky cigars at home, but his suits reeked like smoke when he came in the door. Like this. I know it's a totally weird thing to say, but that was, like, my favorite smell in the world. It meant that he was home."

Josie held his pencil and his letter opener and picked up his phone as if they might all still have a little bit of him left on them. For three months since the crash, our houses had been walked through, cleaned, rearranged. Changed. They were lived in. Reminders of our parents were far from gone, but there were less and less of them every day. The foods they liked went sour in the fridge until we tossed them out. Their shoes didn't live by the front door anymore. Little things they left behind—notes on the corkboard and loose change and single socks—had disappeared one piece at time. Even their smells—aftershave, shampoo, coffee—were drifting away. Mr. Clay's office, on the other hand, was . . . preserved. It felt alive, like he could walk back in at any second. So I let Josie linger. On his books and his cigars and his laptop. She sat down in his oversize leather chair, closed her eyes, and breathed.

"We should look through his computer," she said, finally opening her eyes. "Daddy did everything on this stupid laptop. It was a big thing that Mom made him leave it at the office before their vacation." She slid it over to me.

"I think you should do this," I said. I didn't feel good about going through Mr. Clay's computer. Computers weren't just devices. They collected history. Like a diary, or my sketchbook. They stored what was inside you. Someone combing through your laptop could probably learn more about you than they could in a thousand hours of conversation.

"You're better at the computer stuff than I am." She got up and let me sit in the big chair. I couldn't believe how soft it was, how my whole body sank into the brown leather. As I turned on the laptop, Josie leaned over me and rested her hand on my shoulder. Her face floated right next to mine. I had to stay focused on the job, but she was pressing her body against my back. As she exhaled, I felt her breath on the side of my neck. I took off my glasses and set them on the desk. My stomach tightened. The tightness spread lower, too. I tried to ignore the feelings, but my body wasn't taking messages from my brain anymore. I felt warm and uncomfortable. I shifted in the chair. If I turned my head just a little bit . . .

Josie pushed away and stood up straight. Did she suddenly realize what I was thinking? I gave myself away, didn't I? Did she look down and see that I . . . I mean . . . I wasn't . . . Not fully . . . Okay, maybe I was, but what do you expect? We were alone in an empty office and she was pressing against me and . . . She was Josie.

Josie backed across the room to give herself some distance. She wasn't even looking at me. That's how disgusted she was. I felt ashamed. She brought me here to help her find out how her parents died and I got turned on. What was wrong with me?

The login screen came up. I cleared my throat. "It, uh . . . it needs a password."

Josie looked around at her dad's pictures and memorabilia and rattled off a few options. Family names, their first dog, his favorite teams. None of it got me into the system. "Birthdays," she said. "Let's try birthdays." Without asking I punched in 081301. August 13, 2001. Josie and Jack's birthday.

Josie finally looked at me. "You remember my birthday?"

Of course I remembered her birthday. "Just one of those things that sticks with you, I guess."

Josie started to cry and she grabbed a tissue box from the bookshelves. "It's so stupid how this happens all the time. I didn't let myself cry for, like, three years and now I can't get through a freaking day without going into full-on blubber mode."

"I cried in PE the other day," I said. "Softball. It wasn't that I cared about striking out. I always strike out. But I was swinging the bat and I had this flash of Dad trying to teach me how to hit in the backyard."

"Did it work? When he taught you?"

"No, of course not. I was a complete disaster. Dad just kept moving closer and closer and throwing the ball slower and slower until he was basically placing it on the bat. When we were done he hugged me and told me he was proud of me. Anyway, that's what came back to me on the field behind the science lab that day."

"What did you do?" she asked.

"Pretended I got dirt in my eye. Totally humiliating."

Josie smiled. "I'm sure no one noticed."

"Everyone noticed."

"I'll give you lessons someday," she said. "No more strikeouts." I looked at her. Did she just offer to help me play softball? I knew what that meant for her and I knew she wouldn't say it by accident. She hadn't picked up a ball or a bat since . . .

"Archie . . . ?"

"Yeah?"

"I said earlier that at the table I didn't have anything I was thankful for . . . that wasn't true. I'm thankful for Jack. And even though I don't always show it, I'm thankful for you."

I tried to respond, but my mouth dried up. Whatever words I was trying to say got stuck in the back of my throat. *I'm thankful for you, Josie. I've been thankful for you since I was four years old.* "I—"

"JackJosie081301! Try that. Try JackJosie081301. Daddy used that for our Wi-Fi at home." I typed it in and poof! I was in. Josie celebrated our victory with a little touchdown dance. She wagged her finger in the air and spun around on one leg. My heart felt like it might burst through my chest like a baby alien.

The computer was stocked with files, all labeled by client names and dates. I didn't even know what I was looking for, but it would be easy to sit here for days going through depositions and memos without finding anything. I was okay with that. There was no place I wanted to be more. So I started at the top and scrolled through the files one at a time while Josie went to track down sodas and snacks from the kitchen.

I scanned down the list, looking for anything related to my dad's work at Fort Benson, the government, or my father. Bachman deposition 8.3.15. Baird closing arguments 4.16.09. I stopped at one file with a different type of file name. The Beach.rar. I knew RAR files were compressed, which meant multiple documents or a lot of data. I double-clicked on the file, but a message popped up telling me the file was password protected. An extra level of security. Now I was really interested. I tried all of the passwords Josie had given me and when they didn't work, I decided to grease the wheels.

Junior year I sat next to this kid named Cole in computer lab. Cole was a creepy hacker, like the kind you see in bad movies. Pale skin, greasy hair, the whole deal. Who knows what he was using his skills for? All I know is he liked showing off and he taught me how to get into password-protected RAR files. As Cole had instructed, I downloaded and installed a hacking tool on Mr. Clay's laptop. Then I experimented with brute-force and dictionary methods of password de-encryption. Took less than five minutes to break the code. The password was "mojito."

When the file opened, it didn't reveal a long deposition or list of case notes. It was full of compressed photos. I opened them in order. Photos of a tropical beach. A woman wearing a bathing suit, a wide-brimmed hat, and a small cover-up. She held a brightly colored drink and she smiled at the camera. No, she smiled at the person *behind* the camera. These photos were meant to be seen by him and only him. I could tell by her smile. She was shiny and flirty. There were so many of these pictures. In one she seemed like she was waving for her cameraman to join her in the shot. And so he did. He came around the other side of the camera. And there in the last few pictures was a tanned, shirtless Richard

Clay kissing his colleague Vanesa Calderón. Dayana's mother. Dayana's mother and Josie's dad . . . Josie's dad and Dayana's mother.

Maybe it wasn't what it looked like. They worked at the same law firm. They were on a business trip and maybe they were just having fun for the camera. For all I knew, Nelson and Michelle were there on the other side of the camera. But I didn't believe that. No one who saw these pictures could ever believe that. This was *exactly* what it looked like. If it wasn't, he wouldn't have put these pictures in a protected file where no one but he was ever supposed to see them.

"All right, I got trail mix, Red Vines, pretzels, water, and lots of drink options. How extreme do we want to go?" I hadn't even noticed Josie standing in the doorway. When I snapped my head up, she must've seen the look on my face. "Did you find something?" she asked.

I panicked. What was I supposed to do, tell her about her dad and Dayana's mom? Show her the pictures? She thought her father was the greatest. Was it my business to change that? Rich Clay never thought someone like me would be snooping around in his files. He'd kept it a secret to the end of his life. Was it up to me to blow it, now that he was dead? And what would it do to Dayana's family? I shouldn't have hacked into his private file. That's illegal. It's wrong. But I couldn't lie to Josie. I couldn't look her in the eye and lie about something this important. Could I?

She started to carry the snacks and drinks over to the

desk. I closed the files as quickly as I could. By the time she got around to my side they were hidden away. Look, I know how this is in the movies. The guy learns a terrible secret and he decides to do the noble thing. He's going to protect the woman he loves from news that could break her heart. He'll suffer in silence and take the secret to his grave to keep her from getting hurt. That wasn't me. I didn't make noble sacrifices. I'm not even sure I knew what it meant. What I did know is Josie said she was thankful to have me in her life. I knew that sneaking into an empty law office in the middle of the night was one of the best days I'd ever had. I knew that I would do anything to hold on to that feeling.

"So far I haven't found anything." Lie. "Just boring depositions and case summaries." Lie. "I'll copy the important files and we can share some of them with Harrison." Lie lie lie.

Josie watched me carefully. "You sure you didn't find anything?"

I shook my head. "No, I mean . . . It's just legal stuff. I'm sorry."

Josie let out a sigh. She unwrapped a Red Vine, stuck one in her mouth, and handed me the other. She deserved to know. She was the toughest person I'd ever met. After what happened with the coach, she came back stronger than ever. She could face this, too. If I let her. She came here looking for truth, and I found it. At least some of it.

But what if I told her and she blamed me? What if she

hated me for delivering the news? What if she ran out of the office and we had to go back to ignoring each other? I couldn't handle that again. I wouldn't. So I kept it to myself because I needed her in my life. And, as always, having Josie in my life changed everything.

12

DAYANA

CHRISTMAS USED TO BE A BFD IN OUR HOUSE. When we arrived in the U.S., Papi was all about giving me the big Catholic Christmas we had back home. He brought in a tree that was taller than the ceiling and lined it with enough presents to fill our living room. Mami decorated the house with whatever flowers she could find in the market. We got dressed up for Misa de Gallo at St. Augustine's, where we said prayers for our friends and family back home and those in the States. But when things went to shit for him and we downsized, Christmas took a hit, too. The tree got smaller. The presents got fewer. We even stopped going to church. Every year was a little crappier and a little crappier until the Christmas before the plane crash, when Casa de Calderón finally hit rock-fucking-bottom. My parents had transitioned from arguing all the time to avoiding each other and barely speaking at all.

Honestly, I think we all would've been happier if we'd

just killed a giant punch bowl of eggnog spiked with Ambien and slept from Christmas Eve to New Year's Day. But Papi accepted an invite to his cousin Miguel's Noche Buena feast in our old Patterson neighborhood. I wasn't usually into gatherings of any sort, but I was actually looking forward to the tamales and the music and being around people who still made an effort to have fun. I pulled out a red dress I hadn't worn in two years and borrowed a pair of Mami's heels. When I was dressed and ready to go, I came into to the living room just as Mami was on her way out the door.

"I'm sorry, Daya. There's an emergency at the office. A deal has broken down. The partners are working through the night and I must be there." If she didn't want to go, she should've let her face know. There was no hiding the relief on it. The woman didn't want to spend Christmas Eve with her family.

Papi and I stood in the kitchen, watching her go. "I'm not feeling so good, Daya," he said. "Please call your primo Miguel and tell him I just can't."

"Papi . . ."

He shook his head and trudged off to the bedroom. I hated Mami for doing this to him again.

The one good thing about rock-fucking-bottom is you can't get lower. 'Course I had to admit there were about fifteen times in the last few years that I thought were low points until I realized soon they were just way stations to points even lower. But with a year's distance, I could say without hesitation that last Christmas was the actual, honest-to-goodness, dogshit-horrible, lowest point in the life of the Calderón family.

I'm not saying this year was going to be jingle bells and candy canes and Whos in Whoville, but the dread was slightly less dreadful. Papi had made it past a couple of rounds of interviews for a job at a big construction firm. He was trying. Mami was still too caught up in her own shit to notice, but I noticed. And so I tried, too. I started writing down which pills I took and how many. Maybe I'd been hanging around Harrison too much. Harrison and his lists. But each day I tried to take one less. I wasn't ready to give up on altering my moods altogether, but if Papi could work on it, then so could I.

Harrison had been acting even jumpier than usual since that epically cringey attempt at a kiss, so I finally cornered his ass in the hallway near the science labs. But as soon as I brought it up, he started breathing weird and got this scared look on his face.

"It's okay," I said. "I get it. I'm very kissable."

"You said I'm the weirdest person you know."

"You're up there, pal."

"Well, you're the weirdest person *I* know. Number one. No one else is even close."

"I'll take that as a compliment. Listen, I understand what happens to you. The panic attacks."

"I don't have—"

"Harrison, cut the shit. I've seen you."

He rubbed up and down his forearm. "Glitches."

"Huh?"

"I call them glitches."

"Oh. Glitches. I get it. That's a good word for it. My brain turns on itself sometimes, too."

"What do you do?"

"I get high."

"Right. Have you ever tried reciting pi? It's fairly easy to memorize if you break it up in chunks. I can help you over Christmas break."

"I'll think about it. Hey, what are you and your pop doing for the holidays?"

"I don't know. I have a lot of research to do. Phone calls to make."

"About the crash."

"Yes. I know you think it's just crazy talk."

"Are Archie and Josie helping you?"

"I'm not sure. I thought we were all going to do this together. Now I think they're together without me."

"I think it's more complicated than that," I said. "Just do me a favor, if you start to . . . you know, glitch. Text me."

He nodded and I watched him walk off down the hall.

"I'm inviting everyone for Noche Buena," I announced to Mami and Papi when I walked in the door after school.

"Dayana, we don't have time to prepare a feast for the family. If you want to try going to your primo Miguel's apartment again—"

"Not *that* everybody. I mean Harrison and his dad. Archie and Lucas. The Clays."

She looked stunned. "You want to invite the Sunnies?"

"Don't call them that."

"Jack and Josie, too? Would they come? I'm sure their abuelos are expecting them."

"Then they'll say no. Just like the old days. But we can ask."

"Okay. We'll give it a try."

"And Mami . . . promise this year there won't be any emergencies at the office." She looked away and nodded.

I really didn't think through my suggestion before I made it. And once Mami said yes I started to freak. This could be an absolute clusterfuck of epic proportions. I didn't even know how to go about inviting everybody. Horse-drawn carriage and messenger? Smoke signals?

I opted for a group text. When I say "opted," I mean I spent two hours writing and rewriting it so it wouldn't sound too pathetic or too forward. I wanted casual and real. Like *Come if you want or don't come if you want, but it would be really good if you came. But if you can't, that's cool, too. Not as cool as if you came, but not uncool either. You know, whatever.* I once saw this thing about the new trend of young people getting together with friends instead of spending holidays with their families. They called it Orphan Christmas. Not as cute when the guests are actual orphans.

I settled on *X-mas Eve (Noche Buena) at my house? If you can make it. Vanesa's cooking. Bring whoever.*

I had barely hit send when my phone dinged. Archie'd

already texted back. He must've been staring at his phone with his thumbs over the keypad.

Lucas and I are in
This is Archie
You already knew that
Just making sure
Lucas might want to bring his bf
Sam
They're very close
He's at my house all the time
He'll probably want Sam to come
I'm sure he'll want to be with Sam on X-mas Eve
I'll let you know about Sam. It's pretty serious
Archie plus one or probably two

Archie's text-arrhea might have gone on all night if Harrison hadn't cut in with a well-constructed text of his own: *Dear Dayana, thank you for the invitation. My father and I will gladly join you for Noche Buena. He says to inform you that he will bring his famous nine-layer dip appetizer. I am not certain what level of fame it's achieved nor what makes it famous. Also, I am somewhat concerned it might be culturally insensitive.*

Those responses were not followed by one from Josie or Jack. Not that I was expecting either to write back right away. It was pretty hard to concentrate on a whole lot else while I waited. But what if Josie had changed her number and I didn't know about it? Or what if the network was down and my message didn't go through? Or what if she'd decided that

181

cell phones caused brain tumors and was no longer using a cell phone at all?

I almost sent follow-up texts, but for once I decided to let it be. Josie and Jack were not coming to my house for Christmas Eve, and I was fine with that. It was delusional to think that just because their amazing Mom and Dad were gone, they'd be looking to my screwed-up padres to fill the void.

I'd given up on getting an answer. And that's when Josie came to see me at my lunch table.

I always sat in the same seat in the heart of Lonersville. Corner table, last chair, back to the wall where I could see the whole room. The view offered me protection if anyone was going to mess with me, but it also gave me a chance to watch. Observing everyone else turned what could be a really lonely and depressing part of my day into something I actually looked forward to. Like how Tía Elena used to watch her telenovelas on TV. But a few months into senior year, I got tired of watching. It was no longer fun to witness the hookups and the breakups. The reality show I'd been watching half my life had jumped the shark. I can't explain why it happened, but after the crash, Josie's crew started to look silly and maybe even a little sad. How a girl would be so in love one day and then crying the next and then in love with someone else the day after that. It's like they had no way of seeing five minutes ahead of them.

So one day I walked into the cafetorium and I headed to my table in the corner. Only instead of sitting with my back to the wall, I sat on the other side with my back to everything else. It was just me, my earbuds, my yogurt, and the yellow wall. And it wasn't so bad. I cranked up the music (pop, my secret shame) in my head, and I let myself get lost. There could've been a straight-up orgy going on behind me and I wouldn't have even known or cared. Okay, if it were an orgy I'd hope someone would at least tap me on the shoulder with a heads-up.

When Josie tapped me on the shoulder, I jumped so much my knees crashed into the table, knocking over everything on it. "What the shit?!" I'd forgotten anyone else was in the room. I whipped around and found myself face-to-face with her. She looked tired and maybe a little nervous. She was carrying a brown paper bag and she kept crinkling and uncrinkling the top.

"Sorry. Didn't mean to, uh . . ."

"Freak me the fuck out?"

"Yeah. Anyway, hi."

She came over here to say *Hi*? What was I supposed to say to that?

"Hi."

Josie pulled a napkin from her bag and started scrubbing up the spilled yogurt on the table. She didn't stop until the table was spotless. "Hey, I was wondering . . . is that Nocha Bwen—Christmas Eve offer still good?"

"Do you want it to be?"

She nodded. "If it's okay, Jack and I would like to come. Thanksgiving at my grandparents' was enough."

I tried to sound casual, like my text. "Yeah, sure, whatever. I just need to tell Nelson and Vanesa so they have enough food in the house for Jack."

"Actually," Josie said, "he hasn't been eating much since the concussion. He's not even in school today. Migraine. It happens a lot lately."

"Oh. Sorry." She seemed to drift off and didn't say anything for a while. And then finally: "Can I sit here?"

Was this some kind of trick? I looked around to see if anyone else was watching. Josie didn't turn around at all. She was actually waiting for an answer.

"I don't know," I said. "I'm going to have to put it to a vote." I turned my head and looked around, as if consulting all my tablemates. It took a second for Josie to realize I was making a joke.

She laughed. "If I knew there'd be a vote I would've launched a campaign."

"Oh God, more posters with your face on them?"

"You don't like my student council posters? Come on, you know you have one in your locker."

As much as I wanted to just live in this moment, Josie and I going back and forth like we did a thousand years ago, I couldn't help myself. I had to understand. "What are you doing over here?"

Her smile dropped. "You want me to go back over to my table?"

184

"No. I just . . ."

"Good," she said. "'Cause neither do I."

"Welcome to Lonersville, Josie Fucking Clay."

Getting ready for the First Annual Calderón Orphan Noche Buena™ was stressful. Grocery shopping at the specialty market. Cleaning the house. Mami and Papi bickering and snapping at each other and at me. During a heated battle over the dessert options, I told them both to f off. But I actually said "f" instead of the f word, which is real progress for me. I was down to just a coupla pills a day. And we kinda got shit done. We each took jobs and we put a plan together, and for a couple of days, we upped our family game from HFF (hopelessly fucked forever) to good old-fashioned dysfunctional. Not gonna lie. It felt pretty good.

I even agreed to suspend my veganism for Mami's baked pork legs. Weirdly, I found myself getting excited about introducing something so . . . tico to the others. Like I was sharing a part of myself that I had spent a lot of time trying to cover over. Papi went out and bought a real tree and dug out the box of ancient decorations from the basement. He played some Spanish Christmas tunes on his phone and we pulled out the string lights and tinsel and whatever other old crap was in the box. It had all been purchased in the first couple of years after we moved to America and untouched in at least five. When we got to the bottom of the dusty box, Papi produced an old seashell with a hole in it.

"Do you know what this is, Daya? I found this on the first date your mami and I ever went on. We walked together on Playa Tortuguero. The parrots were singing overhead and I told her—"

"'Voy a casarme contigo un día,'" I said. My Spanish was far from perfect these days, but I'd heard the story a million times before, and he told it the same way each time. It was their first date, and as they strolled together, he told her he was going to marry her one day. She laughed at him, and he made her a bet. Un colón that she'd be his bride. On their wedding day as they stood at the altar she reached into her dress and pulled out a single colón that she placed in his hand.

"Tú ganas," she said. You win.

We had a few minutes under the tree where it was really good. The house smelled like pine. Papi was dressed and sober and Mami wasn't crying. But once he started with the shell and the "feelsies" and the stroll down memory lane, she bolted out of the house without a word and left him holding his seashell. Papi went back to the tree. I chased Mami outside into the cold, where she was lighting up a cigarette.

"You're ruining everything," I said to her. "Haven't you done enough? Why do you have to be so selfish and bitter? Couldn't you try to pretend we're normal for one fucking night?"

Historically, this was the part where Mami would rain down fire on me. She'd tell me I was throwing my life away by being like I was. Dressing like a vampira, talking like a sailor. America doesn't just hand you things. I'd never get a job or a great guy or a fun, exciting life if I just . . . wallowed in oscuridad. Darkness.

She stood in the cold and struggled to light a cigarette. "You can't forget. How do you forget? Or pretend like the last years are gone? They still live for me." She gave up on her smoke and walked slowly to the car. "We need more butter."

Papi came to the door to watch her go. He didn't try to stop her. Instead, he sat down on the steps and placed the seashell beside him.

"We all make choices," he said. "Don't hate her. I don't."

I started to worry I'd made a terrible mistake. Mami had gone to the store and hadn't come home yet. Papi was still in his room with the door shut. The idea that I would have to host this gathering on my own made me want to scream, or better yet, get very, very high. Papi's meds might not make the evening go smoother, but at least I wouldn't notice. I rifled through the medicine cabinet and started to select a few pills to swallow when I heard the doorbell ring. I listened as Papi hurried out of his room to answer the door.

"Archie. Feliz Navidad. Welcome."

Archie was almost a half hour early. "I . . . thought it would take me longer to get here. I mean, I don't know why. It's less than a mile and I did a practice run in the morning to make sure I remembered how. But then I was sitting in the house and I started thinking what if there was traffic or some kind of police stop because of Christmas Eve and so I just decided to leave since I was just sitting there anyway and now here I am and you're not ready. What's the opposite of fashionably late? Unfashionably early? That's me. Is Josie here yet? Of course not. Why would she be?"

There was still time to swallow the pills, but I couldn't bear listening to Archie struggling out there. I stuffed the pills in my pockets in case I needed them for later. But for now, I was going to face the night with all faculties intact. When I came out of the bathroom, Archie was sitting alone on the couch. He was wearing a dress shirt that was both too big and too small for him at the same time.

"Hey," I said.

"Oh, hi. Merry—um—Felice Navi—"

"Yeah. You too. No Lucas?"

"He's with his boyfriend's family. I invited him, but um . . . He chose them."

"Where's your sketchbook?" I asked. "You look naked without it."

Archie looked down at his hand and dropped his head into his shirt like a turtle. I suddenly got an image of the first time I met Archie. Our mothers had shoved us in a room together, hoping that two kids who spoke different languages would somehow play well together. After a couple of attempts to communicate, Archie turned away and started drawing. When he finally turned back he handed me a drawing he'd made of me in my princess dress. We didn't understand a word each other said, but I felt like he understood me.

Archie picked up a couple of plátanos and popped one into his mouth. "This is cool," he said. "Like cultural night in my house. Only real."

Mami made it home fifteen minutes before Jack and Josie arrived. Archie, who had been fidgeting silently on the couch, straightened his shirt and matted his hair. Jack entered first, and I noticed that he looked thinner, like a partially deflated parade balloon. He handed Mami a bottle of wine, which he said he took from their father's collection. It probably cost as much as our house. Mami took the bottle from Jack and ran her hand back and forth over the label. When she sensed I was watching she set the bottle down and wrapped Jack into a hug. It was a bizarre scene on many levels. Did she have that kind of relationship with Jack, just from working with his dad? While Mami was still holding Jack, Josie moved in, wearing a red sweater and a plaid miniskirt. Her hair was down and uncharacteristically messy.

Mami finally let go of Jack. "It's lovely to see you, Josie," she said. "Feliz Navidad. Merry Christmas."

"Merry Christmas," said Josie. "Thank you for having us." Mami suddenly reached out and grabbed her, too. Josie looked like she didn't know what to do. But Mami hung on until Josie finally relaxed and put her hands on Mami's back.

"Mami—"

When Mami dropped her arms, I spotted Archie staring at his feet and moving his lips like he was talking to himself.

Papi cracked the tension by going into host-mode, offering drinks and snacks and taking coats and telling everyone how great they looked.

Josie seemed a little shaken by the hug, so I brought her into the kitchen. "Sorry about that," I said. "Things are intense around here."

"Things are intense everywhere." She gazed out into the living room, where Archie was piling a tower of cheese onto a cracker.

"So . . . what's the deal with you and Archie? Are you, like . . . ?"

"No . . . I don't know. He's . . . Archie, you know. He's not like any other guy I've ever been around. He's not like this big athlete or all popular or buff . . ."

"Might not want to say any of this to him."

"I'm saying it doesn't matter. It's the way I feel around him. He has this way of looking at things, like he's drawing them in his head. Of making them better, you know. And like he hasn't had the easiest life. People made fun of him . . . for his family and for carrying around the sketchbook and—"

"People," I said. "That's what they do."

"Yeah. I guess you know about that. They do it to you, too."

"Some of those people are your friends."

"Daya—"

"It's okay. Everybody makes choices. So are you and Archie hanging out now?"

"Not like you mean. At least . . . We've been trying to

find out about the plane crash. And we were at my dad's office, going through his files. Archie was at the computer and I was leaning over him and we had this . . . I don't know how to describe it. I got a . . . vibe. A feeling. From being close to him like that. He'd always been, well, Archie, but I was touching him and . . . something happened."

"Like *happened* happened? For both of you?"

"I don't know. I panicked. I'm not sure why it scared me so much. I mean, it's not like I've never been close to a guy before . . . but this was different. I, like, ran to the other side of the room. And since then when we've been together I've kept . . . distance. Sorry for rambling. That was a lot of info."

"You're starting to talk like him."

Archie walked into the kitchen and when he saw us, his face got all weird and he started coughing.

Harrison and his father showed up late. H stood quietly by the door as Bobby put on his usual show, cracking wise and telling stories as he *ooh*ed and *aaah*ed over how grown-up we all were and how everybody's parents must've been so proud just like he's so proud of his Harry. The guy was a big, loud blowhard, but I have to admit it was hard not to like him. Especially when I saw how Harrison looked at him.

I sidled up to Harrison and gave him a hug.

"Feliz Navidad," he said.

"Why are you looking at me like that? You're not gonna try to slip me the tongue again, are you?"

"You look normal," he said.

"Huh?"

"I mean not the way most people look normal. I mean you're not high. You've got all these people in your house with your parents and you're totally sober?"

"Maybe I'm changing."

"Maybe we all are."

Papi moved through the party with purpose, chatting people up and making sure everyone was having a good time. I knew he had to be holding on by his fingernails, but he didn't show it. Hard to believe this was the same person who just a few months ago needed me to bring him peanut butter sandwiches in bed. In fact, everything was going well. It felt like what a family feast was supposed to feel like.

Josie found me looking at the seashell on the Christmas tree. "Hey, do you have a hair band? It's, like, an epically bad hair day and I'm tired of fighting it."

The moment she came to my table in the lunchroom was dramatic, but this was even better. Because it wasn't some forced reunion or grand gesture. It was just Josie asking me for a hair band. The way friends do without thinking. The way friends do.

"Sure, let me go grab one." I walked slowly away and turned the corner before racing into my room without even turning on the light. I frantically rummaged through my drawers, looking for one measly band. I don't usually put my hair up. It was too choppy. But I was sure I'd have at least one. Suddenly the desk light snapped on. I screamed and spun around to see Jack sitting at my desk with the lights off.

"What the fuck, Jack? Might want to give me a warning next time."

"Sorry. Waiting for a headache to pass. Not that they ever do." It was then that I noticed the papers spread out in front of him. Shit, I'd forgotten to clean off my desk before the party. It was stacked high with pictures I'd printed out from social media. Pictures of Jack and Josie and all of their friends. Evidence. Jack was looking at stone-cold proof that I was a weird and freaky stalker. He looked up at me and in that instant I saw it all slipping away. Noche Buena, the lunch table, the hair band, everything. He'd realize what I'd been doing all along and who I really was. He'd tell Josie and they'd both run out of this house and never look back.

I did my best to dance my way out of it. "I don't do this shit anymore," I swore, my voice tight. "My friends went away and I was alone, so I   I imagined."

But Jack didn't accuse me of being a psycho. He didn't run and rat me out to Josie. He just stopped to look at the picture I'd printed from their party the night of the crash. Jack and Josie, arms around each other on their front porch.

"It's weird," he said. "I picked this up and I almost didn't recognize us. It's like it happened in a different lifetime."

He gritted his teeth as he squeezed his temples. "Want to know something? I always hated those parties."

"What? People would've given their left tit or ball to go to those freaking things. You just saw that I was basically stalking them. And you didn't even like them?"

"They were Josie's parties. Her chance to put on a show."

"Yeah, but she loved them."

"If you say so."

I couldn't believe what he was suggesting. Josie hated the parties, too. Is that why her smiles never looked genuine?

Jack took the photo, folded it up, and slipped it into his pocket. "She needed them," he said.

I could hear dinner starting in the dining room. "You coming?"

"I'm going to stay in here a little while longer if you're cool with it. Harrison's dad's stories are rough for me."

"I'll bring you a plate," I said.

Jack never made it back out to the feast, and I ended up delivering him three helpings. But overall the feast was a success. People asked for seconds of tamales and casado and complimented the chef. Mami found a red hair band for Josie and even helped her put it in. As a kid, Noche Buena at my tío's was a way of revisiting what life had been like back in Costa Rica. This night was something different than that. Most of my life I hadn't felt fully Tica or Americana. I was neither. But now, watching my friends sit around the table eating the traditional food Mami prepared, I felt like both, maybe for the first time.

After dinner I pulled on my wool cap and went outside to look at the stars and vape. It was a cloudy night, and the moon barely gave off any light. After a few minutes, Harrison wandered out into the yard. Archie followed him. Josie even led Jack outside.

"I thought it would be good to have a discussion out here," Harrison said. I offered the vape pen to everyone. They all turned down my offer except for Harrison, who was, these days, game for whatever. He took a big drag, let it out in a humid cough.

Inside, Bobby was telling another story, and I could actually hear both of my parents laughing. Loud, genuine laughter. We all heard it outside. For me, it warmed up the cold night. I don't think it did the same for Josie, Jack, and Archie. It was Christmas Eve and my parents were actually getting along. It was Christmas Eve and theirs were gone. For them, there would be no presents under the tree on Christmas morning, no happy celebrations. It would be their first Christmas as orphans, the first of forever.

"I think I found something," Harrison said. Josie and Archie perked up.

"About the crash? You found evidence?" asked Archie.

Harrison pulled out his phone, where he'd made notes. "You know about Michael Boddicker, the investigator for the NTSB. We've been exchanging emails. He's made trips to Anguilla and St. Martin on behalf of the US government. He was scheduled to make another trip last week but I never heard from him. Since then, Boddicker has fallen off the map. When I tried his office number at the NTSB, they told me he'd taken an emergency leave of absence. I asked what that meant, and they started asking *me* questions—personal questions—so I hung up. I believe Michael Boddicker knows what happened to that plane. I also believe Michael Boddicker is missing."

"What are you doing?" snapped Jack.

"I'm explaining that I think Michael Boddicker—"

"I mean what the hell is the point of this?"

"We want to find the truth," said Archie, blowing into his hands.

"Why?" said Jack. "Who gives a shit? Does it make them any less dead?"

Josie took Jack's arm. "Jack, stop."

"You're acting like it will change a goddamn thing."

Harrison looked confused. "Don't you want to know the truth about what happened?"

"I know what happened. The plane crashed and they all died. And maybe you can't let that sink in because your mom fucked with your head so much and turned you into a freak."

"Don't say that to him," said Archie.

Jack spun around to face him. "And you, you just want to use this to get with my sister."

Josie was furious. "Shut up, Jack! Stop it!"

But Jack wasn't stopping. "You want to know the truth about my parents? Dad didn't care about anyone but himself."

"Don't say that!"

"All he did was tell me I didn't work hard enough or live up to my potential. And Mom never said a word about it. So you know what? I wouldn't be surprised if he is the reason that plane crashed. When he wanted something, he never cared who got hurt."

"Please," begged Josie. "Please stop."

I felt everything that had gone right that night slipping away. "Can't we all just go back inside?" I offered. "There's tres leches cake."

A cloud bank cleared and I could suddenly see Jack's face in the moonlight. Tears streamed down his cheeks. He wiped them away, over his shaved head, which gleamed in the darkness. It was like he'd completely lost control of his emotions. It was scary to see that happen to someone as big and strong as him.

Josie stepped in front of him. "Stop it, Jack! This isn't you. You can't just keep losing your shit and using your head as an excuse. Mom and Daddy were good people. We loved them. You may not care about the truth, but I do. It's all we have left."

Jack put his hands to his head and winced. Then he turned and ran down the street toward his house. Josie started to follow him, but Archie put a hand on her arm. "Josie," he said. "I'll go with you. There's um, there's something I need to tell you." Whatever he was about to say to her, it seemed very important.

I called after them, trying to get them to come back. But it was too late. The magic of our Noche Buena feast was over. Jack, Josie, and Archie were gone, and I had a feeling we might never find a moment like that together again.

When Harrison and I went back inside, his pop was helping my parents clean up. I took the broom from Papi's hand.

"Let's drive up to St. Augustine's for midnight Mass," I said. "All of us."

"We haven't been to Misa de Gallo in many years, Dayana," Mami said.

"I know."

"It's a wonderful idea, Daya," said Papi.

"Why don't we head home, Bud," said Bobby. "They've been excellent hosts and we're not exactly good Catholics."

"You'll be our guests," said Papi. "Come. Everyone is welcome."

"I'd like to go, actually," said Harrison. "I'm not tired at all."

We arrived at the old church before Mass had started. Papi opened the huge wooden doors for us. When Mami hesitated before entering, Papi gave her his arm and led her in. I took Harrison's hand and walked him down the carpeted aisle to the front, where I'd had my First Communion a million years ago. I picked up a match and dipped it over the wick of a lit votive until it caught fire. I said a silent prayer, and together Harrison and I used the flickering flame to light five tiny candles.

13

JOSIE

"JOSIE'S BACK, BITCHES!" I RAISED THE PLASTIC cup of cheap champagne over my head and drank to New Year's Eve with the rowdy crowd in Cody's basement. They all screamed back my name. How good did it feel to be back at the heart of a party, surrounded by my real friends, the ones I'd worked so hard to collect? Siobhan and I danced and drank and sang along with every song. I was hot and dizzy, but the drinks had never gone down easier.

"You have no idea how Gucci it is to have you back, girl," Siobhan shouted over the beat. "I thought we'd totally lost you."

"Never!"

"What?"

"Never!"

"What?!"

"Never mind!"

Cody came by with a bottle to top off our drinks. He wore a tight white T-shirt and striped board shorts. He leaned down, his lips almost right against my ear. "I missed you."

I tensed up, but pushed the feeling away and flirted back. "So did I."

Cody kissed me on the cheek and disappeared into the sweaty crowd.

"He's been asking about you all night," yelled Siobhan. "Not a bad way to bang in the New Year! I mean ring! Did I say bang?!" She reached up and tried to smooth down the hair on the side of my head. "I'm totally shipping you two. But you need to tame that nest!"

I patted my head and felt the bulge of hair. "I'm going to hit the bathroom."

"What?!"

"I need to fix my hair!"

"What?!"

My ankles wobbled on Mom's spikiest heels as I weaved my way through the mass of bodies.

"It's so savage you're here!"

"Don't ever go cray on us again, Josie!"

It was twenty degrees outside, but Cody's basement had to be a hundred, thick and sticky. I grabbed the bathroom door handle, but it didn't turn. Someone was already inside. I leaned against the wall and soaked in the party. It wasn't as perfect as one of mine. Too crowded. Too hot. But nobody seemed to care. I didn't realize how much I missed all this.

How much I needed to feel good. And to not care. Not about my parents. Not about the Sunnies. Or Jack. And especially not about Archie.

The bathroom door opened and Cody came out wiping his hands on his shorts. He smiled when he saw me. "I'm gonna be looking for you at midnight."

Why would I want to be anywhere else? Everything was here. Every*one* was here. And anyone that wasn't . . . That was *their* problem. I walked into the bathroom and shut the door behind me. The music was still loud, but the door and the fan muted it some. I looked at myself in the mirror. My face was flushed and my eye makeup a little smudged, but I still looked pretty decent. All except that one chunk of hair on the side that wouldn't lie flat. No matter how much I smoothed it down or pulled it back, it wouldn't straighten out. I splashed it with water, but still the freaking thing. Would. Not. Stay. Down. Where was my flat iron when I needed it? My hair had a mind of its own. Just like on Christmas Eve.

I shut my eyes. I did not come here to think about Christmas Eve at Dayana's. I came here to *not* think about Christmas Eve. To not think. Of course, trying not to think about something is the best way to make yourself think about it nonstop. After Jack bolted from Dayana's yard, Archie asked to walk me home.

"I have something to tell you," he said. As we walked and he talked, I kept staring at his breath—how it looked like smoke when it shot out of his mouth and then disappeared.

It took me a while to understand what he was saying about Daddy and the computer and a beach and pictures of him and Dayana's mom. And when I finally got it, I wanted to scream.

"Josie, do you understand? I mean, I know this . . . I know this sucks and—"

"The office? You saw it in Daddy's office?"

"Yes."

"You said you didn't find anything."

"Because I know how much you loved him and seeing you walking around his office, touching his things—"

"You said there was nothing."

"I was trying to . . . I would never hurt you. Never."

"But you're okay doing it now. You let me hang out in their house all night. You let me eat her big feast. I told her it was the best Christmas Eve meal I'd ever had. And *now* you think I need to know the truth?"

"No, I . . . Yes. I should have said it right away, but I couldn't. If it made you hate me—"

"You said you didn't want to hurt me."

"Yes."

"You didn't want to hurt me? Or you didn't want me to hate you?"

"I don't know. Both, I . . . Josie, I . . . When you went away again after Jack came home . . . I don't know how to explain the loneliness. I mean, I should've been used to it, but then you were in my life and you were the only good. The only good. Lucas had Sam and—and being close to you made everything better. To lose it again . . . and then to not even be able to draw . . ."

We were standing in front of my house. And I couldn't look at him. I couldn't listen to any more explanation. "Even Jack keeps secrets from me. You were the one person I thought I could trust."

"You can. I am."

I spun away and left him standing there, alone. I walked inside, closed the door behind me, and turned off the porch light. Jack was already upstairs. I flipped on the living room lights. The house looked different, like someone had snuck in and rearranged everything. It felt so big and cold. The pictures on the wall felt phony and staged. Even the white furniture didn't look so white. I thought I knew this place. I thought I knew the people who lived here. All the trips Daddy took when he couldn't make it to my games. Every time he'd come home with presents for me and Jack and flowers for Mom and would take us all out for a big dinner. I felt sick and stupid. I could see Archie still standing outside as I ran up to my room and shut the door.

The next morning I told Jack I was too sick to go to Grandma and Grandpa's for Christmas. I didn't want to tell him. Either he'd hate Daddy and start punching his fist through walls or worse, he'd defend him. I ignored Archie's calls and texts. There was nothing he could say that would make this better. For seven days I sat in my room, scrolling through Instagram, watching other people live their lives, go to parties, be normal.

And then on New Year's Eve, a text popped up on my phone. From Cody.

NY Eve bash in the basement. Want U there.

Want U there. Suddenly, I wanted to be there, too. I was tired of sitting in my room and tired of being a victim. I mean, what a waste of *me*, right? Josie Clay doesn't sit home on *New Year's Eve.* That's something Archie or Dayana or Harrison would do. And how perfect. A brand-new year. New Year's Eve is when you get to start over, right? So that's what I did. I decided I was going to be the person I was before the crash, the person everybody loved, the person who never let anyone hurt her. I was Josie Fucking Clay. How did I let that be taken away from me after I worked so hard to build it? I went out and bought myself a short new dress and got a fresh manicure. I even invited Jack to come with me.

"No, thanks."

"It'll be fun. You remember fun, right?"

"Is that the thing that makes people smile?"

"See? You *do* remember."

"No, thanks."

"Come on."

"Nah. My head's not up to it. But you have some of that . . . fun. You going with Archie?"

"No." I kissed Jack on the cheek. "Happy New Year."

"Happy New Year, Jo."

I walked into Cody's basement like I owned the place. And I did own it. If only I could get that one piece of hair to stay down!

I don't know how long I was in the bathroom, but when I stepped out, there was a line of people waiting to get in. Siobhan was halfway down the line. "All cool, JoJo?"

"Um, yeah. Sure." It had gotten hotter and even more crowded in the basement. My head spun from the heat and the booze. Maybe just one more. I could barely squeeze through the bodies to get to the bar. That didn't matter, though, since Cody was there to hand me another shot of tequila.

"Looking for one of these?" he asked.

We clinked glasses and I tossed it down my throat without thinking. It burned going down and he had another one waiting as soon as I was done with the first. The room was becoming a blur of people and faces.

Cody leaned in and said something softly.

"What?!"

He leaned in closer, moving his mouth right to my ear again. A chill ran right up my neck. "It's a mad scene down here. You look like you're over it."

"What?"

"You look like you're over it."

"No, I'm okay. I . . ."

"You want to get out of here?"

As I looked around the room, everything started to spin like crazy. Before I could even steady myself, Cody took my hand and led me to the basement stairs. I was sort of aware of people saying my name or looking at me as we headed up, but I was just looking forward to getting some fresh, cool air and some quiet.

Cody did not let go of my hand as he walked me out of the basement and up another flight of stairs. We crossed a landing into a large bedroom filled with guitars, surfing posters, and jars of protein powder. I could hear the thumping coming from downstairs, but it felt very far away. Cody sat me down on the bed. He was so cute with the deep creases around his mouth and his broad shoulders.

"I'm so glad I texted you," he said.

"You broke up with me."

"I'm a dumbass. I never stopped thinking about you."

I couldn't really process what he was saying. My head was fuzzy. "Josie's back, bitches," I said, my tongue feeling swollen and clumsy.

Cody stroked my face. "This is where you're supposed to be," he said.

He kissed me. My shoes dropped off my feet at the edge of the bed. The room spun again. As I squeezed my eyes shut, his hands were suddenly on the zipper of my dress.

It was all going fast and I felt out of control. "Wait . . ."

"I've waited so long for this."

"Hold on. I'm not . . ."

"I love you, Jos. I never stopped loving you."

"Don't say *that* . . ."

"It's true. You didn't belong with those kids you've been hanging out with."

"What?"

"They don't know you like I do."

"That's not true . . . Stop."

"Stop? Why?"

"Because I shouldn't be here. You're just like all of them."

"Like who?"

"The liars. All of the liars . . ."

He pulled me closer. "Josie . . ."

"No!"

I shoved him away and slipped off the bed onto the floor. I teetered to my feet. I wanted out of there. I didn't want to kiss him anymore. I didn't want to be in this bedroom or in this house.

"You're not . . . It's bullshit. It's all bullshit!" I stumbled out of the room and down the steps. I fumbled with the front door and then out into the freezing night in bare feet and a half-zipped dress. Cody came running after me, calling my name, but I tore through a neighbor's backyard and hid behind some trees. I stayed there, panting and shivering, until I was sure no one was going to find me.

It was freezing cold, but even that seemed far away, outside of my body. It didn't bother me. I walked fast down the block and then I picked up the pace to a jog. Pretty soon I was running through the neighborhood. When I didn't turn at the stop sign, I realized I wasn't on my way home. I just kept going.

By the time I made it to Dayana's house, I had to put my hands on my knees to catch my breath. My bare back burned in the cold. Wheezing, I walked up the driveway. Lights were on inside, but I couldn't see anyone. *Thwack!* I banged right into a big blue recycling bin, knocking cans and bottles onto the driveway. I tried to clean up the mess and only made even more of a racket. I had an armful of empties when the front door opened and Dayana walked outside in pajama pants and a black T-shirt. She held her hand up to shield her eyes. "Josie?"

My legs were frozen in place. I suddenly became aware of how cold I was and how silent it was around us. I could hear my heart pounding in my ears. "It's not right. It's not right."

"Did you *run* here?"

"They were lying to me," I blurted. "I thought I had everything. I thought it was perfect. But it was just another lie. Just another liar. Another person who only wanted what he wanted and didn't care what it does to you, how it makes you feel."

She walked toward me. "Why don't you come inside?"

"No! I'm not going in *there*!"

"Okay, but it's cold out here. And you're not even wearing shoes." She took a couple of steps closer.

"I loved him. I trusted him. And now I can't even see him to ask why. You can't ask a dead person how he could . . ."

"Are you talking about your dad?"

"How do you do that to someone you say you love? Why does this keep happening? Everyone I trust. Everyone I ever . . ."

The front door creaked open and Dayana's parents walked out onto the porch. Her mother was holding a phone.

I could hear Ryan Seacrest in Times Square through the open door.

"Josie? Is everything all right?"

"Why don't you ask *her*?" I said.

Dayana didn't turn around to look at her parents. "Go back inside. Both of you."

"Daya?"

"It's fine. I've got it."

I watched Vanesa allow Nelson to lead her back into the house.

Dayana waited for the door to close. "How did you find out?"

"What?

"How did you find out about your dad and my mom?"

"You knew?"

"I knew."

"For—for how long?"

"Since last Christmas."

"A year?"

"She bailed on our family event. She said she had to work. And when Papi put himself to bed, I . . . decided I'd go bring her some of the cake we baked together for the party. I don't even know why. When I got to her office—"

"Stop! Just stop. Shut up!"

"I'm sorry, Jo. Fuck. I hate it, too. I'm so sorry."

"You're not sorry. Why should you be sorry? She's still here! Look at them in there. They're both still here. They're watching the stupid ball drop. They'll see another year. But

Mom and Daddy are . . . I'll never see them again. Nothing feels real. Like I had a life and now it's like it never existed . . . And I don't even know if that makes me sad or angry, but—"

I started to cry. Warm tears down my freezing cheeks. Once I started, I couldn't stop. I cried so much I didn't even hear the Jeep pull up behind me. I'm not sure I ever would've stopped screaming and crying if I hadn't felt big arms encircling me. I looked back to see Jack holding on to me as I struggled.

"Let me go!" I cried. "Why are you here?!"

"Vanesa called me."

From inside the house, we heard the countdown from Times Square. *Five! Four! Three! Two! One! Happy New Year!*

Dayana cut a look inside. "Happy New Year, Josie," she said. Then she, too, went into her house. Nothing more for anyone to say.

"Come on, Jo. Let me take you home."

"Jack . . . I don't think I can do it anymore."

"You don't have to do anything. Just keep breathing. Just keep moving."

Struggling to catch my breath, I fell back into Jack's arms.

Walking through the heavy metal doors of RBHS the first day after winter break, I fully expected to be shunned like that *Scarlet Letter* girl. Instead, everybody treated me like a returning hero. All anybody wanted to talk about was how amazingly awesome it was that I was at the party and how

I totally killed it. They'd posted selfies with me hashtagged #thereturnofJosie. What the hell? Did they forget the part where I blasted out the door with an open dress and no shoes? Were they not searching the neighborhood for me while I hid in the woods like a wounded animal?

Siobhan rushed up as soon as she saw me. "Spill the tea, sis."

"Huh?"

"That night was so iconic. You've always been like an inspiration to everyone. Not just because of how you dress, but how you're so strong. And to watch you hurting after your parents died, it, like—hurt, like, all of us. When you came to the party it was like the world was right again. And you and Cody, can I say it gives me hope for me and Jack?"

When I walked into the cafetorium at lunchtime, I saw Dayana sitting at her corner table. But she wasn't alone in Lonersville. Archie and Harrison sat across from her. Before I could make a decision, I felt an arm come around my shoulder.

"Hey you," said Cody. "Come sit with us."

"Why would I . . . ?"

"Because I want to sit with you."

"But New Year's Eve . . . I totally freaked out and bailed on you."

"Did you?" he smirked. "I don't remember that."

"Cody . . ."

"Oh, that was you? No worries. Happens all the time. I take a girl to my room and she hits me in the junk and runs off screaming into the freezing cold night. Not at all a shot to the ego."

"I hit you in the junk?"

"That's not what really hurt. Know what I was doing at midnight? Standing in my neighbor's yard, scraping frozen dog crap off my shoe. Not that I'm looking for any sympathy."

Siobhan was waving me over to the table. My table. My squad. This is what I wanted from New Year's Eve, right? I wanted cute guys to want me. I wanted the best people to be my friends. I wanted to throw parties and decide who belonged and who didn't. I wanted to be surrounded by people who thought I was the greatest. I wanted to be safe from the things that hurt me. I didn't want to be the gooey snail anymore. I wanted to be bulletproof.

And if I had to walk by Archie, Dayana, and Harrison's table to feel that way again, then that's what I'd do.

The 'rents are gone this wknd, Cody texted in the middle of history. So were mine.

Come ovr? Just U n me. I'll wear my track shoes if you decide to run!

I stared at those texts and read them over and over. *Just U n me.* I knew that any girl in RBHS would kill to be in my place. And for me, Cody was more than just a hot guy who really liked me. He was my second chance. Five months ago, on the last night of the other part of my life, Cody and

I were the perfect couple at the perfect party. Now here we were, almost half a year later with a chance to go back.

C U there, I texted.

I dug into the back of my closet to find the skirt I'd been saving for a special occasion. As I adjusted myself in the mirror, I thought about Cody, about the way he touched my arm when he talked to me or let his eyes travel up my body every time I got near him. Reflexively, I touched the softball scar on my face.

Can't wait to C U

For a long time after Coach Murph, I didn't want to be touched by anyone. But I saw how boys looked at me and I didn't always hate it. The way I saw it, there were all kinds of reasons to be with someone. Sometimes it's not even about them. It's about what's going on in your life. You're having a tough time and feeling bad. Having a guy hold you and tell you he wants you . . . That's not nothing. After it's over, sometimes you feel better. More likely you feel worse. But at least while you were with him, you weren't caught in your own head. And you were a little less lonely. Sometimes that can be enough.

When I came downstairs in the new skirt, Jack was sitting at the piano. "Hey," he said.

"Hey."

"Going out?"

"Just heading to Siobhan's," I lied.

"Tell her I said hi."

"She said she wants to get back together with you."

"I know. We're talking sometimes. But we're not good for each other."

"I'm not sure about that."

"Can we have a night?" he asked. "Next week maybe?"

"A night to do what?" I asked.

"I don't know. Hang out. Talk. What'd we used to do?"

"I don't remember. See movies?"

Jack paused. "Movies are rough for me right now. All the noise and the cutting around. I'd rather not get sick in the popcorn."

"I'll think about it."

The silence hung there. Talking to my twin brother used to be the easiest thing in the world. We could say anything and never worry about hurting each other. He knew everything about me and I knew everything about him. At least I thought we did. Half the time we didn't even have to say anything. Now it was heavy and awkward and I hated it.

Jack slid over to the low end of the piano, put his fingers on the keys, and started playing his bass part.

Boom ba dada Boom ba dada Boom ba dada Boom ba dada boom ba dada . . .

"What are you doing? I really have to go."

Boom ba dada Boom ba dada Boom ba dada Boom ba dada boom ba dada . . .

"You're just going to keep doing this, aren't you?"

Boom ba dada Boom ba dada Boom ba dada Boom ba dada boom ba dada . . .

"Fine. Make room on the bench." I sat down next to him. It had been years since we played, but my fingers knew exactly what to do.

Boom ba dada Boom ba dada Boom ba dada Boom ba dada boom ba dada . . .

Ba ba baaa dada dada dadaaa ba ba baaa dada dada dadaaa daaaa daaaa dada dada da da dada dada dada da

Boom ba dada Boom ba dada Boom ba dada Boom ba dada boom ba dada . . .

We never looked at each other, but our timing was as good as it had been when we were ten years old. He played those bass notes and I moved around inside them. The piano filled the house with the most music it had heard since the night of the party.

When we were done, we sat there for a long time before Jack spoke. "I think we should sell the house, Soul. It's too big for us, and I feel stuck here. Grandpa brought it up with me a few months ago, but I wasn't ready to talk about it. I don't know, for a while I thought we needed to hang on to it forever. That letting go of anything would be letting go of Mom and Dad. But the more we sit in here, the more I start to feel like I'm trapped. Like we're living in this place where we were a certain kind of family, and pretending we're still that thing. And it's the same thing for me. I spent all this time trying to be what I was. I'm just finally starting to realize

I'm not that anymore." His words hung in the air. "Sorry," he said, cutting through it. "I know I'm not making sense. There's been a lot of that lately. It's just the kind of shit I've been thinking about."

We'd been here forever. I thought this was the place we'd come back to on college breaks. Eventually, I'd return home with my serious boyfriend. My fiancé. My husband. My kids.

That was all gone. It was different now. Jack nailed it. No matter how much we pretended, we weren't that thing anymore. "It's a good idea," I said. "Siobhan's dad is a real estate agent. We can ask him."

Jack nodded. "You should go. Have a fun girls' night. I know Siobhan is psyched to have you back."

Jack walked me to the door and said goodbye. *I'm not that anymore*, he'd said. Suddenly, I had an urge to not just hear those words and feel them, but to see them. I took out my phone and typed them into a text. I sent the text to myself and watched it come back to me in a tiny gray bubble.

You're not that anymore
YOU'RE NOT THAT ANYMORE

Then I sent two more texts. One to Cody. And one to Archie.

The Sunny Horizons playground was mostly dark, but the floodlights from outside the school lit up a circle just around the swing set and on the stump where Archie was waiting, hands in his pockets and hoodie pulled up over his head. The lights reflected off his glasses.

"Look, I'm wearing a coat," I said, trying to sound cheery. "I'm learning."

He didn't crack a smile. I started to explain that I wasn't sure why I texted him, that I was supposed to go somewhere else, and something just told me that I needed to be here.

Archie cut me off mid-thought. "I can't do this, Josie," he said, pulling the hood away from his face. "I'm sorry I didn't tell you right away what I found out about your dad. And I'm even more sorry that he wasn't the guy you thought he was. But I can't anymore. Thirteen years. You've been bouncing me around since I was four years old and I never complained. Because it wasn't a choice for me. And for those moments when we were together and I got to feel what it might be like . . . It was worth it. You were worth it."

He kicked at the dirt. "Now you're back at that table and dating that guy again and that's great for you. You landed on your feet. And he's . . . everybody says he's the best. So I hope he makes you happy. But then you can't text me and tell me to meet you here. *Here*—"

His voice broke. Like he was choking on something. It was awful to see him like this, to know that I'd hurt him so much. And standing there in that same spot where he'd saved me three and a half years ago, I wanted him to know how grateful I was. How he's the sweetest, most creative, special person I'd ever met. How much it killed me all of these years to stay away from him. It probably wouldn't make sense to him. How it scared me too much to let him get close, but just knowing he was there, knowing that I could count on him if I needed to, meant more to me than almost anything in my life.

He reached under his sweatshirt and pulled out his sketchbook. A new one, with a shiny brown cover. He handed it to me. I took a breath and opened the first page to a sketch of me in Daddy's office. It was drawn on Daddy's letterhead and taped on four corners to the page.

"I saved every drawing you ever gave me," I said. "The way you draw me . . . The way you see me. I wish I could be that person."

"You are that person. Do you really not know that?"

"I've done a lot of bad things."

"You've been hurt."

Our faces were close, inches apart. Our breath mingled in the air. Our legs brushed against each other and the electricity shot through my body. I shuddered. I was panicked again, feeling that instinct to shut down, to run away.

"The last thing I'd ever want to do is hurt you," he said.

I reached up and took off his glasses and then pressed my lips to his. At first, he didn't move and I wondered if I'd made a mistake. Then he slowly put his arms around me and he kissed me back. I don't know how long the kiss lasted. We broke, but were instantly back together with even more pressure, more intensity. I grabbed the back of his head to pull him closer.

This time I pulled back. Archie was breathing heavily. His eyes were shiny from the cold.

"Everyone's lied to me," I said.

"I lied to you, too. But I'll never do it again."

"I'm scared," I said. "Are you?"

Archie nodded. "If this all goes away again, I can't. I just can't."

I reached out and took his hand. He looked down at it and then back up at my face.

"Lucas is at my aunt's," he said. We never let go of each other as we walked down the street to his house. He took off my coat and led me through the kitchen and down the hall past his bedroom. We stopped at a small guest room with a sea grass rug, a white comforter, and billowy curtains hanging by the window. Black-and-white sketches of the beach hung on the wall. I knew Archie had drawn them. The room was simple and beautiful and clean. He kissed me, and I closed my eyes and felt him gently guide me down to the soft comforter. In between kisses, Archie tried to catch his breath. "I don't have . . . I mean, I've never been with anyone . . ."

"I know."

"You're safe here."

"I know."

I couldn't tell if I was shaking or if it was him. I put his glasses on the nightstand. He undressed me slowly and traced a finger along my back as if he were drawing me.

14

JACK

DAD YOU LYING HYPOCRITICAL PIECE OF SHIT

During one of my follow-up visits with the neurologist, he said I might have some "underlying emotional issues complicating my recovery." He handed me the card for a therapist. I went to see her in her home office, a cluttered room full of books and candles.

"Jack, why don't you try this," she said, after listening to me talk for a few minutes. "Write a letter to your father saying all the things you wish you'd said to him while he was still here."

"Why only Dad?"

"I get the sense that there are some unresolved feeling there."

"But he's dead. What's the point?"

"Give it a try."

"Nobody writes letters anymore." As soon as I got home, I called and cancelled next week's appointment.

But then one day I was walking past Dad's study and I stopped to look at the golden Man of the Year plaque he'd won from the New Jersey Bar Association. And in my head, I started to write the letter. But I was never any good at putting pen to paper, so I took out my phone and texted his disconnected number.

Dad you cheating selfish poor excuse for a father

Look a man in the eye and let him know your character. Act as if someone is always watching. Remember that shit?

Fuck you.

Not sure if this was what the therapist had in mind. But it was what I needed to say. Football was gone. At the gym, the lights were too bright. The music was too loud. And as soon as I lifted anything heavy, I got dizzy again. Without anywhere for it to go, the bad shit started to build. The pressure. So I texted a dead guy and told him to fuck off. I hit *things*. I broke stuff. Shattered most of the trophies and picture frames in Dad's study. Put a couple of holes in the wall, too. Better than hitting a person, I guess. Or tearing up a sketchbook.

Here's the thing about being the biggest guy in every room. Nobody feels sorry for you. Nobody thinks you need looking after. Jo was tougher than me from the day we were born, but she was half my size. Archie wore those thick glasses and babbled when he got nervous. Harrison was wound tighter than a baseball and looked like a strong wind could break him in half. But the scary guy with the bald head—the guy doing the blocking—he can take care of himself. People worry about him. They don't worry *for* him.

I hate you for what you did to Josie

You were her hero

You didn't embarrass her when she made a mistake. You didn't make her feel small

All she ever wanted was to make you proud

So she never told you when that monster took advantage of her. Better not disappoint Daddy. You had no clue your little girl was suffering

Only I knew

The night she slept out, I knew she wasn't going to hang with Siobhan, but I thought she was going to see Cody. Most of the time, I stayed out of her way when it came to guys. Josie was a pro at not letting herself get hurt. Cody would be like the rest. Once he started getting too close, Josie would lift the hammer and end it quickly. No harm, no foul.

As soon as we got to school that Monday, I saw that Cody was history. But whatever had happened that night was different.

"You don't have to walk me to class," she said.

"Who says that's what I'm doing?"

"You have math. It's in the other direction."

"Maybe I'm lost."

"You're definitely lost."

That's when Archie came around the corner. As Jo turned to smile and wave, it was like I wasn't there anymore. Suddenly I realized she hadn't gone to be with Cody at all.

It was Archie. Archie, who'd worshipped her his whole life. Archie, who'd taken care of her when I couldn't. And that scared the crap out of me because I knew she could get hurt for real this time. What I did to Archie's sketchbook was shitty, and I still felt bad about it. But I'd never feel bad for trying to keep Josie safe.

At lunch, they both ate at Dayana's table. Harrison, too. After everything that had gone down between Jo and Dayana, I was sure Archie was the one who convinced her to sit there. I watched as he made her laugh, and I hated it. I saw the danger. Archie was a good guy, but he was not good for my sister. We were all not good for each other. Look at what happened since the crash. Fights, suspensions, trouble. And all that conspiracy bullshit? Where would it lead? "The Sunnies" was not some fun after-school group. We were not the glee club. We were a bunch of messy, fucked-up people whose parents just happened to die on the same plane. When we were together, I always saw the cloud hanging over us. It was like spending your whole life at a funeral. I didn't want that for Josie.

Since my injury, Siobhan and I had gotten back together and broken up a dozen times. She'd try her best to help me feel better, and I'd pick a fight. Or I'd get lost in my own head and ignore her for days. Then I'd text her in the middle of the night, wanting to hang out and hook up. I asked for a lot and gave almost nothing in return. For some reason, she kept coming back.

Guess I'm not so different from you, Dad

This was the worst part of the relationship, the part where I had to lie. To her and to myself. "It's gonna be different this time," I'd promise. "I learned my lesson. I missed you."

You'd be proud of that line of bullshit

I'd buy her flowers or put together a playlist of special songs. I'd Instagram some place that was meaningful to us and write a sweet message for all her friends to see. For about a day and a half she'd play hard to get. Eventually, we'd have yet another teary reunion that would last until the next breakup.

Every time I pulled Siobhan back in, I felt worse about what I was doing to her. I'd blast Dad in a text and then act just like him. Valentine's Day fell during one of those getting-back-together periods. I stayed away from Siobhan for most of the day. And then nighttime came, and Josie left to meet Archie. I sat alone in the house and poured myself a shot from Dad's bar.

Look at me Dad. Drinking your whiskey. Sitting on your stool

Only thing missing is Mom fixing you a drink

So civilized. Such a great couple. Everyone said so.

I'm not like you

I'm not

A few minutes later, I was speeding to the drug store to pick up a card and a lame gift for Siobhan. When I pulled into the strip mall parking lot, it was mostly empty. Just a few cars bunched together under the light poles. I parked near the store, slammed my fists against the wheel, and took out my phone.

I hate that I keep doing this
I hate that I hurt her like you hurt Mom
And Josie
I hate
I hate

Climbing out of the Jeep, I noticed a guy in jeans and an old leather bomber jacket walking out of the Liquor Emporium. Holding a huge bouquet of roses in front of his face. Juggling his keys and a box of candy. Bottle of wine in a brown paper bag. Poor bastard forgot Valentine's Day. Trying for a last-minute save, just like me. As he stepped off the curb and into the light, he adjusted the flowers in his arms and I saw his face. He had a beard that had come in half gray. His face was puffy and his eyes were red. But it was the same face I'd tried not to think about for four years. Mr. Murphy. Josie's coach. Murph.

Suddenly my whole body got warm. The sound of rushing water in my ears, like before the first whistle in a football game. Time slowing down. My vision narrowing so that I could only see what was right in front of me. My heart slamming against my chest. Every muscle in my body tensing at once. Murph walked toward me, balancing the wine and the flowers. He clicked his keyfob and the car beeped twice. His shiny blue Mustang—right next to my car. The same car I used to see almost every night on my street. In front of my house. The one he picked her up in. The one he . . .

He was almost right in my face before he recognized me. "Jack? How are you? It's good to see you, man."

I couldn't speak. There was so much building in my body. Acid rising in my throat. I could see my shadow shaking in front of me. Vibrating. Like it was going to spring up and attack him.

Murph's face cracked into a sad smile. "How's my girl JC doin'?" he asked. "Tell her I said hi and I'm thinking about her."

My body, as if on autopilot, charged forward. I hurled myself shoulder first into his chest. Murph let out a shocked grunt as his back slammed hard against the side of the Jeep and his head snapped back. The roses crunched in his hands and the candy box sailed onto the roof. The wine bottle hit the ground and shattered. Struggling for wind, Murph rebounded off the car and collapsed forward into the dark red puddle. And I was on top of him, raining down blows on his head. There was blood and wine and glass everywhere, and I couldn't stop myself from hitting him over and over and over. I could hear a woman screaming in the background, and Murph was begging me to stop, then whimpering. Then he wasn't making any noise at all.

Someone finally grabbed me and yanked my arms behind my back. I looked up into the bright parking lot light to see two police officers shouting for me not to move. A beefy cop, almost as big as me, pushed me down and slapped handcuffs on my wrists while the other checked on Murph. I finally blinked, and the rest of the parking lot came into focus.

Murph was motionless on the ground, his face a misshapen mess. But he was breathing. I was almost surprised to see that I hadn't killed him. The officer pulled me to my feet and I was suddenly exhausted by the effort it took to stand. I could barely keep my head up. A small crowd had gathered around us. On the far side was a plain, middle-aged woman holding a shopping bag. Mrs. O'Meara, the librarian at the middle school. After the crash, she'd sent us a nice card with an angel on the front. She looked terrified.

One of the cops recognized me. From football or "The Sunnies," I don't know. "We're gonna have to take you in, Jack," he said as they loaded me into their car. "Tell us who you want us to call."

Guess you won't be picking me up from the station this time, Dad.

My hands throbbed. My pants were shredded and my knees were cut up from the broken wine bottle, but I slept more soundly in that jail cell than I had in a very long time. Most nights, I'd wake up with my heart racing. The only way to get calm was to walk down the hall to Josie's room to make sure she was safe in her bed. But on this night, on the lumpy cot of a brightly lit jail cell, I closed my eyes and crashed.

Officer Tobias, the beefy cop, woke me with a cup of

coffee to tell me my visitor had arrived. I looked at an old clock on the wall: 1:37 A.M. The officer led me into a private room with no windows where Vanesa was sitting at a metal table, rubbing her hands together.

"Thanks for coming," I said.

"Oh, Jack."

It was raining hard when we walked out of the police station, but neither of us rushed. By the time we reached her car we were both wet and cold. But she stopped before getting inside.

"I'm sorry, Jack. For everything. It was not supposed to happen. We didn't plan it. I know that is what people always say, right? I just want to say it because you should know. You are a good person, Jack. You always have been. Your father, he was . . . I do not know the right word. He jumped into life. He expected a lot. That could be exciting to be around. Also hard to live with. He loved you. So much pride for his son. I don't know."

I swiped at the rain in my eyes. "Were you guys in love?"

"I don't know. Does it even matter?"

When I opened the car door, Dayana was sitting in the back wearing an oversize black sweatshirt and wool cap.

"She insisted on coming along," said Vanesa.

"Couldn't miss all the jailhouse excitement," she said. Then, quieter: "You okay?"

"I don't know. But thanks for asking."

Vanesa turned on the ignition. She started to put the car in reverse, but stopped. "You two want to know a secret? Something I wish I knew when I was your age? You grow up. You have children. You become someone's mami or papi. People, they say you are an adult now. But just because someone says it does not mean you are any less . . . cagada than you were as a teenager."

The rain was coming down even harder when we pulled into their driveway.

"I will call Gary Grossman at the firm," Vanesa said. "He won't like being woken. But he loved your father. Go ahead inside. Dayana, please heat up some of the soup for Jack."

When we got inside, Dayana grabbed a dish towel and threw it to me. "Use this for now. I'll get you a real-size towel to dry off. She took off her hat. Even in the dim kitchen light I could see she didn't have on any makeup at all. It had been a long time since I'd seen her face like that. I'd almost forgotten about all the soft freckles around her nose.

She gently touched my battered knuckles. "Those must hurt like a bastard."

I shrugged.

"You Clays have a habit of coming here in the middle of the night," she said.

"Sorry if I woke you up."

"I was awake. Not sleeping much lately. I went cold turkey on the Ambien."

"That's good."

Dayana opened the refrigerator. "So who was the guy?"

"No one you know."

"Good. How about a beer to go with your soup?"

I guess she saw surprise on my face.

"You were just incarcerated. I don't think Vanesa's gonna flip about you drinking a light beer in her kitchen. And by the way, she's in no position to be judging anyone." She tossed me a can and I cracked it open. She opened another one for herself.

"Is your dad sleeping?" I asked.

She paused. "Yeah. Since about four in the afternoon. He, uh, didn't get that job he was interviewing for. Sucks for us, huh?" She paused. "Can I ask you something?"

"Okay."

"You called Vanesa to bail you out? That's fucking weird."

"Your mom . . . She used to help me out when my dad was around, but wasn't around. Which was pretty much always. She was. She's . . . a cool person. I'm glad she's still here. I mean not dead."

She changed the subject quickly. "Does Josie know? About the whole jail thing?"

"No, and I want to keep it that way. She can't find out about this. You have to promise me."

"Okay. So from that reaction I'm thinking whatever got you locked up and did this to your hands—it had something to do with Jo?"

I took a long drink from the beer.

"She's lucky to have you," Dayana said. "You look out for her. Always have."

"Not always," I said. " Jo's strong, but . . . not what everybody thinks."

"No," said Dayana. "Not what everybody thinks. It can't be easy though, being her twin."

"You mean being 'the other one.'"

Dayana nodded. "Helluva way to go through life."

I thought about that for a few seconds. "What does *cah-gah-da* mean?" I asked.

"*Cagada?*"

"In the car your mom said parents are just as *ca-gada* as teenagers."

Dayana smiled. "*Cagada* is a Spanish slang thing. I think it means fucked-up. Parents are fucked-up."

"Oh," I said, finishing the beer. "I already knew that."

"Me too."

She rubbed her eyes and yawned. People were afraid of this girl, I thought. Because of the piercings and the clothes and the way she kept to herself. Afraid of her like they were afraid of me. She filled a bag with ice and set it on my hands. "What does it feel like?"

"Hitting someone?"

"Losing your parents. I mean, I know it sucks, but . . . what does it feel like for you? You don't have to answer if you don't want. It's not any of my business."

I took a long time to think about that. Nobody had ever really asked me that question. What did it feel like?

The answer was that the answer changed ten times a day. Sometimes it was sharp and intense. Sometimes it burned like a dull ache or sat like a weight on my whole body. Sometimes I was furious at Mom and Dad for the mistakes they made when they were here, how they'd let me and Josie down. Sometimes I was furious at them for being gone. I didn't think about them every second, but I was never not thinking about them either. It felt . . . like being half-awake. You know how when you pull an all-nighter, the next day everything feels like it's not real? The colors are all dull, and you can't really hear or understand what people are saying. You're just floating along, sort of removed. Like you could drive your car straight into a telephone pole and it wouldn't hurt you because you're already so numb. Saying all of that out loud felt like an impossible task.

"I don't know," I said. "I feel lost."

Dayana let that sink in. "Are you hungry? There's no way they gave you anything good to eat in the Big House."

"Big House?"

"I could try making you something. It's basically morning. How about gallo pinto? It's like rice and beans and eggs."

"I should be getting home. You go back to bed. You don't have to do this for me."

She took my bruised hand and gently wiped it with the damp towel. "Hey, your dad was boning my mom. We're basically family."

15

HARRISON

-Track down Michael Boddicker.

-Demand latest progress on crash investigation.

-Weekly status meeting with Archie (and Josie?)

-Find a girlfriend.

-~~Buy Pop a birthday present and plan his birthday dinner.~~

-Confirm Harvard acceptance.

The letter was waiting in the mailbox when I got home from school. Just an innocuous white envelope buried between catalogues, coupons, and real estate flyers. It was only when I set the stack down on the table that I spied a corner peeking out from underneath the Pottery Barn spring collection. There it was: the Harvard crest. I felt every drop of blood in my body rushing to my head. I steadied myself, put my thumb and middle finger together, and carefully fished the envelope out of the pile.

I could have received my acceptance notification via email or by checking the college's admission portal, but Mom didn't believe in that. Our years of hard work deserved to be recognized in print on real paper. She always talked about that moment when we'd find it in the mailbox and open it together. So even though I knew the date had arrived, I didn't visit the Harvard website. I didn't check my inbox. I didn't even open the envelope when I first found it. This was a moment fifteen years in the making and didn't belong only to me. It belonged to Mom. She's the one who sacrificed for The Plan. She's the one who nurtured it. She taught me what it meant to work hard and to sacrifice everything for a goal. *The day you're accepted to Harvard, we will celebrate with the biggest ice cream cone the world has ever seen.*

I carried the envelope up to Mom's bedroom and gently set it down on her pillow. Her bed was unchanged. That's how I kept it. Even after all this time the pillows were dented in the place her head had last rested on them. She could've been sleeping here last night. She wasn't though. Half a year had gone by since she was in this bed. In this house. Six months. Six months since I'd seen her or heard her voice or felt the touch of her soft hand on my head when I wasn't feeling well. I'd never missed her more than I did right then. I sat down on the bed and put her pillow up to my cheek. Without warning, a sob exploded from my chest. It was followed by another and then I lost control entirely. I didn't even recognize the noises coming out of me. It went on so long I wasn't certain I would ever stop. When it was finally over, I felt spent, but ready.

"Thank you," I whispered into her pillow. Then I slid my finger under the flap and opened the thin envelope.

HARVARD COLLEGE
Admissions and Financial Aid

Harrison Rebkin
5 Fairway Lane
River Bank, NJ

Dear Mr. Rebkin,
The Committee on Admissions has completed its Regular Decision meetings, and I am very sorry to inform you that we cannot offer you admission to the Harvard College incoming class for 2020. I wish that a different decision had been possible, but I hope that receiving our final decision now will be helpful to you as you make your college plans.

. . . Very sorry? . . . cannot offer?! . . . final decision?!! No, that wasn't right. It wasn't possible. I rifled through the open envelope for more material, but there was only the letter, the one letter.

I read it over and over again, searching for an explanation. Maybe it was sent to the wrong address. That could happen. I grabbed the phone beside the bed and called the admissions office in Cambridge. After putting me on hold for ten minutes, a nice woman named Julia confirmed that I had received the correct letter. I attempted to explain to Julia that a terrible mistake had occurred. *You are special. Don't let anyone ever make you believe otherwise.* My grades were perfect; my SAT scores were nearly perfect. My application was impeccable. She explained to me that Harvard University receives hundreds of worthy applications for each slot in its incoming class. She wished me luck at one of my other choices. Other choices?! There were no other choices. I didn't apply anywhere else. I was going to Harvard. It was The Plan. *Early decision was The Plan. You missed the deadline.* Yes, well, I was . . . I couldn't. Not then. You had just . . .

Rejected? This made no sense.

I called back the admissions office, and this time I was forwarded to a voice messaging service. At the beep I identified myself and rattled off my grades and accomplishments. I had slipped to number two in my class thanks to all my absences, but that could be remedied. I could still catch Mackenzie Markowitz. It was just a matter of determination. I calmly (at first) explained that my mother and I had been working toward this moment most of my life and they were not going to take that away. Not from me and not from her.

"Bud?" Pop walked into the room just as my heart started to beat out of control. "What's going on?" He spotted the letter on the bed. He picked it up, scanned it, and whistled. "Okay, okay. I'm not gonna lie to you," he said. "This is a kick in the balls. But here's the thing."

I didn't care about the thing. There was nothing he could say, nothing that would make this better. I wanted Mom. I wanted her here. My knees buckled, but he took me by the shoulders and held me up.

"Look at me," he said. "You're better than this, Bud. You don't need them."

"I . . . failed . . . her."

I tried to slip his grip, but he wouldn't let go. "You're coming with me."

"No, this is where I need to be. In her room. I need to be close to her." This was not going to be solved by mini golf or a strip club or a hike in the woods. "Please. Let me go."

Instead, he drove us straight to the beach. He got out and opened my door.

"It's too cold to swim," I told him.

"We're not here to ride waves," he said. "I need you to hear something." He walked across the sand and up onto the jetty. He waited there for me. I thought about making a run for it, but I knew he'd find me. I wandered onto the beach and up the rocks as the waves crashed over onto our feet.

"This is a good thing," he said. "I know it doesn't feel that way right now."

"But . . . The Plan."

"The Plan was horseshit. I'm not trying to trash your mother. That woman loved you like crazy. But she had issues that she put on you and it's time you understand that."

"Her issue was that you left."

"And I'll never forgive myself for taking off on you. But

after I went away, she made her whole life about you. And that's not fair to do to a seven-year-old kid. The two of you in that house with The Plan. Have you even asked yourself if you *wanted* Harvard and med school and all the rest of it? No, because she didn't let you. It was *her* plan, not yours. I know you miss your mom. I do, too. But this rejection is a gift. Now *you* get to decide. You've got nobody to answer to. No pressure to be anything but what you are. I'll always be here for you, Bud, but I'll never tell you what to do. Take a breath, man. Look around. College will always be there. Your life won't. We can travel to Europe. Hit the road in an Airstream trailer. Live on the beach in Hawaii. We can dream big now."

He reached into his jacket and removed a sheet of paper from his pocket. It was the letter from Harvard. The rejection letter. He'd brought it with him.

"What are you doing with that?" I asked.

He pulled out a cigarette lighter and handed it to me. "Do it," he said. "Let it burn."

"Even if I burn the letter, I still failed her."

"It's not about this letter. It's not even about being turned down by some elitist jagoffs in Boston. It's about saying goodbye."

"To Harvard?"

"To The Plan, Bud. It's about letting go of your mother's expectations for you. And maybe letting go of your mother, too."

An ice-cold wave came up on the rocks and splashed

against my leg. He didn't understand what he was asking. He couldn't know what it was like when he disappeared and it was Mom and me alone in the house. Watching TV. Trading books. Talking about the future. Just the two of us. He didn't know how it felt to catch her falling apart when she thought she was alone in her bedroom. Or to watch her suffer in silence after the cancer scare. The radiation. She took care of me. We took care of each other.

And then one day, she was gone. No warning. No goodbye. I would never see her again. As much as she tried to prepare me, I had no Plan and no idea how I'd find a new one.

The tide was rising, and the rocks we were standing on were becoming wet and slippery. I flicked the lighter and the flame popped up. But I stopped there. I couldn't say goodbye.

Pop grabbed my wrist. "This is something you need to do. For both of us." He pulled my hand over to the paper. "Let go," he said. "Let her go." He brought the flame to the bottom of the letter.

I wasn't ready. I tried to pull away but he didn't let me.

The paper smoldered and then caught. He released my hand as the fire scorched the bottom of the paper, turning it to ash. The flame traveled up, blacking the page before making it disappear until it finally reached the Harvard logo at the top. Pop held on to the letter as long as he could before letting it fly in the wind.

We watched the ball of fire flutter down into the ocean, where it dissolved with a puff of smoke. As the letter flamed out in the water, I couldn't help but note that Mom's Plan ended up exactly the same way she did.

I didn't intend to lie. I didn't even know I was going to do it until the words escaped my mouth.

Mackenzie Markowitz had attracted a small crowd near her locker. Several girls from our AP classes were embracing her and engaging in awkward high fives. From halfway down the hall, I could see that Mackenzie Markowitz was holding up a letter with a familiar crest in the upper left-hand corner. However, her letter from the Harvard admissions department did not look like mine. It was at least twice as long, and I knew what that meant. Mackenzie Markowitz, who had usurped me as number one in the senior class, and who claimed she wasn't sure which school she wanted to attend, had been accepted. She'd taken my spot in the class of 2024. And now I was going to have to walk by her and her squealing friends on my way to calculus. I put my head down, hoping no one would notice me—and my rejection.

"Harrison, hi!" Mackenzie Markowitz called out as I tried to slink past. I could already feel her twisting the knife. The tone in her voice dripped with superiority. Her green eyes sparkled. Even her hair seemed shinier than usual. "I did it," she shrieked. "Harvard! I got in!" She held up the letter with two hands, flashing me the words I'd visualized so many times: "congratulations," "delighted," "invitation to attend."

I couldn't let her win. After all these years, I couldn't

admit defeat. I answered Mackenzie Markowitz the only way I could, with two words of my own. "Me too."

Her smile widened. Objectively, it was a nice, even pretty smile. But I knew better. I knew that to be the smile of a killer, someone who for seven years had wanted nothing more than to grind me into the dirt en route to becoming valedictorian. She bounded over and gave me a big hug. My arms dangled by my sides as she squeezed. She'd never hugged me before. We weren't even nice to each other. Feeling her body suddenly pressed against mine was . . . confusing. That was her intention, wasn't it? She wanted me to feel things so I'd be thrown off my game. I was not going to confess. I would not give Mackenzie Markowitz the satisfaction.

When she let go, my physical responses were still . . . activated. That's when Mackenzie Markowitz twisted the knife. "This is awesome," she said. "My parents are taking me up in a few weeks for the Visitas—the admitted students' weekend. If you want to come with us, there's plenty of room in the SUV."

Mackenzie Markowitz was testing me. First with all the physical contact, and now by bringing up her parents. She knew I'd never say yes to her offer. How could I sit in a car with the entire, intact, Markowitz family? She was trying to humiliate me. We stood there in the hall, staring at each other, before I finally realized she was waiting for an answer. As Dayana would say, Mackenzie Markowitz expected me to "bitch out." That was not going to happen.

"A road trip," I said, digging myself deeper and deeper into the hole. "Sounds like fun."

Her smile widened even more and she put her hand on my chest and gave me a shove. "The battle continues. See you in calc class, Number Two." She rejoined her friends and walked off, tossing one last smile over her shoulder. I watched her walk away, her shiny ponytail swinging back and forth.

When I turned around, Dayana was standing there.

"Why are you looking at me like that?" I asked.

"She's way into you," she said.

"Who?"

"Harvard girl. With the hair."

"Mackenzie Markowitz?"

"First name would've been fine. Yes, the girl who just rubbed *her* body all over *your* body."

I was not in the mood for Dayana being Dayana. "Were you listening to my conversation?"

"My locker is right here."

"Mackenzie Markowitz is not into me. She can't stand me. She may look nice and shiny, but she's the smartest, most ruthless, competitive person I know, and she will do anything to be number one. She's wanted to beat me since we were in sixth grade."

"Yeah, well now she wants a little nerd-on-nerd action."

Dayana was mistaken, of course. Mackenzie Markowitz and I were sworn enemies. She stole my spot at Harvard and my number one ranking. I needed to get to class, but Dayana stood in my way.

"Wait," said Dayana, looking over my shoulder. She called out to Jack down the hall and he started toward us. I tensed up.

She pulled Jack over to face me. "Tell him you're sorry for being a dick on Christmas Eve." Jack shook his head, but Dayana didn't let him off the hook. "Say you're sorry for calling him a freak and that other repugnant shit you said. We're all freaks. Even you. Maybe especially you."

Jack rubbed his hands together. They were raw and bruised. I didn't want to know what—or whom—he'd been punching. "Sorry, man," he said.

"That's all?" asked Dayana. "Come on, Jailbird, you can do better than that."

He took a deep breath. "I don't know why I said those things, Harrison. My head hurt. I got mad. Happens a lot these days."

"I understand," I said. "I know what it feels like to lose control of what's going on in your brain and your body."

"You do?"

Dayana chimed in. "Trust him. He does."

"Next time you feel it happening, you might try reciting pi to as many decimal places as you can remember."

Jack stared at me blankly.

"Or something else that calms you down," I added.

"Good plan," said Dayana.

"I was thinking," said Jack. "Maybe we could start tutoring again. I'm eating it hard in chem."

"Um. Okay. I've been busy with my research into the crash and spending time with Pop, but—"

"If you don't have time, I get it."

"No, I'll find time. We'll talk chem and maybe you can help me with other things."

"You want him to help you with that girl?" asked Dayana.

"No, I . . ."

"Investigating the crash, you mean," said Jack.

"You really don't care about it?" I asked. "You don't want some kind of closure?"

"I don't know," he said. "It's not that I don't care. It's just . . . You loved your mom a lot, right? She was good to you?"

"I was her world."

"Yeah, it's not that I didn't love my parents, too. But since the crash and then my concussion, things just ricochet around my head sometimes. Good thoughts, bad thoughts, memories. Stuff that makes me angry. Stuff there's no way to fix now that . . . now that they're gone. So I think . . . I think the kind of closure I need I'm not going to get from any investigation." He paused. "But I won't get in your way if that's what you need."

Dayana touched his back. "Atta boy, Shawshank. By the way, our fellow freak here just got accepted at Hahvahd." She grabbed my shirt and untucked it.

"No surprise. Nice, man," said Jack, slapping me hard on the back.

I kept quiet. My stomach tightened as I let the lie continue. I was in too deep to get out now.

Dayana suggested that we "hit the diner" this afternoon to celebrate with greasy food. I told them I had plans with my father. I couldn't stand the thought of lying through a whole meal.

Dayana got on her tiptoes and kissed me on the cheek. Her eyebrow ring scratched against my face. "Congratu-fucking-lations. You did it. Wherever your mom is, she's celebrating."

Dayana and Jack walked away. I wished for nothing more than to open a locker and climb inside for the rest of my life.

Every day, I came home from school and buried myself in the plane crash. I couldn't bear to look at Mom's room, much less go inside. Not only had I failed at getting into Harvard, but now I was lying to the world about it. So I did the only thing I could think to do for her: solve her murder. Because that's what it was to me now. Someone wanted that plane to fall from the sky. And these same people didn't want us to know why. Archie and I had our weekly briefings, but he and Josie were definitely together now, and that changed everything for him. He had a reason to focus on the present.

Jack and I restarted our tutoring sessions, but I couldn't get him interested in my research either. I'd stay up most of the night, following internet rabbit holes, pursuing leads, reading the minutes of congressional subcommittee meetings with the Federal Aviation Administration and trying to contact Michael Boddicker, the NTSB investigator, who had yet to respond to my latest emails and phone calls and was still MIA from his office. And then one night, at 2:44 A.M., I was drifting off when an email popped into my inbox, jolting me wide-awake. I clicked on it immediately.

AGENT MICHAEL BODDICKER, NTSB

To: Harrison Rebkin
Re: Flight 206

Mr. Rebkin:
On behalf of the National Transportation Safety Board, let me extend our deepest condolences on the loss of your mother. I understand you've suffered a tremendous loss, one that defies comprehension. Our thoughts and prayers are with your friends and family at this time of tragedy. Our investigation into the crash of Flight 206 off the coast of Anguilla has been comprehensive. I will personally be traveling back to St. Martin and Anguilla in the near future to wrap up the investigation. Please be assured that we will contact you and the other families once we have reached a conclusion.

Once again, I am terribly sorry for your loss. I hope you find solace in the memories of your beloved mother.

Agent Michael Boddicker
National Transportation Safety Board
Washington, D.C.

People say lack of sleep dulls the senses, but I felt more energized, sharper, like I was seeing connections and nuances I'd normally miss. This was it. This was the cover-up and Agent Boddicker was trying to get rid of me. I had to share this information right now. I couldn't keep it to myself. I grabbed my phone and raced down to my father's room and shook him awake.

He was confused and groggy. "What's wrong? Is someone in the house?"

"We have to get up."

"Why? What time is it?"

"It's imperative that we go to the headquarters of the NTSB to speak to them in person."

"Who?"

"The so-called investigators, they've been giving me the runaround. But if I can make them look me in the eye and tell me about Mom's plane— If we get in the car right now we could make it to D.C. by the time their offices open."

Pop wasn't stirring.

I switched on the light beside his bed and he shielded his eyes with his hand. "What the hell is this all about?" he mumbled.

"I'll explain the specifics on the way, but we cannot wait any longer on this investigation. Every day wasted is another day where the cover-up has a chance to take root."

Pop removed his hand and squinted up at me. "You want us to get in the car and drive to D.C.? Now?"

I explained how I'd been researching the crash and how Mom and her friends were caught in the middle of a government conspiracy. The officials were trying to silence me. It was the first time I'd said it so blatantly out loud. It felt good to get it out.

Pop grabbed his watch from the bedside table and checked the time. "It's the middle of the night. Let's talk about this in the morning. You need rest."

"I can't rest. Not now. We owe it to Mom and Jack and Josie's parents and Archie and Lucas's parents to find out what really happened. Someone brought down their plane. Someone is covering it up. We need to get down there and—"

"No," he said, finally sitting up.

"What do you mean, no? You won't drive to D.C. with me?"

"We're not going to D.C. We're not pursuing this. In fact, we're not gonna speak about it again."

"What? Why not?"

"Because it's craziness. A government conspiracy? This is paranoid nutcase talk."

"It's not. I could show you documentation. I have minutes from an FAA subcommittee—"

"It's nonsense. You might as well be claiming they were abducted by aliens. And if you start saying it out loud to people, it's gonna blow up our whole case."

"What *case*?"

He grabbed a glass of water from the table and took a gulp. "I didn't want to bother you with this because you had enough on your plate with school and 'The Plan' and your emotional issues."

Emotional issues. He spit it out like the words disgusted him.

"What are you talking about?" I asked.

"We did what any reasonable person would do in this situation. We filed suit against the airline for your mother's wrongful death. If you want to do some research, look into *those* numbers. There's more money at stake than you can imagine." He started talking about contingencies and precedents and settlements, but I was hung up on the first thing he said. *We.*

"How is it 'we'?" I asked.

Pop swung his legs off the bed and stood up. He puffed out his bare chest and advanced toward me aggressively. "You. Me. We. We're a family. Did you forget that? I had a life somewhere else, but I came all the way back to *this place* to take care of you. Emotionally and financially. This is a huge opportunity. You do see that, right?"

With every word he sounded less like happy-go-lucky

Bobby and more like the guy Mom talked about. He moved in closer, crowding my space. His breath was stale. "You need to get back to sleep, *Bud*." Suddenly, even my nickname sounded like a threat. "You'll think more clearly in the morning."

I was thinking very clearly. Maybe for the first time in months. That word he used: opportunity. "You haven't worked since you've been here," I said. "How have you been supporting yourself?"

"What are you asking me?"

"You get takeout for every meal. You go to concerts in the city. You have a new watch and a surfboard."

"What. Are. You. Asking. Me?"

"Where are you getting your money?"

"Be careful."

"Where are you getting your money?!"

"This is what she would want. She saved money so that it could be spent on you."

Maybe I knew it all along, but I didn't want to see it. "You've been taking money from Mom?"

He snorted. "I transferred some so that we could have access."

"How?"

"Your mother was predictable. She never changed her pass codes."

"You stole her money."

"Stole?!" His voice was getting tighter and tighter. "I did it for you. There are bills to pay. Food. Gas money."

"*I* pay the bills. I've been doing it since the day after the crash. How much have you taken?"

I looked down at my phone and sent a text. *Need your help. Please. If you're awake come to—*

"Put that down!" He backed me up a step. "You sound like your mother right now. Okay, yes, I've used some of the *family* money. I've taken over the family. There's nobody else. You're my son. I'm entitled to—"

"Entitled? Why, because you've been here a few months? Because you took me out for some fun? What about the last ten years?"

"Are we really gonna start rehashing this crap? I heard it enough from *her*. Did you forget what you said at the beach? You were gonna let her go."

"*You* said let her go. If I let go of Mom, it's just me and you and the settlement money. We'd do all those things you were talking about. Travel through Europe, and drive around in a camper, and live in Hawaii. All with my money."

"This is how you thank me? When I showed up here, you weren't a teenager. You were a . . . *veal.* Your mother kept you in a box and crippled you. For once in your life, you're actually living. Think about the fun we can have with that money. We can do anything we want."

"Get out," I said.

"You want me to go? Now?!"

"I want you out of my house." I picked up a bag and started throwing his things into it.

He chased me down the stairs and ripped it from my hand. "You think I'm really gonna leave? Just like that? You have no idea what I've been through. The dues I've paid. I've had more disappointments, more shit than you can imagine. This could be a new life. For both of us. Like hell I'm walking away from it."

The doorbell rang.

Pop looked stunned. "What'd you do, call the police?"

I walked to the door and opened it. Jack stood on the porch, barefoot in basketball shorts and no shirt. He filled the doorframe, his bald head nearly brushing against the porch light.

Pop just looked at me. "You must be shitting me. You called your meathead bodyguard? You need to get your head straight. When I showed up here, you were all alone. Freaking out every five minutes because you didn't have your mommy to tell you what to do. You want that again?"

I looked to Jack. "I'd like him to go now. He can take the car."

My father looked tiny next to Jack. "What're you gonna do, kick my ass if I refuse?"

Jack said nothing.

I handed Pop the bag with his things. "I'm changing all the pass codes and calling the lawyers in the morning."

"Please, Bud. Don't do this." He looked from Jack to me and I saw beneath the anger. I saw the fear and the desperation and the sadness. I actually felt sorry for him.

"It was really good having you here, Pop," I said. "I didn't realize how much I'd missed you. I'll see ya when I see ya."

He stared at me for a while and then he gave up and shook his head. "I'll see ya when I see ya, Bud." And then he was gone.

Jack and I looked at each other for a few seconds. Then he nodded and followed Pop out.

I was alone again.

I couldn't make it to D.C. without a car, but I was too wired to lie down. I wrote an email to Jack and Archie and Josie and then I thought twice and added Dayana.

Sunnies,
Michael Boddicker wrote to me. He's going back to Anguilla to investigate the crash. I think he's onto something. I think we should go to D.C. to talk to him.

Nobody wrote back. So I took an Uber to school. I was barely inside when Mackenzie Markowitz sidled up to me, a stack of books pressed against her chest. The lie. The Harvard lie. I'd almost forgotten.

"Didn't you get my text?" she asked. "I wanted to talk to you about plans for the Visitas in Cambridge. My parents want to leave really early in the morning. Like four A.M. or something inhumane. Since you're on the other side of town,

I thought it might be easier for you to just stay over the night before. You know, in our guest room. We could study or watch a movie together . . . Or not. It's totally up to you."

I did all I could to fight the wave of panic traveling through my body. I could not have a glitch in front of Mackenzie Markowitz. Anyone but her. I looked down at my feet, flexed my hands, and managed to say I'd let her know. Then I raced off to the empty gym, where I closed my eyes and fought it, minute by minute. I recited the digits of pi to forty-seven decimal places before I calmed myself. I wasn't going to give in. I wasn't going to let my father be right about me. I could do this without Mom *and* without him.

I'd never gone deep into a glitch before and been able to stave it off, but this time I managed to keep it at bay, at least for a little while. I listened to the voice in my head. It was my own voice. *You can do this*, I told myself. *You're the person who won four spelling bees in a row. You single-handedly won Math Olympics as a ninth grader. You kicked your father out of your house. You're stronger than this.*

I made it through the first half of the day through sheer force of will. But just before lunch, I was sitting in AP history when Mr. Herrera delivered a note to my desk. The guidance counselor would like to see me in her office. No other details. She must've heard from Harvard. Did she know I'd lied? Was she going to confront me? Or even worse, offer sympathy? Alternatives, other scenarios. Community college. Summer school. As I walked out of the classroom and into the hallway, the glitch overwhelmed me. I could not catch my breath or stop my heart from pounding out of my chest. I was already drenched in sweat and shaking all over my body. Thankfully, the bell had yet to ring, so the hallway was empty. I braced myself against the wall and dragged myself locker by locker to Mr. U's closet. I struggled with my key, but finally got it unlocked. When the door swung open I stumbled in, kicked the door closed, and lay flat on my back. I heard the bell ring and the hall fill with students on their way to classes or the cafetorium.

This was more than a glitch. My body was shutting down. My heart couldn't keep this up. I was running out of air. I was going to pass out and then I was going to die.

A knock at the door. Mr. U's voice: "Harry? You okay in there?" I couldn't answer him. More knocks. I tried to call for medical attention, but all that came out was a soft wheeze. After a while, the knocking stopped. That was it. I was going to die here, alone on the floor of the janitor's closet among the mop and the cleaning supplies.

As my vision started to go blurry, the door creaked open and Mr. U stood over me. "I know you said not to tell anyone, but she's your friend, right?" Mr. U moved out of the way to reveal Dayana standing behind him.

"Thanks," said Dayana. "I got it from here."

I heard Mr. U leave and Dayana close the door. I tried to say something to her, but she told me not to speak. As I gasped for air, she grabbed a mop bucket, flipped it over, and sat down next to me.

"Nice place you got here," she said.

"I didn't . . . get in . . . to Harvard," I gasped. "They didn't want me."

Dayana didn't say anything. She just took off a few of her rings and dropped them into her bag. Then she put her hand on my head and stroked my hair. Her hand was soft like Mom's. I closed my eyes and we stayed like that, listening to my ragged breathing until the hallway was quiet and the glitch had finally passed.

When I was able to stand up, Dayana grabbed me by the back of the neck. "You need to eat something. A butt load of sugar and grease."

We walked together into the cafetorium and she bought me two packs of Pop-Tarts and a plate of fries. I followed her to her table, where Josie and Archie were already sitting next to each other. They looked up when they saw me. I could see on their faces that I looked as shaky as I felt.

"Our boy had a shitty night," said Dayana. "His dad hit the road. And some other stuff." I was so grateful she didn't tell everyone else about Harvard. I definitely wasn't ready for that yet.

Josie asked if I was okay and pushed a chair toward me. Archie opened his sketchpad and asked about the email from the NTSB. I sat down and started to explain, when suddenly a shadow fell over us. We all looked up simultaneously to see Jack towering above us. He'd never been over to this table before.

Josie immediately got tears in her eyes. "You're coming here to sit with us? You're on board?"

Jack swiped a hand over his head. "Do I believe that the government plotted to eliminate our parents?" He took a moment to consider it. "Who the hell knows?"

I said, "There is evidence that—"

"Harrison, let him talk," said Archie.

"I don't know about military contracts and national secrets and shit like that," Jack said. "What I know is I'm stuck. And I can't get unstuck."

"Me too," I said.

"What I've been doing, it's not working. I sit in the house. I get in the car and I drive too fast. I treat my girlfriend like crap. I send these fucking texts to a ghost like they're going to do something."

"What texts?" asked Josie.

"It doesn't matter," said Jack. "I think the problem is that it still doesn't feel real. After all this time. Maybe it's my head, but . . . sometimes I feel like it's a dream. Harrison, you want answers about the crash. I just want . . . I just want to feel that it's real. Finally. I don't know if this will fix anything. But I think we need to go. I think we all need to go."

"Go?"

Jack reached into his bag and pulled out some papers. "It's four hundred twenty-seven bucks per person round trip for spring break. We'll cover the cost of the flights and the hotel."

"You want us to take a trip? Together?" asked Josie. "Where?"

"Anguilla," said Archie. "You want us all to go to Anguilla."

16

JOSIE

OPERATION SUNNIES GO TO ANGUILLA WAS
over a week away, but I'd started packing the day Jack bought
the plane tickets. Or at least planning to pack. At this point,
it was just a mountain of clothes on my bed. Maybe that's
why I woke up every morning feeling so tired. I was definitely coming down with something. Nothing new there. My
whole life, I'd always gotten sick before big events. Every test,
big game, or family vacation would bring with it a cold, flu,
or other random virus. As a little kid, I'd learned to pretend
I was okay. Jack was the sickly one. He was the one with all
the doctor visits and the late night trips to the hospital. Mom
worried enough about him. So I'd always just acted like I was
fine, and nobody seemed to notice. And I did the same when
my body turned on me the week before we headed off to
the island where Mom and Daddy died.

I guess each of us had a different reason for taking this
trip. Harrison was convinced that if he confronted the local

authorities with his research on the crash, they'd have to start talking. Archie was starting to believe it, too. I thought mostly he just loved the idea of the five of us going away together. Jack said he wanted to get unstuck and that made sense to me. And Dayana. We were sitting at the same lunch table, but we hadn't really talked since New Year's Eve. I'm not sure what I believed about the crash, but I knew I needed to be there, to stand on the beach and see where the plane went into the water. So we waited.

After the night I spent with Archie, it wasn't like we became an instant couple. I'm sure he was hoping for that, but I wasn't ready. That night in his house, I asked him if he was scared. I was the one who was terrified. And as good as I felt being with him, that feeling didn't go away when we woke up the next morning. The snail had lost its shell. I don't know what freaked me out more: how easily I could be hurt, or how easily I could hurt Archie.

After I ended things for good with Cody, Siobhan tried her best to keep me in the fold. But the more time I spent with Archie and Harrison, the less I fit in with her and the girls. The Sunnies were no longer the flav of the month. The calls and texts slowed down and finally stopped coming altogether. I was out and I was okay with it.

I'm sure I frustrated Archie. Every time we took another step closer, I took a half step back. Like when he held my hand in the hallway one morning and I acted like I had to go to the bathroom. Or when he asked me to sleep over, and I said no and then changed my mind four times before finally showing up at his house, after he was already in bed. He never complained and he never pressured me. When I went to my locker at the end of each school day, there was a new drawing waiting for me. When I texted him, he was always there to answer. He was kind and patient and he made me feel special like none of the guys in my life ever had before. And it still scared me to death.

Stupid immune system. Breaking down when I needed it most. I couldn't be stuck in an Anguilla hotel room with the flu, so I tried to conserve my energy and let my body recover. That didn't go over so well with my hardass PE teacher, Mr. Morgan. When I told him I was too sick for field hockey he sent me to the nurse's office for a note. I sat in Nurse Leonard's waiting room, checking our flights for the 150th time. Newark to St. Martin to Anguilla. No change to the schedule. When the office door clanked open, I didn't even look up until I heard a familiar jingling of hardware. Dayana gave an awkward half wave and sat down in the plastic chair next to me.

"What're you in for?" she asked.

"General crappiness," I said. "Pre-trip stress. Never fails."

Dayana nodded. "Like when you got that stomach thing before our Girl Scout campout? That was some nasty business."

We both went quiet, staring at a poster depicting the cow-shaped organs of the female reproductive system. It was kinda the same way at our lunch table. When Archie and Harrison and Jack were there, we talked, but if Dayana and I happened to be the first two to arrive—awkward silence.

On the first day of school after the crash, Siobhan asked me if I was jealous of Dayana. "You know, 'cause her parents, like, lived?"

It wasn't until that horrible moment outside Dayana's house on New Year's Eve that it really hit me. And it wasn't because I missed being able to talk to Mom and Daddy, which I did. Or hug them, which I did. What finally got to me that night was knowing that Dayana could yell at her mom. She could call her names, shake her, slap her, demand answers about the affair. Dayana knew for a whole year and she didn't tell me. And it's what I needed more than anything now. To confront Daddy, to scream at him for what he did to Mom. To our family. He was supposed to be different. He was supposed to be better than the guys I knew, better than Coach Murph. Keeping all of that inside was probably not great for my health. Maybe the trip to Anguilla would help. But there would be no confrontation, no apologies. No answers. Somehow I'd have to live with that.

And somehow I'd have to live with Dayana.

"In case you're wondering why I'm here," she said, pulling out her lower lip and showing off an angry red-and-black blotch, "*inffctd llllp prrrrcng*." She winced as she let her lip snap back into place. "Infected lip piercing."

"Okay, that is vile," I said.

"Thanks. You always know how to make a girl feel better." She offered me a closer look.

I made a face. "Um, you need to get that checked out by a doctor."

"It's cool. It's happened to me before. I'm just taking some leftover antibiotics we had in the house. Knock this shit right out. Going to the doctor means I have to take it out and that'll make Mami too happy."

After the mention of her mother we were both quiet again. Finally, she spoke up. "I'm sorry I didn't tell you," she said. "About my mom and your dad. I thought about it. Even wrote an email once, but I never sent it. You and your dad always got along so well. And it's not like we were hanging out. We weren't even talking."

"You never said anything to her? Or to your dad?"

"What was the point?"

More silence.

"Do you, like, hate her?" I asked.

"I hate what she did to your family. Mine was already fucked."

I let that sink in. On the surface, my family *wasn't* like Dayana's. We didn't fight in front of people. We didn't curse at each other. Nobody locked himself in a bedroom or took a bunch of prescription drugs. We looked perfect in pictures. We had lots of friends. We went on great vacations and hosted killer parties. We had a great life. Except Daddy was having sex with his coworker. Mom just kept on buying herself more things and joining more organizations. Jack walked around angry all the time. And a terrible thing happened to me when I was fourteen. We were the family everybody else wanted to be. But maybe that's because they didn't know who we really were.

"We were pretty fucked ourselves," I said.

I stood up and grabbed two ice packs from Nurse Leonard's freezer. I put one on my head and handed the other to Dayana. "When my earlobe swelled up from a bad piercing in seventh grade, my mom told me to ice it. Fifteen minutes on, fifteen minutes off. It kinda worked. Get that lip in shape or they might not let you through security at the airport."

Dayana took the ice pack and pressed it to her swollen lip. Then she pulled it away. "Hey, about that. It was dope of Jack to buy me a ticket and all. But we all know I shouldn't be going on this trip with you. There's gonna be some heavy shit going down. You don't need me getting in the way."

I took her hand and moved the ice pack back to her mouth. "Why do you do that? Why do you always act like you're not a part of it?"

"I'm not," she said. "My parents were not on that plane, remember?"

"So?"

"Seriously, you need me to explain it to you?"

"You did this before there was ever a plane crash. Even before high school. You kept pushing me away."

"*I* pushed *you* away?"

"You always had to be on the outside," I said.

"I *am* on the outside."

"Says who?"

"Everyone. You don't understand what it's like, Jo. When you walk in a room, you don't even think about it. You know who you are and where you belong without even asking the question. You have a place."

"You have a place, D."

"Where?"

"With us. With the Sunnies. You're the only one of us who hasn't been totally falling apart this year. When the heavy shit goes down on the island, we need you. You are a part of this whether you like it or not. Forever."

I could see Dayana's big eyes getting watery. It always killed me when she cried. Even when we were little. Totally shredded my heart. I didn't want to see what would happen to all that makeup if the waterworks started.

"Now go see a real doctor before your stupid lip falls off."

Right after a tragedy happens, when you're struggling to survive, all you hope for is a day when you start to feel a little better. Some little glimmer of hope that shows you're not going to hurt this much for the rest of your life. And then when it actually does start to hurt a little less, you feel even worse because it's like you're forgetting the people you lost. Like if you admit to yourself that you're starting to feel happy because you have a great boyfriend and real friends, then your parents didn't mean enough to you.

We were a week away from the trip and it was all starting to get to me. I'd gone looking for a new bikini, but I couldn't bring myself to try any on. I walked into every store at the mall and walked out without buying a single thing. By the time I got home, I was *done*. I just fell onto my bed right in the middle of all the clothes. Two hours later, I woke up to Jack's heavy steps on the stairs. I opened my eyes as he walked into my room.

"Didn't mean to wake you. Wow, that's a lot of stuff you're packing. Mom would be proud."

"I just can't decide. It all feels wrong," I said. "Let me guess. You haven't even started."

Jack rubbed his hands together. The cuts on his knuckles were mostly healed. He told me he'd punched a wall outside the pharmacy when someone stole his parking spot. Since then, something had changed. For the first time since his concussion, he seemed quieter, more at peace.

"I'm not going," he said.

I sat up in bed. "Not going where?"

"Anguilla."

"What? It was your idea."

"I want you to go without me," he said. "You need it. Archie will be there for you."

"You have to go, Jack. You need it, too. You said it. You're stuck. If I'm going, then so are you."

"I can't, Jo. I can't go."

"Of course you can."

"No. I can't. I mean—I'm not allowed. They just told me."

"Not allowed? *Who* told you?"

"My lawyer," he said. "I got in some trouble and the D.A. said I can't leave the state."

"I don't understand. What kind of trouble?"

He looked down at his hands like a scared, oversize five-year-old.

"It wasn't a wall, was it? You didn't punch a wall."

"Finish packing," he said, starting out of the room.

"Stop," I said. "I'm tired of all the secrets. I don't want to be protected or lied to anymore." I jumped up from the bed. The head rush made me wobble.

"Are you okay?" he asked.

"Fine. I stood up too fast. Listen to me. You can't do this, Jack. You can't go around attacking people."

"I'm dealing with it."

"Was it a fight? Who did you hit?"

"I said I'm dealing with it."

"Tell me what happened or I'm calling the D.A. myself." I reached for the phone.

"Don't. It just . . . happened," he said. "I saw him in a parking lot and I—I barely even remember doing it. He walked up like everything was cool. He smiled. Like we were old friends. His car was right next to mine. That goddamned blue car."

Jack finally looked me in the eyes and a terrible wave washed over me. I knew what he'd done. "Coach Murph."

"I wanted to hurt him for what he did to you. And for how he made me feel weak and scared. And for Mom and Dad and all those years we did nothing. We *said* nothing."

"What did you do?"

"Jo . . ."

"What did you do?!"

"I knocked him down and I started hitting him and hitting him and hitting him. I wanted him to suffer. I wanted him to—"

I grabbed him by both arms. And even though he was twice my size I felt stronger than him. Like there was no fight left in his body. "You shouldn't have done that. I never asked you to. It was over. He was out of my life."

"Soul . . ."

"I can't do my part without you. What if you'd killed him? What if you threw your whole life away? I can't lose you, too!"

"I'm sorry, Jo," he whispered, tears rolling out of his eyes. "I'm so sorry I didn't protect you." I'd never been angrier at him or loved him more. I stood on the bed and wrapped him in my arms as best I could. His whole body was heaving and shaking.

When Archie picked me up later that night, I asked him to take me to the Sunny Horizons playground. This time we held hands on the walk to the stump. He didn't even ask why we were here, which was good 'cause I was not looking to explain.

"Can I see your sketchbook?"

"Why?"

"Please. I just need to."

"I could make you copies of any drawings—"

"I want to see it, Archie."

He didn't like handing it over, but he saw how serious I was and he put it on my lap and opened the cover. I didn't know what I was looking for, but after a few pages I found what I needed. A couple of weeks ago I'd woken up in his bed and he wasn't there. I threw on one of his hoodies and walked into the kitchen. He'd obviously been up for a long time because he'd already set out coffee and toast. And cereal and bagels. And bacon and eggs and toaster waffles and microwave pancakes and Pop-Tarts and granola bars and yogurt. It was everything he had in the house, and once it was prepared, this feast barely fit on the table. "I wasn't sure what you wanted for breakfast," he said.

It was the dumbest, sweetest thing anyone had ever done for me. I took it all in and decided, if he'd made all of that for me, I was going to try to eat every bite of it. Plus I was starving. So I grabbed a fork and a spoon and I dug in. Some of it was burned and some of it was undercooked, but I didn't care. I was on a mission. I attacked the bacon, then scarfed down a bagel and some apple slices. When I looked up from a big bowl of cereal, Archie was looking at me like I'd lost my mind. For some reason his worry was the funniest thing ever.

I started to laugh. I tried to hold it back, but the cereal went flying out of my mouth and landed in a chunk on his glasses. That only made me laugh even more. Archie started to laugh, too. He threw a piece of toast in my direction. I picked up a forkful of eggs to throw back at him, but Archie held up a hand and reached for his sketchpad and a pencil. I'd never seen his hand move so fast. In just a few minutes he was done drawing. But he wouldn't show the sketch to me no matter how much I asked. It wasn't ready, he insisted.

That night on the swings I saw the sketch for the first time. There I was in Archie's hoodie, looking ridiculous and covered in food. My goofy smile took over my whole face. I looked happy. I *was* happy. It was exactly what I needed to see. It was exactly what I needed to hold on to.

I circled the block three times before I finally parked down at the end of the street. As I walked up to the small house, his lights were dim and I could see the TV flickering a Mets game through the window. One of his exterior lights was burned out so that the half of the yard near the driveway was dark. I stayed out of the light. As I headed toward the house, I tried not to look at the blue Mustang in the driveway, but my elbow brushed against Shirley's mirror. I yanked my arm back. I didn't want to touch it. I didn't want to be anywhere near this thing. This tiny, cramped space where it all started. For a moment I was back there, in the passenger seat, his hand on my leg, his heavy body pressing against me, my head crushed against the window. A wave of dizziness hit, and my stomach rolled. I hadn't let myself visit those memories in a long time. They were a weight tied to my ankle. They could always pull me back down if I let them.

Not tonight. I wasn't going to let that happen tonight. I walked up the steps to his house. My arm felt like it weighed a hundred pounds as I lifted it to knock on the door. I heard the TV mute inside and ice cubes rattle in a glass. Footsteps getting closer to the door, a lock turning. And then the door swung in, and he was standing there. Coach Murph was standing there. There were cuts on his face and a jagged scar over his eye that had only started to heal. He looked older. Tired. When he saw me, his face went blank.

"JC . . ."

"Is she home?" I asked. He shook his head, and I walked past him into the house, careful not to touch him. As I went by, I caught a whiff of the alcohol on him. Murph closed the door and followed me into the living room. I could see he was walking gingerly, favoring his ribs.

"Jack did all of this to you?"

He nodded. Being alone with him in his house, it was all I could do to stay in the moment. Don't slip back. Don't let him pull you under. The house felt sweltering. Oppressive. On the wall were photos of all the softball teams he'd coached. I saw myself at age eleven, age twelve, age thirteen . . . More dizziness. I was afraid I might pass out, fall to the floor in the middle of his faded rug.

He saw me looking at the photos. "Those were some great teams," he said. "I still think back to—"

"Stop," I snapped. "Just stop!"

He held up his hands. "Why are you here? To see up close what your brother did to me?"

My hands were shaking. I put them behind my back so he wouldn't see. I thought about Archie's drawing. Just pretend to be the way he saw me. "Jack is a good person," I said, trying to keep my voice from wavering. "He is the best brother anyone could ever ask for. I don't know what I'd do without him. He's not going to jail." My voice got stronger as I went along. "Jack is not going to jail. I don't care what you have to do. Lie. Refuse to testify. Say you started the fight. Claim you pulled a weapon on him. Whatever it takes, you're going to make this go away."

"Josie, I . . ." He took a step toward me and I backed away.

It was terrifying, being this close to him again. I knew he could make me feel small and helpless again, like the kid I used to be. But I wouldn't let him do that. Not again, not anymore. I twisted my heels and dug in my feet. "If this case goes forward, if you press charges against my brother, I will tell everyone what happened. I will tell your wife. I will tell your boss. I will tell the police. I will write a letter to every one of your neighbors. I will post it on Facebook and Twitter. The whole world will know what you did. What you are."

"I'm not. I never. I wouldn't . . . Please don't do that. Please."

He was begging me. Begging for his life. *He* was afraid of *me*. And seeing his fear made mine go away. "What have you told the police about Jack? What have you said to other people?"

"I said I didn't remember what happened. I told Christine it was a dispute over a parking space. She probably thought I was lying, I don't know . . ."

Now I walked toward him, and he seemed to shrink. He looked sad and pathetic. "Make it go away," I said. "If you want to keep your life, you make this go away."

"I will. I'll tell them whatever I have to. I promise. I promise." He paused. "I thought he was going to kill me."

"You're lucky he's a good person." I started for the door.

"JC," he called out, weakly. "What happened between us, I never meant to hurt you. You were a special young woman."

Just hearing him defend himself made me want to pummel him. "I wasn't a 'young woman.' I was a girl. A kid. I trusted you. And then I blamed myself, like I did something wrong. I hated myself all these years because I 'let you' do this to me . . . But it wasn't my fault. It was you. It was all you. It didn't 'happen' between us. You did it to me. It was sexual abuse and you did it to me."

He stood there with his battered face and his bruised ribs and his shabby house with old team photos on the wall. He was done hurting me. But I wasn't done hurting him.

I slid a hand into my pocket and touched the folded-up sketch I'd taken from Archie's sketchbook. I looked Murph in the eyes. "I used to think that you'd ruined me forever. That I'd never get back what you took. And for a while, it seemed like that was true. But I'm getting it back now. Every day it feels like I'm getting more of it back."

Murph reached out like he wanted to hug me. Like we were going to just hug it out. Bygones.

When he got close, I elbowed him as hard as I could in his injured ribs. He dropped to his knees. "Do what you have to do to get those charges dropped," I reminded him. "And don't wait. Jack and I have a trip to take."

I looked back at all the team photos, all the young girls smiling in their uniforms. I decided right then that as soon as I got back from the island and Jack was safe, I'd go to the police and tell them everything. I'd tell my story over and over again, as many times as I had to, to make sure nothing like that ever happened again.

I left Murph reeling in pain as I walked out the door and slammed it closed behind me. When I stepped outside and saw the Mustang again, the rush of dizziness flooded in. I felt my lunch coming back up in a big way. I grabbed the driver's side door handle to steady myself and was surprised to find the door was unlocked. I yanked it open and unleashed the contents of my stomach all over the front seat of Murph's beloved Shirley.

17

ARCHIE

YOU SPEND YOUR WHOLE LIFE WISHING FOR something, and then just when you get used to the idea that it's never gonna happen . . . Holy crap! Josie Clay was my girlfriend! Well, maybe not quite my girlfriend. We never used those words, but we saw each other almost every day. Sometimes we talked or texted all night. I even liked taking care of her when she was sick. I don't think anyone ever did that kind of stuff for her. She wasn't good at letting me help her, but she was trying.

So why, when things were just starting to get good, was I about to possibly risk getting myself killed? Maybe I'd read too many comic books. "The Sunnies" even sounded like a team of superheroes: *On a mystical quest to solve the mystery of their parents' deaths. Was it sabotage? A government cover-up?* But we weren't the Avengers. We were five teenagers going to another country to throw around accusations about a government conspiracy. And getting on the same kind of plane that killed our parents.

Between worrying about ending up just like my parents and trying to be a worthy non-boyfriend to the most amazing girl in the world, I totally forgot my eighteenth birthday until Josie surprised me in my bedroom with a party horn and balloons. She led me into the kitchen, where Lucas was waiting.

"Happy birthday," she said. "You deserve the best one ever." She kissed me on the lips. It was the first time she'd done it in front of my brother.

On every kitchen cabinet, she'd taped a picture.

"The world has opened up to you today. What you see here are all the amazing things you can do now that you are *OF AGE*." She handed me a cup of coffee as she identified each picture. "You can join the military, of course, but I am not letting you leave me. So instead I suggest you start by opening your very own *BANK ACCOUNT*! Once you have money in it you can buy a *LOTTERY TICKET*! Maybe *VOTE IN AN ELECTION* or *SERVE ON A JURY*! Hey, did you know you can skydive *and* bungee jump now?"

"And then what do I do *after* lunch?"

Lucas brought over a plate covered in aluminum foil. "I made angel food cake," he said. "I know Mom made it for you every year on your birthday."

"She did."

"Angel food cake seems kinda lame to me," said Josie. "It's mostly air and there's not even any frosting."

"That's what I always thought," said Lucas.

"It's my favorite, so it doesn't matter what either of you think."

"I forgot candles," said Josie. "But you should make a wish anyway."

"I already did," I said. "A long time ago."

Josie went into the other room and came back with a wrapped present that she said was from both of them. From the way Lucas avoided eye contact, I wondered if she'd just let him in on her gift.

"Happy birthday, bro," he said, without much enthusiasm.

I tore off the paper to reveal a beautiful box made of dark wood. I unlatched a gold clasp in the front and opened the lid. Inside were three tiers of professional sketching utensils. Row after row of different pencils of all colors and material, graphite sticks, charcoal. I ran my hand along the incredible set.

Lucas heard his phone ring and headed back to his room without giving me a chance to thank him.

I turned away from Josie so she wouldn't see me getting emotional.

"Do you like it?"

"My mom bought me my first set when I was three. She told me she saw me drawing with crayons on her wall. She started to get mad, but then she saw that I'd drawn this great picture of her and Dad and me as a family, and it melted her heart. She took a photo of it and she bought me a sketchbook and some colored pencils."

"Archie, I'm sorry—"

"No, it's perfect. You're perfect."

It was everything I'd ever wanted. But even as I hugged Josie and tested out my new drawing set, I was distracted. It was my eighteenth birthday. When Josie had put together her list of things I was now old enough to do, she'd left out the only one that mattered to me, the one I'd sort of been waiting for since I was four years old.

I'd started to wonder about my birth mom not long after Lucas was born. I mean, Lucas was Mom and Dad's *real* son. When they brought him home from the hospital, nobody whispered or asked questions. Everyone who came to visit talked about how much Lucas looked like them, how he had Mom's eyes and Dad's crazy cowlick. I was different from them. And skin color was just the most obvious way. I was a duckling living with a family of swans.

When I'd sit in my room sketching or tell Mom how I didn't want to go the school dance or watch the Super Bowl, she would kiss me on the head. "I love you, Archie. But sometimes, I really don't understand you."

And even though she was the most patient and loving mom, I'd think, "Is there someone out there who *does* understand me?"

In the eight months since the crash, I honestly hadn't thought about my birth mother. I'd always assumed that when I turned eighteen I'd sit down with Mom and Dad and together we'd make the decision about whether or not to find her. While Josie was cleaning up the kitchen, I went into my room and opened a desk drawer. Under a pile of comics, I found all the information I'd printed out and saved when I'd heard they were changing the state adoption laws. Now when an adoptee reached age eighteen, he could file a request online for his original birth certificate, including the name of his biological mother. If she'd already given permission, he'd be able to reach out to her, even meet her face-to-face if he wanted. All I had to do was fill out a form and make a payment, and the birth certificate would be on its way. I was logging onto the website for the state registrar when Josie came into the room.

"The last time I read the computer over your shoulder we almost had a moment." When I didn't respond she looked closer at what was on the screen. I heard a little gasp.

"You're eighteen," she said.

"Yeah."

"So, you're going to try to find her? The woman who gave you away?"

The woman who gave me away. That was one name for her. Bio parent. Birth mother. "I don't know," I jabbered. "I mean, I don't know anything about this person. She could live in a van and roam the country, kidnapping dogs and babies. She could be a serial killer or even one of the *Real Housewives of New Jersey.*"

"None of them are black," Josie pointed out.

"She's like this total stranger even though at one time I was *inside her body*. I have half of her DNA." I stared at the instructions on the screen. "Thirty-five dollars plus shipping. It could be here even before we go away. It's insane. I don't know. I mean, my mother . . ."

Josie leaned down and kissed me. "I think you should put in the request."

I drove Lucas back to Aunt Sarah's a few days before we had to leave. As usual, he played his music loud the whole way. When we got there, I popped the trunk and kept the engine running.

He sat there staring at me. "You're not even coming in?"

"I don't feel like getting into a whole thing with Aunt Sarah," I said.

"You mean you don't want her knowing you're going to the island where Mom and Dad died." I had never actually told Lucas our plans. I didn't think he needed to know. I said it was a school trip. "You don't think I heard you and Josie talking about it for weeks? Or when I'm in the house do you just forget I'm there at all?"

"Did you and Sam get in a fight?"

"This has nothing to do with Sam. This is about you lying to me."

"If you knew we were going, why didn't you say something?"

"Because I wanted to see if *you* would. I kept waiting for

279

you to ask me to come with you. But that was stupid. I'm not one of *The Sunnies*. Of course you wouldn't ask me." He turned away from me and looked out the window.

I turned the radio down. "What's going on? What's this about?" I asked. I really didn't have time for this. I wanted to get back home to see if the delivery guy had arrived with my birth certificate.

"They were my parents, too. You don't own them dying just because you were first."

What was he talking about? If anyone "owned" them as parents it was Lucas. He was the favorite. He was the real son.

When he turned back to look at me, his eyes were red and watery. He dragged his sleeve across his runny nose. "Forget it. Just forget it." Lucas kicked open the door and stepped out of the car. Then he ducked his head back in. "You know you've been a shitty brother since they died, right?"

"What?" I climbed out of the car and walked around to his side. "That was harsh. Do I not make you dinner when you're home and drive you around when you need rides?"

"I don't even . . . Just fucking go, okay?"

"What did I do so wrong?"

"Okay. You're right. You didn't do anything wrong 'cause you didn't *do* anything! You didn't come in my room, you didn't even ask how I was feeling. You sent me off to live here most of the time so you wouldn't have to deal. You barely looked at me."

This didn't make sense. That's not how it was. I made

sure he was fine. I *would've* gone into his room. I wanted to, but he was always . . . busy. He had so many friends . . . "You were okay. I saw that. You didn't need me."

"I was *okay*? I was starting eighth grade and Mom and Dad died in a plane crash!"

"Well, I mean—"

"You didn't even tell me they were dead until the next morning. I sat in my room that night playing *Fortnite* and my parents were dead and you didn't even bother to let me know."

"No, I . . . I didn't know how to tell you. And I thought I'd give you one last night before you knew."

"It's not about that night. It's about every night since."

"I would've said something."

"But you thought I was okay."

"Not okay, but . . . I mean, you weren't like me. I didn't have anybody and you have all those friends . . ."

"You mean my Instagram followers? Lonely, scared boys looking for someone to tell them it gets better?"

"What about your real friends? Your soccer team. And Sam. You had Sam. You were happy. You had someone to love . . ."

"I don't love Sam. He's fun and he likes me and all. But mostly he was just *there*. And when you shut me out—"

"Shut you out? That not what happened—"

"I needed someone to . . . whatever. Make the house not so quiet. Not so *alone* without them."

"I was alone, too. You could've said something."

"But you never asked, Archie. You never fucking asked."

My birth certificate arrived via UPS two days before our flight, but I was too jumpy to open it. I texted Josie and begged her to come over. She'd gone home again the night before when she wasn't feeling well. At least that's what she said. She took off so fast I wondered if I'd done something wrong.

Josie arrived looking pale and shaky. But she took the envelope and tore open the top. The document was a crisp, blue rectangle with a raised seal. State of New Jersey Certificate of Live Birth. On the top line was the name of the child: Archie Austin, born April 19, 2001. St. Francis Medical Center, Trenton, NJ. Archie Austin; that was me. Name of mother: Talia Austin. Date of birth: July 16, 1982. Mailing address: 432 Eastern Boulevard, Apt. 5H. Trenton, NJ. The line for father was left blank.

I wasn't sure what I should be feeling. Talia Austin. Was her name supposed to stir something in me? "1982," I said. "She was nineteen when she had me."

"Eighteen," said Josie quietly. "Her birthday's in July. Eighteen like us."

I sat there wondering what Archie Austin's life would have been like. He had a cool name. Archie Austin. Too cool for me. If I'd grown up with Talia, would I have liked different things? Would I have been a different person if I grew up in a house that was, as Grandma called it, "culturally appropriate"? I reached for Josie's hand. It was trembling. She seemed like she was fighting tears. This was one of those times where I really didn't know how to read her feelings.

"What's wrong?" I asked. "You thinking about your parents?"

Josie shook it off. "Today's not about me," she said. She grabbed my laptop. "Do you want to see her?"

One Facebook search later and she was there on the screen, flashing a big, wide smile in her profile picture.

"She's pretty," said Josie. "She looks like you."

I guess she was, although she looked older than her age. Her photo wall gave me an instant glimpse into her life. Sometimes she wore her hair pulled back in a tight ponytail thing and sometimes it was down. She had chunky glasses like mine, but she only wore them for work. She lived in what looked like a nice little house in the suburbs. She worked as the manager at a restaurant connected to a hotel in a place called Burlington Township. McGwynn's. Twenty-five-cent wing special on karaoke nights.

She had a medium-size black dog with a furry white chest, named Elsie, who dug giant holes and slept on furniture. She was religious, or at least spiritual. Her page was filled with inspirational quotes and links to self-help articles. There were men in her life, I guess, but her relationship status was "It's complicated." I wondered if any of those complications were my father. And she had a son. A son she'd decided to keep. Amos—my (half?) brother—looked like he was maybe six or seven years old. He was on a tee-ball team and liked to swim and play with his puppy. As far as I could tell, she seriously loved this kid. I scrolled down picture after picture of the two of them together. I watched him grow up in her photos and I saw all the fun they had together at carnivals and arcades and parks.

Josie made a call to the restaurant and confirmed that Talia would be working that day. "If we get right on the road we'll be there before the dinner rush so the place won't be busy. You'll be able to talk."

Five minutes later we were in the car and on our way to meet my birth mother. As soon as we hit the highway Josie fell asleep and I was glad. She needed rest and I needed time to think about what I was going to do. Would I just march in there and ask for the manager? Then what? "Hi, Talia, it's me, your son. The one you gave up." I wasn't sure those words would even come out of my mouth. What if I made some other excuse for talking to her? Like I was planning a graduation party for me and my four friends. That way I could figure out if she was a nice person. Would she recognize me? Would she know who I was because I looked like Amos?

We arrived at the restaurant too soon. I wasn't ready. I drove around for ten minutes before I settled on a parking spot. Josie woke up while I was circling. She must've known I was stalling.

When I finally parked, I sat behind the wheel taking deep breaths. "What if she's not happy to see me? She gave me up for a reason. And I'm showing up here with a bunch of baggage. Not just the usual adopted kid baggage, but Sunnies baggage. Messed-up-plane-crash-orphan baggage."

Josie grabbed my hand. "She's gonna love you. She and Amos would be so lucky to have you in their lives."

Lucas would disagree. I got a sick feeling thinking about how we'd treated each other since the crash. My baby brother needed me and I wasn't there. And I'd needed him, too. But it was too late to turn back now. Not with Josie here holding my hand all the way across the parking lot.

When we stepped into the vestibule I could see her standing at the hostess desk. Her face was blocked by a specials sign on the door, but I recognized Talia's striped shirt from the photo of her and Amos and Elsie at the dog park. Josie reached for the inner door, but I stopped her. I let a family of five go ahead of us. The two younger kids were arguing over a phone and the mother threatened to take it away if they kept this up. When she saw me watching, she became self-conscious and apologized for her children. I waved it off and let the door close.

"What's wrong?" asked Josie.

"I don't want to meet her. Not now."

After eighteen years, my birth mother was less than ten feet away from me, but that was close enough for today. This woman with the big smile and over five hundred Facebook friends seemed like she'd made a pretty good life for herself. She had a cute kid and a dog, and a good job. She kinda looked like me and she had my smile. No doubt that she was my mother.

But she wasn't my mom. My mom slept in my bed when I had a nightmare, made the lightest, airiest angel food cake in the world, and when she caught me drawing on the wall she gave me my first sketchbook and pencils. My dad waited in line two hours with me to show the great Stan Lee one of my drawings. And my brother was a soccer star and the coolest person I knew and he needed me. They were my family. Maybe someday I'd come back here to meet Talia and we'd sit down together over a big plate of cheap wings and we'd talk about our favorite movies and whether she can do that thing with her tongue where you turn it to the side like I can or if she's a good artist. I'd ask her about why she had to give me away and we'd talk about Amos and Lucas and Mom and Dad and how much I loved them and how grateful I was that she'd allowed me to be their son.

But now I was going to Anguilla because that's where they died. I needed to be there with Josie and my friends and to find out the truth. For me and Lucas and for Mom and Dad. I walked away from the restaurant and from my birth mother because I already had parents. Even if I couldn't see or talk to them anymore, I already had parents.

On the morning of the flight, I drove to Josie's house. I carried my bag up to the porch just as Jack opened the door. It was here in this exact spot where Jack ripped up my sketchbook and tossed the pages into a puddle. I wondered if he was remembering it, too. Even now, I felt anxious standing this close to him. I knew what he'd done to Josie's softball coach. How did he feel about her boyfriend?

"Josie's upstairs," he said. "She's still not feeling great." He stepped aside to let me in. I put down my bag and we lingered by the stairs in silence.

I'm not good with silence. "I heard the meeting with your lawyer and the prosecutor went okay. Not that it's ever good to meet with a prosecutor, but if you have to, this was a good one, I guess. Right?"

Jack slid his hands back and forth over each other. "Still details to work out. Paperwork stuff. But they lifted the travel ban. They're letting me get on the plane."

"I'm glad," I said. "I know you're coming isn't that you believe someone sabotaged the plane. But that's okay. We just wouldn't want to do this without you."

"Thanks."

"For what it's worth," I said, "that guy deserved it. And more. I wish I'd been there to see it. Not that you needed me there. So how'd you get the charges dropped?"

"Believe it or not, the sonofabitch went to the D.A. and said he started the fight. Even claimed that we got in an argument about a parking space and he hit *me* with the wine bottle. Guess he didn't want anyone asking *why* I kicked his ass. Luckily none of the witnesses saw how it actually started. It kinda killed their case."

Jack seemed calmer. Less angry. I started to relax around him. "Probably no glory in prosecuting one of the Orphans of Sunny Horizons," I said.

"She's going to the police when we get back," he said.

"I know. She told me."

"It's gonna suck for her."

"Yeah. But she doesn't have to do it alone."

"No. Not anymore."

Josie appeared at the top of the stairs in an oversize sweatshirt and leggings. Her hair was up and she looked tired. She was lugging a giant pink suitcase she could barely move. Jack and I both rushed up at the same time to help her carry it down the stairs. For a moment we jostled over the handle, each trying to take over the heavy lifting. That was a battle I was sure to lose.

Josie sighed heavily and Jack let go of the handle. He gave me a nod. This time, we each grabbed an end. The case was heavier than I expected, and as we carried it down the steps, I was glad to share the load with him.

In the car to the airport, all three of us sat in the back. Jack was on one side, me on the other with Josie in between us. None of us had any idea if we were headed into something crazy and dangerous. We had no idea of what we might find. But at least we were going to find it together.

18

DAYANA

I THOUGHT WE WERE SAFE. WE'D MADE IT through security, stopped for breakfast burritos, and spent an hour in the waiting area without anybody in the airport recognizing los huérfanos de Sunny Horizons. It had been eight months since the crash and the novelty had mostly worn off. People had moved on to some other horrible tragedy: girl down the well, missing hiker in the woods. But you're never truly safe from the assholes of the world.

As we lined up to board the plane, two idiots in flip-flops and board shorts came running up to Josie and Jack like they were celebrities.

"Hey, it *is* you guys! The Sunnies, right? It's all of you. I told you, dickhead."

"Holy crap, are you, like, all getting on this plane together? Doesn't that freak your shit out?"

"Can we get a selfie?"

Archie stepped in front of Josie protectively and Harrison

covered his face with his briefcase. I saw the flash in Jack's eyes as his fingers curled into a fist. Before he could land himself in airport jail, I stepped in front. "No selfies today, fuckwads. Go away."

The smaller of the two fuckwads looked me up and down. "Who the hell are you supposed to be?"

"I'm sorry. I should've ID'd myself. I'm Dayana, the other one. And if you don't crawl away in a fucking hurry I will walk over to the desk and tell the nice lady in the jacket that you two were bragging that you know how to break into the cockpit during a flight." Johnny Flip-Flop tried to call my bluff, but when I started walking with purpose toward the desk, he and his asshole buddy went scattering, calling me unpleasant names under their breath.

Jack's hand unclenched.

Archie sighed. "Can I take you everywhere I go?"

"Sure. I'll be your designated dickhead repellant."

Josie smiled. "And you thought there was no reason for you to come with us."

"I'm glad I'm here," I said.

"Me too," said Harrison, finally emerging from behind his briefcase.

"Do me a favor though," said Josie. "Don't ever call yourself 'the other one' again."

I tried to imagine what it must've been like for Jack, Josie, Archie, and Harrison, waiting to get on that plane. For weeks, they'd been excited, looking forward to this trip and to getting answers about their parents. But now it was here.

Now they would actually have to sit on an airplane, buckle themselves in, and fly over the ocean.

Archie babbled nonstop about what movies he hoped they'd have on board. Jack put in his earbuds to shut out the world, but couldn't stop looking out the window of the terminal. Josie made half a dozen trips to the restroom. Each time she came out, she looked greener than the last. Harrison stared at his three-ring binder full of research on plane crashes. I suggested he stash it back in the briefcase before any other passengers could see it. Yet somehow, with everything the four of them had going on that morning, I was the one who almost hadn't made it to the airport.

The night before the flight did not go as planned. I hadn't told my parents about the trip. They would've tried to stop me from going if they'd found out. I had to wait until they were asleep before I could pack. In the early morning, I'd slip out the back door and meet Harrison at his car down the block. Simple, right?

The problem was that Papi had a bad day. It had started as a good day. I'd come out of my room to find Papi in a suit, headed for the train into the city for some meeting he was excited about. From what I could tell, when he got off the train, there was a message waiting on his phone cancelling the appointment. By the time he turned around and came home, he was ready to pop some pills and disappear into the bedroom. Mami and I had to work extra hard to keep him going. I smuggled the pills out of his room and she took him for a walk.

My escape plan was screwed. I listened quietly from my room, but they didn't go to sleep until after one in the morning. When I was finally sure they were out, I snuck down to the bathroom in my pajamas to grab my toothbrush and makeup kit. The fact that it was too big to bring on the plane with me gave me the shakes. I flicked a look at the mirror. I didn't like to look at myself with no makeup on, my freckly skin unprotected from the world. I thought about what Josie said to me in the nurse's office. They *needed* me to come with them? She said *I* was the only one who wasn't falling apart for the last six months? The only reason I wasn't falling apart after the crash was that—unlike them—I was *already* broken in pieces. But I had to pull it together for her. For all of them.

I opened the bottom drawer under the sink where I'd stuffed Papi's collection of prescription bottles. It had been a while since I'd done this. My brain was telling me not to—that I didn't need to take pills anymore. I could get through this trip on my own. But that same brain was also racing with bad thoughts of what might happen on the plane: Harrison freaking out, Josie melting down again, Jack getting in another fight.

I caved. I uncapped one of the anti-anxiety meds, placed a pill on my tongue, and stuck my face under the faucet to wash it down. Get a good night's sleep. Be ready to go in the morning. Like Josie said, they were counting on me. After further review, I realized this might require a stronger dose, so I swallowed two more pills and went out to the yard with my vape pen.

I sat down in a lounge chair and scrolled through my phone as I inhaled. No social media activity from Josie tonight. She'd only posted three pictures in the last month. One was a sketch Archie had drawn of the two of them snuggled on a couch together. They looked happy. Content. The other picture was a selfie Archie took of all five of us at the lunch table. His head took up half the frame, nearly blocking Josie entirely. Harrison was looking in the other direction, Jack was half out of the shot, and I had my eyes closed. I saved the photo to my phone and closed my eyes as the pills eased their way through my system. I let the tension escape from my body.

I opened my eyes a millimeter. When did it get light out? Mami was standing over me and I was confused as shit. My mouth felt like I'd swallowed a big gulp of sand at the beach. "What time is it?"

"Did you sleep out here?" she asked. I jammed the vape pen into my pocket as I bolted out of the chair. My phone had line after line of increasingly concerned texts from Harrison. He was down the block. We were supposed to leave ten minutes ago. I started running toward the house even as I typed to Harrison.

Shit. B there soon.

Mami called after me as I tore ass into the house. "Cálmate, Daya," she said. "It's spring break."

But I was not relaxed. I was in a full-blown panic. I hadn't packed or even located my passport. I was still wearing pajamas. I could not miss this flight!

Mami followed me into my room as I yanked clothes from drawers. "Where are you going?"

I had no time to make up an excuse. "I'm going to the airport. We're flying to Anguilla today."

"Anguilla? With who?"

"All of us. Josie, Jack, Harrison, Archie. It's a long story. They want to find out what happened to their parents. Get closure. Whatever. Could you please not ask questions and just help me pack? I have no idea what to bring and Harrison is waiting in the car."

She grabbed a duffel bag out of my closet. "I'm coming with you."

"No, you can't."

"I should be there. I was supposed to be on that flight the first time. I can help. Please let me help you."

"How is you being there gonna help Josie? You think she wants to sit on the plane with the woman who was sleeping with her father? What she's going through right now—it's hard enough. Please don't make it worse for her."

I could see on her face that those words stung. "Open the bag." She went to work, yanking things from my closet and throwing them in as I held the bag open. "It will be warm, but it might get cooler at night. You'll be flying over the

Caribbean Sea," she said quietly. "Look down and see how blue the water is. Like in Tortuguero. I was looking ahead to that."

"You were looking *forward* to that."

"Yes."

We worked as a team, running down the list and packing in record time. Finally, I zipped up the bag and we stood looking at each other and breathing heavily.

"I'm sorry," she said suddenly. "When all of it was happening, I didn't think about who I was hurting. I didn't think about Josie or Jack. I didn't think about your father. I didn't think about you. I couldn't. I'm sorry you felt like you had to keep the secret. I went through this when I was a child. My father . . . your abuelo . . . he wasn't a good husband to Mami. And I swore to myself that I . . . As much as you hate me for what I did, I promise you I hate myself more."

"I don't hate you," I said. And I meant it. "What you did to Papi and to the Clays sucked big-time. But if I'm being honest, our family was already way messed up before you had an affair. We were all trying escape in our own way."

"Escape. Good word. We have done a lot of escaping."

"Do you think about what your life would be, if we'd stayed in Costa Rica?"

"Sometimes. You were little, so maybe you don't feel it so much."

"Feel what?"

"Desplazada. Displaced."

"Are you kidding? My whole life."

"Really?"

"Josie says I always put myself on the outside."

"Josie's very wise."

"Mami, are you glad we came here?"

She took a long pause before answering. "Your papi, he said we came here for the American Dream. I don't know that we found it, or even if it's a real thing. But we found friends. Familia. They were our new home. And that's all I would ever wish for you."

Harrison's car screeched up in front of the house.

I started for the door when I realized, "My passport!"

"I'll get it," she said. "Go to the car. I'll meet you out front!" Mami started out of the room, but she stopped in the doorway. "I'm proud of you, Daya. For everything you've done for them."

"I haven't done anything."

"You've been a good friend to them, even when they didn't know it. You try to hide it, but you have a big, open heart. Like your papi. That's why the world hurts you both so much."

My phone buzzed.

Where are you?! We can NOT be late.

I scooped up my bag and rushed out.

Harrison was waiting by the front door and he helped me put my bag in the car. "I waited down the street like we said. Where were you?"

"Look, I'm here now, aren't I?"

The door swung open and Mami came charging out of

the house with the passport, two bagels, and two bottles of water. "Hi, Harrison. Sorry to keep you waiting."

"Um, hola."

She handed everything to me. "I'm going to call the company and have them turn on your international calling. You call me when you get there, okay?" She didn't step away from the car. She hovered there right beside my window.

"Did I forget something?"

She leaned down, stuck her head inside, and kissed me on the cheek. "Te quiero, princesa." She spun away quickly and walked back toward the house.

Harrison started up the car just as Papi came out of the kitchen with two cups of coffee. He handed one to Mami. I could see she was emotional as she told him what was happening. Harrison hit the gas and as we pulled away, I looked back to see Papi holding Mami in his arms.

It felt like hours before we finally made it down the aisle of the plane. Every jerk in front of us had an oversize carry-on that had to be hammered into the overhead compartment. Harrison walked in front of me, his briefcase of research in his arms. A couple of times, he stopped dead in the middle of the aisle and looked back over his shoulder as if he might be considering making a break for it. Each time he slowed down I gave him a nudge with my bag to keep him moving.

"No turning back now, kid."

"I hope that wasn't supposed to be a pep talk," said Josie,

walking behind me with her own enormous bag. "Because it sounded like a warning."

"Why don't you let someone carry that bag for you, Jo."

She shot me a look. "I'm fine. I got it."

"So what am I *supposed* to say right now?" I asked.

"How about something in Spanish that we can't understand," said Archie.

"Buen viaje."

"I know what that means," said Josie. "And that is wishful thinking."

Josie and Archie slid into seats directly in front of Harrison, Jack, and me. When we reached our row, Harrison swiveled his head around like a trapped animal.

"No," he insisted. "I can't sit in a window seat."

I slid past him and took the seat myself. Harrison started to sit on the aisle, but Jack grabbed him by the shirt.

"Look, man, I get the whole panic thing. We're all a little freaked out," said Jack. "Remember how you liked my size when I helped you kick your dad to the curb? Well, I'm six four and two hundred and forty pounds and I don't do middle. Plus, my doctor warned me that flying might make the post-concussive stuff in my brain worse. So I need every inch of space I can get. Any questions?"

Harrison quietly took his place in the middle and buckled his seat belt.

While we waited for takeoff, Harrison narrated the preparations like he was reading a flight manual. "Cockpit doors closed and locked. Cabin door closed and secured. Flight attendants check seat belts and deliver the safety instructions. Flight attendants take their seats. Engines on. Brakes released. The plane taxis to the runway . . ."

I could tell that the running commentary was making Jack mental, but he let it be and just gripped the armrest even tighter. I could feel the nervous energy coming off both of them as the engines fired up and we started to move. A rush of speed as we raced down the runway, the nose lifted up, and we were in the air. Next to me, Harrison had not taken a breath since we left the gate. Jack's back was rigid, his eyes focused straight ahead. In front of us, Josie and Archie didn't seem to be doing much better. Through the gap in the seats I could see their tightly clasped hands.

I poked my head through. "You okay, Josie?"

She managed a nod.

"Jack?" I asked.

"The doctor didn't lie," he said. "It's like someone jabbing a fork into my brain. But I've felt worse."

When we passed through the clouds I leaned into Harrison's space. "Breathe," I said. "In and out. Or do that freaky pi thing if you have to. We're good." I hoped I sounded calm, because I wasn't sure I was breathing much myself. I was so focused on the four of them that I barely noticed my whole body had been tensed up since the moment we sat down. It *was* going to be fine. Maybe not fun, but fine. Harrison was still on alert, though, bracing himself for a sudden drop. On the ground, he was always just a few bad thoughts away from a panic attack. Up here, I was afraid he might completely snap.

"Still climbing," he muttered to himself between deep breaths. "Level off will begin at approximately thirty-five thousand feet."

"Hey, Harrison, I was thinking," I said.

"Light turbulence at this altitude is perfectly normal."

"Right. So I had this idea. It might sound crazy. Just hear me out. I was thinking about how your dad's gone and I know it turned out he was kind of a shit burger. But he was fun, right? At least most of the time? He took you to strip clubs and all that. You liked having him around. And now you're alone in that house again."

Somehow the mention of his dad cut through his fear of falling from the sky. He looked at me like I *was* crazy. "I'm not asking my father to move back in the house. He was taking my mom's money."

"That's not what I'm saying. Look . . . We have an extra room in my house. It's the little one next to mine. It's pretty cramped and the window has a view of the Olsens' nasty garbage cans instead of Josie's pool. But it's got a sweet twin bed and lots of outlets for your devices. What do you think?"

Harrison tilted his head like a confused dog. "You want me to live with you?"

Jack gave me a look as he rubbed his temples.

"And my delightful parents. For however long you need. You've been in the house. We only have the one bathroom, and the shower never gets hot enough. But you can rent out your place and save some money for college. Or sell it. I just thought: You don't know what you're doing next year. Neither do I. Vanesa can be a pain in the ass, but she's very organized. She'll help you get your shit together for school and we'll figure it all out. Better than being alone, isn't it?"

Harrison was taking a long time to think about it, so Jack chimed in. "It's tons of fun there. I mean, last time they served me a beer at two in the morning."

"I don't see you offering. And you probably have *eight* guest rooms."

"I'm kidding. Not an easy thing to do when your brain is exploding in your skull. But I think it's a cool idea. Very generous. You should do it, man."

Harrison bounced his head around like he was weighing his options. "Dayana has always been generous with me," he said. "Did you know that right after the crash she came over to my house with a big bag full of drugs?"

"*Medication.* Prescribed by a doctor."

"Not *my* doctor," said Harrison. "And not yours either."

"I said *a* doctor."

Harrison smiled. "Or two. Or five."

Jack asked, "How big was the bag?"

"Huge," said Harrison. "Like Santa Claus's toy sack." They both laughed and I felt them finally start to relax.

Josie and Archie turned around. "What's so funny?"

"You missed it, Jo. We were just talking about Dayana bringing Harrison drugs," said Jack.

Archie whispered, "Today? On the plane?"

Harrison laughed again. "No. When I was sitting shiva."

"Aren't you supposed to bring, like, sandwiches or a casserole?" asked Josie.

"Listen, he was a total mess," I said. "So I brought him a thoughtful gift to help him relax. Just some things I had lying around the house."

"Drugs," said Josie.

"Medicine," I said. "Okay, sort of drugs."

It's going to sound corny and weird coming from me. But maybe for the first time in almost fifteen years this group felt like . . . a group. Friends. And whether I liked it or not, I was responsible for them.

Spoiler alert: I kinda liked it.

It wasn't the loud bang and the violent jostling of the airplane that startled me awake. It was Harrison's death grip on my arm. It felt like he was squeezing right through to the bones in my wrist. The *Fasten Seat Belt* light binged on and the captain warned us of choppy air ahead. But "choppy" was not the word for it. In an instant, the plane was being bounced around, whipping us from side to side, up and down. Harrison was gasping for air and I could see Jack's fingers digging into the armrest, his jaw clenched tight. In front of us, Josie was clinging to Archie. I lifted the shade and looked out the window as we dipped and jolted. Nothing but endless blue water below us.

19

JOSIE

WE WERE GOING DOWN! THAT'S WHAT EVERY cell in my body was screaming. This wasn't a *patch of turbulence* or *choppy skies* or whatever they say when they're trying to convince you you're not going down. The plane was breaking apart and we were going to crash in the water and die. Archie was trying not to look terrified, but I could tell by the way he was clutching my hand that he felt it, too. What the hell were we thinking, coming on this trip? Was somebody trying to get us, like they got our parents? Behind me, I could hear Harrison hyperventilating and Dayana trying to talk him down. The plane was shaking like crazy and taking huge drops. Big roller coaster drops that slam your stomach into your throat. Why weren't they making any announcements?

A piece of luggage slammed inside the compartment over my head. I whipped around, expecting to see a big hole in the side of the plane, but instead my eyes caught Jack's.

They were wild with fear and I hated it. Jack didn't get scared. He scared *other people*. He was the one who told me that the sounds in the night were normal house noises and checked out the yard when I thought I saw someone through the window. Only now, he looked as frightened as I felt and that made everything worse. In the row ahead of ours, a baby was screaming its head off. Of course the baby had to be right in front of me. Nothing the mother did was working to calm it down. I scanned the rest of the plane. Some people looked properly freaked, but others were casually reading or watching movies or flat-out sleeping. What was wrong with them?! Why were they not panicking?

The rational part of my brain tried to explain that they weren't panicking because this *was* just turbulence. If something horrible was really happening to the plane, the flight crew wouldn't be so calm. I could see them strapped into their seats, chatting away. But what if they were trained *not* to react? That's what I'd do if I ran an airline. I'd make them learn how to stay calm and pretend to be joking around with each other even if we headed for a watery grave. Were they secretly saying prayers and texting goodbyes to loved ones? That's ridiculous, said my brain. Nobody keeps a poker face when your plane is about to crash in the ocean. Okay, but what about how people always say you should trust your instincts? If you get a bad feeling in your gut, follow it. Right now my instincts were screaming louder than that wailing baby.

The plane kept rising and falling with loud clunks, and

the baby kept wailing louder and louder. I wanted to be any-where but here. I felt the pull. It would be so easy to slip down to the bottom of the pool. Shut down like I did after Mom and Daddy died. It's what got me through those first few days. If I let go now, I wouldn't feel any of it. No fear . . .

Archie squeezed my hand as the plane lurched again. Squeezed it as if he knew exactly what I was feeling. No, I wasn't letting go. No matter how scary this was I had to stay here. For him and for Jack.

"We're gonna get through this," said Archie. But I heard the hitch in his voice.

What did they tell Mom and Daddy and their friends when their plane was going down? Did they call it *choppy skies*? A *patch of turbulence*? Or were they honest? Maybe there wasn't even time for honesty. If someone did cause the plane to crash, maybe it just . . . fell without warning and none of them even knew it was happening.

But I saw the pictures of the crash. The plane didn't explode before it dropped into the water. They knew they were going down. They had to.

What did they say to one another in those last moments? Did Daddy try to clear his conscience? Did he confess to the affair? Did he apologize to Mom for cheating on her with her friend? I hated to think that those were the last words she heard. And yet as angry as I was at Daddy, I found myself hoping that in the end he found some peace. The more I thought about it, the more I wanted to believe that he did confess. I hoped that in those last moments Mom even forgave him. So as our plane was dipping and diving through the sky and Archie and I were holding on to each other for dear life, that's what I did. I confessed.

I hadn't been feeling good in a long while. Months. When it started I just felt tired and . . . off. Like I was exhausted all the time but I couldn't really sleep. I'd be crazy hungry, but as soon as I tried to eat, I'd feel too sick to get anything down. I didn't overthink it, though. It was just another one of those times when my body broke down due to stress.

Only I wasn't that stressed. Things were starting to go really well with Archie. What the hell, I might as well say it. I was in love with him. I'd finally said it to him on the drive home from seeing his birth mother. Or not seeing her. It wasn't one of those movie moments where you're on the beach with the waves crashing down and the music swelling. We were on the Garden State Parkway, exit 98, which is pretty much the opposite of that.

"I'm not feeling so good," I said. "Car sickness."

He screeched the car onto the exit ramp and pulled over. Then he ran to my side of the car and helped me out. "Take deep breaths. There you go. Can I get you ginger ale? There's a store right down there. We don't have to drive. I can run and get it."

I looked up at him and before I knew it, I said, "I love you, Archie."

He waited to see if I was kidding.

"I do," I said. "I love you."

"Oh," he said, breaking into a wide smile. "I love you, too."

Booting into Coach Murph's Mustang had been hella satisfying. I hoped that he'd never get the smell out. Throwing up had never felt so . . . cleansing. Like getting rid of poison from my system. But then it happened again. Jack and I were opening our acceptance emails from Rutgers and I had to run to the bathroom. I puked a third time when Jack and I were meeting with his lawyer outside the D.A.'s office. I barely made it to the bathroom on that one. Each time it happened I came up with excuses for myself. I was feeling anxious or upset or I ate something weird and or didn't get enough sleep. But then a couple weeks ago I'd *woken up* sick. And since then I'd felt like I could throw up from the moment I woke up *every* morning.

Anyone with half a brain and a day or two of sex ed class would say I was in major denial. I even managed to explain away my first missed period. Stress can cause that, too. And I wasn't always that regular anyway. Archie and I were careful, I told myself. This couldn't happen to me. But it's not like I was one of those girls who thinks she's just getting fat until she goes to the prom and then . . . surprise! Of course I knew it somewhere in my brain. I just couldn't go there.

So I just . . . went on. I shoved it out of my mind like it didn't exist. I kept up the lie to myself that I had a lingering flu or something. But one night Archie and I were watching some bad reality show on his couch and a commercial came on for one of those home pregnancy tests. A young couple was so excited about their first child! It was a blessing! It was like those two cute actors were looking right at me. *Are you that stupid, Josie?* they were saying. *Are you going to keep pretending like it's not real, like it's not happening to you?!*

Archie got up to refill the popcorn and I just sat there, finally letting it wash over me. My period wasn't *irregular*. I'd missed it. Twice! I wasn't sick in the morning. I had *morning sickness*. I jumped off the couch. The whole room was spinning. Now I was really going to puke. Archie came back and I mumbled some excuse about not feeling well.

His face dropped. "You were supposed to stay the night. Is something wrong?"

I could barely manage to put together a decent story. I even forgot to kiss him goodbye as I rushed out the door. As soon as I got outside, I pulled out my phone. I was panicking, but I couldn't tell Jack. Without thinking, I called Dayana and she answered on the first ring. I'm not sure if she even understood what I was saying, but it didn't matter.

"Come pick me up," she said.

She came out of the house and walked to the driver's side. "Slide over, Clay."

I asked her to drive to a pharmacy far away to make sure no one would see me buying the test. I imagined the headlines on some gossip site. *Sunny Horizon Orphan Knocked Up! Sunny with a Chance of Child!*

In the store, Dayana held up two boxes from the shelf:

one blue, one pink. Both claimed to be the most accurate test on the market. "Which one? Ah, fuck it, let's do both."

She took them to the counter for me. When the clerk eyed her she stared him down. "It's for my grandma."

Dayana drove me home and walked me into the house. Jack was eating pizza in the kitchen. "I thought you were sleeping at Archie's."

I couldn't even look at him.

"I called her with an emergency," Dayana said. "I'm going through some stuff. *Girl stuff.*"

I knew Jack could tell something was up. He could always tell. "Everything okay, Jo?"

"Yep. All good." My voice sounded high and fake.

"You and Archie are good?"

"Uh-huh."

"So this is the real deal, huh? You two. Have you two talked about what happens next year?" he asked.

Dayana grabbed one of his pizza slices. "Honestly, Jack," she said. "Can the girl just get through today? We're having a sleepover. Don't bother us."

Dayana kept me from sprinting up the stairs into my room. She led me to my bathroom, closed the door, and locked it. "You can do this, Jo." She opened the blue box first, unwrapped the stick, and handed it to me. "Have at it."

Hand shaking, I held the stick under the stream and put it on the counter to wait. Three minutes. "What do I do for three minutes besides panic?"

"Know any good jokes?"

"I am one."

"Don't say that."

"You're right. It's not funny."

"So . . . you and Archie, huh?"

"Yeah. Me and Archie."

To take my mind off things, Dayana told me about Connor, the guy she used to like. How he slept with her and then pretended it never happened.

"I'm sorry," I said. "That's the worst. And you didn't even have someone to talk to about it."

"No, I didn't."

"You do now." The time on my phone ran out. "Can you look?" I asked.

Dayana picked up the stick. "It's a plus, Jo."

"No. No. There could be false positives, right? The tests say they're not a hundred percent accurate."

"Let's give the other one a shot."

This time I sat down to pee on the stick and I couldn't get anything to come out. Dayana turned on the water for inspiration. Finally, I squeezed out enough and put this stick on the counter next to the first.

Another three minutes of hell. Washing my hands. Drying them off. Then washing them again.

Bing. In the window a tiny pink YES popped up.

I wanted to scream and throw the boxes across the room, but I knew Jack would hear and come running. Dayana stuffed all of the evidence into her bag as I sat down on the floor of the bathroom and wrapped my arms around my knees, hugging my body in as close as I could. Dayana put her arms around me and held on tight. I buried my mouth into her shoulder so that Jack wouldn't hear me crying. Neither of us said anything.

I didn't want to be a mother. I didn't want to be an orphan. I just wanted to be.

I heard my phone buzzing on the sink.

Hope UR OK.

Goodnight. Love you.

Dayana stayed with me all night.

I woke to my phone buzzing again. "That's Archie. You should go home."

"You sure? I'll stay as long as you want."

"I've got to get out of this bathroom some time."

"What're you gonna do? You know, about—"

"I don't know. I don't know."

"I'm here . . . for whatever. Whenever."

"Thanks. Love ya, D."

"You too, Jo. It's gonna be all right." She left and I picked up my phone.

Good morning. Hope U slept well.

Let me know if you want to talk.

UPS guy!

Birth certificate. Aaaaaah!

Ok. Don't want to beg. But please can U join my panic party?

P.S. UPS guy was wearing shorts. Is it spring already?

Archie could always make me smile even at the worst of

times. And this was pretty bad. I couldn't ignore him. I couldn't make him go through this on his own. I looked through a stack of drawings he'd given me. I had to do this. For him. I texted back. *On my way.*

I didn't know how I was going to face Archie, but he needed me and that was all that mattered. I mean, he and I . . . We were . . . This was our . . . God, it was hard to admit, even in my head. Hard not to drive my car into a tree, too.

When Archie opened the door, I went into his arms. For a second I almost told him right there, but he handed me the envelope from the state.

"I couldn't open it."

Archie's mother was eighteen! That was the first thing I saw. I watched him read it and I knew I couldn't say anything today. I had to help Archie and not make things any more complicated for him. He'd been waiting a long time for this day. He deserved to have it. But keeping the secret from him was even harder than I could've imagined. I don't know which part was worse, dealing with it alone or lying to him. On the drive to his birth mother's restaurant, I pretended to be asleep. It was easier that way. I promised myself I'd tell Archie the next time we were together.

But I didn't tell him. And then I didn't tell him again. And again. Guess I was just waiting for the right time.

Of course, none of that would matter when our plane broke apart and crashed in the Atlantic Ocean. We were still thrashing about more than ever. The overhead bin kept opening and closing with a thud behind me. Every time it slammed shut, I jumped and felt the seat belt, tight across my middle. It felt like this had been going on for hours. And still no word from the flight crew. At least the baby in front of me had stopped crying. Through the space between seats, I could see that he had fallen asleep in his relieved mother's arms. She kissed the top of his head.

"What were you just thinking about?" Archie asked.

I told him. I spoke softly so that only Archie could hear me, but I was surprised at how easily it came out.

"I'm pregnant."

He looked at me like I was making a crazy joke. "Trying to take my mind off the turbulence? That's desperate."

"It's true," I said. "I took a test. Twice. I'm pregnant, Archie."

"You're serious?"

I nodded. Archie's lips moved, but he didn't make a sound. It was like he was doing one of his rambling things, only nothing was coming out.

"Good timing, huh?" I said.

"You were feeling sick. This is why?"

"Yeah."

"How long? How long have you known?"

"A few days," I said. "I don't know why I waited to tell you."

"But . . . we were . . . careful?"

"Not every time."

Archie looked like I'd just dropped a weight on him. He probably had a thousand questions. But he didn't ask any of them. I don't really remember him saying much at all. He just unbuckled his seat belt and held on to me. The plane was still chaotic, the luggage and the cans and the carts banging around the aisle. Archie was untethered now, and a heavy jolt might send him flying. So I held on to him.

I don't know how long we clung to each other, but at some point the plane stopped rocking as it finally traveled into smooth air. The captain removed the fasten seat belt sign, and the flight attendants got up to start putting the cabin back in order. All over the plane, people were laughing and breathing easier. I saw Jack pry his fingers off the armrests.

Archie let go of me. "I have to use the bathroom," he said. I thought it was strange that he was taking his sketchbook with him. But he gave me a smile and kissed me on the cheek. "Be right back."

The plane was steady and quiet.

We were going to make it.

20

ARCHIE

I LOCKED MYSELF IN THE AIRPLANE BATH-
room with my sketchbook so that Josie wouldn't see me
FREAK out. When she told me she was pregnant, I managed to keep it together just long enough to survive the turbulence and stagger up the aisle. But now as I looked at myself
in the mirror, I wasn't sure I'd ever be ready to come out.

I let my glasses fall into the sink and splashed water on
my face. This was not the face of someone ready to be a
father. This was the face of someone who still read comics
and had a room full of action figures. Look at the job I did
taking care of Lucas. Imagine what I'd do with a baby. A
baby with two teenagers for parents, with no grandparents.
A baby who was black and white and would feel everything
I'd felt growing up. Confused and lonely and unsure of
where he belongs. Only he or she didn't have my mom and
dad. This kid would be relying on *me* to make it better. I sat

down on the closed toiled seat, opened my sketchbook, and started to draw.

Bang! Bang! Bang!

"Archie, you okay in there?" Jack was knocking on the bathroom door.

"Be out in a sec!" My voice sounded unnaturally high and shaky.

Bang! Bang! Bang!

"Hurry up, man. We're landing soon."

"Coming!"

I wiped off my face and shoved my glasses onto my nose. Josie was waiting for me. I knew she was just as scared as I was. Josie had been disappointed by so many people she'd counted on. Her coach. Her dad. I couldn't add myself to that list. I wasn't sure if I could be strong enough for her, but maybe I could *pretend* to be strong enough. I'd spent my childhood telling lies. I was prepared to tell the biggest one of my life.

I unlocked the door and slid it open. Jack was standing there staring at me. I didn't know what to say. I didn't want him to see what might be on my face or in my eyes. I just needed to be away from him. So I gave him a thumbs-up. Jack look surprised, but gave me a thumbs-up in return as I squeezed past his enormous body to return to my seat.

As I walked down the aisle, the baby started screaming again. It was a terrible, piercing cry that went right through me. Dayana was in my seat when I returned. She got up as soon as she saw me. I could see on her face that she knew.

"Are you okay?" Josie asked. Her eyes were wide and clear, but she nervously chewed on her bottom lip.

I took a deep breath and did what I needed to do. "I'm good," I lied, ignoring the baby's screams. "Great."

For the rest of the flight, I stuffed down the urge to panic and played the part of the caring, selfless boyfriend. Like I was an actor in a movie. I asked how she was feeling and how far along she was. (Nauseated and about two months.) I told her we'd go see a doctor as soon as we got home and we wouldn't have to tell anyone else until she was ready.

Every time the baby cried, I felt my eye twitch. And I could see Josie flinching, too. I imagined what someone cool and together might say in this situation if he was cool and together. I promised her that whatever decisions had to be made, we'd make together. Neither of us mentioned the infant yelling its head off two feet from our faces.

The good thing about trying to keep Josie from seeing me wig out about the pregnancy was that I didn't have time to be afraid of the second flight. And there would've been plenty to be afraid of. The plane was small and ancient. Just like our parents, we were flying from St. Martin to Anguilla, and just like them we were the only five passengers on the flight. There was no rampway to the plane, no connection to the terminal. Just a rusty set of metal stairs in the middle of the hot tarmac. But there was only so much room in my panicky brain for fear. The needle was already pinned on red.

As we walked out to the plane, Harrison looked back toward the terminal.

"Move it along, Rebkin," said Dayana. "What's the holdup?"

"Nothing," said Harrison. He tapped three times against the outside of the plane as he climbed up.

That's a guy who is not good at lying, I thought. I saw *everything* that was going on inside him.

All the seats on the tiny plane were singles. We were each on our own. Josie took the seat directly behind me; I kissed her before I sat down. Still keeping up the lie. But I made sure not to look to see if Jack was watching.

For a small plane, the engines were incredibly loud. But even if they'd been silent, I'm not sure any of us would've talked during that flight.

We were about to relive our parents' last twenty minutes on earth. I thought about Mom and Dad and the others boarding a plane just like this. Laughing, excited to be with their best friends in the world. Together they'd had fifteen years of good times and difficult ones. There were fights and divorces. Illness. Money problems. Kid problems. Lots of kid problems. And they had their secrets. But these were the people they'd chosen to share their vacations with—to share their lives with.

I was with my best friends, too. We hadn't chosen to be thrown back together, but we'd chosen to be here, on this flight, together. And we *were* together. Behind me was the girl I loved, and she was pregnant with our kid. Mom's and

Dad's lives ended on a flight like this. Mine was never going to be the same.

The plane bounced along the runway before lurching into the air. We stayed low enough where we could still see boats and the reef under the water. In front of me, Jack reached across the aisle and squeezed Dayana's hand. I looked over at Harrison, whose eyes were fixed on his watch. I knew exactly what he was doing. Counting off the exact amount of time it had taken before our parents' plane crashed. I saw him mouthing the numbers. Three, two, one. When we passed that milestone, he let out a long sigh. I craned my head around to see Josie behind me.

She was looking out the window with tears streaming down her face. "It's so beautiful." I could barely hear her over the engines.

The water was crystal blue below us. It was so close in color to the sky that it was tough to tell where one ended and the other began.

The plane passed over the beach and landed gently on the runway in Anguilla. I walked down the metal stairs and touched the ground. My parents had never made it this far.

I gave Josie a squeeze. "I'll catch up to you in a minute," I said.

"What's wrong?"

"I need to make something right."

As Josie walked away I reached into my pocket for my phone and made an international call.

Lucas took a few rings to answer. "Archie?"

"Hey."

"Where are you?"

"I'm here."

"Anguilla."

"Yeah."

"Oh."

"I just wanted to say . . . I'm sorry, Lucas. You were right about me being a shitty brother. But you were pretty shitty, too."

"Yeah," he said. "I guess I was."

"I'm sorry I didn't ask you to come here with us. I'm sorry I wasn't there to be your brother . . . I'm sorry about Mom and Dad . . ."

The phone had gone silent. "Lucas? Lucas, are you still there?"

"I'm here. What's it like?"

"I'm still at the airport, but . . . we flew over the beach. The sand is very white and the water is so blue and . . . It's . . . I feel them here. I can't really explain it, but I feel them."

"Yeah . . ."

"How about we come back here when school ends. You and me."

"Really?"

"Really."

"I'd like that."

". . . Lucas?"

"Yeah?"

"I'll never let you down again. I promise."

He didn't say anything for a long time, but I could tell he was still there.

"Archie? We were lucky to have them, weren't we?"

"Very lucky."

The sun was beating down on our necks as we exited the Anguilla airport to look for a taxi. Josie was flushed and sweaty, but she wouldn't let me pull her suitcase to the taxi stand. The rush for cars was total chaos. Every time a car would pull up, there would be a mad dash to claim it. Harrison spotted an open taxi and sprinted across the road, just barely missing being struck by a minivan. He waved us over with both arms. Dayana tried to point out that the car was too small for the five of us and our bags, but Harrison insisted it would be fine.

Jack squeezed in up front, his knees pressing into his chest, while the rest of us piled into the back. Josie sat on my lap and I put the seat belt carefully around both of us. In the process, my hand touched her stomach. The moment was not lost on either of us.

I was barely aware of the driver, who did nothing but complain for the entire ride. Jack did his best to ignore him, too, but he was getting more agitated as the trip went on.

Dayana leaned over. "Hey, how much cash do you guys have on you? 'Cause I'm thinking this ride is going to be fucking expensive."

Reaching for our wallets in the cramped backseat was like playing Twister. I was very aware of Josie being pushed or jostled. We each fished out our money and Harrison added up the collection. It was clear we were going to be short. When the driver realized we didn't have enough money to get to the hotel, he started yelling and cursing. Jack told him to stop at an ATM, but the guy wasn't having any of it. He didn't want to take us all in the first place and now we were costing him money. He was ranting about goddamn entitled American kids and threatening to call the police and Jack finally told him to pull over. I took in our surroundings. Nothing but open fields of grass and rocks.

The driver pulled the car over to the side of the road.

"What the hell," said Dayana. "He expects us to get out? In the middle of freaking nowhere?"

"Better than getting arrested," said Jack. "We'll flag down another cab. Let's go. We're not giving this asshole our money." Dayana tried to reason with the driver, but Jack was already unloading all of our bags. We had no choice but to climb out. The second the door closed, the driver sped off and left us.

Josie shoved Jack. "How did you let that happen? Why couldn't you just apologize? Look around. There are no cabs here. It's a hundred and ten degrees. How the hell are we going to get to the hotel?"

Harrison studied the GPS on his phone. "It's approximately a fifty-five-minute walk," he said, looking around at the area. "I can get us there. But we should start moving right away."

Josie looked even more flushed and exhausted.

"Have a seat on my bag," I said. "We'll call another taxi service."

Jack slung his bag over his shoulder. "By the time one comes, we'll already be there."

"He's probably right," said Harrison. "We saw the shortage at the airport."

Jack started to walk. "We didn't come here to wait around. Let's move."

"It's too hot to walk," I said, keeping an eye on Josie. "We don't even have water."

Jack shook his head. "Oh. Are you hot and thirsty? You want me to carry you?"

"Jack, just wait for the car," I said.

"Waste of time. Walking will suck, but at least we'll be there. Let's just go."

"No," said Josie.

"Come on, Jo," said Jack. "You're holding us up. We walk, we jump in the pool, we have a drink . . ."

Josie kicked over her suitcase. "I said no!"

Harrison stood the suitcase back up. "You overpacked your suitcase. That's why you don't want to drag it. You really didn't need to bring more than—"

"You don't know what the hell you're talking about," Josie snapped. "I can't believe we followed you down here."

Harrison looked stunned. "I never forced anybody . . ."

"What the hell are we doing?" Josie asked. "How are we going to find out what happened to our parents when we can't even find a cab! You want to walk? Fine, let's walk. And when I pass out, just leave me on the side of the road until someone finds me."

Jack stopped. "Are you feeling sick again? Why didn't you tell me? Here, let me take your bag."

She shoved him away. "I'm not sick!" she blurted. "I'm pregnant. I'm fucking pregnant."

The group went silent as her words sunk in.

Then Dayana rushed to hug her. "At least it's out there now and we can deal with it."

Josie took a step back. "I don't want to talk about it. I just want to get out of here."

Harrison was stepping into the road. "I'll call for another taxi."

Jack stared at Josie.

She waited for him to say something, to hold her, to do *anything*.

Instead he pressed his palm into his forehead and turned on me. "You must be psyched." His face was red and his shirt was soaked through with sweat. A vein throbbed in the side of his head.

"I just told him, Jack," said Josie. "On the plane. He didn't know."

Jack kept his focus on me. "You love this, don't you?"

I didn't know how to answer. I was still trying to keep up the lie, but he was attacking. "What? I . . ."

"You had to be scared before. It's only natural. You had to worry that someday Josie would leave you like she did all the others. You'd just be another guy she used and tossed away."

"Jack, don't be a dick," said Dayana.

He didn't stop. "Now she's locked in. She can never leave you. You've got her for the rest of her life."

"No. It's not like that."

Josie tried to step in. "What's wrong with you, Jack? Stop this."

But Jack was only getting himself more worked up. "On the plane. When you came out of the bathroom, you knew, didn't you?"

"Yes, but I—"

"You gave me a thumbs-up. A fucking thumbs-up!"

"It's not what you think."

"Is anybody getting more than two bars?" asked Harrison, holding up his phone.

Jack ignored Harrison. "You're ruining her life and you couldn't be happier about it."

"Jack, stop it!" said Josie.

"Yeah, take it easy," said Dayana.

But Jack was advancing on me, just like that night with my sketchbook. Only he was even angrier now. Out of control. He kept coming forward. "Admit you love this!"

"Stop!" I said.

"Did you try to get her pregnant?!"

"Of course not."

He was going to hit me. I could feel it. They wouldn't be able to hold him back, and I'd end up in the hospital like

Coach Murphy or bleeding in some field in the middle of an island.

"Jack, come on!"

"Leave him alone!"

Nothing they said was stopping him. If I didn't do something he'd be on me. He was inches away now. His giant hands squeezing into tight fists. "Why should I believe you? This is the best thing that ever happened to you. You got what you always wanted. All those years following her around, drawing her in your book, and now she's finally yours."

"You think I wanted this?"

"Stop, Jack."

He grabbed my shirt. "Didn't you? Didn't you?!"

"No! No, I didn't want a baby! I'm not even close to being ready. Josie and me as parents? It's a disaster. A train wreck. I was just pretending to make her feel good." The words weren't even out of my mouth before I tried to take them back. But it was too late.

The look on Josie's face absolutely crushed me. "You think it's a disaster . . ."

I was too upset and confused to even defend myself. "Josie . . ."

She backed away from me.

Dayana moved in to comfort Josie and glared at me. "That was a fucked-up thing to say." She didn't have to tell me that.

"It's not unreasonable, though," Harrison offered. I don't

know if he thought he was defending me, but he just made it worse. "They're eighteen years old. Statistically, they are not the most suitable parents."

"Stop talking," Josie snapped at Harrison.

"He didn't mean it," said Dayana. "Nobody knows what to say in a situation like this."

"It's not a situation, Dayana," said Josie. "It's my life!"

Dayana looked hurt.

"I'm trying to be practical," added Harrison. "Which is why we need to get to the police station and . . ."

"Tell me the truth, Archie," said Josie, zeroing in on me. "Just you and me now. What do you really think about me being pregnant?"

I looked into Josie's eyes and I couldn't. The fake smile. The nice words. I couldn't find them or any others. The lie was over. "I don't. I mean, it's just that . . ."

As Josie turned away from me, Jack shook his head. "This is the father of your baby. Congratulations."

When a taxi appeared down the road, Harrison yelled and waved his hands to flag it down. The car pulled over. It was even smaller than the first one. "You get in, Josie," said Jack, loading her bag.

He tried to get in after her, but she blocked him. "You're not coming."

"I'll go with her," said Dayana.

"Me too," I said.

"No," she said. "Both of you. All of you. Please. Just let me go. Let me go."

21

JACK

I SMELLED THEIR COCONUT SUNSCREEN before I saw or heard them. It cut through the dust in my nose.

"Hold the elevator!" I stuck my foot out to keep the door from closing before two girls around my age, one blonde, the other with dark, curly hair, jumped in. Both were a reddish tan, wearing bikini tops and sarongs. They carried towels and smoothies in plastic cups. They both smiled at me as the elevator door shut. I was suddenly very aware of how I must look after running halfway across the island searching for my sister.

As soon as Josie had taken off in the cab, I threw my duffel over my shoulder and started to sprint. I left Archie, Dayana, and Harrison standing there on the side of the road calling after me.

"Jack, where the hell are you going?!"

"You don't have to do this," yelled Archie.

I could barely hear Harrison's voice as I turned a corner. "Please don't leave!"

I ran as hard as I could down small streets and past grassy fields. I wanted to get to Jo, to tell her—I don't know what. But I couldn't stand the thought of her alone somewhere. Pregnant. All these years I'd waited for my chance to protect her. And I'd let her down again. So I ran all the way to the hotel, hoping to find her and make it right.

The girls in the elevator didn't seem to care that I was dirty and sweaty. "Thanks," said Blondie.

"Thank you, sir," added Curls. "Wow, you're big. You just get here?"

"I did."

"You look hot." The blonde shared a smirk with her friend. "I mean, you should check out the pool. It has a swim-up bar."

The other girl put her hand to the side of her mouth and pretended to whisper. "They don't check IDs either."

The elevator landed on the fifth floor and the doors opened. "Aw, is this your floor? Already? Too bad," said the blonde.

"We're just going to grab a phone charger. We'll be back at the pool in a few," said her friend. "Maybe we'll see you there?"

I dragged my bag off the elevator and heard them giggling as the door closed behind me. It's like they were from a different world, the one that existed for me before the crash, before my brain got all mashed up and long before my twin sister got knocked up.

I found the room, swiped the key, and went inside. "Jo?" The suite was large and tropical with a view of the beach and the pool. But it was empty. I tried calling Josie's phone but got her voicemail seven times in a row. I went into the bathroom, peeled off my wet clothes, and jumped into a cold shower. I had to duck to fit under the shower-head and I watched dirt swirl around the drain by my feet.

I stepped out of the shower, wrapped a towel around my waist, and walked out to the balcony with four small bottles of rum from the minibar. In the pool down below, a father was throwing his little son up in the air as the boy laughed and screamed. I watched as the two girls from the elevator returned to the poolside, ditched their skirts, and lay out on a couple of chairs with fresh drinks.

I glanced at my phone. No messages. I picked it up and started to text Dad.

Great news Dad
Jo's pregnant!
Why R we here?
You died out there but so what?
You were here and now you're not
We were a family and now we're not
I'm sorry
I said I'd protect her
She doesn't even want to talk to me
I'm sorry

I unzipped my duffel, dumping its contents over the bed.

I grabbed a bathing suit from the pile, yanked it on, and banged out the door without a shirt or shoes, but with a couple more bottles from the bar tucked under a towel.

I finished the bottles in the elevator and tossed the empties into the bushes on my way to the pool. I jumped straight into the water, creating a large splash on my way in. When I resurfaced, I could see that my entrance had attracted attention. Blondie and Curls were on the other side of the pool, whispering to each other. I swam to their side and lifted myself from the water right in front of them. They smiled and removed their sunglasses as I shook myself off like a dog. I snatched a nearby lounge chair and dragged it loudly across the concrete.

A nearby hotel worker hurried up. "Can I help you with that, sir?"

"I'm good. But you can get me a drink. Whatever they're having. And two more for them. Room 537."

As he walked up, I sat down next to Curls. "I'm Jack."

She took my hand and shook it. "Lacey."

"I'm Sierra."

"Nice to meet you both," I said.

Lacey handed me one of her towels. "Who are you here with, Jack?"

"Nobody. What are we drinking, by the way?"

"Some kind of rum punch. It's strong. So you just came on vacation by yourself?"

"It's not a vacation," I said.

"Work?"

"Why does it matter?"

"We were just curious. We're here with our families. That's my big brother across the pool." I didn't even glance over.

"I'm rewarding myself. It's been a shitty year."

"Your parents let you come down here all by yourself?"

I opened my mouth and out shot a laugh. A loud, harsh laugh that made my head pound again and startled me as much as it startled the girls. I saw them cut a look across the pool and the brother got off his chair and walked over.

He was almost as tall as me, but a lot skinnier. He had long hair and a hipster beard. "How's it going, Sierra?"

"Okay. Perry, this is Jack."

"What's up, Jack? Sierra, why don't you two give us a second."

The more my head hurt, the harder I laughed. "Look at you, playing the hero brother. Trying to protect your sister, huh? Good fucking luck with that. Nothing you can do . . . *bro*. Nothing you can do."

"Lace," said Sierra. "Let's take a walk on the beach."

"The . . . beach," I choked out between laughs. "Sure, nothing bad could happen out there."

Lacey got up from her chair. "It was nice meeting you, Jack. We really need to go."

"That's where they died." It felt like the words came out before the thought fully appeared in my brain. Like someone else put them there.

Lacey and Sierra stopped walking.

"My parents. That's where they died. Right out there, a few miles down. They were supposed to stay here, right in this hotel. I came here to see it with my sister, only she's missing. She ran away from me and I don't know how to find her."

"Excuse me, sir, can we escort you back to your room?" I turned to see two men in golf shirts. The guy talking was wearing an earpiece.

"I haven't gotten my drink yet."

Lacey and Sierra and her brother were already on their way to the beach.

"Sir, come with us please."

"I don't want to come with you. I want to find Jo. I want to go home. I want to go back."

"That can be arranged, sir."

"Can it? Can you make it go back?"

The two men each grabbed one of my arms. "Let's go."

"Don't touch me," I growled. "Get your hands off me!" But as I tried to rip my arms free, I suddenly felt tired and weak. Instead of fighting, I sagged down and gave up as they dragged me away from the pool deck and toward the lobby.

"Wait! Please don't!"

Suddenly the security guards stopped pulling me, and I picked my head up to see Archie standing in the way. His glasses were covered in dust and his shirt was soaked through.

"Please move," said one of the security guards. "This man was creating a disturbance."

"I'm sorry about that," said Archie, his voice not cracking

333

at all. "But he's not going to cause any trouble. Right, Jack?"

"Archie?"

"Who are you, young man?" said the other guard.

"My name is Archie Gallagher. I'm eighteen and I live in River Bank, New Jersey. This is Jack Clay. He lives there too."

"He's your friend?"

"He's . . . Yes, Jack is my friend, he's been my friend since we were four years old, even if he didn't always know it."

"Stop talking," I said. He did the opposite.

"Jack and I and his sister Josie and our friends Harrison and Dayana we came down here because our parents died in a plane crash well not Dayana's but she's part of us too we came down here for answers and because we didn't know what else to do and because Jack made us realize we need it and because we were stuck. I know Jack looks big and scary and he has a temper but he's a good person and a great brother and please don't arrest him or throw him out or whatever because I kind of need him right now and so does his sister."

When Archie was done jabbering the security guards looked at each other and one shook his head.

"Take him up to your room and don't let him out until he's sobered up. And if this happens again, we call the police."

"Yes," said Archie. "That's what we'll do. Thank you. Thank you both."

The guards walked away and Archie stood there looking at me, like he was waiting for something to happen. I turned my back on him and walked toward the beach.

He followed me. "You're just gonna walk away again?"

I stepped on the sand just as Archie grabbed my arm as hard as he could and spun me around to face him. He took off his glasses and put them in his pocket.

"Go ahead, hit me. Knock me down. Do what you have to do to feel better about this. I know you hate me right now and you think I ruined Josie's life by getting her pregnant. You think I'm not good enough for her and you're probably right about that. But . . . just know that if you don't knock me out or kill me or at least maim me severely—which are all possibilities—I'm gonna get back up and I'm gonna keep getting back up because Josie needs me. She needs me whether you like it or—"

"I knew it was going to happen," I snapped.

"What?"

"I knew she'd get hurt again. I saw it and I did nothing."

"Hurt by *me*?"

"I swore I'd never let her down again and I did. Just like I did back then."

"Back then . . . You mean with her coach?"

"I could've stopped it. One word to Dad or Mom. Or even if I'd said something to Jo. It never would've happened like it did. Instead he just hurt her over and over. He showed up in that car, and I let her walk out of the house. I let him do it. He changed her. He made her sad and lonely and scared. And I let him. She was just a kid."

"So were you, Jack. You were just a kid, too. Your mom and dad should've seen it. The other parents on the team. So many people who could've done something. It's not your fault. It's not your fault."

My whole body started to shake and heave as I turned away from him.

Archie just kept going and as he went, he seemed to get more confident. More in control. "And this . . . I know you think Josie's in trouble, and I'm not going to pretend like this isn't a mess. You already heard me admit that. And so did Josie. But this is not like when she was fourteen. I'm not that guy. I'm not saying I know what to do or exactly how to make this any easier for her. This is crazy and scary and I just turned eighteen and I don't know anything about anything. I don't even have parents who can help or give advice or just tell me we're gonna figure this out. So I guess I have to say it myself and believe that we're gonna figure it out. Because what I do know is that I love her, Jack. I love her. And I will spend every second of every day treating her the way she deserves to be treated."

When Archie was done, he was breathing hard, but he held his back straight and his chin still stuck out. "So go ahead. If you're gonna hit me, just get it over with so I can get back up and go find Josie."

22

HARRISON

-~~Survive flight from Newark to St. Martin.~~

-~~Survive smaller flight from St. Martin to Anguilla.~~

-Meet Agent Michael Boddicker at Royal Anguilla Police Headquarters.

-Show MB results of my investigation.

-Demand answers about the crash.

-Justice for Mom and her friends?

-Develop new Plan.

I paused on the veranda of the Royal Anguilla Police Headquarters. I had never been inside a police station before, and certainly not one surrounded by lush grass and palm trees. I was exhausted and I had blisters on both feet from walking here with Dayana. When Josie fled in the taxi, Jack took off running. He didn't even say anything before he left. He just grabbed his bag and disappeared. And then Archie went after him. My bags were heavy with research and books. I couldn't have kept up.

"Go ahead," I said to Dayana. "Go to the hotel. Find Josie."

"What about you?"

"I'm going to the police station. I need to talk to the agent. I thought that's why we were all here."

"I'm not sure that's why everyone is here. But you're not going by yourself. Lead the way."

I reached for the door to the police station. My hand shook so much I had to steady it with the other.

"We don't have to do this now," said Dayana. "We can find everybody else, come back tomorrow."

"I came here for my mother."

"She'd understand."

"No. Jack and Josie and Archie may have left us—"

"They didn't leave us. They're just figuring shit out."

"So am I."

Inside, the station didn't look all that different from the gritty precincts I'd seen in movies. Desks with landline phones and stained coffee mugs. I approached the desk and announced myself to an officer in a white uniform. She looked me up and down.

I brushed off my filthy shirt and tucked it into my pants.

"Hello. Hello. My name is Harrison Rebkin from the United States. We're here to meet with Michael Boddicker of the NTSB."

The officer looked at me as if I were speaking a different language. "I'm sorry?"

I reached into my briefcase and produced a copy of the email Agent Boddicker sent me. "I informed him that my friends and I would be coming down here during our spring break. Here's the email he sent back, promising to meet us here on this day to discuss the findings of his investigations."

"Investigations?" Her accent was thick and pleasant.

"Investigations into the plane crash that killed our parents."

Her eyes got wide and she opened her mouth, then closed it again. "Come with me if you please." She led us into a small, windowless room.

As soon as she closed the door, I started to feel warm and nauseated. "We're not going to find anything, are we? There's nothing here."

"You don't know that," said Dayana.

"He's not here. He didn't mean it. He's not here and nobody is going to tell us anything about the crash. We'll never know the cause or the meaning of any of it. Jack was right all along. It was a colossal waste of time and energy."

"You're giving up already?"

"Do you have any pills with you?"

"You don't need them."

"Don't *you?*"

"Sometimes, but I'm trying not to. Harrison, stay with me. You okay?"

My hands tingled and my jaw clenched tight. My heart was pounding and my lungs wouldn't fill.

"Is it happening?" she asked. "A panic attack?"

"Glitch."

"A glitch. Whatever. Stay with me. You'll get through this."

"3.14159 . . . 3.14159 . . . 9 . . . 59 . . ." I closed my eyes trying to summon more digits, but they wouldn't come. "What's wrong with me? I can't remember . . ."

"You don't need to count. You can do this, Harrison. Just breathe and hold on."

"Can't—can't breathe . . ."

"Yes, you can."

"Mom . . . would be so disappointed."

"What are you talking about?"

I gasped between words. "I . . . failed . . . her."

"Don't say that."

"It's . . . true. She's . . . dead and I . . . failed her."

"No way."

"She would be so—so . . . disappointed . . ."

Dayana banged her hands on the table. "Then screw her."

"What?!"

"Screw her if she'd be disappointed. Look at you. Look at what you've done this year."

"I . . . failed."

"Bullshit! Tell me how you failed."

"The investigation . . . Harvard . . . The Plan."

"Are you fucking kidding me? You *failed*? Harrison, look at me. Your mom died in a goddamn plane crash the week before school started. You lived alone for months before your deadbeat dad finally showed up. And when he turned out to be a douchenozzle, you had the balls to kick him out of your life and start over again. All of this while still being at the top of the freakin' class."

"Second in the class—"

"If you ask me, second in the class is nothing short of an honest-to-God miracle. Emotionally, you may be a basket case like the rest of us, but in the world, you're a fucking rock star. I don't know anybody else on the planet who could've pulled off what you did this year. Not me. Not Mackenzie whats-her-face. And definitely not your mom."

"Don't say that! She had dreams. I still hear about them in my head."

"Fuck her dreams. And if your mother would be disappointed with you after what you've accomplished, then fuck her, too. Fuck her a million times. If she put that voice in your head, then she was a terrible person, and you're better off without her."

"Stop saying that! She was the best person I've ever known. She gave up everything for me. And all she wanted was for me to be happy."

"That's not what you just said."

"Then I was wrong. I was wrong. The voice in my head . . . It wasn't her. She was my mom. My best friend. She was all I had." My eyes were blurry from the tears. "When Pop left, you know what she did? She slept on the floor of my room every night so that if I got scared or lonely I could put out my hand and hers would be right there to hold it. It didn't matter if it was two o'clock in the morning. Her hand never wasn't there. Never. And still . . . when I turned thirteen for some reason I decided I wanted to go see Pop. He was living in Florida at the time. So I bought myself a train ticket and I tried to sneak out in the middle of the night. When I got to the porch, she was waiting. She knew."

"Was she pissed?"

"No. She put her arm around me and kissed the top of my head. 'Sometimes I look at you and I just marvel,' she said. 'Because the universe seems so random. I'm twenty-three years old and I show up late to my friend's party. Your father is looking for some other house down the block and he stops to ask me for directions. If I'm on time, if he's not lost, thirty seconds in either direction and we never meet. We never fall in love. Random events produce something so incredible: my son, the gift of my lifetime. I marvel.' That's what she said. 'I marvel.'" I wiped my eyes and looked up at Dayana. "She was all I had and now she's gone."

I looked down at my hand. Mom wasn't there to hold it anymore. But before I could even process that thought,

Dayana was grabbing my hand and squeezing. "She's not all you have. Not anymore."

"We should be with Josie," I said. "She needs all of us."

The door opened and a large man in a blue shirt stained with sweat walked in holding a file.

"Hello, Harrison. My name is Michael Boddicker."

23

JOSIE

IT WAS JUST A BEACH. NOT A WIDE ONE OR A beautiful, pristine one like on the postcards Daddy used to send us when he'd go away. Just a small, rocky stretch of sand and water on the edge of a little town. I took off my shoes and dug my toes into the sand. There was no plane debris or police tape or any other reminder that something terrible happened near here. I don't know what I was expecting. Just, *more* than this. I thought being here, it would feel like walking into a cemetery. Hallowed ground, I think they call it. Out there was the place where my whole world changed, and it felt like . . . *nothing.*

In my mind, I'd step onto this stretch of beach and Mom and Daddy would be here with me. Comforting me. The night before we left, I'd been in the shower when I had this crazy fantasy. I'd show up here and suddenly I'd hear their voices in the surf.

"I'm so sorry, jellybean," Daddy would say. "I'm sorry I didn't keep you safe. I'm sorry I let you down."

"We're sorry we left when you needed us," Mom would say.

In the fantasy, I could talk to Mom and Daddy about Archie and Jack and my friends. Somehow they'd help me make sense of the crash and the pregnancy and how the people we love the most are the ones that hurt us.

I didn't feel Mom or Daddy with me at all on that beach. Standing with my feet in the sand, I could barely remember what they looked like, the sound of their voices. If anything, the sound of the waves made them feel farther away than ever. This wasn't a place to reconnect with them. It was a dead zone, a giant reminder that they were gone forever. There were no memorials here, no markers, nothing to tell the world that they ever existed at all. All that was here was sand and rock and a flat, empty sea.

I walked down to the sea until the warm water was lapping my ankles. I squinted up at the sun, my head suddenly feeling light and fuzzy. I looked down and tried to focus on seeing my feet through the water. But the world became washed out, too bright. I leaned down to splash water on my face and felt my legs going soft underneath me. I looked up again. The sun flashed and everything went white and I was falling. Falling into the water.

When I opened my eyes, my back was wet and sandy and there were four worried faces hovering over me.

Dayana was practically right on top of me, staring into my eyes. "I think she's awake. Jos, can you hear me? You want some water? I snatched a bottle from the police station."

Jack and Archie were kneeling on either side of me, each holding one of my hands. I saw the fear in their eyes. I was still trying to piece together what happened.

"You're gonna be all right," said Archie.

"Let her answer that," snapped Jack. "Jo, you there?"

Harrison studied his phone. "Fainting can be a common symptom of pregnancy, due to the dilation of the blood vessels. Excessive heat, stress, and low blood sugar."

"Blah blah blah," said Dayana. "We got it, genius."

Dayana gave me a sip of water while the guys argued about whether they should call a doctor. I lay there and watched them try to take care of me.

"Hey, aren't you guys the Sunnies?" I croaked.

Dayana shook her head. "Seriously?"

"Somebody want to explain how I ended up down here?" I tried to sit up, but Archie put a hand on my shoulder.

"You passed out just as we were getting to the beach," he said. "You fell right in the water."

"So that's why my butt's wet. That's a relief."

Dayana spritzed me with water. "You just can't resist being dramatic, can you?"

I grabbed Archie's hand and pulled myself up. "How did you know I was here?"

"We didn't," said Archie. "We just showed up."

"All four of you?"

"Just me and Jack."

"You and Jack?"

"Yeah," said Jack. "How about that."

"Harrison and I had a feeling you'd come here," said Dayana.

I picked up some sand. "It's not even that nice of a beach."

For a long time, no one said anything. We all just stared at the water.

"There's nothing here," said Jack. "Nobody would even know. At least when there's an accident on the highway, they put up those little crosses and people leave flowers."

"We should put a marker here," said Archie. "To remember them. I could make a little sign or . . ."

"It won't last," said Harrison. "The water will wash it away."

We all let that sink in.

Then Archie spoke again. "Someone could say something. You know, some words for them."

"That's a nice idea," I said, but nobody said anything. We all avoided eye contact.

Finally, when nobody volunteered, Dayana cleared her throat. "Fine, if you cowards aren't going to step up, I'll start. What do I have to lose?" She took a breath and flicked a look up at the sky. "Hey, everybody. Bet you're surprised I'm here. I am, too." She paused for a moment, looked at me, and kept going. "Look, I'm sure you don't want to hear a lot from me, so I'll make it quick. I just want to say that your kids . . . They loved you a lot. *Love* you a lot. Losing you was the shittiest of all breaks. And they miss the hell out of you. Every day. Nobody knows that better than me. So even though none of you was perfect—some less than others—you must've done something right. 'Cause I look around at these four weirdos . . . and I can see they're gonna be all right. Even if they don't know it yet. Okay, so, uh, rest in peace, I guess." Dayana started to sit down, but I had an overwhelming urge to hug her. I practically tackled her and we fell down into the sand.

"Thank you," I whispered in her ear.

Harrison turned and gave a wave to a large man standing beside a black car parked at the edge of the beach. The man's face was severe and weathered. He wore a shirt with the sleeves rolled up and his forearms bulged. As he got close to us, he reached into his pocket and revealed a shiny badge in a black case. "Hey folks."

"This is Michael Boddicker," said Harrison. "He works as an investigator for the NTSB. He came to the police station, but I asked him not to give me the results until we were all together."

"Nice to meet you all." Boddicker spoke with the hint of a southern accent. He opened up a satchel and produced a manila file folder. Boddicker tapped the outside of the folder. "As of two days ago, our investigation into the crash of the Island Hopper flight 206 is closed."

"I don't understand," I said. "Over?"

Boddicker looked to Harrison, who nodded. Agent

Boddicker paused before opening the folder and looked around at us. "Are you sure you all want to see this? It's not graphic, but it has some hard truths about the crash and how it happened. Do you all want to know what happened to your parents?"

I met Jack's eyes. He nodded. "Yes," I said. "We want to know why they died."

"Okay then." He handed the folder to Harrison, who slowly lifted the cover. The first pages were a typed report. Behind that were color and black-and-white photos of the beach and the water and sections of the plane that had been recovered. Harrison skimmed through the report, making little noises and clucks.

Archie pushed him along. "What does it say?"

Harrison cleared his throat and read from the NTSB report. "Examination indicates that the left outboard wing lower-attachment lug fractured through an area of preexisting-fatigue cracking in the lower lug ligament."

"What does that mean?" I asked.

Boddicker turned to me. "Ms. Clay?"

"Yes, I'm Josie. Now please tell us in a way we can understand."

"Josie, there was damage caused over time to the part of the plane that holds the wing on. This damage, it reduced the strength of the fitting to the post so that operational loads produced what we call an overstress fracture. Basically, because this one part was cracked already, it weakened to the point where it couldn't withstand the force of the wing.

These findings matched up with eyewitnesses who reported seeing one of the plane's wings snap off midflight."

We were silent, probably all imagining what it was like for them when that wing broke off. "Would you like me to stop?" he offered.

"No. Keep going," said Jack.

"The pilot lost control. The plane rolled to the left, at which point it descended rapidly and went nose first into the water. There was nothing anyone could have done. Those were our findings."

"You said it was a . . . lug lower ligament that caused it," said Archie. "What is that?"

"Well, I guess you'd say it's a bolt," said Boddicker. He made a space with his thumb and finger. "'Bout this long. Not much bigger than your pinky, but when it wears out and nobody catches it . . ."

The size of a pinky . . . That's what did all this.

"There's a photo inside," he said. "Number 17B. You can see it for yourselves." I reached into the file and found the picture. He was right. It looked like an old bolt. Reminded me of the kind Daddy used to put together the IKEA bookshelves in my bedroom. Maybe even smaller. How could something so insignificant be the cause of something so big?

Harrison took the photo and studied it. He shook his head back and forth. "It had to be more than this. It had to. 'Planes want to stay in the air.' That's what the pilot told me. They don't want to crash. This was not enough. It had to be something more. What about Archie's father's job with the military? What about Mr. Clay's dealing with the government? Who had access to the plane?"

"I looked into all that," said Boddicker. "Just to be sure. After your emails raised those questions. I called around. Mr. Gallagher was a civilian. His job was mostly budgetary, ordering supplies, hiring other civilians. There was no connection to Mr. Clay or his law practice."

I could see the disappointment on Archie's face. "Budgetary," he said.

"The lug was left in the plane too long. That's the simplest way to explain it. It should've been replaced after a couple of years. We're working to make certain that this sort of thing never happens again. We're not sure how it got missed in the first place. We've gotten several different stories. There may never be an answer."

"That's not good enough!" said Harrison. "What aren't you telling us? Why should we believe that this little—"

"I understand, son," said Boddicker. "Believe me, I understand. It doesn't seem possible. Or right."

"How could you," said Harrison. "How the hell could you understand?"

The agent removed his sunglasses and put them in his pocket. I was surprised to see that his eyes were red and moist. He dabbed at them with his sleeve. "The reason I didn't answer your emails and why I took a leave of absence from the NTSB is that I also suffered a loss. My wife. We were married twenty-one years. Till lung cancer took her seven weeks ago. She was forty-eight years old. Never smoked a day in her life.

I used to make fun of her for eating organic and never missing a workout. Try and explain that one to your kids. Or to yourself for that matter . . . You want to know how many times I asked the doctors for an explanation? Some *reason*. They had nothing. They told me over and over again that they couldn't explain it. She got cancer. She died. It just is."

He stared off into the water. "I wish I could give you a more satisfying answer. Damn, now I sound just like them. How I wanted to beat the hell out of those doctors every time they said that. *Satisfying*." Boddicker took back the file. "I'll leave you to it. Please call if you have more questions. Have a safe trip back. You seem like good kids. Take care of each other. I'm very sorry for your loss."

"Yours, too," said Archie.

Boddicker looked at him and nodded. Then he put on his sunglasses and walked back to the black car.

Good kids, he'd said. I'd never in my life felt less like a kid.

We watched the black car speed off until it disappeared.

"I'm sorry," said Harrison. "I pulled you all into my stupid conspiracy theory and wasted your time."

Archie walked away and sat in the sand, opened his sketchbook, and buried his head in it. Jack picked up a rock and hurled it across the beach with a yell. Harrison took off for the parking lot.

Dayana grabbed him. "Where are you going?"

"I was so sure," he said. "I spent six months on this. I did all the research. The phone calls, the emails. I was convinced we'd find something, prove something. It was more than an accident. I was certain there was a reason. And if there was a reason, there was something we could do. If they were killed, then we'd find out who did it. We'd expose them. I'd do it for Mom. I'd make it right and people would know why she died and it would be for something. They would've died for *something*. And now it's just a rusty bolt. It's *nothing*. They died for *nothing*. It means *nothing*."

I stood in the middle of that beach and watched them all dealing with the reality in their own ways. And as Archie drew and Jack fumed and Harrison retreated, I pictured us going home and going off in opposite directions, just like we'd been doing since we were kids. Harrison to his studies and Archie to his sketches. Jack and I, we'd be heading off to college. And Dayana, she'd be on the outside again. The thing that brought us here, all of us, was over. Our parents were dead. There was no mystery behind it. No secrets. The rest was just . . . life. We came together to find something and we didn't find it. At least not what we thought we were looking for. But as I watched them all in their private pain, it hit me. Maybe we'd found something else.

"It wasn't for nothing," I called out. They all turned back. "There may not have been sabotage or murder; my father wasn't involved in a government conspiracy; Archie, your dad was just a guy with a job. The crash wasn't anything more than bad luck. There was no reason. But it did mean something. It had meaning."

"What?" asked Harrison. "What did it mean?"

"This," I said. "Us. The crash took Mom and Daddy. It

took away our families. But it gave me the person I'm in love with. It gave me back my best friend. It gave me a new family."

Archie dropped his pad and moved over to join me.

Dayana sniffled. "A new, fucked-up family."

"Exactly. We might have no idea where we're going or what's gonna happen next, but we're not doing it alone. And we're definitely going to need every single one of you to figure out what the hell to do about this baby."

Archie just looked at me for a long time. Why wasn't he talking? It was killing me. "You can say something now."

"Oh," he said. "Right. I'm with you. I'm always with you." I walked into his arms and he lifted my feet off the ground. There was no question we were going to make mistakes. Possibly big, catastrophic mistakes just like our parents did. They lied to us and they pushed us too hard. Or they didn't understand us or listen enough. They weren't perfect. They were people. But they loved us.

"We would so mess this kid up," I said, laughing and crying at the same time.

"You won't be doing it alone," said Jack.

Archie laughed. "No, we'd all mess up that kid together."

Dayana came and hugged us both. "Please. That little bastard would get the full fucking Sunnies experience."

By now the sun was already halfway down into the water. We barely noticed as Harrison rolled up his pants and started walking right into the ocean. He went in up to his knees and then his waist. When he got to his chest and still wasn't stopping, we finally started paying attention.

"What're you doing, you freak?" Dayana called out.

Harrison didn't look back. He just kept walking, his head getting lower and lower until he was fully submerged. For a few seconds, there was no sign of him. We all looked around at each other. He was gone. There wasn't even a ripple in the water where he'd gone under. As a suddenly panicked Dayana called Harrison's name, Jack yanked off his shirt and sprinted down to the water. But just as he was about to dive in for a save, Harrison surfaced with a splash, spit out a large plume of water, and let out a primal scream.

"You little shit," said Dayana, kicking off her shoes. She went charging in after him, did a face-first plunge, and came up with her hair matted down and makeup running off her face. She jumped on Harrison's back and dunked his head under. Jack gave me a shrug and then he ran in, too, doing a front flip into a wave. When he came up, Dayana started splashing him and soon he fought back, laughing and splashing her and Harrison.

Archie and I met each other's look.

"We're really gonna do this?" he asked.

"We're really gonna do it."

"Then let's do it."

He tossed his glasses in the sand and took my hand. We sprinted into the ocean to join our friends—our family. When we were deep enough, we dove under the water together, and together, we popped back up.

EPILOGUE

DAYANA

I won't pretend I wasn't sweating it out those last few weeks before graduation. I was a fucking wreck and a half. I barely slept, and I'm sure I was not my usual delightful self to be around. Poor Harrison took the brunt. But as much as I wanted to smoke, drink, or swallow something to lower my anxiety level from a 10 to a 9.9, I resisted. I'd come this far. That last semester, I'd kicked more academic ass than I had in my whole high school career. Got my averages up to a rock-solid C plus. Living in the room right next door to Harrison certainly didn't hurt.

The guidance counselor, Ms. Bryson, who'd spent four years calling me hopeless, called me into her office one day and informed me that I'd passed with room to spare. "Fuck yeah, I did!" I screamed out. And for a second there, I was afraid she was going to change her mind. But instead she hugged me and told me she was proud of me.

I woke up the morning of graduation and put an extra

streak of RBHS red in my hair to commemorate the occasion. I even left the lip ring at home out of respect. Still kept the two in my eyebrow, of course. Couldn't let Mami be too happy, could I?

I sat there with the other 327 members of the senior class on the hot and humid turf field in my metal folding chair, wearing my polyester cap and gown and my favorite combat boots. Principal Walters stood at the lectern on the fifty-yard line and welcomed family, friends, and the graduating class of 2020. As she droned on with her opening remarks, I looked down the end of my row to where Jack and Josie were sitting. I rolled my eyes and Josie pretended to stifle a yawn. I saw her look behind me and I followed her gaze to Archie, sketching away with a small pencil on the graduation program. I loved seeing her happy.

When we'd landed in New Jersey after leaving Anguilla, Josie made good on her promise. "Let's go to the police station," she said.

"Now? Are you sure?" asked Jack.

"Now," she said.

"I'll order the car," said Archie.

Jack, Archie, Harrison, and I sat in the waiting area while she gave her statement to the police. She walked out of the interrogation room and Archie gave up his seat for her.

"Is it done?" I asked.

"It's just getting started," she said. "But that's okay. I've been waiting a long time for this."

Coach Murphy was arrested that night and Josie never

wavered in telling her story. And we were all with her, at every step.

"And now, without any further ado, I'd like to introduce our first speaker of the day. He's a very impressive young man who had to overcome a great deal this year. The entire RBHS community is proud to welcome Harrison Rebkin . . . your class salutatorian." The applause through the stadium was quiet and respectful.

"Harrison! *Wooo!*" I yelled as loudly as I could. Everyone looked in my direction, but I didn't care.

Jack and Josie joined in.

"Yeah, baby!"

"Go get 'em, H!"

From the side of the stands, I heard another loud yell. "Go Harry!" I turned around to see Mr. U, the custodian, wearing a tie and cheering his head off for Harrison.

Harrison walked up to the microphone and tried not to laugh. Just as he was about to speak, we started a second wave of screaming and cheering until Principal Walters silenced us with death stares.

Harrison reached for the mic and opened his mouth, but the PA system squealed with feedback. He backed away until the ear-piercing noise stopped. The stadium was silent, other than the sound of people fanning themselves with programs and a few stray coughs. Harrison approached again and this time his voice was clear and solid. "I had a Plan, with a capital P," he began, speaking without any notes. "The Plan was formulated when I was a little boy and my mother and

I worked it out to the smallest detail. The Plan dictated how I would study, what activities I would participate in, how I would live my life in pursuit of certain goals. My mother and I spent every day of my life working to achieve those goals, working on that Plan." He paused and looked out at the crowd. "You all probably know that before this school year even started, that Plan crashed and sank into the Caribbean Sea. Today, I look out into the bleachers and I see some empty seats. Five empty seats, one of which belonged to my mother."

At the end of the aisle, Jack handed Josie a tissue from his pocket as Harrison's voice echoed across the field.

"Today is different than I expected. *Everything* is different than I expected. Mom isn't here. My father turned out not to be the man I hoped he'd be. I didn't get into Harvard. I'm not the valedictorian." He took another pause and this time looked down across the lectern to the other special guest on the stage. "I would like to say congratulations to Mackenzie Markowitz, who deserves to be sitting there. I have to admit, I thought I could best her, but she was too strong, too determined. Don't feel sorry for me, though, because she's my girlfriend now and that's better in so many ways."

Mackenzie's cheeks turned bright red as the senior class erupted in laughs and murmuring. But I could see by the way she smiled at Harrison that she kinda loved it. Principal Walters stood up and put an angry shush finger to her lips, quieting the stadium.

Just as everyone settled down again, I let out another even louder "Hell yeah!"

Harrison gathered himself and took a few seconds to look over all of us in the folding chairs. "Traditionally, graduation speakers are supposed to deliver some sort of wisdom or helpful advice. I can't say that I have much of either to impart to you, although I feel as if I've lived more this year than I did in the seventeen years before it. The truth is, I am still attempting to figure things out in my life. Unlike Mackenzie Markowitz and most of you sitting here—and Harrison Rebkin ten months ago—I don't have a Plan. But believe it or not, I've come to embrace that. After years of avoiding surprise and uncertainty at all costs, I like that I don't know. I like that I get to choose and make mistakes and take detours and get lost. Because when I do that, there's a chance I'll find even better things along the way."

He turned his head to address Jack, Josie, Archie, and me directly. "One thing my dad did was introduce me to some classic rock, like the Beatles. John Lennon once said, 'Life is what happens to you while you're busy making other plans.' One of my best friends has a way with words and I think she'd phrase it this way: 'Life is what happens to you when The Plan gets royally fucked.'" As a shocked and horrified buzz erupted from the crowd, Harrison gave me a big old, cheesy grin.

Once the speeches were over, Principal Walters read the names of the graduates. I tapped my foot waiting for him to get to me.

"Dayana Osanna Calderón."

I clicked my boots and walked up the stairs to the stage. As I got up there, I peered out into the stands. A few rows up, Mami was sitting by herself, tears running down her face. I started across the stage when a loud whistle cut through the stadium. I turned to see Papi, wearing a tan suit and rushing up the bleachers with two fingers in his mouth. He'd come directly from work and he'd arrived just in time. He kissed Mami and slipped an arm around her as they both cheered like maniacs. I was so distracted by them, I almost forgot to walk over and take my diploma. Principal Walters had to repeat my name to get me moving.

I was heading back to my front row seat when Jack and Josie received their diplomas. Jack went first, shaking hands with the football coach on his way to the stage. Josie walked up right after him, the slightest bit of belly showing through her gown. I heard some tittering behind me.

"They should give her an extra tiny diploma for the baby."

I turned around in my seat and flashed my teeth at Siobhan. "Hi there. Before we leave this place forever, I just wanted to say you're a horrible, judgmental bitch and Josie was always too good for you. That's all. Sign my yearbook later?"

When the ceremony was over and we'd tossed our caps, we all gathered near the bleachers. Harrison was stuck in an awkward conversation with Mackenzie Markowitz's father. Jack and Josie's grandparents were chatting with some of Archie's relatives. Their smiles looked just a bit stiff.

Archie picked up his cap and stuck it on Lucas's head. "As soon as we're done with dinner, I'll take you to Aunt Sarah's to pick up the rest of your stuff."

"You sure? I mean, if you're moving into Josie's house—"

"We want you there. Stop trying to talk me out of it."

Josie popped her head in. "It's a big house. It's supposed to have a family in it."

Papi rushed over and picked me up in his arms. "Who is better than my little girl? No one. So sorry I was late. I kept trying to get out of the meeting, but the client wouldn't stop asking questions."

"It's cool," I said. And it was.

Papi hugged Jack and Josie together and then grabbed Harrison's arm. "I heard your speech from the parking lot. Fantastic job. If only I could've seen the principal's face when you quoted my princesa."

Harrison shrugged. "I didn't turn around."

"How do you know he was quoting *me*?"

Mami laughed and slipped her arms around me. "You are my hero, Dayanita," she said.

"Even if I didn't take out my eyebrow piercings?"

"They have begun to grow on me."

"I see what this is. Reverse psychology." We both suddenly noticed that Jack and Josie were right next to us.

"Your parents would be so proud," said Mami. "I know I am." She hugged Jack and then stood face-to-face with Josie. I was ready to step in and referee if I had to. "Anything you need, I'm here. Your mother was a special person and I would never try to . . ." Josie reached out and embraced my mother. Neither of them said another word.

Papi broke the moment, calling for attention as he took out his phone. "Okay, graduates, stand together with each other for a picture. We weren't sure this day would happen. We need proof." I stood between Jack and Harrison, our shoulders touching. In front of us Josie and Archie were arm in arm.

"Are we ready?" asked Papi.

"Wait," I said. "Should we show them off?"

Mami looked alarmed. "Oh no. Show what?"

"I think we have to," said Josie. "Especially since we've learned I wasn't supposed to do it in the first place."

"It's fine," said Jack. "Stop worrying."

"Okay," I said gently. "When we were all down in the Caribbean, we decided we needed to . . . bring something home to remember the experience. So before we left we each got a little memento of our time together."

"Let's just do it," said Jack. "On three. Explain later."

Papi held up his phone. "Okay then . . . Everybody smile. One . . . two . . ."

Just before Papi snapped the picture, we all pulled up the sleeves of our graduation gowns and held up our right arms to show off our matching tattoos. There, on the inside of each of our forearms, was a small, winking yellow sun.

JACK

I wasn't used to planning a party without Josie. I lifted heavy things and she did the heavy lifting. I didn't decide on food or music or decorations. Josie wouldn't let me near anything that mattered. But with Josie otherwise occupied, it came down to me to make this worthy of a Josie Clay production. Thankfully, I'd made it home in time from basic training in South Carolina. I thought I'd have a week to plan this thing, but like Harrison said, plans don't always work out. It all went down a lot faster than we expected.

In a couple of months, I'd be headed for medic training in Texas. But for now, I was happy to be home, where I could spend time with Josie. Even if I'd forgotten how freakin' cold New Jersey could be in December. Josie and I had decided to hold off on selling the house. She and Archie and Lucas were settling in. Even without Mom and Dad, this was home for both of us.

When our acceptance letters came from Rutgers a couple of months before graduation, college didn't feel right to me. I couldn't imagine myself going to football games, sitting in a library, or pledging a frat. I honestly didn't know what I was going to do until I bumped into an army recruiter in the school parking lot. We started talking and it suddenly all made sense. I didn't want to fight, but I wanted to help. I signed up to be an army medic a week later. Basic training was hard as hell, but I'd been through worse. And I loved the discipline. I loved having a purpose.

But now my purpose was to get this house in shape for guests. The last party we'd thrown here was supposed to be the biggest our school had ever seen. Josie's mission was to make it perfect. It didn't work out that way.

I straightened the couch and moved the ottoman to reveal a dark spot on the rug. A year after the party there were still scratches on the floor, stains on carpets, remnants, reminders. *That* party left permanent scars on our house and our family. *This* party was another step toward healing them.

Dayana and Harrison showed up carrying soda and plastic cups. She saluted me as Harrison handed me the drinks.

"How's school?" I asked him.

"It's good," said Harrison. "I'm applying to transfer for next semester."

"Harvard pre-med?"

"Brown. But I'll still visit Mack up there a lot. And I haven't decided on a major yet."

Dayana gave him a punch in the gut. "He's our little rebel."

I started to spread out the drinks when I realized, "Ice! We don't have ice!"

"Ease up, Sergeant," said Dayana. "It doesn't matter."

"It does matter," I said, remembering the lessons Josie drilled into me. "Every detail matters."

Harrison said he'd text Mackenzie and have her bring a couple of bags. Crisis averted. Was it good enough? Did I pull it off? "What do you think?" I asked.

Dayana took it all in. "You know, I've never officially been invited to one of these. Crashed one once. It's not quite a Josie Clay joint, but it'll do."

I hoped so. I wanted it to be perfect for her. For all of them. The guests started to arrive in small groups. Grandma and Grandpa. Archie's aunt and uncle. Nelson and Vanesa. Friends. Family. They slowly filled the living room with noise. I knew some of them were less supportive of Jo and Archie than others, but I didn't care. The music was playing and the drinks were flowing when we heard a car drive up.

"It's them," Lucas called. "They're here!"

Everybody stood by the front and waited. I opened the door, and Josie walked in to a chorus of cheers and applause. I took her coat, her hat, and her scarf and she ruffled my buzz cut.

"I love coming home and seeing you here," she said. She looked tired, but beautiful and happy. "Thank you all for being here. And now it is my pleasure to present the guest of honor. It took him seventeen hours to arrive, but I think you'll agree it was worth it. Celebrating his third day on this planet, Clay Phillip Gallagher!"

Archie entered, carrying my baby nephew in a car seat. *My nephew.* He already looked bigger than he did in the hospital. A collective *Awwww* went through the room. I reached in and stuck my finger in Clay's tiny hand and let him squeeze it. Three days old and the kid already had a killer grip.

"There's only one?" I teased. "Everybody knows you're supposed to bring two babies home."

"One was plenty," said Josie, unbuckling him from the seat.

I couldn't believe he was real. He had Josie's eyes; Mom's eyes. He was seven pounds nine ounces and he was the most incredible thing I'd ever seen.

"You did good, Soul."

"I like to think so, Heart."

I moved onto the couch and put my arm around her. "Maybe later we hit the piano for a duet?"

"We'll see. I'm a little tired."

"From what?"

She smiled at me.

"It's going to be okay," I said.

Josie looked up at me. "You said that to me the day of Daddy and Mom's memorial service. I was on my bed and you were trying to get me up."

"I didn't know you heard me."

"I heard. I always hear you. You were right, by the way."

I was sitting on the couch holding the baby when Archie came over, planted a kiss on his head, and shook my hand. "I'm glad you're here."

"Me too," I said. "Now, you know I'm not gonna be around all the time, so I need you to do me a favor. I want you to make sure my nephew knows about his grandparents. All four of them. And Archie . . . take care of our girl."

"You know I will."

"Yeah."

Josie led Dayana and Harrison over to take their turns holding the baby. We all sat there together and stared down at baby Clay Phillip Gallagher. I know they say newborns can't really see much, but I swear he was looking up at us. If he was, I hoped that he would see the five of us and know that we were his family and that we always would be.

It was the best party we'd ever thrown.

AUTHOR'S NOTE

In *The Year They Fell*, Josie is suffering from the after-effects of sexual assault. And like many survivors, she feels all alone.

Sexual assault is any sexual interaction or conduct that takes place without the consent of everybody involved. If this happens between people who know each other, between people who are in a romantic or sexual relationship, or even between people who previously consented to be intimate as recently as a second earlier, it is still sexual assault.

Sexual assault includes rape, attempted rape, forced or coerced sexual activity, and unwanted sexual touch. These are just examples; no definition can encompass every survivor's experience of sexual assault.

If you've experienced sexual assault and you want to talk to someone about it, here are a few resources:

- **RAINN** (Rape, Abuse & Incest National Network) is the largest organization in the United States dedicated to anti-sexual violence initiatives. You can call RAINN's National Sexual Assault Hotline at 1-800-656-HOPE (or 1-800-656-4673). You can also talk to someone online at online.rainn.org.
- **The VictimConnect Resource Center** (run by the

National Center for Victims of Crime) provides crime victims with resources for learning about their legal rights and options for next steps. You can call VictimConnect at 1-855-4-VICTIM (or 1-855-484-2846). You can also talk to someone online at chat .victimconnect.org.

If someone you know has been sexually assaulted and they tell you about it, listen to them, believe them, and help them get the resources they want and need. Anyone can be part of a support network for survivors, helping to dismantle the culture of sexual harassment and sexual assault. Listen to survivors and encourage others to listen, too.

And if, like Josie and her friends, you are mourning the death of a loved one, struggling with depression, or simply feeling lost, it's important that you tell someone else how you're feeling. A parent, a friend, or someone at school can help you find support. If you don't want to talk to someone you know, there are many services that provide free, confidential help. One well-known provider is the National Suicide Prevention Lifeline, available twenty-four hours a day, seven days a week. Its toll-free number is 1-800-273-8255, and its website is SuicidePreventionLifeline.org. You can also reach out by text to the Crisis Text Line for free, 24/7 support (in the United States). Just text 741741; a live, trained Crisis Counselor will receive the text and respond quickly.

ACKNOWLEDGMENTS

Like Dayana, Archie, Josie, Jack, and Harrison, I have learned that the world can be a scary, complicated, and confusing place, but it's a whole lot better with the right mix of people around to support you. I owe an ocean of thanks to everyone in my life who made this book possible. I may not have met you all when we were four years old, but you are my own personal Sunnies.

I could write an entire book about my agent and friend, the inspiring and heroic Marietta Zacker. You loved this story from the moment I hit you with a two-minute pitch at the food truck festival in South Orange and you have been its tireless champion ever since. I know the Sunnies themselves are as dear to your heart as they are to mine and you've never stopped fighting for them to be seen and heard in the world. Can't wait to get our matching tattoos.

Thanks as well to Marietta's partner Nancy Gallt and colleague Erin Casey for keeping me honest and always being a great sounding board.

Thank you to my insightful and sensitive editor, John Morgan. You made this a better book in every way, guiding and protecting the story and helping the characters become even more of who they were meant to be.

Many thanks to the wonderful Erin Stein and the entire team at Imprint and Macmillan Children's Publishing Group. I've been so impressed with your vision and care at every step of this process.

To the endlessly creative Benee Knauer, you helped me take this from an idea and a few chapters to a fully realized novel. You always pushed me to go deeper and to find the heart of the story. Your influence is on every page of this book.

Cindy Kanegis, you helped me find my focus and keep my eye on the finish line. Scott Miller, thank you for your hard work and belief in this project.

Mark and Rachel Calveric; Alisa and Dan Cohen; Steve Horowitz and Cathy Roma and Patrick Henigan, none of whom were harmed in the making of this book—you are my peeps, my travel companions, my tribe, the greatest group of friends anyone could ever ask for. We got off a plane from St. Martin a million years ago and I said, "I think I have an idea." Love you all. Beth El preschool forever!

Much gratitude to my podcast partners in crime, Ben Strouse and Chris Tarry. I'm proud to have my book on the office coffee table next to yours.

My two oldest friends—pre-preschool—gave me some much needed guidance in the writing of this book. Steve O'Hagan, thanks for the criminal law expertise and, more importantly, for being the large, situationally aggressive older brother I never had and desperately needed. Meredith Frankel, my friend since birth, my friend for life. I can't tell you how much your love and support have meant to me. I am so lucky to have you.

Thank you to fellow authors and *Guiding Light* alumni Jenelle Lindsay, Josh Sabarra, Danielle Paige, and Rebecca Hanover for your advice and inspiration. And to my pals Matt Savare and Tom Means, for always being on Team Kreizman.

Natalia Feigin, thanks for sharing your personal story with me. Nancy Donoghue, thanks for the use of your Pocono retreat so this father of three could spend some time writing in rare solitude.

To my brilliant little cousin, Maris Kreizman, who was killing it in the literary world long before I put a toe in the water. You may not have realized it at the time, but you talked me through a crisis of story faith that helped shape what the book became.

Thank you to the world's best in-laws, David and Arlene Katzive. You have lived a life full of art and books and culture. Thanks for sharing it with me, Tash, and the kids.

To my amazing parents, who didn't know I was writing this book until after I sold it. Mom and Dad, sorry for keeping it a secret, and thank you for not freaking out too much when I said I wanted to be a writer but had no idea how to make a living doing it. You gave me a love of reading and writing when I was barely more than a preschooler. Try to leave a few books on the shelves for everyone else.

Dashiell, Fiona, and Oliver, you were never far from my mind while I was writing this. Thank you for inspiring me, for keeping me up-to-date on current slang, and for being understanding when Daddy marches up to the third floor to pound away at the keyboard. I love you guys.

And finally, to my wife, Natasha, who read this first and never stopped believing in it and in me. Tash, you're the single biggest reason that this novel exists. I share it—and everything else great in my life—with you, always.